LAWRENCE MATRICK M.D.

THE QUISLING

Cover designer: Ana Chabrand, Chabrand Design House
www.anachabrand.com

Interior Formatting: Marla Thompson, EdgeofWater Designs
edgeofwater.com

ISBNs:
978-1- 77374-008- 9 (Paperback);
978-1- 77374-009- 6 (E-book)

Bellevue Publishing
Vancouver, BC, Canada
Printed in USA

THE QUISLING

LAWRENCE MATRICK, M.D.

DEDICATION

To my wife, Jean, and also to our children: Marilyn, Diana and Michael for their love, encouragement and support while writing this book and for traveling with me on this journey.

ACKNOWLEDGEMENTS

With gratitude and appreciation to my editors, Gordon Thomas and Michelle Balfour.

CHAPTER 1

Acapulco

Zack had nothing else to do for the weekend, and the cooler breeze off the Pacific would be a welcome reprieve. It was a four-hour drive west of Mexico City, through the town of Taxco, the silver city popular with busloads of tourists.

For Camille, Taxco meant a gas-up stop for the limo and a place for her to urinate, hydrate, restock the bar with tequila, and shop for some expensive silver jewelry she didn't need. She was also a compulsive shoplifter, but resisted the temptation this time.

Once they left Taxco, Zack drove the short distance to the beachfront just north of Acapulco, where he was directed by guards to a secure area surrounded by a barbed wire fence. Zack parked the limo in a lot, guarded by well-armed sentries, which rested on a secluded, private stretch of beach. He escorted Camille, now slightly tipsy and unsteady, to the sheltered, heavily-guarded beachfront. It was full of Salazar's bodyguards and crime bosses.

As he sat back in a beach chair wearing a large-brimmed Panama hat, feeling the cool breeze across his bare chest, he watched Camille attempt to seduce some of the generals, who were friendly, but wary of their boss's wife, and her advances. He lit up another Cuban cigar of good quality and sipped on a double single-malt scotch, with a few drops of water.

As he surveyed the busy scene, he observed there to be three distinct camps on the beach. The first were the wealthy, bejeweled wives of the drug cartel generals splayed out on beach chairs: drinking, laughing and lathering their corpulent bodies with oil. They attempted to seduce the muscular, young waiters and bartenders, who plied them with more tequila and margaritas.

The second camp consisted of the nubile, skinny, bikini-clad prostitutes from Mexico City, who were cavorting on the beach with the cartel husbands and waiters who flashed American dollars their way.

The third camp were the men—the drug lords gathered in small groups here and there, smoking, drinking, cutting deals, and, in hushed tones, discussing what to do with Carlos.

Filling out the tableau of beachside humanity were the waiters, bartenders, cooks, guards, nursemaids, and limo drivers: baking in the hot sun wearing dark uniforms, waiting patiently at the beck and call of their bosses, and hustling for tips in American dollars.

Alongside this collection of weary, sweaty men were the babysitters, playing in the sand with little children who were sent away to cavort in the waves.

The ones who made the most money of all were the so-called "massage therapists". These beautiful young men and women stood outside tents near the water's edge. The tent openings boldly revealed cots and tables that held an array of body lotions, salves, dildos of all sizes, vibrators, and other sex toys. Gloves and tissues were provided to wipe up the semen of male customers who requested a "full release" massage. Cool towels, floating in ice buckets, were provided to calm the fiery aftermath of a women's engorged vagina after clitoral stimulation by hand, tongue, or with the dildos during a sensual massage.

Customers could choose a male or female masseuse to satisfy their own personal sexual proclivity. The males were striking, young, muscular hunks in their early twenties parading close by their tents. They were preferred by the women, but also by a few of Salazar's male drug lords. As a customer entered the tent, it would then be closed by a flap.

Zack relaxed with his drink, and could hear the squeals, cries, moans, and sounds of orgasmic release as one or all orifices were manipulated by fingers, dildos, or vibrators.

The dildos for the women were of all sizes: small, vibrating, smooth, colorful sausages or large, twirling, rubber apparatuses that were twisted, like a screw, and thrust in and out. Some were dipped in cinnamon, or brushed with hot peppers or Tabasco sauce, in order to enflame the vaginal or anal canals, producing a more excruciating, sadistic climax.

The customers could choose from a hot young man or a beautiful teenaged girl who stood outside her tent, licking her ruby red lips and sucking on a large, cold Popsicle, dramatically suggesting a very enticing fellatio.

Whether they desired a quick hand job or a long session of fellatio, the men exited the tents red-faced and sweating, having shot their wads both figuratively and literally; for these masseurs accepted US dollars happily, but never pesos.

Zack never participated in anonymous sex. As a physician, he was well aware of the inherent risks and dangers such sexual activity produced, which he witnessed and helped to diagnose in hospital emergency wards as a teaching assistant.

He pulled up a chair for Camille and was pleased to see her join him under the cool palapa, somewhat unsteady in her walk and careful not to spill a drop of the full glass of tequila she carried.

"You don't like the pretty young girls in that tent over there?" she asked, taking a sip of her drink and pointing to a tent by the water.

Zack sat up to make room for her next to him on the beach lounge before she fell over. "No, Camille, I never partook of such dalliance, knowing that the human papillomavirus is passed freely from the mouth," he explained.

Camille turned to face him and then confessed in a whisper, "My doctor spoke of such a virus, when I went to him for my itch. You know"—she paused briefly—"down there." She pulled up her beach sundress and pointed to her naked thighs and a few genital warts, now displayed for all to see.

Pulling her dress down to cover her sexually transmitted disease, Zack then continued, feeling concerned for her plight. "Yes, Camille," he offered to help, "that virus originates in the mouth, goes back to the hand, to the mouth, to the anus, to the vagina, and back again; to and fro, by the newly-infected, ignorant masseuse and to the unknowing, unenlightened participant, or, in your case, your lover."

"That lover is a fucker; my Salazar, who sees those whores in Mazatlán, or Tijuana—wherever he meets the cartel," she swore, downing the rest of her tequila and violently throwing the empty glass at the tree.

"Be careful, Camille. It could also be Miguel. This virus, commonly called 'HPV', causes cervical cancers in women, genital warts in men and women, and leads to cancers in the mouth, pharynx, anus, and genitalia in both sexes. Vaccination to protect against this most common of all sexually transmitted disease is available, but is rarely asked for or suggested by doctors."

"Miguel is good to me, Doctor. He puts a cream on that itch for me," she chastised Zack, pouting. She then called over a waiter for a refill.

"Camille, there are over a hundred and fifty types of HPV viruses, with almost one third of them being pathogenic. That is infective and problematic to the anogenital region of both sexes. It is believed that over fifty percent of sexually promiscuous men and women will be infected in their lifetimes."

"Miguel is clean. He said so. That fucker of mine isn't, and he fucks me after fucking those whores in Tijuana."

"I hope your men are circumcised, Camille," he said with compassion. "Male circumcision at birth, or later, is a protective surgical practice that prevents the virus from inhabiting the area under the foreskin, making it less likely to develop into cancer. Without circumcision, the dreaded disease is freely communicated to others."

Camille had had enough. She swore at her 'fucker' again, and pushed herself off the lounge when she saw one of the cartel generals beckoning to her. "Miguel was cut. Badly. His prick has a crook in it now, but I like it that way." She laughed and stormed off.

Zack watched her leave, waving in glee to the man who was making sexual gestures toward her. He shuddered to think of how many of those entering the tents on the beach would be scratching their crotches by next week. But he was inwardly pleased to see that money was freely exchanged, and that the economy, at least on the beach, was flourishing for those most in need, infected or not.

Zack settled back again, pulling his Panama hat down over his eyes to rest. If such sexual activity wasn't sufficient, for another fistful of dollars you could purchase anything you wanted to smoke, suck up your nose, or inject into your veins.

As he rested, he heard the crowd exchange ideas and money. They were all anxiously waiting for one grand and momentous occasion: Salazar's arrival.

Zack's comfortable repose was interrupted, and his attention again shifted to Camille. Her devotion had also shifted from her attempts to titillate the generals to her daughter, Maria, who had just arrived. Maria smiled at Zack, but blatantly ignored her mother and sat a short distance away, talking to another young woman.

Camille, displeased at her daughter's spiteful entrance, approached Zack, and apropos of nothing, commented, "You will soon be out of this country, where you were exiled in poverty; like your hero, Napoleon, as you once told me, away from all these wetbacks." He held her up as she staggered about, now completely drunk after emptying the liter of tequila and iced margaritas she'd mixed on the drive from Mexico City.

Zack nodded absently as he watched the tanned, topless girls parade themselves in front of the handsome *gringo* from America. Any one of them would kill to be taken back to America with Zack.

As the beach party continued, tequila and expensive scotch flowed freely alongside joints and numerous lines of cocaine. Zack was becoming increasingly nervous, aware that the people surrounding him were already quite high.

The cartel generals were close by, talking in huddles, their volume increasing with each drink or toke. One man dragged his finger viciously across his own neck, indicating violent decapitation, and then he laughed hideously. He also heard them mocking Carlos, using such words as 'collaborator' and 'rat fink' and offering threats of what his punishment might be.

Zack finished his drink and was ready to leave. He feared being a witness to a beheading and wanted to get out, Camille or not.

As he was thinking of how he would make his way back to the city, Maria approached him. He decided to stay a moment longer, spellbound by her beauty.

She sat down next to her mother, and Camille began to braid her hair. Zack was near enough to hear the stern tone in Camille's voice.

Zack had heard that Maria lived in the city in the wealthy district, the *Zona Rosa*. Camille had also told Zack that Maria was involved with Carlos the snitch: the stool pigeon, the informer. Not only was Carlos wanted by Salazar, but also by the *federales*, the police. His face had been severely slashed by Salazar's generals for being an informant, but he escaped—somehow.

Zack listened as he basked under the palapa, and was intrigued to hear his name mentioned often. Camille nodded toward Zack as she brushed her daughter's golden hair. "Maria, this nice young man in his thirties—Zachariah, he calls himself—is a doctor at our University, a psychiatrist; single and handsome, he is. A good catch, my baby, a very good catch for you," she clucked, combing Maria's tresses. A cool breeze gently bathed the trio.

Zack smiled approvingly to hear Camille calling him a 'good catch'. After all, he was. Dark haired; a muscular, strong body; clean shaven; Roman profile; cunning and driven to succeed.

Zack moved his chair and shifted himself closer to mother and daughter.

Maria was shouting. "You only want to marry me off, bitch, so you can continue to fuck that one-eyed stud with the foot-long prick," she sneered.

Camille lowered her voice as children ran by to play in the ocean. "Shush, my dear one. Be still. Pedro? He is good to me, my sweet. That doctor, he could be good for you, too, baby. Doctor Zack, he soon returns to America, soon to be the director at a famous hospital. He could save you from that man of yours, Carlos, who is a dead barracuda as soon as Salazar finds him. He'll slit his throat for betraying the cartel to the *politicos*, and you will lose that one and only love in your life."

Maria swore at her mother again and Zack heard her throw her handheld mirror against the sturdy tree trunk.

"Be still, my dear. I heard this doctor speaking with his friend in England who gives people a new face by surgery. Maybe he can give your Carlos a new face also, my sweet," Camille whispered, holding her daughter back.

Zack was surprised that Camille had recently overheard him talking to Sam, his close friend in London, England. Sam was a plastic surgeon, who perfected total facial transplants on those who had their face burned away in accidents or mauled by animals; Sam was now very famous. The newspapers wrote that the Queen might soon bestow an award on him, to recognize his surgical skills.

Maria broke her mother's grip on her arm, and she stomped away, swearing and shouting that her mother, Salazar, and Pedro were all fucking pigs.

Zack shrugged and allowed his imagination to wander. Maybe, just maybe, he could charm Maria, suck up to Salazar, manipulate the alcoholic Camille, and save Maria from Carlos. He imagined he could marry her, and live the good life as a prominent psychiatrist in Mexico City. Treat wealthy, neurotic, histrionic rich women all day long.

Life might be easier in Mexico than in competitive California, after all, he thought to himself.

"Pardon her language," Camille said, moving her chair to be closer as she downed another sambuca on ice.

Camille, the conniving mother, was now determined to have her Maria—her only child—not only meet a rich American doctor, but avoid potential death once Salazar found Carlos.

It was during the stop in Taxco that Camille confided in Zack, stating that she wanted her daughter to marry before the girl was sent to Salazar's brothels in Tijuana; a likely result after Salazar found and butchered her lover.

Camille had explained that Carlos was one of Salazar's henchmen, but after rescuing Maria from her sordid lifestyle, he collaborated with the authorities and exposed many of the cartel generals for a generous reward. Camille feared that Maria would be sent to Tijuana, where she would be used and abused at the will of Salazar's guards, cronies, henchmen, dealers, and pushers after Carlos was caught, slaughtered, quartered, and hung out to dry in the hot desert sun.

"The vultures would nibble on his flesh and leave the bones to dry and rot in our beautiful Mexican desert," she concluded with an air of *just desserts.*

Zack had heard the rumblings earlier from Camille about Carlos. Some newspaper articles lauded him as a hero, a courageous whistle-blower. They were quoting authorities, the police and the politicians, vowing to clean up the drug trade to make Mexico safe for its citizens and its tourists.

Camille said it was Salazar and his drug lords who called Carlos a 'quisling': a filthy, conniving rat; a stool pigeon; a man with a badly scarred face, sliced up as a warning to others.

As Zack watched the bizarre scene before him, Salazar's cartel generals continued to drink, talk, laugh, and drink some more. He noted that a number of them were also snorting coke and frequenting the tents for added pleasures. The masseurs were making a small fortune.

But the generals, and those who were hungry, were waiting anxiously for two major events to happen. The pig was nearly finished roasting on the spit, and their drug lord, Salazar, would be arriving shortly. The fat pig, ready to be carved, and the corpulent 'wolf'—called *El Lobo*—soon to appear, were the most highly anticipated events of the day.

Teenagers played volleyball, small children laughed and cavorted in the pounding waves, whores made money, and the cartel generals dealt drugs while the sun was slowly setting. A cool breeze carried the enticing smell of the roasting pig. Burning grease spurted and flamed from the pit as the chef tapped his ladle and poured more grease onto the beast to the tune of the Mariachi band playing close by.

CHAPTER 2

El Lobo

Suddenly, the band stopped playing. Mariachi trumpets on the beach blared in unison. Children scurried to be with their parents. The young whores squirted perfume over their bodies; men stood at attention. The chef covered the pig in a tarp, and a deep hush fell over the crowd.

Zack stirred from his recurrent thoughts of leaving, curious to witness the next act in this drama.

Conversations ceased, parents cleaned sand from their children's bodies, whiskey glasses were emptied and dropped into pails, and all eyes turned toward the iron gates protecting the crowd, far behind the gathering.

A lone trumpeter, decked out in his finest black suit, festooned with pearl decorations and beads, walked through the crowd. He blared out a welcoming blast as other guards raised their rifles in salute. One fired off a volley in tribute.

Zack watched as Salazar made his grand entrance. Salazar's convoy of three, shining, black Bentleys drove up to the elaborate iron gates, guards stationed and waiting. Pedro jumped out of the lead car and ran ahead of the convoy in order to get the gates to open on time.

The limousines spat sand as they drove into the conclave. They came to a halt in front of Camille. A young boy ran to open Salazar's door—a great honor for the youth—as "The Wolf" maneuvered his rotund, sweating body out of his vehicle. He pressed a handful of pesos into the lad's hand.

Salazar waved to his adoring crowd, but he continued talking to another man who was also exiting the Bentley: a colossal, swarthy Mexican man named Gomez. Gomez, with a trim mustache and bushy eyebrows, sporting wide, heavy braces that held up massive trousers, a gun belt, and a machete, was a formidable presence.

Ever persistent, Camille's once again introduced Maria to Zack after Maria joined her mother in quiet deference.

However, Maria, now ignoring her mother, dragged Zack away from the crowd that was fawning over Salazar to a rickety bamboo bench, located near the water.

As they sat on the bench, the wind picked up, and Zack could see a fishing boat in the distance slowly moving toward them. A flock of pelicans flew past, dipping and diving here and there to catch small sardines or herring.

He moved closer to her tanned legs, hidden beneath the gossamer wrap, and he inhaled deeply, smelling her perfumed body. He wondered how he could use this temptress to his own advantage, since he was certain she wanted something from him. He felt he could test her out and reveal something of himself.

She was the first to speak. "Tell me why you came to our country, Zack," Maria asked, gently holding his hand, being much warmer and softer than she had been in their earlier meeting.

"I was happy to leave Boston and a disastrous, painful, five-year marriage, followed by a lengthy divorce."

She gripped his hand tightly. "Oh, what happened to you then, my Zack?"

'My Zack'? He was already hers? He liked the thought of that.

"After medical school, I specialized in psychiatry. There is an open director position in San Diego on a psych ward that I want to apply for. I just need to move a creepy, pervert of a director off that ward and out of his position. He's a pervert from way back. We all knew him well in the east."

Maria, not picking up on the pervert theme, looked at Zack intently. "Why ever psychiatry, Zack?"

There it was again: a simple question often asked, but begging a long and tedious answer. He wanted her to know something about him and gave her the pure, simple answer. "I was always interested in human behavior. I was impressed that those who were so ill were able to be healthy again. Not many doctors were interested in helping them."

Before Zack could explain further, Maria suddenly stood up. "There, Zack. Now. It is five o'clock," was all she said.

He looked up, following the wave of her hand back to the crowd. He was sure one of the guards suddenly dropped over the parapet at the gates. Zack watched as another guard fell to the ground. He heard cracks of several rifles coming from that fishing boat, now close to the beach near the roasting pig.

"They're shooting. Is it a police raid?" Zack shouted.

Maria was calm, almost dreamlike. "No, it is Carlos and his friends. We are safe here, my Zack; do not fear."

Zack wasn't as certain about that, but there was nowhere else to go. He was caught with the ocean in front, a stinking, rotting slough behind, and the rattle of gunfire ahead. He stood briefly stricken with panic, but he quickly regained his senses as Maria pulled him toward the approaching fishing boat, which was still firing into the crowd.

He stopped and ducked behind the bench, pushing Maria with him as an explosion tore at the iron gates. The entrance collapsed as pieces of bamboo and metal flew into the air, piercing the crowd, felling the young lad still clutching a handful of pesos from Salazar.

Suddenly, several large, armored jeeps sped through the rubble and circled the crowd. Women and men were screaming, and children scattered as the roasted pig tumbled over and sand flew in the air.

Jeeps wheeled in and out, causing utter chaos. Men and women, some totally naked, ran out of the massage tents as one jeep smashed into the nearest one, running over a young masseuse clutching a wad of bills.

Men in the jeeps were firing into the crowd as guests tried to run for safety. There was no cover: only low Yucca brush and coconut trees. Grenades were lobbed toward the fleeing guests, aimed at Salazar and his guards.

Maria stood and laughed as she pointed at Salazar attempting to hide his corpulent body behind his guards. "There's Salazar, my stepfather, that fat, pervert pig who used me when I was young. He's dead, for sure," she shouted to Zack over the mayhem.

Suddenly, two of Salazar's three Bentleys disintegrated into balls of fire. Zack crouched down, pulling Maria by the arm, as small pieces of metal crisscrossed the area. The stench of gunfire smoke, combined with the odor of the roasting pig, overwhelmed them.

Zack, now aware of Maria's close relationship with Carlos, was amazed at her courage and fortitude in her quest to help him and be rid of Salazar.

Pushing Maria ahead of him, he started for the back roads behind the beach villas, along the filthy marsh toward the small village nearby.

She resisted him, and said, "Don't be afraid, Zack. It is Salazar we want, not you." She stood there with a satisfied smile, enjoying the bedlam.

Zack, beside himself now in terror, saw that the jeeps carried four men each, all blazing their guns at the crowd. Grenades sporadically went off and bullets zinged about. Pedro, Salazar's lackey, pushed his boss under a table and rolled on top of him in protection.

Acrid smoke from the burning Bentleys and gas tanks billowed from the massive explosions engulfing Zack and Maria.

Through the smoldering haze, Zack could just make out Pedro, who now stood up with Gomez, Salazar's general in the drug trade. He was firing point-blank at a jeep mired in the soft sand. With the frantic driver gunning the motor, the jeep flipped over onto its side, pinning the men underneath.

Gomez calmly went to the struggling foursome and shot each one in the head at close range. Another jeep was cornered, and the four men inside were quickly slaughtered with machetes.

Thinking he should help the wounded, Zack carefully tried to make his way back to the group, leaving Maria, who was slowly walking to the water's edge.

He crept low to the ground, seeking out Camille. Once in sight, he watched as she ran amok, unsteady and drunk, trying to flee from a jeep that was attempting to run her down.

The jeep suddenly flipped, pinning the men underneath, narrowly avoiding Camille, who fell to the ground in shock.

Gomez calmly walked over and fired point-blank at the men desperately trying to free themselves. He left Camille for dead.

The last lone jeep accelerated in reverse and left as quickly as it came.

"My God, Maria; we need to get help. Use your phone," Zack yelled as he ran toward the chaos. He watched in disbelief as the Mariachi band members opened their musical cases and removed hand pistols and Uzi machine guns. They began firing in Salazar's direction.

Zack ducked behind an overturned jeep, hugging the sand, fearing for stray bullets. He looked back at Maria.

Maria waved him away and began running to the edge of the beach, toward the boat, which was near the shoreline. One man waded to shore and helped Maria get into the waiting vessel. She called out to Zack to join her.

He waivered slightly. *Should he go with Maria?* Maria motioned again for Zack to join her, waving her arms wildly and shouting. His heart sank to see her disappear as the boat sped away, destroying what he thought was his only chance to escape. He had waited too long, conflicted between joining Maria and fulfilling his duty as a physician. He looked about, struggling to move through the pandemonium, but he knew he had to help those still alive.

Zack looked over the painful madness. Many guests lay dead. Wives, husbands, and children left behind were wailing over their loved ones' mangled bodies.

A few remaining guests had their drivers pull them into waiting cars, abandoning Salazar, who was still cowering under a heavy wooden table, still protected by Pedro.

Zack made his way through the chaos and found Salazar standing near the collapsed bar, swearing in Spanish. He brushed off blood and sand from his rotund body. "You can't do anything here, Doctor. All dead."

Zack looked back to see the fishing boat Maria was in speeding off into the distant setting sun, a red ball of fire being consumed by the blue Pacific. "That bitch; it was her, Carlos, I know," Salazar swore, waving a stubby fist at her.

Zack left Salazar and walked about the dead and dying, covering his face with a kerchief in order to stop the black smoke from filling his nostrils and stifling him. "Salazar, are you all right? Where's Camille?" Zack asked.

"There," Salazar spat at the body. "Dead, by the daughter's hand. That daughter, Maria, borne from this bitch's womb, and that son of a bitch, Carlos," he added as Gomez forced him away into his one remaining SUV, leaving his wife to rot under dead bodies.

Zack turned away from the vitriol and spied her lying in a heap. Her inert body was half-covered by four dead men sprawled on top of her. They were in army fatigues: black bandanas covered their heads, and many were still holding their Uzi machine guns. Some of their necks and arms had been partly chopped away by Gomez.

He was ready to leave Camille's body for the ambulances and police officers, whose sirens could be heard, wailing in the distance. He had to return to the city and be ready to leave the next day for America.

Just as he turned away, he heard a whimper. He turned around again and saw Camille's hand trying to push a body off of her torso. He stopped, conflicted again about the need to escape the chaos and his duty as a physician to save Camille, if she was still alive.

Nauseated and holding a towel over his face to protect him from the stench, Zack removed distorted, crushed bodies off of Camille and kneeled down beside her. She was barely breathing, but alive. She had been spared from death by the mangled corpses that covered her blood-stained body.

CHAPTER 3

Taxco

Zack lifted Camille's head gently, and, as he did, she opened her eyes wide and spontaneously flung her arms around him. She was sobbing wildly and babbling; her face was contorted with fear.

He brushed the matted hair from her face, soothing her anguish. He spoke gently to her, reassuring she would be safe now that she was with him.

She gradually became oriented to what had happened, and she shuddered. But she wept with joy that she had survived, and she was happy to be in his strong arms.

Camille clung to him as he carried her amidst mangled bodies and vehicles still aflame, fearing other explosions. He made his way toward her SUV, still parked in the distance near the bushes, free from the chaos.

Struggling through the sand with Camille clinging to his neck, he found the keys, opened the passenger door, and quickly buckled her in. As he drove toward the demolished gates, they passed women still in bathing suits, men staggering with open wounds, and parents with small, naked children who all tried to flag him down, pleading for help.

With Camille beside him, he feared stopping to help, lest others might recognize her and still want to kill her—and him, who appeared to be her apparent bodyguard.

He looked back in the rear-view mirror to see hungry vultures already hopping about, picking at swollen eyes, torn-apart bellies with bowels protruding here and there, and at other contorted corpses in the sand. He could see Pedro near the gates, pushing Salazar and Gomez into another shiny, black SUV that had two armed guards on each side.

They paid no attention to him, since he was just one of many cars on the roadway trying to escape.

Zack shook his head in disbelief when he saw the white banner stuck on the back panel of Salazar's SUV as it roared past stating, *"Jesus is coming soon."*

The sun had set, but there was still a small amount of light in the sky as he drove as carefully, but as fast, as he could on the crowded highway out of Acapulco, passing fire engines, ambulances, and police cars swooping onto the confusion of the beach.

He told Camille, who was finally awake and aware of who he was, but still in shock, that they would stop for the night in Taxco, just far enough away to make sure they were safe.

As they neared Taxco, she was more coherent. She recalled the fear of the jeep running at her, and trembled at the vivid flashbacks flooding over her of her traumatic experience.

Zack was relieved that she didn't suffer a permanent concussion or open head injury. He glanced at her from time to time, wondering if he should just take her to a hospital instead. He reassured himself that her pupils were equal, there was no paralysis or weakness of her arms or legs, her memory was decent, she was talking, and she was not bleeding from any wounds.

Once off the highway in Taxco, he turned into the town, parked on a quiet, dark, side road just off the *zocolo* square. He looked around. There were no other cars. It felt safe.

"Stay in the car," he instructed Camille, and he went into a nondescript hotel and booked a room. He returned with a bottle of water and some chocolate he had bought from the hotel lobby machine and gave her some of both. He looked her over. She had no visible severe wounds and was coherent. He felt comfortable tending to her without additional medical intervention.

The clerk smiled knowingly at the young man and an inebriated older woman renting a cheap room. Zack helped Camille into the elevator and pressed the button for the third floor. He found the room, bolted the door, turned on the lights, and pulled the shades down on the windows.

Camille was still unsteady on her feet as Zack helped her undress and step into a hot tub. She sat there, more aware and calmer in the soothing, warm water. He gently washed her down, toweled her body clean, and helped her to the bed.

He pulled up the bed covers over her and told her to rest. He freshened up, checked the scene out the window, and told her he'd be right back. He secured the door and went out for some food, bottled water, whiskey, and a pack of Cuban cigars—but no tequila for Camille, even though that is what she'd requested.

The hotel felt quiet and safe as Camille recovered. Zack calmed down by smoking cigars and drinking scotch most of the night. He didn't talk to Camille about Maria, Salazar, Pedro, or the cartel, as he feared having too much information would be risky for him.

By the next morning, she had made a good recovery, and there was no more news of Acapulco on the old, scratchy Toshiba television. It was safe to drive back to Camille's villa in the city.

When Zack pulled into the driveway to the massive, high gates guarding the villa just after noon, three guards with guns drawn and two others with Uzi machine guns pointed their weapons at the SUV. Zack, with his heart in his throat, stopped the car.

Unable to see the driver since the windows were dark, one heavily armed guard barked in halting English and some Spanish to roll down all the windows. Another passed a mirror on a long handle under the car, seeking any hidden explosives. A third had his dog sniff for explosives inside the van once the doors were opened.

The one who appeared to be in charge kept Zack's driver's door ajar with his foot, holding back a snarling Labrador retriever who looked at Zack suspiciously. They recognized Camille, who spoke calmly to each of them and identified him as her savior, and assured them that she was safe. They all saluted and let them pass.

Camille looked back through the rear window and waved at the well-trained dog barking and straining at the leash, wanting to chase the vehicle. "I'm so glad that the guards used a Lab and not a German shepherd. My favorite kind of pet, once upon a time."

Zack drove slowly, not wanting to cause any new distress for the guards at the gates as other well-armed men scurried about the grounds. "Those German shepherds were the kind seen in the movies, and the kind that were used in Afghanistan to sniff out IED's—improvised explosive devices—used by the Taliban, Camille. I read about it in the Med journals. Those dogs have a keen sense of smell, with a well-developed trigeminal nerve, the fifth cranial nerve that innervates the nose with the brain."

As he parked the van he recalled that one of his physiology professors lectured that while humans can smell a spoonful of sugar in a cup of coffee, a well-trained dog can smell that same spoonful in a million gallons of water.

Zack held onto Camille's arm as she exited the van, and he helped her into her room. The villa was quiet. No one had heard from Salazar: not Fernando the chef, Miguel the masseuse, or the gardener. Several guards wandered about the villa and camped outside on the streets in vans at night.

Camille slept for the afternoon while he lay near the pool, reading the papers and listening to Taylor Swift singing "Shake it Off" on his iPhone.

The local news described the politicians' promises to the people, ridding the country of corruption, prostitution, crime, drugs, and poverty after Acapulco's bedlam. Headlines were rife with news of the drug wars, murders, and slaughter of the various gangs; hundreds had been killed, tortured, and had gone missing. Many of those killed were innocent citizens, tourists, and bystanders: people who were just in the wrong place at the wrong time during the street gunfights.

Zack was startled to read police had certain information from an 'unnamed informant'. Zack knew it was the quisling Carlos, Maria's '*hombre*'. They were now raiding the cartels, which could include Pedro, Gomez, and Salazar.

Zack's gut churned as he thought of Pedro, and what might be revealed about his own, personal deals with him if caught. Still, it wasn't as though he was pushing real drugs, or was a part of the cartel.

He read how the citizenry were worried about the violent war between Salazar's men, the police, and other crime bosses, and they were calling for quislings, like Carlos, to receive protection. A few local *politicos* were already in jail for receiving huge bribes from the cartels, often escaping or being pardoned at great expense by corrupt judges and prosecutors.

One judge, having convicted Salazar's deputies a short while ago, was ambushed. He had been beheaded in front of his children, and his house was torched with the children and their nanny, all bound and gagged, still inside in order to serve as an example. The judge's headless body was left, smoldering after being doused in gasoline, at 3 AM in the *zocolo*, Mexico City's grand public square.

The corpse was still ablaze, and the stink flooded the *zocolo* as the cathedral bells tolled in the square, bringing people to early mass on Sunday. It was not only the reek of burned flesh that appalled arriving churchgoers, but also the vision of the judge's wife. She was hanging from a light standard by her ankles. Her throat had been sliced, and her face was covered in red, congealed blood, which flowed down her breasts and dripped from her fingers.

Zack gagged as he read the details on the front pages, and his eyes twitched as he envisioned the dreadful scene. He could read no more. He could be next. He had to get out of Mexico, soon, and get to San Diego.

All of those headlines made Zack apprehensive. He had a good thing going with Salazar's bodyguard, Pedro. Amphetamines and Ritalin, a psychoactive stimulant used for autistic children, were both freely available to Zack at the university hospital. Pedro had involved Zack in selling such stimulants to university students and others on the streets for a good price, lining Zack's pockets to pay off his wife and the legal bills.

The Mexican pharmaceutical drug companies gave Zack whatever he wanted for his research on women suffering from severe depression. He simply substituted their research antidepressants for sugar tablets, and told the company that he was doing double-blind studies with amphetamines and Ritalin. That was acceptable. After all, it was research, and the company would make a fortune on Zack's soon-to-be-published, favorable conclusions.

Zack was doing well with Pedro's contacts. Pedro sold the drugs on the streets and in the schools, and then passed the profits to Zack, less ten percent for his troubles.

Zack rationalized that it wasn't like he was selling cocaine or heroin to those kids. They got high, mixed a tablet with beer or whatever, got their girlfriends stupid on additional date drugs and alcoholic potions, and had a good time. As long as they didn't pop pills, drink, and drive. But some did. That was too bad.

Zack's secret account in the Bahamas was safe and burgeoning quickly, paying off his massive legal bills and university bank loans. But there were storm clouds on the horizon, and Zack could smell trouble. Pedro's secret delivery of a satchel of cash in Acapulco was the last. After all, Zack had a hundred thousand American dollars in his Bahama's piggy bank, and that was enough.

Even in the aftermath of all he had witnessed, the doctor was still mesmerized by the dramatically beautiful, but potentially dangerous, Maria. She was so different to his ex, Selma, who was always angry and critical. She was an alcoholic manic-depressive, who was also addicted to drugs supplied by her own doctor. He was not only disqualified for prescribing too many oxycodone meds, but he also developed a sexual relationship with her. That had been the last straw. Zack lost all empathy for her and her illnesses.

He had tried to lead a quiet life in Acapulco, minding his own business—although that included his business with Pedro—but now there was Maria. He preferred to keep his sexual appetites quietly confined to Carmen, a pretty Mexican law student at the university.

However, he never had intercourse with Carmen, fearing being infected with HIV or some other venereal disease. He thought he would see less of Carmen, now that Maria had entered his life, if she might return before he left Mexico.

Zack was nervous about asking Camille about her daughter, as she might inform Salazar. Camille had kept her mouth shut about Zack's extracurricular financial activities. She knew all about the healthy grant from a large, international pharmaceutical company he received in order to work at the University of Mexico, after completing his residency in psychiatry in Boston. Zack had talked too much with Camille after several margaritas at the villa's pool some time ago.

She put two and two together when she kept seeing Pedro at her city residence, and saw Zack passing large packages to Pedro. Zack also found out that 'Doctor' Salazar actually funded Zack's income to a large extent in order to make his department appear more legitimate. This 'Doctor' Salazar was not a doctor at all, and his department was only a front to launder drug money. Having Zack there gave the department, and the research, a certain degree of credibility.

It was later that afternoon when Zack was determined to leave Mexico; he would have to tell Camille.

Once Camille had recovered from her trauma, she was back at the pool sipping on her favorite drink. Zack, unfortunately, told her more about Sam, his close buddy from medical school who was doing facial transplants in London.

It was at that same time when Camille's newly-found bodyguard, Miguel—his previous position being house boy, masseuse, margarita mixer, or whatever else Camille needed—came out to the pool with a jug of ice cold drinks for his mistress.

As Zack accepted a margarita, he almost spilled it when he looked up and saw Miguel in the daylight.

"My God, man. What happened?" Zack asked.

Miguel, stoic and aloof, didn't try to hide the scars on his face. In fact, he seemed to be proud of them as he turned and showed Zack both cheeks. "Fire, *señor* doctor. Bad fire at the hotel I worked. Back at my home in Puerto Rico," he said. He then took off his shirt and showed Zack his back. More scars were revealed on a powerful, muscular man.

"My friend in England does facial transplants, Miguel. He could help you. Maybe someone could send you there if the cost is difficult," Zack replied sympathetically, giving Camille a sideward glance.

Miguel bowed. He looked at Camille. She just rolled her eyes, not looking up. Miguel left.

Camille was suddenly interested. "Maria's friend, Carlos, needs a new face, my Zack. It was sliced badly. Someday Maria will tell you."

That's all that was said about that. Camille was silent. Brooding. Drinking more quickly as she looked back to see where Miguel had gone. Zack imagined she was thinking of Miguel, blushing, excitedly getting ready for Miguel's deft fingers.

Zack broke the silence. "Salazar is still away, *señora*. Any word?" Zack asked, somewhat anxiously while he stretched out in a pool chair beside her.

Camille nestled in beside Zack, closer to his chaise longue. "*Sí*, Doctor. He often travels on business to Tijuana, but this time with his bodyguards, Pedro and Gomez, for protection," Camille said as she bent over, revealing her well-shaped breasts, recently uplifted and now tantalizingly close to his face.

Camille continued in her seductive, cloying manner as she squirted body lotion onto one hand and rubbed up and down her arms and legs. She whispered to Zack that they could move into her bedroom; clouds were moving in, and her room would be warmer. She said she wanted to thank him for saving her. It would be her way of giving him a reward.

He shook his head, fearing that the chef or Miguel could show up and inform Salazar. "Not a good idea, Camille. Not here in the open. It is too risky for me with your husband," he said.

Camille pouted. "My husband, he lets go all over my breasts during sex. He says that it is clean, and he calls it something in his poor Spanish, *el sperma*. Where did that word come from?" she asked, downing another margarita.

Zack looked at her curiously, surprised that she was sincerely interested in a part of Salazar's human physiology. "A Greek word. It means seed."

"Is all that white stuff clean, though?"

"Yes, Camille." Zack again shifted away from Camille; he saw Miguel talking to one of the guards by the house, who was looking sideways at Camille and snickering.

Camille pouted. "I know that I am a good woman, like your mother used to be. You told me the story: before she died, when you were still a young boy. You loved her deeply. She was very good to you, you said. You did well with your inheritance, and after your father left, my dear one, to graduate, and to help your sister with your money, even as she lay dying from that dreaded disease," she said quietly to Zack, silently accepting his decision to keep her hands to herself.

"Yes, Camille. Multiple sclerosis. Poor girl."

Zack, concerned for her risky adventures with Pedro and now Miguel, offered her some simple advice. "It is dangerous for you to take the sexual risks with some of these men that you see. I am worried for you. Please be careful."

Camille listened, touched his hand in quiet gratitude, "I will. I just need it."

This is one woman who is open to speak her mind, Zack thought. "It is written that sex keeps one young. It is good for the skin and the constitution, and some say those who are sexually active live even longer. Their minds are sharper—cognitively, that is—and they think with better memory."

Camille nodded and poured herself another margarita. Zack liked Camille and their verbal dalliance, but he had heard of Fernando's tale of woe some weeks earlier. The chef talked, and listening to such a story caused Zack's own delicate *cajones*, as Fernando called his testicles, to tighten up. He needed his testicles to stay where they were, and not at the end of Salazar's machete.

Sleeping with the boss's wife was not a good idea. It was in the kitchen that Camille's chef, Fernando, had told him the story. It appeared that Camille was depressed and vengeful after her young gardener fled with his life. She needed another bed partner, and not the services of her perverted husband, who preferred the nubile teen whores living in the pink zone in the city, *Zona Rosa*, as it was called.

The chef had sliced a head of lettuce and divided tomatoes into a salad as he spoke in low tones. "She had taken her whole bottle of sleeping pills a month after our gardener never returned. When Salazar came home a day early and found her vomiting, he just left her to sleep it off for two days."

Zack nibbled on a papaya. "Poor lady. Why?"

Fernando washed three cucumbers for the salad. "Poor? Not so. Jose, her gardener, was truly a veritable stud with a dick as long and thick as this cucumber. But he was well paid as a gardener by our lady. He serviced some of the female help and then our lady. Then our chief came home unexpectedly, and found her in her room tied up to the bed posts, as she liked it with Jose. The chief was going to kill both Jose and our lady," the cook told Zack, pouring olive oil on the greens.

"*Mamma mia*, Fernando. What happened?"

Fernando brandished his butcher knife in the air. "He threatened to castrate Jose with his machete. Jose pushed the overweight Salazar aside and jumped out the window. He fled naked across the courtyard and never returned."

"*Mamma mia*, that Jose, he was stupid to be fooling around with his boss's wife. Dumb, man, very dumb," Zack added.

Fernando thought for a second, looked at a fruitcake he had just baked, pointed to it and said, "Yes, Doctor, well, life is like that fruitcake I just baked."

Zack was expecting a lecture on baking fruitcakes. "Really; life is like a fruitcake. How so, Fernando?"

"Well, if you dig around long enough, you'll always find some nuts."

They both laughed. Fernando was the original culinary philosopher, Zack thought as he had left the kitchen nibbling on a piece of cake.

Zack recalled that Camille was not a happy camper at the villa after that incident. She was out to get her husband. He had left her tied up to the bedstead, whipped her mercilessly, abused her in all orifices, and then left her for Maria to find.

Camille complained bitterly to Salazar that she needed massage therapy after such abuse. Salazar agreed, after constant nagging, and he hired Miguel as her private masseur. He thought that Miguel, hideous with a face like rough sandpaper, and looking like a shriveled prune after it was scorched by a fire, would never appeal to his wife.

Salazar was happy to not hear Camille's complaints again.

Miguel, a hunk of a man, with strong arms and upper body strength, but nimble fingers, was happy to have work. Camille had never been more satisfied. Fernando claimed he had heard the squeals coming from her bedroom as Miguel massaged every orifice, which had once been abused by Salazar, with his fingers, his tongue, or with his massive erection.

Zack was surprised about Camille and her sexual preferences, although nothing could surprise him anymore after what he heard from all his patients as a psychiatrist. But being tied up for sex was novel for the young man.

Zack once asked Camille why she preferred to be tied up, after she had, at one time, invited him into her parlor for similar sadomasochistic sex games. He was interested, but after what he heard happened to Jose, he quickly declined.

"My dear, Doctor," she confessed, "I will explain. It gives me a complete feeling of helplessness. It frees me up. I can fantasize about sex without needing to do anything. I am quiet, still, and just accepting without responsibility. It's exhilarating. The more I struggle, the more intense the sexual orgasms. I can have several," she said without blushing or embarrassment.

Zack recalled studying Freud and the Marquis de Sade. Freud was sure that sadomasochism was a delayed immaturity of the young girl's infantile psych or ego. De Sade wrote about the practices, but not about the psychoanalysis of the sexual acts. The word sadomasochism was coined after de Sade and Sacher-Masoch, two Europeans who wrote about the so-called 'perversions'.

He knew that women's magazines, like *Cosmopolitan*, now wrote about bondage and S&M practices. Nothing was sacred anymore. They were called perversions many years ago, but no longer.

Zack was worried. Just knowing about Maria and her Carlos might be enough to court disaster.

He had returned to his room to ready himself for his trip back to America. He threw his empty margarita glass at the garbage can in the corner of the room and swore at Maria, and then at himself, for letting her lure him into a hornet's nest.

The crack of gunfire, an explosion, and screams could be heard coming from the front gates, drowning out the shatter of the margarita glass hitting the garbage can.

Zack instinctively ducked down and scrambled behind his bed, still reminded of the trauma on the Acapulco beaches. The window in his room vibrated from the blast.

"What the hell's going on?" Zack shouted as he eventually ran out into the dining room.

Fernando was out of the kitchen brandishing his large chopping cleaver. "The attack, Doctor. On our lady," he shouted, running toward the pool area.

Zack, still uncertain what to do or where to go, cautiously went to the pool patio door and peered out. He saw Miguel picking up Camille and rushing to the side of the villa, away from the front area.

Zack waited as a police siren came to a halt in front of the gates. Fernando reappeared, still holding his cleaver, but sweating and swearing. "They bombed the guards, Doctor; the autos are destroyed, and two guards are dead. Some poor dog had his throat cut. Some pedestrians walking by were killed, but the police are here now. We are safe, Doctor."

"Camille? Where is she, Fernando?"

Fernando put his cleaver down on a table as he pulled out a large kitchen towel from his back pocket and wiped down his brow and neck. "Safe. With Miguel and the gardener. Safe, Doctor. We are safe now."

Zack opened the patio doors. Several police were walking about with guns drawn. Camille was talking to an officer who appeared to be in charge. She offered him a cocktail and watched him take a drink as they spoke.

Fernando, calm and at ease again, went back to his kitchen. Zack assumed that he had seen this before.

Zack made a decision. He packed his one bag and left his room, thinking he must find a cheap hotel, and lose himself for the night in the seedy side of Mexico City. He would then hop a plane for America the next morning.

As he walked through the gardens, he looked at the chaos on the street. Four ambulances and several police cars were out front. A van the guards used was smoldering after being doused by the fire truck. Two of the guards were covered in sheets, and the dog was in a sack.

Zack presumed the men were being taken to the morgue.

As he debated whether or not to tell Camille of his decision, he felt his cell vibrating in his pocket.

It was Maria. Unsure whether to answer, he pushed the button. Her voice was warm and inviting. She apologized for abandoning him at the beach, and she invited him to her apartment in the *Zona Rosa*, the Pink Zone, of Mexico City.

"I just heard from my mother. Terrible for the family of those poor guards just doing their jobs. You are safe?" she asked.

Zack thought it had to be Carlos again who attacked Camille and the villa.

"Yes, I'm okay. Too risky for me after what went down on the beach. You're a part of it, and now this," he said anxiously. He hesitated to talk more with her, and yet yearned to feel her warm body against his.

Zack could hear the tension in her voice as she pleaded, "Carlos disappeared. I'm frightened of being alone. Please, just stay awhile. It is safe here for you." She hesitated for a second, knowing what Zack must be thinking. "Carlos was not involved with this attack on our house, Zack."

Zack didn't respond to that reassurance, but he was relieved. Not having anywhere else to go for the night, he reluctantly agreed.

Zack decided to tell Camille of his decision to move for his own safety, but he did not mention Maria's invitation. She gave him a big hug, but was not sorry to see him go, since she had just heard from Pedro. He was back in the city, and would be visiting her with Salazar still in hiding in northern Mexico.

Zack had finished his business with Pedro, but he never trusted him or Camille. Pedro was unreliable, and could be vengeful. The sultry Camille could not be trusted since she was, after all, married to Salazar. She, too, could seek revenge if she didn't get her own way, and she could be angry that Zack was leaving.

He recalled the late 17th century playwright, Congreve, who opined, "Hell hath no fury like a woman scorned."

CHAPTER 4

Zona Rosa and Maria

Zack closed his bedroom door, carrying his small suitcase out the front door to the gates. He avoided Camille and lied to the guards, saying he would be back in a bit. They were not interested in him, as they were busy piling up sand bags around the gates and setting up a protective guardhouse filled with machine guns.

Zack walked to the corner of the block, and took a cab through the city on the main boulevard into the pink zone.

The *Zona Rosa* was the upscale area of Mexico City, with five-star restaurants, boutique shopping, and five-star hotels. It was a much safer area for tourists, where street hookers, the homeless seeking hand-outs, pushers, or addicts were kept out by the police.

When the taxi dropped him off at the plush Rialto Rosa Hotel, Zack marveled at the opulence of the *entrada*, replete with a concierge wearing a fancy black suit with tails and a valet who was busy parking Mercedes and Jaguars.

He walked into the massive, ornate lobby, where the concierge insisted on carrying his meager case.

Once at the check-in desk, the manager, an older snooty man who was also wearing black tails, said he was expecting Zack, once he'd confirmed his ID photo. The manager smiled knowingly, winked, and said Maria, a single, young lady, had checked in and was expecting him. He gave Zack an envelope and the room key.

As Zack moved into the elevator past a gaggle of nurses who were there for a convention, he tore open the letter. It was a brief note stating he should wait in her room.

The room was on the top floor; not quite the penthouse, but it was an immense, plush suite with two bathrooms and a king-sized bed. It had state-of-the-art electronics, a plethora of chandeliers, and gold-gilded doors. There was wainscoting and buttons here and there to open the drapes, turn on lights, or to start the TV.

Zack sat and waited for Maria. He stayed up until midnight watching old movies on TV, draining the scotch from the hotel room bar, smoking, and walking back and forth, worrying and thinking he should just head for the airport.

Given that she hadn't yet shown up, he finally fell asleep on the couch after consuming too much Johnny Walker Black Label with the TV on, still alone.

At two in the morning, he awoke with a start. Just as he was about to move into bed, he heard her quietly entering the room. He feigned sleep as she closed the bathroom door, washed her face, and then crawled in next to him.

Naked, she snuggled up to his back and gently massaged his chest and arms. He didn't budge and said nothing.

She deftly maneuvered her hand down his waist and reached for his erect phallus, which was now rock-hard from feeling her body against his back. Still pretending to be asleep, he let her stroke him until he came, his orgasm devoid of sound or groans, but relieving him of all tension, anxiety, fear, and anger that had been bottled up inside his body.

The next morning, she made breakfast in the kitchen without many words. They sat on the balcony and drank coffee as she smoked a joint and passed it to him.

He accepted it just to be sociable, and hoped it would get her talking. He needed some answers. He was never fond of smoking grass, and opted for the excellent quality Mexican cigars she had bought for him in the lobby gift shop. He wanted to talk about the beach, but she said she would tell him more as the day went on.

Zack simply accepted that. He was just happy to be with her, and to be safe where no one knew where he was. They just stayed together, ate, drank, smoked, drank more, and had more sex. He asked questions, but she just chided him, told him to be patient, and delayed answering. "Later, later. I'll tell you everything."

Maria, strange and secretive, had returned wearing an expensive pantsuit, carrying bags full of clothes and shoes from Gucci and Louis Vuitton.

Zack had been patient, but finally confronted her. He couldn't accept her secretive lifestyle anymore, and he told her he was ready to leave.

Maria ran to Zack and flung herself into his arms, crying bitterly. "Don't leave me. I'm sorry. Sorry, my love. I wanted to see our home for the last time," she confessed, occasionally trembling with sporadic gasps and spasms as he held her.

"That was risky…very risky. Was Salazar there?"

"No. Only Fernando. He and another gardener."

Zack waited for an explanation, knowing to not push her, as she might just rebuke him, as she did before. He moved her onto the couch, and poured her a glass of tequila.

She swirled the tequila with the clink of the ice in the glass, quickly gulping the whole tumbler, which seemed to revive her.

"Fernando? Nice guy. Great cook."

She took Zack's hand, composing herself as she drained the last dregs, and said, "He was dead. A bullet through his head. He was dead. On the patio, dead. Next to the new gardener and Manuel."

Zack reared back. "Holy shit, Maria. The same guys who shot up the beach party? Your mother? Was she there?"

"No. She was dead. They…" She hesitated. "Someone, I don't know who, rammed through the gates in a semi-trailer, killing all the guards and blowing up the guardhouse, driving into the patio. It ran over my mother, throwing her into the pool. Drowned. The house was torched. All the help were slaughtered. Then the semi exploded"—she tried to compose herself—"blew up. I found empty gasoline tins all over the house. Huge fire. No police were around after the fire trucks, which must have come."

Maria was exhausted as she described the scene, and she gagged at finding her mother facedown in the pool. She emptied her glass, sucking on the ice cubes, got up, opened the liquor cabinet, and drank straight out of the tequila bottle.

Zack took the bottle away from her and started to pace about the room. He came at her and grabbed her shoulders. "For Christ Sake. My God, Maria. Camille? I loved that lady. She was kind to me." He paused, reminiscing his friendship. "And she was kind to you, too. Fuck. Was that your Carlos' doing? We better get the hell out of here. We'll be next, woman."

Maria covered her face with her hands, crying hysterically and holding on to Zack. She finally babbled, "No, not Carlos. It wasn't him." She stopped and began sobbing again. "He wouldn't harm my mother. It was…just don't know…the cartel. They were after Salazar. Don't be angry with me. Please, Zack. Please."

Zack just held her. Eventually, she let go and went into the bedroom, where she crawled into the bed and pulled the sheets over her head. As she was quietly whimpering, Zack went to her and lay next to her body. He just held her. They both fell asleep.

The next day, Zack called Salazar's secretary to terminate his position at the university, and he made preparations on the phone to fly to San Diego. He never went out. It was too risky. He told Maria that he had to phone a Dr. Forzani in San Diego to confirm his position at the hospital.

He was fearful of asking more questions, since knowledge of what was going on could be too risky. While she was in the tub, soaking in hot water to calm herself, he used the speed dial on his Blackberry. He called his good friend, Sam, in London.

CHAPTER 5

Sam, the Facial Transplant Man

"You got me at a good time, Zack."

"Sorry to call so late." Sam was six hours ahead. "You were probably in the OR again, right?" he asked.

Sam never minded being pulled out of bed to talk to his best man from his wedding. "It's okay. Just wait 'til I go to the next room. My Bev is sound asleep," he whispered.

Zack waited. He heard the rustle of bedclothes, a kiss, and the door closing.

Sam was back on the phone, yawning.

"Sorry, Sam. How's the micro-surgery going—the Frankenstein stuff—the facial transplants?"

Sam was weary. Zack heard Sam open the fridge and pour himself some orange juice. He always drank juice in the night when they were in medical school together.

"Real good. This one was a twelve-hour facial micro surgery on a

"

lady. Face burned off in a house fire. Awful—poor woman."

"Ouch, sorry. Must have been exhausting."

Sam yawned. He was tired. "What I just did…well…it was worth it. We had a good transplant from a young woman who recently died in a car accident in Soho. I'm sure it will take. The sutures held, the blood vessels took, and the nerves will grow back in. My patient will be pleased."

Zach heard the fridge close.

"So, what about you? Maria's photo came through from your mobile. Nice beach, nice sharks, and a real good-looking woman. Lots of flesh and nice tits. You always liked them well-formed, taut, knockers, pal. Nice fuckin' body."

"Thanks buddy. The sharks were not only in the water, Sam. Some guy, Maria's friend Carlos, or his gang, shot up the beach party. It was chaotic, man."

Zack told Sam about the firefight in detail, and then the loss of Maria's mother.

"Really? Holy shit, man. I saw some of it on the BBC, and a bit in the local rag papers. A collaborator, stool pigeon. A rat fink, the Mexicans called him. A fucking quisling, man. It's drugs, man. Christ, I hope you're not involved again. We did well in medical school, selling weed and speed shit to all those kids at the university, but with this beauty, well…the gangs and so on." He hesitated. "You're in deep shit, man. You really know how to pick them, buddy. Know what I'm saying?"

Zack was fed up with Sam's usual prophetic lecturing, but he had to agree. "Yeah, it was a drug war. This Maria, she's a stunning beauty, all right. She put me up in her city condo. Nice place in the *Zona Rosa*, real plush."

"Don't knock her up, or her father will use those machetes on you next."

Zack chuckled, sucking on his cigar. "No, not really her father. He's some big, drug-rich, powerful Mafioso-type who had shacked up with her mother. Strange, this Maria; she often whimpers after sex, whenever we have it. She holds back on me until the final moment, just as I'm about to shoot my load. She's a ball breaker."

"Aha, there you go. Remember what our psych tutor, Abrahams, told us about a girl's past sexual abuse history. Post-traumatic history. No doubt about it. Poor girl."

"Yeah. That's what she said: by this Salazar, her step-father. Her mother told me she was with the local mafia briefly. Maybe a hooker. Some guy by the name of Carlos rescued her from Salazar's nightly prowls in her bed some years ago, when she was still a young girl. Now Salazar is after Carlos, and now, maybe me."

"No shit? So are you going to marry her, know what I'm saying?"

"She's a bit off the wall. Neurotic, melodramatic girl: stressed, paranoid, histrionic, and over the top. Has something to do with this Carlos guy, who finked on the cartel to the authorities for a wad of cash, but was one of the cartel types. He's now on the run, but she's clean. No drugs around. I checked."

"Paranoid? You mean she's suspicious?"

"You know, maybe not. I think she's hooked up with that drug dealer, Carlos, who set up that attack on Salazar. Big trouble, Sam." Zack whistled into the phone and finished his glass of scotch and stubbed out his smoke.

Sam whistled back into the phone. "Damn. Drama and trauma, right up your alley, boyo. Know what I mean?"

"Yeah, I know what you mean. It's exciting, but risky for me. I think I'm going to get out of Dodge, man."

"You always took big risks, Zack. Even in med school—pushing dope, running around with those loose women after the divorce. Her father, or whatever he is, the pervert, could set you up for life in the city in a lucrative practice, if he survives. Zacharias Scarlatto: handsome, dark, Mexican shrink extraordinaire." Sam whistled into his Blackberry again and laughed.

"Don't know. Maybe a good idea, but I might be a dead shrink, too.

What I need is that psych ward job in California, then a private practice."

"You told me your boss in San Diego was Forzani. Is he the same pervert who fingered little girls when we were in residency? The guy who was kicked out of practice? He's in California now?"

"The same. Maybe he's been rehabilitated."

"Doubtful. Heterosexual perverts are never cured. You know that. They're all immature; but, good luck, buddy. Look, pedophiles like Forzani have some cerebral dysfunctions, including problems with self-control, extreme urges, and cognitive distortions."

Zack was pleased to talk with Sam in medical parlance. "Yeah, yeah. Probably was abused himself in childhood, molested by others. Complete role-reversal now gives him some upper hand, but, with his immaturity and sexual urges, this has been ingrained in his nervous and cognitive system, and is now uncontrollable, compulsive activity."

"Give Maria a kiss for me and call again. By the way, put her on some meds. Do your psycho stuff on her."

"Not sure, Sam. Maybe I should lead a quieter life, like you do in London."

"Marry her. There's lots of money there. Like you always wanted. You've always taken risks to reach for the brass ring. The high life, with good restaurants and big cars were always your style. Not mine."

"Yeah. Maybe I can help her get over that post-traumatic sex abuse. I try hard. Do my best every night in bed, whenever she's here. Know what I mean?"

"Look after yourself, buddy, but maybe get the hell back to the States. Much safer there for you. Know what I'm saying? Marry her and maybe take her with you."

"Thanks, Sam. I do know what you're saying, and I will do. This Maria, she wants to go with me. So, maybe I'll take her. Good enough in bed, for now. Give my love to Bev. How many months now?"

"Going well, and she's holding on to this one. Third month. Might be a boy. I want her to quit working soon. Listen, all the best, buddy,"

Sam said as he swallowed the last gulp of juice.

"Okay. I'll call you from San Diego, after I get rid of that prick, Forzani. I want that psych ward for myself. You're happy doing what you do, but I need more."

"You always wanted more. You're restless, and maybe too pushy. Reaching for the gold. Careful, good buddy."

Zack ignored the truth. "Oh, say! I must tell you. Maria was impressed. 'The finest plastic surgeon in England doing facial transplants'—that's what she read on Google. She was very interested and excited. Said she knows a guy close to her who needs a facial transplant. Maybe that Carlos guy. His face is a mess, so I hear."

"Refer him to me. I'll give him a new handsome face," Sam said and laughed as he closed his phone.

Zack always felt better after talking with Sam. He never had anyone else with whom he could really confide. His wife loved her drugs and booze more than him, and Camille was a close second to Sam, he thought.

CHAPTER 6

Gomez

Maria, always the charmer and the temptress, was now regretful for her secret jaunts, and she became more candid with Zack as she felt more at ease with him.

Just before going to her favorite restaurant that evening, after Sam's phone call, she came to Zack, hugged him tight, and rubbed her body against him. "I just needed to find Carlos and get him safe," she confessed. "I found him two nights ago. I was going to tell you. He's safe now, my love," she whispered.

Zack didn't question her further; instead he just let her pull him down to the floor. She slid into her favorite position, sitting on top, as he slowly slid his dick inside her. She always had to be in control.

That night after a dinner, at her favorite, quiet Spanish restaurant, they walked arm in arm in the *Zona Rosa* district, having agreed that they would both fly to San Diego in the morning. Zack was listening to Elvis Costello on his iPod as Maria hummed along to "All You Need is Love."

Zack was surprised that, at the restaurant, the more she drank, the more she told Zack about Salazar. She confessed that he came into her bed when she was in her late teens, and her mother ignored her pleas for help.

"As many mothers do," Zack said, trying to be sympathetic.

The more details that spilled out of her mouth about Salazar forcing himself on her, the more she drank. Zack listened intently, and was understanding as he held her hand with compassion.

Leaving the restaurant, it was near midnight and Zack had his arm around Maria's waist in order to keep her steady from too much wine.

They staggered into the hotel lobby. The desk clerk snickered again and winked at Zack. They ignored the rowdy crowd at the bar, beckoning them to join the party. Instead they shot a quick wave to the drunks, and laughed as they stumbled into the elevator.

Maria had insisted her room be on the top floor, a quiet one, with very few tourists.

On the tenth floor of the hotel, Zack escorted her out of the elevator, keeping her on her feet. Maria struggled finding her key in the darkened hallway.

As they approached her room, Zack heard the fire escape door open and then shut with a loud bang, but brushed it off. Although it was next to Maria's suite, he was too busy holding Maria steady, and never saw the two men come out of the stairwell.

As she continued to fumble with her key in order to open the door, Zack's heart shot up to his throat. He turned and recognized Gomez and Pedro just as the goliath, Gomez, jumped Zack from behind. Zack let go of Maria's waist, and the black beast with the eye patch, Pedro, grabbed her by the neck, putting her in a head lock.

Zack struggled for air and tried to free himself, but Gomez held him tight and then threw him to the ground. He held Zack down by twisting his neck in a vice-like grip, and leaning his knee into Zack's throat. Gomez brandished a red Swiss Army knife, and moved the open blade close to Zack's face.

"Quiet, little man, or you lose an ear, or your fucking nose," Gomez barked.

Zack said nothing. The edge of the blade was at his right nostril.

"Where is C-C-Carlos, with the face that I c-c-cut, that fucking bandit who stole our money?" Pedro stuttered to Maria.

Maria, throttled by Pedro, could barely speak. She tried to push him aside, but her efforts were in vain. Eventually she squeaked out, "We…I don't know; we're looking for him, too. Please." She struggled. "Let me go! You're hurting me."

Pedro turned to Zack. "Fuck face. You screwed P-P-Pedro out of his p-p-p-percentage the last time. You and this b-b-b-bitch are dead."

Zack could only shake his head slightly. He regretted cheating Pedro on that last drop. It wasn't that much. A few dollars, but Zack didn't think Pedro noticed.

Zack's head was pinned to the hall carpet, left side down, but with his right eye he watched Pedro open up his fly, and pull out his throbbing erection.

Pedro, turned on by the thought of raping another woman, was in a lather, spittle foaming on his chin. He stuttered as he forced his erect penis up against Maria's thighs.

Zack could see the black Mexican on top of Maria was squeezing her breasts and running his hand up her skirt, but Zack could do nothing. Instead he watched in horror as Maria gasped for breath, slowly turning blue, with Pedro's other hand now on her throat.

Pedro clenched her neck in a steel grip with one hand and ripped at her blouse with the other, forcing her legs apart with his knees. Her skirt was up to her hips. Pedro tore at her panties.

"I haven't seen him. Your men killed him in Acapulco," she wheezed in desperation, struggling to move Pedro off her body.

Zack could only watch helplessly as Pedro tried to thrust his erection into Maria's vagina. Maria tried to force her legs together, but failed to do so. She begged, again and again, but with those last words, she fainted on the hallway floor.

Pedro wasn't finished with Maria, as he desperately tried to enter her. She was almost lifeless, but still instinctively tried to close her legs, something she consciously did with Salazar in her youth. "He's not d-d-dead, b-bitch. He'll be easy to find with a scarred, cut-up f-f-face like that," he stammered, lips and good eye throbbing in unison, as he pushed himself into her panties, searching for her vaginal opening.

The large man with a grizzled beard who was kneeling on Zack's chest barked out, "Stop groping her tits, Pedro. Go check her room. Take her later. Stop fucking around."

It was too late for Pedro, though. In his eagerness, he could no longer contain himself, and while still pushing to get through Maria's undies, he ejaculated all over her pelvis.

It was just as Pedro let go and gave out a loud, throaty, orgasmic gasp that Zack saw the legs of a young man who was wearing red sneakers, red socks, and blue jeans walk out of a nearby room. He was shouting. "What the hell is all the racket about?"

Zack then saw him run at Pedro.

Zack tried to struggle against Gomez, again, ever so slightly. Gomez was furious. He took the knife blade and poked it into Zack's nose.

Zack pushed with all his might to get Gomez off of his body and to help Maria. Gomez swore, pushed his knee in harder, and poked his sharp knife into Zack's right nostril again.

Zack watched the intruder jump on Pedro as he was cleaning himself off on Maria's skirt. The youngster was strong enough to pull Pedro off of Maria. Just then Gomez let go of Zack's neck in order to help Pedro.

As he pushed to get some air, Gomez turned to Zack and, with a quick stroke, sliced through Zack's right nostril, just close to his upper lip. Gomez then jumped up and slammed his body at the young man.

Zack was in a daze, bleeding from the sliced nostril, blood trickling into his mouth, but he was conscious enough as he watched Gomez pull a long, slender, silk rope from his back pocket and quickly threw it around the young man's neck.

Zack struggled to get to his knees, and he watched in horror as Gomez wound the silk around his own wrists and quickly throttled the hapless visitor.

Gomez turned the man's face toward Zack. Zack could see that he was a young man: athletic with a small beard, wearing a Toronto Blue Jays jacket, a large maple leaf button attached.

He was an unfortunate tourist from Canada, who was in the wrong place, at the wrong time. His eyes bulged out of their sockets with the noose tightened. His face turned purple as he was slowly strangled. His bladder emptied all over the carpet, and he let out a final gurgle, went limp, and died.

Pedro kicked Maria to the ground again as she struggled to get up, pleadingly looking to Zack for help. "Let's g-g-get the fuck out of here, Gomez," he shouted, pushing his still-oozing erection into his pants and pulling up the zipper. Gomez picked up the limp body of the young man. Pedro put his hands into the victim's pockets and came up with his wallet, keys, and some peso bills. He then opened the fire escape door.

Gomez pulled a small package out of his back pocket, tore it open, and flung the white powder around the young dead man's nose. He then pushed the rest of the package into the man's jeans. They picked up the body and threw it down the flight of concrete stairs, closed the door, and quickly moved toward the elevator. Pedro rifled through the wallet, took out a number of American dollar bills and credit cards, and then threw the pesos and wallet on the floor.

Zack, shaken by Gomez's attack, blood still dripping down the front of his shirt, managed to pull himself up and labored to help Maria into their room.

Once in the room, he wiped the blood, which was now oozing down his chin. His lip tasted of salt. Maria was lying on the floor, shaking from the trauma.

"Salazar's henchmen from the beach. Now we're in a deep shit hole and witnesses to a fucking murder. Pedro was right…you're fucking around with that Carlos got me in deep shit." He groaned, angry, but still dazed, still bleeding.

Maria winced from his hostility, but, with great effort, she managed to pull up herself. She put her bra back in place, removed her skirt, and feverishly tried to clean the ejaculation from her legs with a bed sheet.

She whimpered, "We must leave right now. One of them was called Gomez, the big one. He's a disgraced army general. The other gorilla with the eye patch, Pedro, was a hit man with the dreaded mafia. You saw him at the beach."

After some time, Maria became more composed. She walked to the door and used the chain to secure it. She pulled a small couch in front of it, and used it to lodge the door shut.

Zack struggled to clear his throat, swallowing large gulps of water in the kitchen. He covered his wounded nostril with a tissue from a box on the counter. He packed the right nostril with more tissue, and he went to find a bandage in the bathroom.

He found a heavy, white strip of a bandage and taped it to his nose. He returned to the room, where he watched Maria tear at her remaining clothes, trying to free herself of Pedro. The strip on his nose stopped the bleeding.

He went to Maria and grabbed her by the shoulders. "No, Maria; we must stay until morning, as though nothing happened. If we leave now, the desk will implicate us once they find the body."

Maria nodded in agreement, but she was still visibly shaken: trembling and shivering, as though she was out in the freezing cold. She pushed herself away from him, and began pacing back and forth, holding her bruised right breast. She then feverishly wiped her pelvis and thighs clean using soap and a wash cloth from the bathroom.

She came back to Zack, tears flooding down her cheeks, and moaned, "It was this way when Salazar would come into my bed years ago. He did what he wanted with me, holding me down like Pedro did—choking me. And then I had to clean up what he had spent all over me, like Pedro did, using my own nightie."

"You're quivering, Maria. It's post-traumatic stress disorder. You're reliving the trauma you went through as a young girl," he said, taking her into his arms and holding on to her.

Maria just held on until she quieted down. After some time, she looked at Zack's large bandage on his nose. "Yes, you're right, but, oh, so sorry, you poor boy. Does it hurt?"

Zack wanted to give her a good smack in the head, but he had never hit a woman before, and wasn't going to start now, especially with what she had just gone through. "No, no," he replied. "Only when I breathe."

Maria, bewildered by the joking remark, shivered from fear, feeling his wrath. She was cold, and was weeping silently.

Zack helped Maria into a chair, and then went into the kitchen and soaked a few towels in warm water. He placed one of the wet towels around her bruised head, and another over her breasts.

As he paced back and forth, massaging his neck, he barked out, "You said you were finished with the mafia, Maria. I'm outta here. Too fucking risky; so, *adios*, sweetheart!" He removed his shirts and another pair of trousers from the closet and started packing his only bag.

Maria held the towel over her forehead, and, with the other towel, she wiped her thighs clean again. She waited. "They think I know where Carlos is. I don't have anything to do with Salazar's mafia. Zack, I'm not involved," she lied.

Zack circled the room, frantic and kicking at the furniture here and there. He came right at her. "And Carlos? His face is all scarred and cut up? That's why you wanted a new face, Maria. For him?" he said, lifting her chin and staring into her eyes.

Maria averted her eyes from his face and the question. She sprayed her perfume between her legs. Her hand trembled as she took his hands away, and then showed him the colored card.

"The black beast left his blue calling card with the letter 'M' on it, Zack. *La Eme*. It is a bad sign."

Zack snatched the card from her. "M? What the fuck is that, Maria, and who the fuck is Carlos?" He pitched the card on the floor.

Maria buried her head in her hands, looked away, fearful of Gomez, but now more frightened of Zack.

"Someone I used to know. Yes, Salazar watched Pedro slash his face as a warning some time ago. When they were partners; Carlos turned on Salazar. Carlos and I were very close once. It is over," she lied again, turning away from his glare.

Zack wasn't convinced. "Salazar called Carlos a thief."

Maria slowly walked about the room, opened the liquor cabinet, and brought out a small bottle of gin. "It was years ago. I hated my life on the university campus, and ran with a different crowd. I wanted to be tough; not like the other debutantes Salazar and my mother wanted me to be. I had to be different."

Zack flexed his back muscles to relieve the spasms, but he suddenly felt sorry for her, and he went to her to hold her in his arms. She gently pressed the bandage over the cut on Zack's nose. The bleeding had stopped.

"It's not too bad, Zack. It should heal," she added, peeling back the bandage slightly. She cleaned off the remnants of blood with a tissue.

"You look like Jack Nicholson."

"Really? Nicholson? What the hell are you talking about?"

"Yes, you know; like in that movie, *Chinatown*, where he had his nose cut like that by some bully. He walked around with that huge bandage on it."

It wasn't funny, but it cut the icy atmosphere in the room. They both laughed, but not for long.

Zack pushed her hand away. "I read in the papers that the Mexican mafia met in Acapulco six months ago. The gang had murdered several of their men. Those were the traitors."

"They were cruel men."

"Others had their fingers cut off, their eyes gouged, or their faces slashed, tattooing the letter 'M' on their foreheads."

Maria was quiet, nodding, but she began sobbing again. Zack was right in her face, holding her by the shoulders, glaring. "That's what they did to your Carlos, is it? Cut up his face; and now you want me to fix that fucker?"

Maria nodded, pleading, "Don't be mad, Zack. Please help me, and my friend. Your friend, Sam, can do the micro surgery, so he won't be recognized by Salazar, or the police authorities. He could help the police, and your country also."

Zack, furious, grasped Maria by the arms and spat out the words, "The big ape, that pig, Gomez, used Salazar's name just before I blacked out. God damnit, Maria. Now I'm in the shit house with you, your Carlos, Gomez, Salazar, and now a fucking dead man in the stairwell."

Maria pushed herself from Zack's arms and covered her face from his glare. "Zack, if Salazar finds Carlos, he will kill him for cooperating with the police. Carlos wants to help the police and the government authorities. He has all the information to help them. The cartels, the drugs, it is destroying our people. It is damaging to our beautiful country; and to yours as well."

"So I heard. It has nothing to do with me. I'm the fuck out of here. Gone."

"It has to do with you. You are a medical. You are of help to many addicts. Millions of dollars are siphoned into your country. Many millions of drug dollars. There are many in California who launder money for the cartels. Drugs have been seized from shipping containers, private boats, planes, and from my people shoving drugs up their asses in condoms, just to get drugs into your country."

"So? They can swallow it, shove it up their vaginas, or shove it up their asses. I could care less."

"Your border agencies have doubled, tripled in size in order to stop the distribution. Billions of dollars are spent to catch a few. When one is caught, there are ten more to take his place."

"Yeah, yeah. They'll catch the big boys. Salazar and his generals," Zack said.

"There are too many of them. The others find mid-level groups like biker gangs, younger people, and Middle Eastern gangs in order to fill in the gaps. The circus goes on."

She ran into the bathroom, took her toothbrush and make-up, and insisted they move to a hotel blocks away.

Zack calmed her again as she emptied the gin bottle, and said, "We must wait until the morning. No one will check that stairwell this late at night."

They went to bed. It was a fitful night for both of them. She came to his body for warmth and comfort, but she still whimpered from periodic nightmares.

They checked out at 6 AM the next morning. As Maria paid her bill with a credit card, four policemen walked through the doors.

"What's going on here? Police?" Maria asked. Zack pulled her away, and as far as possible from the desk, fearing exposure from too much talk.

"*Si*, a very bad robbery, *señora*. Bad man and bad, *mucho* bad, drugs, *señora*. Cocaine," the clerk said, pointing to the policeman.

CHAPTER 7

Good-bye, Maria. Or was it?

They walked two blocks away, onto a side street in order to find another nondescript hotel. Once they checked into a basement room in the one-star, "Mirabella Hotel", Zack gave the cot to Maria. He elected to sleep on the couch. Their ardor had cooled.

"Have no fear, Zack. My aunt, Jacinda Chapala, has many rooms for you and me. It is in her beautiful mansion in the hills, outside of San Diego," Maria announced the next morning, putting another cold towel on her bruised breast.

"Really? You have an aunt? In San Diego?" Zack asked laughingly, pulling on his pants.

Maria, sleepy from having a restless night with nightmares of Pedro groping her, was working hard at trying to be calm in front of Zack. She avoided any talk of last night. "*Si, si.* She is a strange lady. My aunt, she loves the liposurgery. She wants to be beautiful, like all the Hollywood women on *Desperate Housewives*. She is my mother's older sister. You will like her, my love."

Zack, still shaken, steadied himself against the filthy, cracked, kitchen counter slate, trying to get the coffee machine to work. He worried about being saddled with Maria now that he was still 'my love', and, later, with a neurotic, crazy, aunt-of-a-woman—if he agreed to live there.

Maria could see his worried look. She reassured him as she led him to the cot, to try and relieve him of his tensions. "You will also like my uncle, Hector, very much. He is a guardian to my people. He saved so many Mexicans from poverty, in both countries."

"I'm looking forward to meeting him," Zack said sarcastically as she pulled down his pants, massaged his groin, and pushed him onto the cot.

She mounted him and started grinding her pelvis. Maria wrapped her legs around his strong torso in bed. He fell onto his side and felt the tension slowly ease out of his body.

After they finished, she lay next to him and continued. "My poor Mexican migrants, who swam across the Rio Grande to illegally cross the border into your country, were assisted by Hector. They are the 'wetbacks', as your countrymen called them."

He let her lay there, very gently caressing the breast that wasn't abused or hurting. "Wetbacks? What the hell, Maria?"

Maria was still stirring inwardly after sex with Zack. Her nipples remained erect from the caress. "*Si*. My people swam across the Rio Grande River into the US of A. They were illegal immigrants, and the American patrol soldiers were waiting for them on your side, my love. They arrested them. My people, they were soaking wet from the swim. And so…wetbacks; that's what they were called by your policemen."

"We need them now to do all the work, my dear girl."

Maria smiled, and pushed his hands away when he attempted to move down her belly and between her legs. She blew him a kiss, jumped up, and got dressed.

She came to him and used a swab with peroxide she had found under the hotel sink. Ever-so-gently, she removed the small bandage from the cut on his nose and dabbed it with solution.

"There. Much better. Almost healed. No longer like Jack Nicholson, my sweet," she said, throwing away the bandage.

He saw Maria not as the brightest star in her family tree, but she was still wealthy, attractive, pleasantly seductive, kind to him, and fleshy; as Sam had said, just as he liked his women. Now, at least, he had a bed in a fancy mansion in San Diego with the crazy auntie, he thought. He would take her with him, he decided.

"You go straight to the airport. I'll pack a bag and I'll meet you at the departure lounge," Maria said, nibbling at his ear.

Zack agreed, finished the weak cup of coffee, and packed his bag again. He kissed her good-bye and took a peso cab to the airport.

The airport was a cacophony of sounds and smells. Locals and tourists ran about confused, munching on tacos and wiping off the sauces that had dripped onto their shirts and blouses.

He bought a paper and turned pale when he read of the murder of a young Canadian cocaine addict who died in a plush, Mexico City hotel. There were details from the police chief extoling on the drug trade, and blaming foreigners for moving cocaine across the borders.

As he waited in the airport lounge for Maria, he became restless. The longer he waited, the more he feared she wouldn't come.

Zack knew the Aero Mexicana flight for San Diego wouldn't wait. He finally gave up his search in the crowded departure lounge.

"It had to do with those two overgrown mafia goons. Maybe they caught her. Shit, she's probably dead or in the whore houses in Tijuana; poor Maria," he said, fretting as he pushed through the noisy throng.

Zack put out a call for her, and he listened to the loud speakers calling her name in vain. Their flight on the departure board was blinking steadily, and the final call was posted. He gave up and was able to change both tickets to an open flight in the future. He prayed that Maria would somehow join him again, and he craved for her body. He developed a full erection as he thought of entering her as she straddled him.

He left the terminal and hailed a cab, returning to the sleazy hotel room. The overweight Mexican lady at the desk, with poorly-dyed orange hair, simply shrugged when he asked about Maria. She let him back into the room, which he found to be vacant. There was no sign of Maria.

His full, day-long search—wandering the streets of the pink zone in the relentless rain and checking the posh shops—was futile.

"Damn that woman," Zack shouted. A young school girl stopped to look at the man who was talking to himself on the street. He was frustrated, confused, and sad. Thinking of his loss, tears welled up in his eyes.

He stopped at a local bar, pulled himself together, and, in desperation, decided to quell his anger by calling Carmen. He needed Carmen and her services: her small, deft fingers and tantalizing mouth.

"She should be studying for her exams. Should be in," he prayed as he dialed her number.

CHAPTER 8

Carmen

Carmen picked up the phone, expecting it to be one of her many *politicos* requesting a hand job, or more. She was surprised to hear it was Zack, and she heard the pleading despair in his voice.

"Zack; nice to hear from you. I thought it was someone else. That badass still hasn't paid me, so I probably won't hear from that impotent prick again. I'm just reading about marital law and divorce for my next law exam. I only have one more year to go. Dull reading for sure; boring, but, yes, I can meet. At least you're gentle with me, and fulfill our contract on time," she replied to his subtle entreaties.

Carmen met him at the three-star hotel she always used, and Zack paid for the one night with his credit card. She was waiting for him on the bed, reading a journal on marital law.

He joined her, sitting up next to her. She put her journal down and snuggled closer to him. At first they just settled in and relaxed, watching the local TV news, drinking margaritas, and smoking a fat joint. The news still showed brief scenes of the bloody attack on Salazar's villa, including pictures of mangled bodies and canine carcasses taken away in body bags and ambulances.

Carmen could sense the angst in Zack's voice as he revealed some details of his life with Camille at the villa. She was very sensitive to every client's moods, and that was one reason she was so popular.

Zack, exhausted, frightened, and still panicky about remaining in Mexico, didn't reveal anything to Carmen about his last few days in the hotel with Maria. At least she could comfort him in her arms, together again, and do what she always did well for him—relieve stress and bottled up anger. This time, she may not ask him for money, since he had been so generous with her in the past.

As he lay with her, gently caressing her body, he thought he should give her some pleasure, instead of always taking.

He smiled and recounted how they first met. "Remember how we met, Carmen, at the university cafeteria? That was a great day for me, and, actually, for you, too. We established a mutually-profitable relationship." He then added, "Profitable for you, especially, but very satisfactory for me."

It was she who actually insisted on meeting Zack. She sought him out through her two elderly professors who were her best, most reliable, customers. They only wanted a hand job, or a blow job at most. The one hundred US dollars she received per service, plus a good meal in a nice hotel, was the easiest money she could make to pay for her education.

Carmen, a vivacious, dark-skinned, twenty-two year-old law student who claimed to be from Chiapas—the southernmost state of Mexico—did what she did best. It paid for her law school tuition, her bank loans, and even some extras so that she could send money to her family in Turkey.

Zack was more than pleased to meet Carmen during the first few weeks that he was at Mexico University. However, it was on that very first visit that Zack received his first surprise from this sultry and pretty woman. The shocker was that he simply didn't have to pay her in cash anymore.

After he took his clothes off that first night and they were lying in bed, she halted his wandering hands, gently turned him aside, and said, "Zack, I heard from one of my professors that you are offering tablets of speed through a contact. No one else is aware of that; but, I don't want your money anymore. Hereafter, all I ask for is thirty tablets of your five milligram amphetamines each Friday night that we meet. No need for money. Would you be so kind as to agree? Could we make a deal?"

Zack was so surprised by her knowledge of what he was peddling with Pedro that his sexual eagerness cooled, and he immediately lost his erection. He feared some kind of a threat, or extortion.

Once he recovered from the brazen offer, and realized that she was reliable and credible—honest in her presentation, not a flake or hysteric—he quickly agreed. This was a good deal for Zack. And a better deal for Carmen. She simply and quietly sold the thirty tablets of speed for five American dollars each to her University friends.

He saved one hundred American dollars each time they met, and she made one hundred and fifty dollars each time she sold the tablets.

They both laughed at recounting their first visit and the deal. They smoked some more, and drank from her canteen. However, Zack had one more, even greater, surprise once Carmen turned toward him and started to stroke his erection again.

Now that he was more at ease with the alcohol and the occasional toke, he quickly got hard. He had never tried to excite her in the past, never wanted to enter her, fearing disease. He always remained passive while she did all the work for her thirty tablets with her nimble fingers or her mouth.

Once she did what she did best and he was satisfied, they lay quietly together. She waited, sipping from her canteen, while he caught his breath again. This time, he was in no hurry; neither was she as his hand moved slowly from her small breasts down to her pubic area. He wanted to give her an orgasm as a tribute to their relationship, and to not be selfish this time. It was then that he got the shock of his life.

His fingers caressed her pubic hair, which she never shaved, knowing that it was more appealing to many mature men than the cleanly-shaved pubic area that some men liked. Shaved vaginas were perceived by some as more virginal: unsullied, prepubescent, and adolescent.

He remembered his anatomy class professor referring to this area as the *pudendum*: a Latin term, meaning a place where one should feel shame. Now it was commonly called 'the bush'.

He also recalled a well-known female comedian referring to the pudenda, the female genital area, which caused some embarrassment for her audience. She then berated women for shaving their genital areas in order to appear more teenaged and juvenile, and, thus, more appealing to men.

He reached down to caress the soft, pink, inner vaginal lips enveloped by the larger, outer, protective lips, which slowly opened as she became excited. As her legs spread, and as her breathing became more intense, he continued to slip his fingers into her vagina. He was pleased that she became easily aroused and moist.

Suddenly, he was taken aback, and, just as unexpectedly, realized she didn't have a mound there, between her upper lips area. A button, some called it. His anatomy professor called it a clitoris, or a clit. He searched further, but it was not to be found.

Is this simply an anatomical aberration? he thought. *An anomaly, a deviation, a very abnormal congenital malfunction, for this one and only young girl?*

No, it wasn't there, and it was nowhere to be found. The area was just a smooth, soft valley, totally devoid of that highly-sensitive little organ that should give Carmen—and all women—real climactic pleasure, and the only way many women achieve the ultimate orgasm.

Zack had never encountered this anatomical void before: this emptiness, this total lack of highly-required need for female sexuality.

Carmen remained passive, and she knew that he was searching around down there, hoping to feel her aroused clit. She said nothing, did nothing, and didn't move away. She just lay back with her legs still spread apart.

She knew, in the past, he had simply and gently fondled her breasts, and then, after a short while, she would continue to massage his erection and perform fellatio on him. Sex would be over after a short time, since he usually came quickly, always withdrawing, spending himself in tissues she provided.

She knew that he feared getting gonorrhea, or some other venereal disease, from her since she was promiscuous with others at the university: students and professors, mostly males, but occasionally some females, too.

"It is too risky. That's why the condoms, Carmen," Zack told her early on. She simply agreed. No others had ever considered commenting on this aberration on her body, since others simply didn't know about such delicate anatomy, or they didn't care. Many could care less about her pleasure; they only cared that she had a vagina available for them.

He stopped the search. She slowly closed her legs. He turned to her slightly, facing her. He looked Carmen up and down, and then got up and walked away.

"What happened to you, Carmen?" he asked, perplexed, but quizzical, and not in anger.

Carmen looked up at him. She wasn't shy or apologetic. "You're a psychiatrist, Zack. A medical doctor. I trust you. You have been good to me. You don't hurt me like some of those other men do, so I'll tell you."

"No, I wouldn't hurt you, Carmen. Do tell me. What's that about? What happened? You were born that way?" Zack asked, bending down again, gently putting his right hand tenderly over her pudendum.

Carmen told her brutal, traumatic story. She sat up in bed, naked; silent, at first, but intent on telling her story and gripping his hand. "This is something I've never told before, to anybody, Zack," she said.

CHAPTER 9

A Sad Tale of a Thousand Cuts

Zack sensed her nervousness and kept quiet, listening to her amazingly bizarre story as they sat together.

Carmen slowly began telling the details of her sadistic tale of the cruel excision of her body parts. She spoke with hesitation and paused often. "My name is not Carmen. My father named me that when I was still a young girl, hiding out in Chiapas State. After I killed my aunt back in my own country, we both escaped and ran to Mexico. My given name is Azmera, named by my father—it means 'harvest' in my country. My light-colored father was originally from Lisbon, and he worked as a coffee producer, harvester, and exporter of coffee beans to China and Germany."

Zack, captivated by her confession, did not interject. He moved closer to her on the bed and listened. She poured out a few ounces of margarita from the thermos bottle, took a sip, and passed it to Zack.

She went on. "It was the surgical removal of the female clitoris, Zack. It's a common cultural and religious practice in certain tribes of

Africa and throughout the Middle East."

"My God, Carmen; I had heard about it while in med school, but never in detail. Why?"

"I researched this at the university, and I learned a few statistics through my law courses. The United Nations had outlawed the practice, but only after over a hundred and twenty-five million young girls had been subjected to female mutilation of the genitals, or FMG."

"I read about it in the medical journals years ago. Those damn men should have been castrated; they should not have defiled you, and all those young girls."

Carmen remained calm. "It wasn't the men; it was the women." She paused. "My aunt held me down, not the men. It was my aunt. She held me from behind, grabbed my legs, and opened me so wide that I screamed in pain. It was another woman, her friend, who used an old, used razorblade on me."

"A razorblade?" Zack asked indignantly, but already knew the answer. He was visibly shocked and horrified by what he heard, but he remained composed.

"Calm, be calm, Zack. Look, I've never talked about this before. My father knew about it, but he was powerless against the women in my family. It was the women in Africa and the Middle East who insisted on this."

"Okay. Go on, Carmen."

"My aunt, and then her friend, spread my legs apart. My aunt held me in a grip. Her friend used forceps to grasp the hood of my clit, and with the razorblade, she cut it off. All of it. Then she removed the inner lips."

"The labia minora. The smaller, inner lips?"

She stopped. He said nothing. What could he do but bend down and embrace her? Through the embrace, he felt her heart throbbing, her body sweating from the stress and embarrassment. He just held her.

"Yes. Those small lips. Very small to a little child."

All Zack could say was, "Yes, so tiny and pure to a small girl."

"I was maybe five or six. Maybe; I don't remember. I fainted from the pain. When I woke, I saw another ten or twenty more young girls, my friends, in the large room. That beast used the same, blood-soaked razor on all of us."

She lay there, trembling as she recounted the suffering. "Men felt it was needed for girls to remain pure, free of sexual lust; to be modest, virginal, and unsullied, like all the other women. It was mostly the women who performed the surgery, but it was the men who allowed it to happen.

"At times, the entire labia would be cut off, and the vulva would be sewn shut, leaving just a tiny hole for urination. Later, that hole would be enlarged for sexual intercourse after marriage, or for child birth."

Carmen was exhausted from the confession. She turned away from Zack, crying from re-experiencing the trauma.

Zack, embarrassed by his maleness at this point, could only say, "I'm so sorry that this happened to you, Carmen."

"I'm so embarrassed, Zack, but you seem to be kind, and I never told this to anyone before. No one cared. I still have nightmares of a bloody sword hovering over me as I lie helpless, tied down."

"Post-traumatic stress, Carmen. Humans can be so cruel and sadistic; but I read that Egypt outlawed the practice a few years ago, and it's against the law in England, where there are many Muslims. Although it is still done by *imams,* secretly, and in Africa, openly."

Silence.

There was more. It was a confession. She could trust him. He only listened: didn't berate her, criticize her, tell her what to do, or give her advice. She wanted to tell him, and to relieve herself of the remaining story, even though it contributed to her post-traumatic stress disorder.

"I still have nightmares of that blood-spattered razor, and flashbacks of the wails of my friends in that torture room.

"When I was a teenager, maybe fifteen, my aunt, that woman who held my legs apart, became ill. She was in bed, in my father's house, dying of cancer."

"Good. Sweet revenge from her own God."

"Maybe, but it was me, not her God, who took her. I killed her." She knew what he was thinking. Murder? She tried to clarify. "It's okay, Zack; I didn't really kill her. I just helped her on the way, with a pillow over her face," she whispered, almost fearing the walls could hear, praying he would understand.

Zack lay down beside her again. Held her in his arms. "It was a long time ago, and it was in another country. So you came here, to Mexico?"

"My mother died. My father became depressed. I got frightened. The police were suspicious. Father had a contact in Mexico with his exporting business. I looked Mexican enough," she said with a silly giggle, holding on to him.

"So you do. You're from Turkey, but you're not dark. How come?"

Carmen laughed for the first time. "My father was Portuguese, and my mother came somewhere from northern Europe. Maybe Denmark or Sweden. I didn't know her; she was blonde. I was lighter skinned."

Zack looked at her and smiled. Now that he knew something about her, he could see that she indeed looked like Jessica Alba, the actress in the series *Sin City*, who had a European mother and a Mexican father. She had dark, narrow facial features with black hair, dark eyes, and full lips. She was petite, lithe, and with a beautiful smile.

As Carmen relieved herself of this burden, she became more relaxed; comfortable, at last. She told him she'd give him something for his kindness. She tried with her hand, but to no avail. He was impotent from anger, sadness, and guilt after hearing about such an atrocity, not being able to do anything about it.

Carmen removed her hand. "Now, there are some women who speak up against it. A well-known celebrity and model from Africa, living in your country, lectures against the practice."

"I read about her once. Look, I'm very proud of you. Good for you that you were able to talk about this. You went through a lot, very courageously, and you've done well," Zack said as he held her close to his body.

Carmen held on to him and wept. "Zack, no one, ever, said anything nice like that to me."

They lay there. Together, silently.

As he got dressed, he explained to Carmen how his med professor lectured on cultural psychiatry. "Theories posited that female sexuality caused mental illness in the 19th century. Doctors, at that time, were convinced that female hysteria, a prolonged disabling neurosis, was due to the presence of female genitalia and a woman's sexual arousal, which, at certain times, would cause them to behave unpredictably and appear nearly psychotic.

"They concluded that it was the uterus, or the womb, having left the pelvic area and traveled uncontrollably here and there throughout the body that caused nervousness and insanity in women.

"Hysteria and hysterectomy are commonly associated terms. The cure for hysteria then, and all the supposed female woes, was treatment by radical hysterectomy. Thousands of women throughout history had various parts of their genitals removed, including a hysterectomy, in order to cure their mental disorder."

"I read about that," Carmen said proudly.

"*Hyster*, a Greek word, means 'the womb', the uterus. Thus, the term and diagnosis of hysteria. Therefore, the uterus was often surgically removed in order to cure women of the neurosis," Zack explained. "The last such 'medically necessary' hysterectomy to cure a woman of her mental or emotional illness was documented in a hospital in the USA, in 1956."

Zack was good for Carmen, and she was good for Zack. With the money she made from Zack's Ritalin, speed tablets, she was able to cut back on peddling herself to unsavory characters that were sadistic and abusive. With his weekly meeting with her, a routine part of his life, Zack could concentrate on his research and also have his despair and pent-up frustrations relieved by the dark and beautiful Carmen.

She felt relieved after her confession. She told Zack that, as a lawyer graduating next month, she would go into forensics, and then work with the United Nations in order to eradicate female genital mutilation around the world.

She told him one more statistic as he put on his pants. "Zack, in your country, there are over a half million girls who are having their clit surgically removed. They are the immigrant families. It still happens," she said as she dressed.

As they parted Zack offered a suggestion. "Carmen, you have been very brave, and faithful to your cause. When you are in New York with the UN, go onto the social networks and develop a clinic, a group: maybe even online. Meet up with that woman you mentioned, and set up an organization. Work with a large group to help you eradicate that sadistic scourge to women."

Carmen listened thoughtfully, kissed Zack good-bye, walked him out to the street, and called herself a cab. Zack thanked her for the evening, held her close, kissed her on the cheek, and said he hoped that they would meet again sometime soon.

She waved to him as the cab left, and, in desperation, Zack walked down the street carrying his bag. He decided to give up on Maria. It was finally time for him to depart.

At a corner car lot he bought an old Toyota. The passenger door was rusted shut, and the driver's door was a different color, but he was assured it would get him to the border.

He drove straight through to San Diego during a Pacific thunderstorm, crossing the border with hundreds of other tourists driving into California at Tijuana. He turned on the radio as the windshield wipers struggled with the downpour.

The *Evanescence* song, "Listen to the Rain" was playing on the radio. His thoughts were about Maria, but also about Carmen.

Zack hummed with the song, "I stand alone in the storm, I stand alone…"

CHAPTER 10

Dr. Alberto Forzani

The very first day back in San Diego, Zack went to the first pharmacy he could find and wrote out a prescription for himself for sublingual lorazepam—a very good, fast acting anti-anxiety agent.

The young Chinese lady pharmacist looked at him sideways and hesitated. It was Zack's looks. He looked tired, wan, bleary-eyed, unshaven, unwashed, and appeared more like a homeless person than a doctor, especially when she looked out the window and saw the beat-up car he just got out of.

When he saw the hesitation, he handed her his medical number and his driver's license for ID. She checked it on her computer, and only then did she stop questioning the prescription.

As soon as Zack left the pharmacy and got back into his car, he put one tablet under his tongue. It dissolved quickly, like a shot in the arm. He massaged his bruised neck and felt his painful Adam's apple, still smarting from Gomez's stranglehold.

His heart rate settled and his gut stopped gurgling as the meds slowly did their work. He looked into the rearview mirror. His nostril was healing nicely.

He made sure to wear a lightweight turtleneck sweater to hide the blue marks under his chin. He moved his Adam's apple gently to and fro, fearing that it might have been damaged by the steel grip on his throat. Swallowing was still a problem, but it got better every day. His stomach settled down, and his diarrhea, a common anxiety symptom for Zack, cleared up.

Zack made his way through traffic to a motel near the hospital. He was certain he had the position, but he still had to be interviewed by that pervert, Forzani, whom he hoped would now be his boss.

The motel across from the hospital looked decent enough. It was clean and newly painted, with a 'AAA Approved' sign outside and a good number of late-model cars in the parking area. There was a sushi bar attached to the motel that had a 'closed' sign hanging obliquely on the front door. This place would do until he called Maria's auntie. He took his suitcase out of the trunk and rolled it into the small foyer.

After checking in and having some small talk with the middle-aged, female, Japanese desk clerk, he found his room on the second floor. He immediately walked to the bedside table and used the room phone to call Maria's aunt, hoping she would have a room for him, as Maria promised.

The motel would max out his credit card shortly. He needed another bank loan, fast. It was risky to transfer funds from his account in the Bahamas. After the third try to the aunt, all he got was the whining buzz of a fax machine.

"Click off that damn fax and answer the phone," he shouted, cursing the stupid woman.

Zack had a shower, shaved, and went to the barber shop in the mall to get a trim. He bought a fifth of bourbon, a few decent cigars, some new trousers, shirts, and a jacket, and returned to rest in his room. He slept and awoke early the next morning in anticipation of his meeting with Forzani.

He was shocked when he approached Dr. Forzani's office, located in the glass and marble surgical building right next to the adjoining psych ward. Forzani, the head and director of Psychiatry, was in the new surgical unit, and his office was not on the psych ward. Zack was nervous, but felt optimistic about negotiating a full-year position, and hoped Forzani wouldn't recognize him from the past.

In the hallway, he combed his black curly hair, now neatly-trimmed. He straightened out his only tie, and buttoned the jacket he had bought at Wal-Mart across the street from his motel.

He found Forzani's office on the main floor of the new building, next to admitting. He opened the office door and walked into a large, opulently-appointed waiting room.

The room had large hibiscus plants with blooming red flowers near the window and expensive paintings on the walls, probably all originals. There was a fancy, glass-and-metal desk just past the door, and two French provincial couches against each wall. A small water cooler sat next to the desk. Forzani must be doing well, he concluded.

A blonde woman sat at the reception desk. On the desk was her name plate: Josephine. Just Josephine. She wasn't working on anything, but was instead reading a magazine, and never looked up. Zack waited.

She finally closed the magazine and gave a wide, toothy smile. "*Ja?* Ve vere expecting you, Doctor…ah," she said in a broad Scandinavian drawl.

"Scarlatto."

"*Ja, ja.* I remember it. *Ja,* that's it," she said, opening and looking at an appointment book. She smiled again and buzzed her boss.

Josephine was a Nordic blonde, and was most likely wearing a false wig with false eyelashes, false nails, a totally tattooed left arm, and a boob job that left her enormous tits overflowing her tight, low-cut, V-neck sweater. Maybe they were real, but not likely. Zack could also see that her teeth were bleached, and she had had a poorly-done nose job.

As he wondered if there was anything original on that tattooed body, they both heard a throaty voice coughing and shouting for Zack to enter.

Forzani's door was ajar. Zack walked in.

Sitting behind a large, ornate, oak desk, Zack saw a short, overweight man in his mid-sixties, whom he remembered from his residency days. But now, Zack noticed, he appeared to be very well fed. His head sat squarely on his shoulders, bereft of a neck, with ruddy cheeks, silvery, white hairs protruding from his nostrils, and a bulbous nose. He desperately tried to catch his breath after each spasmodic coughing spell.

Here was a perfect example of an unhealthy lifestyle, Zack thought, especially on the ward of the 'worried well', as Forzani had called it on their first telephone meeting, back when Zack was still in Mexico.

On Forzani's desk sat five bottles of pills and two bottles of water. Zack recognized the medication used for high cholesterol, hypertension, diabetes, asthma, and nitro tablets for angina.

Here was a heart attack just waiting to happen, Zack surmised. Those coronaries had to be blocked, and were desperately struggling to pump oxygen through the partially-blocked arteries, into the cardiac muscles, and then throughout the corpulent body.

Zack looked around the office in the bright, new surgical wing. "Your office is not on the psych ward, sir?"

No answer.

Forzani scanned the young psychiatrist, avoiding eye contact.

"Young man, ah, you'll do, ahem…just fine," he wheezed as he squirted a shot of bronchial asthma spray into his mouth.

Zack was pleased not to be recognized. "Your office isn't on the psych ward, sir?" Zack asked again, looking around the expensive suite.

The man still didn't look up, or answer the question. Instead, he rifled through a maze of papers on his desk. "Glad to, to have you, Doctor, Doctor…ah…," he fumbled as he searched again through his messy desktop. "Yes, ahem, ah…welcome to the Sean O'Flanagan Medical Center, Doctor, ah…"

"It's Scarlatto. Thank you, sir. Great honor to be here. Beautiful receptionist, sir." he said with a grin.

"Ah, yes. Yes, er, she is from Stockholm, I think. Last month."

Forzani shuffled more papers on his desk and finally found Zack's application and curriculum vitae, which detailed his medical professional history. "So, aha, I see you graduated"—he coughed twice—"with honors. You did some research." He paused, searching his paperwork. "Ah, on anti-depressants." He coughed again. "Excuse me…bad cough. In Boston? Good work, but you wrote a…" He paused for a very long time. "Paper, ah, criticizing…er, ahem, psychoanalysis?"

Zack took a deep breath. Here was a slow talker. Was Forzani an analyst? That wasn't on his website. "Yes, sir. Meds are better. Faster. Cheaper. Sir."

"Right…ah…ah…ahem. Listen, my boy…er, I hope you're as good as it, yeah, as good as it, ah, gets," Forzani said with a guttural laugh.

Glad that is over, Zack thought. "Sir?"

"You know, like that flick, *As Good as it Gets*. That nutcase with the… the, you know, the OCD guy…uh…he needed a few good electro shocks."

"Ah yes, sir," Zack replied with a forced laugh. "That was a good movie. Jack Nicholson, an obsessive compulsive neurotic, on medication. I heard about him in some other pic: China-something, with a slashed nose."

Forzani forced his rotund body out of the oak chair. He walked to his bag of golf clubs leaning against the window frame and took out a putter.

"Yeah, heh, yeah, that's him: Nicholson." He paused to cough again. "Listen, son, my fraternity friend's daughter…" He wheezed and gasped. "Annie, yeah, needs a little TLC from a good…ah, man like you, and a few good"—He coughed again—"Excuse me, uh…meals. She's a suicidal anorexic, but a nice, sweet girl. A real hysteric flake, but you'll love her. You'll meet her…on the ward."

Zack gulped, but the saliva was stuck in his throat. "She's suicidal, sir? It's an open ward. There are no locked doors, I heard. She could take off at any time," Zack said guardedly, afraid of offending his chief on his first day.

Forzani went back to his desk and squirted a stream of spray from his asthma bottle. He spoke without hesitation after the liquid cleared his bronchi.

"Nah, nah. She's not that suicidal. She only…um…she only threatened to jump off the Golden Gate Bridge. It was a…what would you call it? A veiled threat," Forzani said flippantly as he putted a golf ball into a large, empty, opened milk carton propped against the wall.

"A veiled *threat*? The *bridge*? Well, I feel much better knowing it was only 'veiled', sir," Zack said sarcastically.

Forzani snorted and pointed the club at Zack. He didn't like a wiseass. He waddled to Zack and set his putter on Zack's shoulder. He gave him a slight tap with the iron. "See to her. Her stepfather is too nosy as to her treatments, and pay, yep, pay attention to what I say, keep your nose clean, and you…you…and you and I will be just fine. Know what I'm saying?"

Zack lifted the putter away. "I think so, sir."

Forzani waved Zack out. The interview was over.

At the door, Forzani pointed his stubby finger at Zack. "You'll love Annie. She's a sweet, young girl. Lots of promise. I'll be in Palm Desert for a while now that…you're…ah, here, Scorino."

"It's Scarlatto, sir. Scarlatto. Shall I spell it out for you, sir? Glad to do it," Zack said, maybe sarcastically, maybe not.

He knew that if he could get this oaf stressed, anxious, and very angry, he'd have a coronary, and then he would be out of Zack's hair for good. Then Zack would take over the ward. *Suicidal Annie may just be that trigger*, Zack thought.

Zack followed Forzani out, and Forzani continued to the waiting room door.

The old fat-ass opened the door, and then shouted through the doorway, hurrying to the golf course. His head bobbed back and forth as he wheezed, coughed, and snorted. "We got a timid one this time, Josey. Tell that ball buster, Baker, the good news. We're still in business, old girl."

The ball buster. Baker? Zack recalled reading in the online local newspapers that the city councilor, Marcia Baker, a Filipino troublemaker, had recently toured the 100-year-old, two-story, adjoining brick building that housed the psych ward.

He recalled that, back in their apartment in the *Zona Rosa*, Maria had looked at the photos of the psych ward on Google. "There is the building. Your psych ward is connected to the modern, ten-story surgical unit," she said, dejected.

Zack had said to Maria. "The psych ward building looks like a festering bunion, screaming for amputation. Baker hired the local newspaper to write articles on the ward. She wanted to show how the mentally ill living in the city core are so poorly treated, my love."

Zack was already looking forward to meeting this "ball buster", Baker. He thought he could use Baker one day in order to get rid of the coughing, sputtering, wheezing sleaze bag, Forzani.

As Forzani left the waiting room, Josie shot him a toothy, bleached smile, winked, and then immediately called Baker.

Despite the less than ideal interview, Forzani was going to get a lesson from this 'timid' one, he thought. Zack waited at the desk as Josie left a message for Baker on her cell.

She looked up from her phone after hanging up, opened her small purse, and spread a sheet of red, rouge lipstick over her already ruby-red lips. She smiled. Waiting. Dumb-looking, but cute.

Zack wondered what else she did for Forzani. He wanted so desperately to ask, but contained himself.

"He's going to keep his business *and* his balls this time, old girl," Zack whispered to Josie as he left. He was sure the old man was porking Josie, if he even could with all those pills he was taking. He would need one more bottle of pills to get it up. Viagra.

CHAPTER 11

Zack and the Snake Pit

After the meeting with Forzani, Zack felt subdued in thinking of how he would be rid of him. He was even more deflated as he walked into his ward.

His ward was in the crumbling, brick annex building. It was barely holding on, with decaying, ancient bricks, and mortar that was peeling, shifting, and cracking. It was just barely holding on to the sparkling, new, glassed-in surgical wing.

He winced at the dark, dismal north side of the building, where the sun didn't appear to shine. It sat under the constant shadow of the majestic surgical wing. He had phoned the ward clerk to meet him at the entrance to introduce him to the staff.

When Zack walked through the exterior doors, he looked up at the sign over the entrance to his ward. It had a dusty, metal plate with a wooden, block sign reading 'sychiatry'. The "P" had slipped off, and was never replaced.

"Get that sign fixed. The best thing the city could do is to demolish these two stories and start over again," he said to the clerk who met him. She was a cheerful, very tiny, East Indian woman. She was in her early fifties, and wore a clean blouse and blue jeans, partly covered by a white smock.

"Yes, Doctor," she said with a twinkle in her eye. She made notes of Zack's order.

"I heard that Forzani named this ward after himself,"

"Yes, sir. But little Jasmine here will be leaving soon. I hate bedbugs, and Dr. Forzani won't call in an exterminator, Doctor."

"Bedbugs? I hate them, too. Listen, you call in an exterminator right now, PDQ and ASAP. Understand, Jasmine? Send the bill to O'Flanagan, the chief of this whole hospital. Pronto. Where are you from? With that accent?"

"Grandma's name, it was. From Bali, sir."

"Sorry to be nosy, Jasmine, but I've always been curious about people's whereabouts. Bali? Heard about it in that movie, *South Pacific,* with Mitzi Gainer. Must go sometime. Nice name, Jasmine; like the tea."

Jasmine blushed and returned the focus back to the ward. "Yes, sir. The Forzani ward. He's the golfing friend of the hospital director next door, Dr. Sean O'Flanagan, a good Irish Catholic, whose personal priest visits everyone here. Dr. Forzani admits most of the patients here, but he never makes rounds, and he rarely sees them."

"You're serious? What do you mean, never?" Zack asked as they walked down the hallway. He eyes blinked from the naked neon bulbs attached to the high ceiling by flimsy wires. The lights flickered, and often failed. Some had never been replaced.

"Well, by phone he does, to leave orders with Dr. O'Flanagan's son, Paddy—our orderly—and on the discharge of his patients. Sometimes he comes to push the button for electro-convulsive treatments. Oh, except Annie. He sees her in his office."

Zack stopped in his tracks. "An orderly taking orders? Won't happen again. In his office? Annie, the jumper?"

"Yes, Doctor. Nurse leaves her there."

"Strange. We'll make some changes about that, if she's as suicidal as I heard she was," Zack assured her, poking his face into some of the rooms. He saw paint peeling off the walls, mouse droppings visible in some corners, graffiti over one woman's bed, bed sheets stained from urine, vomit, blood, and random feces.

Zack pointed at the mess. "I want all these rooms cleaned up: new bedding and the walls painted, Jasmine. Make a note," he ordered.

Jasmine scribbled in her notebook as he talked. Patients were walking about, bored. Some were in the lounge watching an old, static-laden TV. Others were in bed, sedated.

Jasmine was apologetic. "Sorry, sir. No money to hire cleaners, or more nurses, Dr. Forzani said. No other psychiatrist would work here, Doctor. They come. They go when they see this hole. Sorry to say that. They leave. After one or two days. One stayed three days. A record," she said remorsefully.

"Understandable. Wow. This place. It is a 'putrid boil needing lancing', someone said once," Zack opined, fearing to look into another room.

"An abscessed tooth needing extraction. Or a bleeding hemorrhoid needing excision," Jasmine countered, this time laughing heartedly.

"Enough already! Carry on like that and I won't last two hours," Zack said laughing with her and touching Jasmine on the arm gently. He liked making physical contact with people. But just a touch. No funny stuff with nurses. Harassment and sexual overtones with staff was not his thing. Some complain, and then get a lawyer.

After a brief tour that made him nauseous from the dank, musty smell, Zack decided to see suicidal Annie. Jasmine brought him Annie's chart from the nurse's station and then left to call in the exterminators.

Anorexics are generally quiet, reclusive, passive types who have an obsession with food, food odors, and food tastes. Zack recalled that they were mainly females, who hated the smell or taste of food. They had a fear about gaining weight, and a faulty, self-perceived image of their bodies.

The disorder starts in adolescence, often after some stress, like a loss in the family, a trauma, or death. They are obsessive. They may live in a culture, like America, where thinness is valued, and they may have relatives with similar problems. Zack was convinced that the malady was biochemical, or an organic brain disorder.

They also have a higher suicide rate.

This should be interesting, Zack thought, *except for the high suicide risk.* He felt somewhat nervous as he carried Annie's chart into her room.

CHAPTER 12

Little Orphaned Annie

When he walked into the room, Zack found Annie hiding under her bed sheet. Her roommate was watching *Bonanza* in the lounge, according to Annie's special nurse.

He called out to Annie, but to no avail. He sat on her bed, reading the weighty chart full of multiple admissions.

Annie's special nurse, sitting in the corner, put her *Cosmo* magazine down and irritably rapped her fingers, waiting even more impatiently for her coffee break.

Zack nodded to the nurse in greeting. He gently pulled the sheet from Annie's face. "Hello, Annie. I'm Dr. Scarlatto, psychiatrist. Dr. Forzani asked me to see you."

"Fuck off," was all Annie said, pulling the sheet back over her face.

Zack remained patient. "My immediate concern about your anorexia, Annie, is your severe weight loss. Your kidneys could shut down, and you'll have to be force fed," he said.

Annie repeated, "Fuck off!" and covered her face with a pillow. She let out a soft groan, rolled over, and turned her back on Zack, spouting, "Force fed? Fuck you."

"It says here you've had psychoanalysis. Many therapists see anorexia to be a purely psychological disorder in need of analysis, and not a biological, genetic, or organic disorder, as I see it," he said firmly, and loudly enough for the private nurse to hear.

Annie finally sat up. Being force fed was no fun. She had endured that in other hospitals. She muttered something inaudible as she played with a small key dangling on a thin silver chain around her neck.

"However, I'm convinced it's genetic or metabolic, and it is basically an organic brain disorder, due to a chemical imbalance of the serotonin enzyme systems. Probably inherited," Zack said as he flipped through the file.

He heard Annie give a loud snort as she pulled her sheets tightly over her head once more.

Zack stood and took her nurse aside as she was delivering morning medicines to Annie. "She shouldn't be on an open ward. Many anorexics commit suicide, so I want someone with her twenty-four seven. They have the highest death rate of any psychiatric illness."

Annie's nurse didn't have a name tag. She was unkempt, and disheveled, with messy hair and no make-up. She was wearing an old, shabby, and stained uniform. "It's Dr. Forzani's orders to have her here, Doctor. I'm here in the daytime. I don't work nights. I just follow orders," the nurse replied, unconcerned and chewing on a stick of gum.

Zack remained calm, but firm. "Those orders will be mine, here on in, Nurse. What do you know about her?" he asked, looking again for her name tag. She had none. Nor did she have any designation of being a nurse, or where she graduated from, if she ever had.

"Not much. And by the way, I only report to Dr. Forzani and Paddy, not you. I escort her to his office before I leave at six," she answered.

Zack stiffened. "I asked you what you knew about her, Nurse."

She didn't reply. He waited patiently. Nothing. He went on to read that Annie was twenty-eight years old, an obsessive compulsive with severe body image distortion, and that she weighed ninety-eight pounds, soaking wet.

Annie, sitting up in bed now, interested in the conversation she had just heard, downed her vitamins with a glass of water. She could have been an attractive young woman if she put on a few pounds.

Her hair was bright orange, and she had three rings in each earlobe. Tattoos of spiders and snakes crawled and wound their way around her neck and shoulders. She sat there, smiling to no one in particular, and seemed to be a simple, intellectually deficient woman. One of her previous therapists had confirmed that in a report.

Zack thought differently. He thought she was probably severely depressed, rather than a moron.

Her 'nurse' finally spoke, rudely. It was clear to Zack that she didn't care. "She has a ten-year history of an eating disorder, Doctor. I think. She purged with diet pills, starved herself, vomited, and was so compulsive about her weight that she jogged ten miles every day," the nurse said as she left more pills on Annie's table, blew out a bubble with her chewing gum, and abruptly walked away.

Zack was furious. "Hey, you can't just leave the pills here. You have to make certain she takes them first."

Too late. She had already left for her coffee break. He settled back again and read the emergency doctor's admission note. She was admitted two months ago from the Bay area.

He read, "*The police talked her down off of the Golden Gate Bridge. She had lost her bit-part in the musical <u>Oklahoma,</u> after she vomited on stage during the rendition of 'Corn is as High as an Elephant's Eye'. Questionable intelligence. Dramatic girl.*"

"Losing that audition plunged you into a severe depression. Must have precipitated your suicide attempt," Zack said to Annie as she sat in bed.

"No one ever told me that before," Annie said. But that's all she said.

He read further into her file and read out loud to Annie. "*She was transferred to this San Diego hospital by her wealthy stepfather to maintain anonymity. They were socially embarrassed by her adolescent dramatics and her simple, dull intellect, and wanted her as far away as possible.*"

"Bullshit."

"Are you that dramatic, with such a simple intellect? Where's your family now, Annie?" he asked, hoping to get a rise out of her and some conversation.

"Dramatic? Simple? No one said so before. Mother killed herself," Annie finally offered.

Annie's nurse returned with her coffee and sat on the end of the bed as she heard the last few words. "Her mother had died from a drug overdose, and her wealthy stepfather travels. He's with some Hollywood model now," the nurse whispered, stirring her latte with a wooden stick from Starbucks, licking her fingers clean from the accompanying sugar donut.

"No need to whisper, Nurse. Annie needs to deal with reality."

Before Zack could say anything more, Annie suddenly leaped out of bed and bolted for the window.

Zack, at first dumbfounded by this brazen, unexpected act, threw the chart on the floor and made a run for her. He missed her, and continued to sprint across the room, diving at her body. He caught Annie's scrawny hips as she was working hard to clear the window sill.

Annie continued to wiggle and worm her way toward the open window, yelling at the top of her lungs. The ward was on the first floor, as the other stories had been closed down by the fire marshal. Annie wasn't going far, even if she did fall.

Zack had strong hands, but his grasp on Annie's legs was slipping. "Annie, you're a drama queen, and we know you love performing on stage, but give it up. Come back in here," Zack shouted, knowing that hysterics could still die, sometimes accidentally.

Zack's heart was thumping as he watched one convertible stop on the street below. The woman got out as the drama unfolded inside, and she began shouting into her cell phone. She then ran under the window and snapped pictures with her cell's camera.

Shit, Zack thought. *This will go viral in minutes.*

Within minutes, two ambulances, a block-long fire truck, and three checkered police cars were outside the hospital window.

"Damn it; the only thing missing is a newspaper reporter to capture this drama," Zack swore.

Annie slowly allowed herself to be pulled back in with the help of her nurse and the ward's male orderly, Paddy, son of O'Flanagan, the chief of the hospital.

Zack recalled the sarcastic words from the ward clerk earlier that day. "Patrick kept his job on the strength of his father's position: a prominent surgeon in the city, married to a beautiful model half his age, who is now in surgery after severely burning her body. She's suing her husband, and everyone else, including this hospital. With the promise of a multi-million dollar donation from him, a priest on the board renamed the hospital after Dr. Sean O'Flanagan.

"The young Patrick O'Flanagan, oh, I mean Paddy—that is what he calls himself—was set for life, working here. Forzani gets him to report to him after Patrick's so-called ward rounds."

Patrick seemed to be bewildered as to what to do. Annie writhed on the floor, screaming and threatening to sue everyone in sight, while she clasped her torn and bleeding nubile chest that had been scraped on the window sill.

Paddy was obviously a very shy young man. As Zack sized him up, he almost felt sorry for him being the son of the chief. He appeared lost, confused as to what to do, and just stood there, red in the face, dancing from foot to foot. He was almost in tears.

As the room filled with nurses and patients, Zack ordered, "Patrick, make yourself useful. Clear the room and get a stretcher for Annie, and then call the special nurse. Get this young lady cleaned up."

Patrick hesitated, being uncertain now as to where such orders were coming from. With a flourish, he threw his dyed-blond locks aside, and then pranced about, not knowing where to find a stretcher. A nurse led him out of the room to help.

Leaning over Annie and checking her pulse, Zack looked up to see Annie's nurse calmly walk in and put her quarter pounder, large fries, and hot latte on a table. She pulled a sheet from a bed and threw it over the naked anorexic, who resembled a concentration camp victim.

"Take your fries out of here, Nurse, and don't bother coming back," Zack ordered as he easily picked up Annie and put her on the bed.

He watched, horrified as three nurses came in and forcibly threw Annie onto a stretcher. A nurse shoved an intramuscular sedative into her buttocks. They all waited while Annie slowly became drowsy, but was still feisty: she kept swearing at anybody and everybody.

"Dr. Forzani left the order with me, just in case," Patrick said knowingly, exercising his important role as Forzani's flunky.

Zack looked at Patrick. Very carefully, but with intensity so that the nurses could hear, Zack ordered, "Look, Patrick, or Paddy. You are the orderly here, not a nurse to be taking orders any longer. You do as I order, or you'll be an orderly on another ward. Father or no."

The nurses whispered something to each other. One seemed to smile. Patrick spun around on his heels and walked out dramatically.

"Halleluiah, Doctor. But he's off to see his papa," one nurse said, glowing admirably at Zack.

Zack listened to Annie's garbled obscenities as she slowly fell asleep, and was then wheeled into a padded side room.

His heart rate slowly settled as he thought of how he was going to modernize such a wretched psych ward, and also how he was going to deal with the publicity, which was sure to come after Annie's squeals out the window.

"With padded rooms straight out of Bedlam, we have to clean up this snake pit. No padded rooms from now on in," he said to the nurses.

Annie's roommate, Kim, heard that order as she walked into the room. Kim nodded. "God will have to save poor Annie, also. Writes in a journal every night, she does. I watch her, I do." She paused, slightly nervous. "After her therapy in Dr. Forzani's office; twice a week, it is."

"Good that she can write how she feels."

"Yes, but she locks the book up, she does. Locks her cupboard with that key around her neck, she does. It fell off once, it did, and I read her diary as she slept," she said, embarrassed. She pointed to a stained, scruffy cabinet next to Annie's bed.

"Write? What about, Kim? It's good that she can express herself," he repeated.

Kim hesitated. "I don't know if it's true. It's what the doctor has her do, what he makes her do. In his office. After hours, he does," she whispered, shaking her head with a disgusted look on her face.

"Has her do? Like what, Kim?" Zack asked pointedly, after the room had cleared.

Kim tried to put on a brave smile, turned away, red with embarrassment. "I read some of that what she wrote, I did."

Zack watched Kim slowly back away. He wrote orders on Annie's chart, noting that she was to have twenty-four seven observation. He went to the window and took in a few deep breaths to clear his head.

As he leaned out the window to get some fresh air, a newspaper reporter looked up and snapped his picture.

"Fuck. That's all I need," he said, leaping back, banging his head on the window jamb.

When he jumped back, he fell and slammed into Annie's bedside table. The door to her side table flew open, and her diary fell out. It was a large scribbler, with her name and the date of when she came into the psych ward written on the jacket. As he opened her diary, he was shocked. It was all about her clandestine meetings with Forzani in his office, in the late evenings.

Kim ran to help Zack regain his composure and sat him down on the bed. "She wrote that, that's what she wrote, Doctor. I seen her write bad stuff like that; after she comes back, she does."

"Let's see, Kim. You watch the door for a minute."

Kim closed the door and Zack read. Annie had details in her diary that confounded Zack. He was appalled by the perverted acts that Annie had written. The writing was rapid, but very legible: concise, with good grammar, and it was obsessive in detail with dates, hours, and locations of every meeting she had with Forzani.

Her writings were graphic as to the ongoing explicit sexual acts that she was forced to perform on Forzani, or that he forced on her. She wrote of her going down on him, performing fellatio, and he going down on her, performing cunnilingus.

He read how she refused intercourse, at first, but she then wrote that he was impotent anyway, and couldn't get an erection unless she went down on him, and that took a half hour of sucking.

She left nothing to the imagination, writing notes after Forzani sent her back to her room. She spared no detail about the different kinds of sex acts, including the fact that he was uncircumcised, told her that he preferred young, innocent, prepubescent girls, and he insisted that she shave all pubic hair clean away. She wrote, time and again, that Forzani threatened to send her to a mental hospital for shock therapy again, if she didn't comply.

The diary details were extensive, and Zack was impressed that there was no apparent drama, embellishment, or exaggeration. It all looked very credible and reliable.

Zack would have to act. *But how?* He thought, as he snapped pictures of all the writings, page after page, on his cell.

"You take the pictures, Doctor. I'll watch the doors," Kim said as she stood guard.

"Thanks, Kim. When I'm finished, I'd like a photo of you holding her diary open, with the calendar on the wall and the date circled by you."

Kim took the diary, held it up high near the calendar, circled the date, and called out the time and date again. "Glad to, Doctor. Glad to help."

Zack snapped pictures of Kim and included a video of her talking of the date and time. He saved the diary to a folder and would transfer it later to his laptop with a secure number. This was one of the nails he would use in Forzani's coffin. Maybe there would be others. Maybe Councilor Baker would be one of those hammers and spikes if he sent the diary to her.

He put the diary back and snapped shut the small door on her side table.

"Getting this place accredited as a serious, teaching psych ward will be a challenge. Maybe Baker will help me, but we must get rid of Forzani, first. That diary will help," he said to himself.

Kim took the corn broom from the small closet in the room. She swept vermin, feces, and silverfish from the corners of the room and from under the beds.

"I'll clean up this snake pit," Zack said to the young woman, blowing his nose from the reek of stale rooms that hadn't been properly cleaned in years.

Kim stopped sweeping. She looked at Zack who was about to leave. "If I can help some, Doctor, let poor Kim know. She likes to help, she does."

Zack thought for a quick moment. "Kim, maybe so. Perhaps you could make a note every time Annie goes to see Dr. Forzani. Detail the exact time she leaves and returns, and what she is like upon return. For the record. Thanks."

"Glad to do, Doctor. Glad you is here."

He left her as silverfish slithered about, feeding on drops of Annie's blood that were scattered on the floor.

CHAPTER 13

Cleaning Up the Snake Pit

Zack anxiously walked into the hallway, hesitant of what else he would find.

Annie's nurse, just fired by Zack, carried her tote bag over her shoulder, talking angrily to herself. She walked off the ward, munching on cold fries. She turned and gave him the finger.

Zack smiled, waved, but fretted about her relationship to Forzani.

One of the day nurses met him in the hallway.

"She's the only one here who wears a uniform," he said to the nurse, pointing to Forzani's niece.

"Yes, no more uniforms, Doctor. Dr. Forzani's orders. Everyone is equal on his ward."

"Equal?"

She smiled, feeling the discomfort. "Nurses and doctors in uniforms represent parental authorities in our fragile unconsciousness. That's what Dr. Forzani said."

"Now we blame our parents for everything, Flora," Zack replied, looking at her nametag.

As they walked along the hallway, he confronted a young woman whose arms had rows of deeply-scarred razorblade cuts. She had just left her room, babbling to herself. She was naked from the waist up.

Flora called the ward clerk to get the patient back in her room. She turned to Zack. "All that cutting. Her poor arms, Doctor."

Zack took off his jacket and gently draped it around the woman's naked shoulders. "The use of physical pain temporarily diminishes the emotional anguish she must be suffering."

The clerk took the old woman by the arm, covered her in a blanket, and led her back into her room.

Flora helped Zack put his jacket back on. "She does that often, Doctor."

"Masochists deal with painful inner anxieties and painful traumatic memories by inflicting outward physical pain. It is so much easier to deal with outward, physical pain, and it masks the inner turmoil," he explained.

Zack nodded thoughtfully as he read the woman's chart pinned to her bed. She had just completed ten electroshock treatments and suffered a severe memory loss, according to the nurse's notes. He read her diagnosis. It was a Psychotic Disorder.

"Why did Dr. Forzani order ten electroconvulsive treatments for this patient? Six to eight would be enough, and then review the progress." Zack questioned.

The young clerk shrugged her shoulders as she gave the woman a blue capsule and a glass of water.

He slowly plodded to the nurse's station, surveying the chaotic ward. The nurse's station was situated halfway down the long, dreary passageway. The station wasn't secure, and it only had a plywood, bottom half of a door that wouldn't lock.

"The nurses have no privacy. Your station is open to any disturbed patient. I want all those patient charts in this office, not pinned to their beds," Zack said, bewildered and angry with the mess.

"Those were Dr. Forzani's orders, according to Patrick, sir," Flora said nervously.

"Well, they are new orders, Flora. Patrick is an orderly. He takes orders from nurses; he doesn't give them, from now on in."

Flora looked up to the sky, threw her hands up and said, "Halleluiah. Finally."

Zack carried on and used his cell phone to take photos of the dismal hallway. "I'll e-mail these to the hospital director, and to that woman councilor, Baker. I wonder if Sean O'Flanagan's ever been here."

"He's afraid of psych patients, Doctor. Baker writes articles in the newspaper, but no one does anything. She's afraid to come now," Flora said.

"Afraid? Baker? Frightened? Of what?"

"Not sure. Forzani treated her uncle here."

Zack stopped and looked hard at Flora. "On this ward?"

"Yep. With his cranial magnetic stuff," she replied, avoiding Zack's eyes.

"So? This Baker woman. What's she afraid of?"

"Her uncle hung himself. In his room, over there," she said, pointing to the end of the hallway.

"Christ. Oh, sorry. If he was suicidal, he should have had twenty-four seven nurses, around the clock. Like Annie," Zack said, apologizing for swearing.

"We all thought so, too."

"What did Baker do?"

"Usual. Lawyers and all that. Dr. Forzani is Dr. O'Flanagan's golfing buddy. In the same club. Settled out of court, I heard."

Zack was furious. "I'll get Sean O'Flanagan here, PDQ, once I call that lady, Baker, and her reporter," he promised as he walked through the clutter in the hall.

He took more photos as he looked into the filthy rooms. There were two beds in each room for the men patients. On the other side of the hallway, each crowded room housed four beds for the women patients.

"Women always outnumbered the men by two to one," Flora said as she walked with him.

Zack held his nose dramatically, indicating his aversion to the smells of humans crowded into a small space. "The first leading cause for women, aged eighteen to forty-five, of being admitted to a hospital is for obstetrical reasons. The second leading cause is for a depressive disorder, Flora."

Flora nodded, handing him an order sheet. "I'll get some deodorants for the ladies, and some cleaning aerosols for all the rooms. To clear the stench."

Zack signed the order and returned to the nurse's station and scanned the blackboard. He found that twenty-eight out of the forty patients on his ward were slated for electro-convulsive shock treatments that week.

They were all under the care of Dr. Forzani.

"I've got a chance to do something right here. I've got to do this, and I can't screw it up," Zack thought to himself as he left the hell hole.

But how, when, and by how much?

CHAPTER 14

Auntie Jacinda

A little after five o'clock and back in his hotel room after a hectic day, Zack stifled a yawn and packed his one bag. Maria's aunt, Jacinda Chapala, had finally called his cell and given him her address. Her voice was brusque and not very hospitable. She had refused to answer his question about Maria.

Zack followed her poor directions and finally made his way to a cul-de-sac at the end of Escondido Drive, on South Ranchero Terrace, high above the city.

When he turned into the elegant driveway, he abruptly slammed on the brakes. "I can't afford a room in this high-income neighborhood," he said, marveling at the massive, iron gates fronting the Chapala residence.

Still Zack continued, maneuvering up the hill. His car belted out black, acrid smoke, and it sputtered as it turned through the gates, which opened slowly as he approached. He then drove into the curved driveway. The mansion was still a long drive up a further incline.

He saw a small, Mexican woman on all fours plucking off the heads of dead flowers in a garden, a cigarette dangling from one side of her mouth.

As she looked up, he rolled down the window. Zack said clearly and slowly, "*Perdon señora, perdon*," taking her for a simple migrant worker. "I'm looking for *Señor* Hector Chapala."

The woman stopped weeding, pulled a few strands of tobacco from her lips, and looked up at the car. "You no find him, *amigo*. He my *marido*, my husband. He in a room at the back of house. Come from 'Frisco with his niece. I am Jacinda, still his wife," she said with a strong Mexican accent. She pushed herself up, and, with difficulty, ambled over.

Zack rolled up his window partway as he saw a black lab in his rear-view mirror charging downhill toward the car. "You the new *medico* here, *señor*? Phone message from my niece, Maria," she asked, kicking the dog in the ribs as it scratched and barked at the intruder's car.

"*Si, si*. That's me, *señora*," Zack shouted, moving away from the partially opened window as the lab showed his teeth. With another fierce kick from the woman, the dog crept away with a mournful yelp.

Zack cautiously opened his door and left the car. The young dog, now looking for a friend, came back and jumped all over Zack, hoping for a gentle pat.

Jacinda held the dog by the nape of his neck as Zack took off his baseball cap in respect for the woman. Jacinda was a good two feet shorter. She shooed the young dog away, and then wrapped herself around Zack in an affectionate squeeze. Her stubby arms could hardly reach around his waist. He nervously bent down to meet her.

When he straightened up, he looked down on the dark complexion and leathery facial features of the woman from the Yucatan Peninsula. She smelled of cigarette smoke. She puffed on the last few dregs, stomped on the butt, and then bent down to put it in her pocket. Her strong, upper body was supported by short, stumpy legs. A flowered blouse covered an empty space where a breast should be.

She followed his eyes to the vacant spot. "Big operation, *amigo*. Cancer, like Hector's mother," she said cupping at her half-empty chest.

"I'm so sorry to hear that, Jacinda."

As Jacinda started walking toward the house, she told him to move his car into a section off the driveway. Zack did so, and then followed behind his landlady, whose varicose veins on her bowed legs were like tangled blue ropes showing through the slit of her jean skirt.

Jacinda stopped, lit up another cigarette and spat the tobacco bits into the bushes. She whirled around. "You pay rent. On time, *amigo*? You have name, *amigo*?" she asked, looking him up and down once again.

"*Si*. Yes, it's Zack. Zack Scarlatto."

"Sack? You say, Sack. Funny name, Sack; like, potato sack."

"No, Jacinda. Zack," he said, pronouncing it slowly.

No response.

He gave up on that one as she scrambled up the hill. The dog playfully ran around the two of them, barking and nipping at Zack's trouser cuffs.

"He needs a good wash and a grooming, Jacinda."

"Not Jacinda's. No one want or need him," she replied coolly, and then smacked the dog with her broom.

Zack looked at the large, young, male dog with greasy, matted, black hair and one eye running with yellow pus. "That's too bad. He could be a beauty if he was cleaned up. Poor thing must have mites in his ears. His eye is infected. I'll clean him up for you, and take care of him."

"*Si*. You do, Sack. Welcome to Chapala Hacienda. Those bad mafia men here with questions. 'Fuck this and fuck that, and mother fucker this and that'; bad men with bad mouths. Called me a mother fucker," she said, fearfully looking around to see if the bad men were still around.

"Bad men? One with an eye patch? Why?" Zack asked nervously.

"*Si, si*. They here, look for Carlos. One big hombre with black eye patch and one with huge, *grande,* suspenders. I say to them, no Carlos here," she answered fearfully and finished her smoke.

"Two men looking for Carlos?" Zack asked, sensing the tightness in his throat again.

Jacinda pulled a beaten up, dirty, half package of Marlboro cigarettes from her back pocket, lit a wooden match that she struck on her jacket zipper, and, in a hushed tone, said, "*Si, si.* They do bad to his face in Acapulco. Show Jacinda photo. He like that man in movies, Frankenstein."

Zack looked around to see if there was someone close by for the quiet whisper. "I saw them some time ago. Is Maria here with Carlos?"

Jacinda didn't answer. She hesitated a moment and then turned, stopped, and looked Zack in the eye again. "Six hundred dollars rent, *amigo.* Three meals a day."

"A good deal, *señora.*"

She stopped, hesitated, puffing heavily from the climb and the effects of tobacco smoke on her already ravaged lungs. "Why they use such bad word, fuck this and that?"

Should he explain the word to this woman? He tried. "It was used hundreds of years ago, to accuse men or women of having sex outside of marriage when that was illegal in England. They were accused before the judge of having sex, and it was legally called 'For Unlawful Carnal Knowledge', or FUCK."

"Not nice then, *señor* doctor."

"No, but it probably came from the German language, as many of our English words did. It was *'fucken'* meaning to penetrate. Do you understand, Jacinda?"

Jacinda put her finger to her brow, and shrugged. Then, as though she forgot someone, she added, "And my niece, Maria, she here, too."

"Maria? She is here? With you?"

Hearing her name again evoked the obsessive anxiety he had been riddled with in Mexico. It had dimmed with time, but she was back. Maria. Maria. Over and over. Her name; the full lips and flashing dark eyes; her soft breasts; that tantalizing smell in the hollow of her neck, behind her ears; the musky and intoxicating odor between her legs. Her voice. He could still hear her voice. Soft. Pleading for help.

That damned Carlos. He had to get rid of Carlos, or help Gomez get rid of him. Then Maria would be his, he was sure.

"*Si, si*. She with her husband, Carlos. Saved his life in *México City* and hides him in this city. Away from the bad…ah, bad mafia men." She hesitated, and then scratched at her belly.

"She hides him? Here?"

Jacinda shook her head indicating not here, but she refused to say more; she pointed to her home. "There," she said, pointing again. "We eat. You hungry, no?"

She didn't wait for an answer.

The house before him was a large, pale yellow stucco and red brick two-and-a-half story grand palace, with large, Roman archways that majestically covered the patios with shade.

Red, white, and blue bougainvillea vines cascaded over the arches and crawled up the high columns. Every corner had a balcony, with large, earthenware vases covered with geraniums and low yucca and cactus plants. The roof had California red tile interspersed with the occasional black, giving it a dramatic character.

Zack marveled at the large, ornate, black, wrought-iron lamps hanging from the middle of each archway, just like in the Mexican *haciendas*. An American flag fluttered from one corner of the house. There was a spacious, four-car garage attached to the house, with apartments above for the help.

Zack watched the black dog stand on his hind legs and lap water from one of the elaborate marble fountains. The dog kept a wary eye on his mistress as he cowered away. His tail went between his legs when she yelled at him.

Crystal clear water bubbled over tall statues of Eros and Aphrodite on either side of the tiled pathway.

As the two approached the entrance, a slight breeze carried the pungent odor of a cigar. The smoke floated down from above.

Jacinda pulled on the sliding glass doors to her kitchen. Zack looked up to see a man standing in the shadow of the archway.

The man was on the upper level, around the side, watching the two of them make their way into the house. The sun cast a shadow over his face, which was also covered by a broad-brimmed Panama hat, pulled sharply down over his eyes.

Zack motioned to Jacinda. "Who is that man, Jacinda?"

"He just go away again soon: my husband, Hector. You no see him again, my friend, Sack."

Zack followed her into her kitchen. His gut made noises in response to the cooking smells coming from the stove. The spicy odor of cooked fish and a pot of simmering chicken took him back to the Mexican outdoor street cafés, where he had spent a few evenings with Maria.

She waved her wooden spatula in Zack and the dog's direction. She barked out, "Sit outside, in the corner, or at the kitchen table. I get lunch."

Man and dog looked at each other, wondering who goes out and who stays in. One took the chair and the other limped to the patio corner. The zesty smells made the dog drool. A small puddle fell from his chops onto the patio tiles, near the open sliding doors.

"His name Hidalgo, *señor* doctor," she said pointing to the dog. She threw him a piece of stale bread, which he deftly caught and devoured.

"Really? How did this young mutt get such a strange name?"

"*Si, amigo.* That dog born on September sixteenth, last year, they say to me. It *México's* Independence Day. Hidalgo a good priest. He led the revolution, and free my country from the Spanish pigs. Then you *gringos* come along…later on, you know, after the…" She stopped and put her hand to her temple.

"The Spanish?"

The light came on for Jacinda. "*Si, si,* the Spanish men."

"No. I didn't know that. *Gringos?* Why did they call us *gringos?*" Zack asked, stretching out and patting his leg to have the dog come to him.

He recalled seeing a painting by Diego Rivera, in the Mexico City town hall. It was a wide mural depicting the freedom of the Mexican people. Hidalgo was included in that painting, inciting the Mexican natives to revolt against the Spaniards.

After hearing his name being called, the dog sat up and slowly crept on his belly, on all fours, to his new master. As he leaned in, Zack scratched the floppy ears and patted his head. The dog nestled against his leg, finally resting his warm body on Zack's foot.

Jacinda continued as she stirred in chopped onions and peppers into the two pots on the stove. "*Amigo*, when your soldiers from America came to my country, in 1846, they all in green uniforms. They came so far south that they were even in Mexico City. My people, they no like that. As they pass the invaders, they pointed to the green uniforms and said, 'green go, green go'."

"Green go. I get it, Jacinda. *Gringo*."

"My people all shout at your soldiers on the street, 'green go, green go, green go'."

Zack laughed, the dog barked, thumping his tail on the kitchen floor, Jacinda stirred the pot.

"So we all became *gringos*."

"*Si, si*. But now we Mexicans take over your country. You maybe take Alamo, but we take California. You'll see"

Zack chuckled. The dog wagged his tail. Jacinda cooked.

CHAPTER 15

Duke the Savior

Zack felt very comfortable with his new Mexican auntie. She was a good cook, and it was better than living in some sleazebag motel. "Jacinda, you said Maria was frightened. Why?"

"One big man with big suspenders, General Gomez, he call himself, leave blue card…big 'M' on card. That all, *amigo*. Salazar make them come…He say to me, to Jacinda."

The blue card. Same as the one at Maria's hotel room. Shit.

Jacinda ladled food onto a large, floral blue plate and set it down in front of Zack. It held a whole fish that spilled over the sides. Then she brought out a small dish with a spicy sauce and some flat, thin bread.

Jacinda sat down and waited for him to eat. "It *huachinango* red snapper, my Sack," she said as she pointed to the fish with a large spoon. "You like red snapper?"

Zack nodded, saliva filling his mouth. She got up and brought the salad with prawns.

Zack inhaled the rich aromas of olive oil and the ocean fish. He patted the dog, who was slobbering at Zack's feet. "I'm going to give him my first dog's name, Duke. He looks regal, royal even, and now needs a noble title. He's starving, Jacinda. Please give him some leftover food. I'll look after him. I had a dog once, when I was a kid."

"You have him still, Sack?"

"No. A car ran over him. My ex was drinking that morning, left the gate open."

Jacinda shrugged, put down an old blue and yellow chipped bowl, and filled it with stale taco shells, chicken bits and tomato sauce for the dog.

"You have children, Sack? *Niño*, no?

Zack hesitated. This was a painful subject for him. "No, Jacinda. A week later, she was drunk at lunch time, backed up in the driveway, and ran over our two-year-old girl."

"Oh. Sorry, Sack. Little girl. Sad, sad little *chica*."

"That's when I left her. Or maybe she left me. She moved in to drink and sleep with my neighbor."

"No worry. Now you have Duke," she said pointing to the dog and throwing it more bits of taco shells.

Duke, his new name by his new master, was panting with eyes wide open in expectation as he gobbled up the food. He looked around for more. The dog licked his chops. He then grew tense, and gave a low growl as his ears perked up.

Jacinda turned. Zack and Duke had their backs to the patio door. They both heard a car door slam.

Zack moved his chair to look to the patio, but all he felt was the sudden rush of wind as one patio door came crashing to the floor.

"What the hell's going on?" Zack screamed, but he was too late. He felt the cold steel of a baseball bat clamped against his throat. It was held by two burly arms from behind.

Zack recognized the other man, Pedro, who ran at Jacinda and knocked her to the kitchen floor, tossing a black hood over her head.

"Check the house, Pedro. And this time, don't forget the fucking car port," the man growled as he tightened his grip on the steel bat.

"Okay, okay, G-G-Gomez," Pedro yelled, pushing down the hood around Jacinda's neck.

Zack could feel his eyes popping out as the cold steel compressed his wind pipe. His carotids were cut off. He was rapidly losing consciousness.

The man pushed Zack's chin up, giving him some air.

Zack desperately tried to pull the bat away with both hands, but to no avail. He helplessly watched as Jacinda squirmed on the floor. The heavy foot of the dark Mexican with one eye held her down, as he had with Maria in her hotel apartment.

Jacinda, wailing in Spanish to the blessed virgin and then to Jesus, pleaded for her life. The dog growled, hiding under Zack's legs, which were trying to kick at Gomez and seek freedom.

Duke stirred, becoming wild and frenzied, yowling as Pedro ran to the car park. Zack felt the man behind him kick at the frantic dog.

His assailant snarled in Zack's ear, "Give up Carlos and his bitch that you are fucking, or you won't see another day, mister fucking doctor, and you will lose more than your nose this time."

Zack twisted his head in the chokehold, trying to get some air. "I don't know any Carlos, and Maria is gone," he croaked as he struggled to catch his breath.

As Pedro rushed back into the kitchen, he swept pots off the stove, spilling hot, greasy chicken onto the floor. The kitchen table tipped and Zack's dinner tumbled, adding to the chaotic mess.

Pedro pushed Jacinda aside and threw her to the floor. She gave out a muffled scream under the black hood as it tightened around her neck.

Zack kicked frantically under the table, gasping for breath. The room was turning black. The pots flying and Zack kicking precipitated a panic in the black lab.

The dog leaped out from his refuge under the table. Zack felt the dog rush through his legs as he jumped at Pedro, knocking him over.

Both man and animal slithered about in the thick goo of soup, fish, shrimp, and chicken stew.

The dog had a better grip on the floor with all four legs clawing and scratching. Duke whirled and turned on Gomez. His fangs were dripping with slobber, and his claws were covered in chicken scraps. He bit into the man's thigh.

Zack felt the bat give way as Duke clamped his teeth, now higher, into the man's crotch. The dog grabbed his balls and held them in a vice-like grip as the man hollered, dropped the steel bat, and tried to pull away.

Zack's eyes slowly refocused on the chaotic scene. The room was ablaze in the smells of the chicken stew that was splattered over the walls and the fish strewn over the tiled floor.

Jacinda was bellowing under her hood and Duke was growling, fiercely chomping at Gomez. Gomez was trying to free his testicles of Duke's fangs, and poor Pedro was stuttering gibberish in terror, sliding about in the mess on the floor.

Pedro tried to get up on all fours, but he kept skidding on the thick, greasy soup covering the tiles. Jacinda sat up and pulled off her hood. She rolled over and found the heavy, iron chicken skillet next to her. She swung it at Pedro's back with great force for such a small person.

Gomez was desperately trying to find his bat on the floor as Duke held on to his pant leg, thrashing about.

Finally, Pedro rolled over on the floor, reaching for his pistol. He shouted as his hand jerked wildly, "Let me s-shoot that mother f-f-fucker of a d-dog for you, G-G-G-Gomez."

"Don't, Pedro. Your hand is shaking. You'll hit me," Gomez pleaded. Groaning and sputtering, Pedro pulled Duke off by the tail, and then reached for his knife in his belt loop.

Pedro was too late; Jacinda swung the heavy steel pan again. She hit the man full-force on his knee. Zack heard the patella, the thin bone covering the right knee, splinter as the man wailed in agony. He dropped his knife and fell back.

Gomez dropped his own knife that he had pulled out just as Duke jumped at his arm, snarling and frothing at the mouth.

Gomez kicked at Duke and finally freed himself. He ran for the patio, holding his balls. The dog followed, nipping at his heels and yapping, howling in pursuit.

The other Mexican, holding his fractured knee, skated on hands and one good knee through the thick grease on the floor. Pedro pulled himself up and crawled out the door as Jacinda continued to thrash her pan at his buttocks.

Zack, uncertain of what else he could do, watched as Gomez came back to hold up his friend. As the two hobbled out, Pedro shouted back, "Next time that old b-b-bitch, mother f-fucker is d-d-dead for sure, and we torch this place, G-Gomez."

Zack put the table back in place, sat on the chair, and rubbed his neck to loosen the muscles, still gasping for air. He looked out. He heard the roar of the Hummer in full throttle turning around over the manicured lawn. It took off. Grass and dirt spewed from spinning tires, tearing up the pristine garden.

He looked out the patio in order to get the license plate number, even though he didn't really know what he would do with it. All he saw was the white sign on the back of the Hummer as it sped away: "*Jesus is coming. Will you be ready for him?*"

Zack, still fearful, cautiously stepped over the shattered patio door. He was worried for Duke, who took off after the Hummer down the driveway.

He called Duke back and turned to see how Jacinda was. "Jacinda, are you all right?" Zack shouted.

Jacinda gathered up her pots from the floor and was cleaning up the stew. "*Si*, Sack. I alive. That beast, he saved us. Brave, well dog, *bueno, bueno.*"

"Duke, the savior," Zack agreed. He pulled Duke into the house and cleaned his paws of the gooey mess that stuck to his claws with a towel.

"I will call Detective Gennero. He save us from these bad men," Jacinda said, patting the dog. Duke was happily licking up all the chicken pieces on the floor as a reward.

CHAPTER 16

Seema, the Wise One

The very next day, back on duty at the hospital, Zack couldn't believe what he read as he scanned the charts on the ward.

Zack saw that most patients were on government assistance. The services were paid for by Medicaid or Medicare. He also saw Forzani was ordering twice the recommended number of ECT treatments for each patient.

A fair-skinned East Indian nurse, with her gold and blue sari hitched up to her knees, showing her jeans underneath, was slowly pedaling on a stationary bike in an empty room.

Zack recognized her badge to signify a graduate. "Good morning, Nurse. On your break?"

Startled, she stopped pedaling. "Yes, I'm done now."

She had been doing a crossword puzzle while pedaling, seemingly accepting the madness around her as ward clerks busily cleaned and changed bed sheets.

"Nurse, when you're finished, please call the fumigators again. There are bedbugs in the mattresses. Kim's room is infested, and I hate bedbugs."

She got off her bike and walked beside Zack. "I complained, but no one listened, sir."

"Complained? To whom?"

"Dr. Forzani, sir. He said…ah, 'no money' was what he told me this morning," she answered, embarrassed.

"Get rid of them, and those old cots, in every room on this ward. I want new, comfortable beds for everyone here," he ordered, scratching his leg and fearing flea bites.

"Yes, Doctor. I'll put in a requisition immediately."

"Who's the charge nurse here?" Zack asked, searching for her name tag on the colorful sari. It read Seema.

"I am, sort of, until Alicia gets back, Doctor. She's the real head nurse. I'm leaving for the hospital across town tomorrow. Good to have someone who is really in charge for a change," she said as she made notes, took off her Adidas, and put on white nurse's shoes.

"You got that right. Change is coming, Seema," he said with a vengeance.

"Change would be good, Doctor. I'm also leaving because of a certain situation. I don't want to be involved with the police."

"Police? Why?" Zack asked, wondering if they already knew about Annie and Forzani.

Seema pulled Zack away from open doors. "It's Paddy, sir. Dr. O'Flanagan's son, our orderly. He steals pills off the ward. Orders them through his father. He may be an addict, or else he sells them on the street, Doctor. I don't want to be here if the police come," she whispered.

"Well, thanks for telling me, Seema. I'll look into that, and don't worry. I'll take full responsibility for that, and you won't be implicated," he reassured her.

"Oh, thank you, Doctor. Thank you. I wouldn't want to be deported if there was trouble."

"So far, in my first real job as a psychiatrist, an anorexic was saved from a headlong plunge, I had my picture taken, which some newspaper is sure to buy, and I fired Annie's special nurse, which might prompt an unlawful dismissal suit. The changes I've ordered will cost the hospital a bundle. I might get lucky yet, nurse," Zack said worriedly.

"You've got to be good to be lucky, Doctor."

"And lucky to be good."

Zack liked Seema's bright smile and beautiful teeth. She had dark, flashing eyes and an alluring figure under her sari. Three bangles in one of her ears softly jangled as she walked with Zack to the station.

"We'll get this bedlam ward fixed, but hard to do. Like pushing a rope up a hill, Seema."

Zack watched her slim body, admiring her tight jeans under the almost see-through sari as she walked to the nurse's desk. Zack closed the small, plywood door, and he told Seema to call in a carpenter to make a secure door to the nurse's office.

The office was barren except for a small desk and a chair. There were cupboards holding meds, which were also unsecure. On the desk was a photo of a beautiful little girl playing in the sand by the beach.

He picked up the photo. The little girl was about the same age as his daughter was when she was killed. "Your daughter?" he asked Seema.

"Yes, Doctor, mine. Aesha is her name…It means, love."

"Beautiful. Father not in the picture?"

Seema pulled out the chair for Zack to sit in. She opened a small fridge in the corner of the room and brought out a plate of samosas. "No. He hit me bad once. He didn't work, so I left him. I look after her, Doctor."

"Sorry to hear, Seema. Aesha is the same age as my daughter was when she died. Good you left your abusive husband. Shouldn't be tolerated."

"Thank you, Doctor. It was hard to do. That's why I need this job," she said as she put four samosas on a pan and turned on a small hotplate by the fridge.

He decided to check the name 'Forzani' as he sat at the nurse's desk. He took out his Blackberry and typed in the name 'Alberto Constantine Forzani'.

There were six sites with his name.

The first had a website with the Forzani clinic. It listed three psychiatrists, four psychologists, a massage therapist, a Pilates instructor, and one group therapist.

As Zack scrolled down, he found a photo of Forzani.

Chubby Forzani was dressed in a blue suit, with a large photograph of Freud hanging on the wall over his left shoulder. It had been taken years ago, when Forzani was a younger, more handsome man, but still very overweight. He was pointing to his newly-acquired transcranial magnetic stimulator.

"It is the most advanced treatment for all types of mental illness", the ad read. There was no mention of his dismissal from the eastern hospital.

Seema sat beside Zack at the desk. She had just sprayed herself with a lilac scent that wafted through the office and helped clear the air of doom and gloom. She got up and turned up the hot plate sitting on a small table in the corner.

Zack inhaled. Seema smiled. Lilac and curry flooded the small room as the cooker warmed up.

"I'll have a vegetarian samosa for you in a minute, Dr. Scarlatto."

Zack nodded. They both looked at the padded fee schedule on the website. Seema rolled her chair closer to the cooker and turned over the samosas sizzling in the pan.

"I'll save the information for Baker and our Dr. Sean O'Flanagan. Lilac, is it, Seema? Very nice," he asked as he scanned his *highly respected psychiatric institution'* down the hall.

"I have other fragrances at my apartment, Dr. Scarlatto. And some decent wine to go with curried chicken and rice."

"Thanks, Seema. I'll remember that once I get settled. Forzani and his website remind me of the snake oil charmers I saw every weekend in the *zocolo*, the enormous square, in Mexico City."

"I remember when my parents took me there many years ago."

"They sold gimmicks and charms, including colored water, crushed iguanas, small snakes, and dead spiders that guaranteed a cure for whatever ailed you, including baldness," he said as she filled in requisition forms.

She looked at the video once more. "Now they are no longer on the corner or in city squares. They all have highly-technical websites, Doctor," the nurse said regretfully. She placed a hot samosa on a paper plate and added a dash of mango sauce, handing it to Zack.

Zack sampled the samosa. "Very tasty. Forzani has to be back from his golf game by now."

Zack called him on his cell as Seema busied herself counting out medication for the patients.

Forzani's secretary, Josephine, answered, but she put Zack off. "He's resting after his long morning at the clinic, Doctor. I'll have him call you later."

"Clinic? I'm at his clinic. He's not here. You mean the golf course. Wake him up. I'm the live one, Josie. Remember? The only live one around here. Wake him up or I'll call that ball buster Baker right now," Zack shouted.

Zack heard Forzani answer quickly, putting him on speakerphone, in his office.

"I saw your friend's daughter. Nice hysteric, as you called her, but depressed, sir. I fired Annie's nurse. She was incompetent. I don't want Annie in a padded cell. I closed that cell, and we'll use it for the laundry. I hired nurses around the clock for Annie."

Zack heard him gasp and splutter. "You did what? That nurse, she happens to be my…uh…ah." He paused and coughed. "My niece." Forzani, suddenly awake, spat angrily into the phone.

Zack hesitated, but pushed on. It was now or never. "And we need three special nurses for Annie around the clock. We don't want another suicide on this ward, do we?"

"Suicide? Shit, man, not Annie. You get my niece, get her back. You hear what I'm saying? You hear me? Specials are over my budget," he stopped to cough, and then wheeze. "Far over, so get those other shiftless nurses on the ward, that ward, my ward, to keep an eye on my Annie 'till my niece is back," Forzani ordered.

Seema gasped and reared back as she heard Forzani shouting through the phone. She put her hand over her mouth and moved away.

There was a long silence. "I also told Sean O'Flanagan's son to stick only to his job description as an orderly."

"You mind your own…uh…business, Mister. Dr. Sean O'Flanagan is my neighbor, a good friend; a family friend," Forzani said, abruptly coughing again into the speaker phone.

"This is my business, sir. I'll talk to the chief about this Dante's inferno, and this mad house, and Annie's depression, and her bouts of crying after each time she visits you for therapy."

"She needs that special therapy."

"I should also tell you that I've referred Annie to the eating disorder clinic at the university hospital. She must have a consultation with an internist to check her kidneys, and she also needs to see a dietician," Zack said, taking a bite of samosa.

Seema saw his hand tremble slightly as he put the rest of the samosa down.

"Bouts of crying? No damn way. Depressed? Bullshit. A dietician is also gonna cost this hospital a lot of money, Doctor." He broke out into a series of coughing fits again. "Get Sean O'Flanagan's approval first, you hear…uh…before you do anything stupid, Stupid," Forzani slurred, gulping down a tablet and slurping a sip of water.

Zack's ears turned red. Seema came to Zack and put her hand on his shoulder.

With that encouragement, he plodded on with an ace up his sleeve. "Yes, despair, but I'll get her through it, after your therapy with her, sir. You bet. There's something else. There was a reporter snooping around here, taking pictures of this God-awful place. It's not as highly a respected institution as your website suggests."

Zack heard the glass of water falling off the desk. "A reporter? You really…you really…think so. That bitch, Baker, is up to this. Out to get me," Forzani yelled, now breathless, coughing and wheezing.

Zack push it. It's now or never again, he thought. "This ward is a disgrace, and Councilor Baker is coming back with that reporter. She's going to puke when she smells this stinking hole."

A fierce coughing spell interrupted the call.

Zack waited patiently, holding his cell away from his ear now.

He had Forzani on the ropes. He hoped he played his cards right.

"Big problemo, Doctor. She's a real, ah…shit…A real ball breaker. That Filipino bitch tried to…ahem, she tried to sue me for what her uncle did. She's out, out…out of line. Listen, you tell that reporter that this is my ward, and to get his ass, his big ass, the hell out. You hear me?"

"I do hear you, but if she's a real ball breaker, then we have to be careful. I'll do my utmost to put you in the best light with that newspaper and that ball breaker. Don't worry, sir," Zack said. Seema grinned.

He thought of telling Forzani about Annie's diary, but decided he would keep that one for the final nail in his coffin.

Forzani took a minute to digest that remark about Baker. "Look here, you're new in these parts…ah…um…so you be careful what you say and do. You know what I'm saying, Scarlatto?" Forzani said, and slammed down the phone.

"I'll see what I can do for you, sir." But it was too late.

Zack hung up, glad Forzani got his name right, finally, but he was worried about Forzani's overt hostility and fiery anger.

Seema sensed that, came to him and reassuringly patted him on the back. She gently offered another samosa on a clean paper plate.

Zack took the new plate with another samosa, inhaled the wonderful odor of pungent sauce, and licked his finger of a bit of mango. "I'm looking forward to meeting this Baker lady," he said as he quickly e-mailed her at city hall, inviting her to meet him on the ward.

Seema nodded. Bewildered by the turn of events, she added, "I'm enjoying the drama, Doctor."

"That so-called director of my psych ward, he's not the brightest candle on the cake," he said as he filled out the medical referrals for Annie.

Seema patted Zack on the shoulder again. She let her hand sit there. "You've got the balls, Doctor. Baker likes that in a man."

Zack laughed. He liked this gritty lady.

"Great samosas, Seema. Very tasty."

"This is getting really exciting. I love this, and I think I'll stay awhile longer, Dr. Scarlatto."

"I need you, Seema. We can get this snake pit cleaned up."

"Snake pit? I've heard that once. Where did that come from, 'snake pit'?"

"An old movie, called just that. The lady was committed to a mental institution. The doctors were thinking of performing a prefrontal lobotomy on her for her schizophrenia."

Seema put her hands up to her face and gave a shriek. "My God. I heard about that done in my country many years ago."

Zack explained further. "It was common all over the world. Two burr holes would be drilled into the top of the patient's skull, just above the eyeballs, once the anesthetic took hold. The neurosurgeon would then punch a scalpel into the hole and slice the frontal lobe of the brain. Cut it away from the rest of the brain."

"Did it cure people?" Seema asked. She brushed her hair back on her forehead, where she imagined the burr holes would be.

"It was done for severely aggressive patients, paranoid schizophrenics, manic-depressives, and even obnoxious, hostile cretins, morons, idiots and imbeciles, as we used to call the intellectually-challenged at that time."

"How the devil did such an operation come to be popular?"

"The devil? You are right about the devil, as it was a fiendish, evil, and devilish procedure. It made the person no longer human. Patients were left without any feeling, emotion, or sensitivity, forever. Often the cut was too far back, and the patient became a total vegetable. Just like President John F. Kennedy's young sister."

Seema covered a samosa in Chutney sauce and bit into it. "Really? Oh, the poor, dear child. How awful for the girl and her family."

"Indeed it was. Her father was afraid that she was far too interested in young boys and sex because of her faulty intellect. So he had it done on her. She was one of over fifty thousand patients in North America alone who had the procedure. It was stopped in the mid- to late-fifties, once medications became available for such people."

"Who devised such surgery?"

"A neurologist, Moniz, in Portugal. He knew that violent people were cured of their aggression if their frontal lobes were smashed in during a war or in an accident. He started to cut those lobes in monkeys, and they were cured of their aggression. He then tried it on humans at the local asylums. It cured them of their schizophrenic delusions and hostility. There were twenty thousand performed in Europe after that. He received the Nobel Prize in Medicine for it. Not done anymore, Seema."

"Thank God for that," Seema said wiping her hands of sweet Chutney sauce, using a warm, wet cloth.

Zack gave a small laugh. "Yes, thanks be to God, but also to Joseph Stalin of Russia. Although he murdered millions of Russians and Ukrainians in his country, he also outlawed prefrontal lobotomies in Russia. He said it was too barbaric."

Seema shook her head in wonderment. "It's good that it was before Dr. Forzani's time here. I fear what he would have it done with his patients."

Zack wanted to get back to Annie, and what Forzani was doing with her. "You must know that Annie is escorted to see Forzani late evenings. Do you think he does psychotherapy with her at that late time?"

Seema looked away, put her plate down, and stopped eating her last samosa. She looked down at her plate. Said nothing. She twirled her fork over the sauce. There was a long silence. Zack waited.

"I'm sorry, Doctor. I'm not at a liberty to think about or say what goes on here or there. Sorry. Not my affair. I need this job. I'm a single mother with a small child, and I look after my mother also. Alzheimer's. She is in India still."

Zack got up. He walked about, seething. "Okay. I get it. I have Annie's diary copied out on my cell. Her roommate is a witness. Can I show you what she wrote?"

Seema, frightened, put both hands up. "No, Doctor. I'm afraid to be involved. I saw that kind of practice in my country's hospitals as a student there, in India. Those who complained of abuse—sexual abuse, whatever kind of abuse—were fired and never to work again. I can't do that. Sorry."

Zack understood, and felt sympathetic for Seema's plight. "Okay, Seema. I understand. Look, I'll forward that diary to Baker and let her and the police have it out with Forzani. It's against the law and unethical. I won't have it on this ward."

Seema took Zack's plate and put it in the small sink. She started cleaning up. She washed the cutlery and said nothing.

She stopped. She turned to face Zack. "Doctor, don't underestimate Dr. Forzani. He has friends in powerful places, including Dr. O'Flanagan, Priest Father Roberts, the Catholic Church, and many others on council who don't agree with Miss Baker. She caused trouble by suing the hospital after her uncle's suicide."

Zack listened. He didn't know what that was about, yet. "Maybe so, but…"

Seema didn't let him finish. "Dr. Scarlatto. Forzani, Dr. O'Flanagan, and others will say that those writings, whatever they are, whatever she wrote, and what you have there are the ranting and ravings of a dramatic, hysterical, immature young female."

Zack was taken aback. Maybe he should listen to this woman. He waited. "What else, Seema? What else?"

"We all know that Annie was on stage; she attempted suicide often. She was on other psych wards. She is a whiner, a complainer, a drama queen, who has no support. You probably don't either, being new to this place. Bide your time, Doctor. Think."

Seema smiled, took Zack's hand, and held it briefly. She left him and finished cleaning the small counter, putting the dishes away in the cupboard.

"Yep. I guess you're right, Seema."

She turned to him and pulled a chair closer to Zack. "Look, just wait. Work on Dr. O'Flanagan. Work on him, and he'll get to Dr. Forzani for you."

"Yeah? How?"

Seema looked away, thought for a minute. "Not sure. He must have some weaknesses. Some weakness that you can exploit."

Zack shook his head, downcast. "He's a Catholic, Seema. You said he's buddy-buddy with that priest, and the church. He must go to mass. He must go to confession. He must be squeaky clean."

"Weaknesses. Doctor. Weaknesses. We all have them. Look, his wife is a young model from the Islands. I heard there's trouble in that marriage. Oh, and Patrick, his son. He is a nice guy but…he just came out of the closet. He told some nurse here that some priest used to abuse him, years ago."

"Closet? I couldn't use that business of possible sexual abuse, or of his exiting the closet. Not with his father, Dr. O'Flanagan. I don't think I'd go there, Seema. Not in this climate of inclusiveness. No way," Zack said, but remembered the possibility of using Paddy somehow.

Seema pushed her chair away and got up to leave. "Yes. Sorry. You're right. That kind of slander, corruption, and bribery was often used where I came from, to get what you wanted. I was still back there, in my own country, for a moment. Sorry."

Zack got up. He wanted to give her a hug, but feared it might be misconstrued as sexual. "That's okay. Thanks for those wise words, Seema.

You're right. I won't do anything rash," he said with a very light touch with one finger on her shoulder.

To Zack's great surprise and astonishment, she quickly whirled about and took Zack's finger, and then his hand, and held it briefly, but intentionally and warmly. "It's been a pleasure to be here with you, Doctor. A pleasure," she said sincerely.

"And with you, Seema. I hope you'll stay."

"Yes, I will now. Come and visit. To my home. Aesha would love you. Come for dinner one day."

"I'd love to, Seema. Love to see Aesha also."

Seema turned and left the office.

Zack sat down. He was alone. But he felt much wiser and smarter, thanks to Seema, and maybe to a new love, a child. At that point in time, Zack didn't know that he soon would have that opportunity with O'Flanagan.

CHAPTER 17

Lani O'Flanagan

Several days later, Zack was still waiting to hear from Baker. He was still considering sending her Annie's diary and details of Annie's "therapy" with Forzani. However, after what Seema, the wise one, advised, he didn't do that yet.

That morning, while driving to his hospital, he checked out his reflection in the rearview mirror, and he liked what he saw. He was clean shaven. He had trimmed back down to his college weight. He had cut his hair back, and he was sporting a new, white sport shirt under a blue summer jacket. Unlike his drab and dismal appearance during his last year of psychiatric residency with his mentor, Dr. Abrahams, the analyst.

He was depressed after his divorce and the death of his child. Abrahams saw his despair during a clinic he was supervising. He told Zack he needed therapy.

His experience with Abrahams was unpleasant, as he never really agreed with psychoanalysis. Too lengthy, too tedious, and Zack was too impatient. All psychiatrists in their final terms of residency had to endure a personal analysis. At one point, Abrahams explained, "The purpose of this year's analysis is to give you some insight into your own aggressive personality disorder and depression, Doctor."

Zack smirked as he recalled the Austrian analyst with a faulty memory. "Personality disorder, sir?"

"You are far too resistive, holding back repressed hostility, and possess an unwillingness to expose yourself, young man. You must let your mind wander freely. Your dream last night, Doctor. What was it?"

Zack laughed as he thought of an answer, but never voiced it.

"I always resisted talking about my erotic dreams. That old pervert would spend an hour on wild interpretations saying that all I wanted was to screw my mother, but only after I killed my father, all that, according to Freud and the Oedipus complex."

As the light changed, he turned onto the freeway. "My analyst only liked to treat young, attractive, sexually-frigid, wealthy women who experienced a plethora of erotic dreams. My athletic, six-foot-tall bulk and size eleven shoes always hung over the end of his damn couch," he said to the sexy weather girl's voice on the radio.

At one session Abrahams chided Zack. "What do you spend your hard-earned money on, young man?"

Zack grinned in the rear view mirror as he recalled his apologetic answer, "Well sir, only on booze, loose women, and strip bars. The rest I just fritter away."

Abrahams, devoid of humor, hastily scribbled notes.

On the last day of his therapy Abrahams summarized, "You have five distinct problems. Two are with that obsessiveness of yours to succeed, and then that aggressive personality. The only three positive attributes are your self-esteem, cheerful outlook, and brutish confidence. You need another year of therapy, young man."

"Well, sir, three out of five ain't bad," Zack said as he stood up off the couch.

As he walked out on that last day, he got the phone number of the pretty blonde sitting in the analyst's waiting room.

"Abrahams will be disappointed. She doesn't look like my mother, and I'll listen to her erotic dreams for free." Zack laughed as he had stepped into the elevator.

As he entered the main hospital to meet Seema again, he bought a bottle of water at Starbuck's in the lobby and then made his way to his psych ward.

He pushed through the grubby swinging doors, still waiting for the painters, but the "P" was back up for "Psychiatry", handwritten with a large felt pen. The ward was cleaner, but there was still much to be done. Now he had a twitching irritation in his nose from the heavy stink of Clorox disinfectant, lingering fumigation smells, and air fresheners used by Seema and Flora.

Annie had been discharged by Forzani, much to Zack's surprise and dismay. When Seema called Zack earlier that morning he was furious.

"Seema! What the hell is he doing? She's still seriously depressed," he ranted.

"Yes, we all thought so, Doctor. Dr. Forzani said she would still be seeing him, but it was more therapeutic for her to be in the community, and placed her in a group home for anorexics. Thanks for telling me about her daily notes in her diary. He insisted that we bring him all her diaries."

"Damn. Oh, sorry. Did you?"

"No, Doctor. I have them locked up in my desk for you. I told him that she had destroyed them. He also refused to pay for a new sign, and told me to use a felt pen for the letter 'P'."

Zack could feel the stress and fear in Seema's voice for disobeying an order. They both knew that Forzani had to get Annie off the ward so he could control her better.

Zack thought for a moment. "Good for you. Maybe he knew what I know and he didn't want anybody else to know."

"Maybe, Doctor."

As he walked down the corridor to his office, his Blackberry vibrated in his breast pocket. He flicked open the cell phone.

"Dr. Scarlatto? Are you the new psychologist here? You're needed at sixth floor surgery. A suicidal patient. Urgent," the operator shouted in a panic.

"Not a psychologist, Miss. It's Dr. Zack Scarlatto, I'm a psychiatrist—" he tried to explain, but she had hung up.

Zack ran into his office and quickly took off his sports jacket and donned his white lab coat. He put a black pen into the breast outer pocket and grabbed a clipboard with last month's psychiatry journal front and center. All of that, he thought, made him look professional, confident, and more important when he visited other areas of the hospital.

He ran out of the old, brick building and through the glass doors of the sparkling surgical wing. "She doesn't know the frigging difference between a psychiatrist and a psychologist, and I'm sure could care less," he muttered.

Nurses, staff, and patients made way for him as he raced to the elevators.

"Sixth floor? Hope she's not teetering on the ledge like Annie. I hate heights," he said as the emergency elevator quickly whisked him to the top.

When the elevator doors opened, he was immediately met by a surgical resident. "Good you got here, doc. I'm Dr. Spinoza, Dr. Sean O'Flanagan's chief resident. I'll take you to his wife. She's the suicidal one," he said, breathless.

Zack followed Spinoza as they ran down the long surgical corridor. "Sean O'Flanagan's wife, you said. The chief?" Zack asked, breathing in the antiseptic flavors of the surgical ward.

"Yeah. She tried it before, by overdose, but she's going to do it this time, doc, with scissors," Spinoza said.

Nurses pushed patients back into their rooms in order to protect them from the crazy one on their ward, and to clear a path for the two doctors. There was tension in the air. Zack felt it.

He also felt the hostility toward a psychiatrist visiting their sacred surgical halls. Surgical wards did not like behavioral problems in their system. Definitely not neurotics or psychotics. And definitely not loony men or women who are threatening to kill themselves. It was simply too distracting. Surgeons and surgical nurses were busy people. There was no time for that kind of nonsense. They saved lives, not catered to hysterics.

At the end of the long corridor were the single, very exclusive rooms for those special patients who could afford the luxury. As Zack sped along, other surgical patients gawked from their doorways as nurses gathered in bunches. Everyone looked worried. The oppressive air could have been cut with a surgical scalpel.

They got to the end of the hallway. Zack couldn't see beyond the crowd outside the door, but he had visions of a woman standing on the window ledge, ready to jump, jabbing at her wrists with scissors.

"She's in there, Doctor. It's Lani O'Flanagan," a security guard whispered in Zack's ear.

The young surgeon spoke softly as he pulled him through the hushed multitude that reluctantly made way. This was high anxiety drama, and those at the stage door weren't going to be shut out that easily.

Act one.

Zack knew that they all wanted to see a jumper. Everybody stops to watch a jumper, whether it's from a bridge or a building. Some even shout and encourage the jumper to leap. Probably some even bet on it. Zack tried to listen as the surgeon talked about "fires, a motor vehicle accident, broken mirrors, glass, suicide, carotid arteries, open windows, facial surgeries, and a husband who drives his wife Looney Tunes."

"Is her husband here?" Zack asked.

"No. In surgery. Lani is back on this ward for a few days. She had plastic reconstruction to her right hand. Face is disfigured. Scars are bad. Her husband, our chief, Dr. O'Flanagan, came to visit this morning.

Bad, bad fight, doc. Their marriage is on the rocks, and she's suing him for all he's got. A real shit storm, man."

Zack hated shit storms. He strained to peer over the heads and into the room.

The surgeon pushed Zack into the doorway as he lowered his voice so that Lani wouldn't hear, "O'Flanagan was swearing, Lani was crying." He paused, and then continued, "Major, major friggin' fight. I gave her a shot. It didn't help. What should we do? She's suicidal, man. She's all yours. Into the psych ward, man. Where she belongs," he said.

Zack knew he would have to sign papers to certify her into a psych ward, but that wasn't going to happen with the chief as her husband. He felt hands propelling him to the front of the group and into the patient's room. He stopped from taking the next step as he heard the frantic shout from inside.

Act two.

"Sthay away or I'll use it on my neck," a woman with a pronounced lisp shouted from deep inside.

The good news was that Lani was not hanging out the window. Now that he could see her, he felt relieved seeing she was in her bed.

The bad news was that Lani was holding a pair of scissors with her right hand and pointing them at the crowd. A large shard of glass, held in her left, gloved hand, was next to her neck.

As Zack looked around the room, he saw splinters of a mirror on the richly carpeted floor. Lani, sitting up in bed, was a darker-skinned woman with a grossly disfigured face. She was shouting hysterically, dramatically jabbing at the air, often crying out indistinctly with a marked lisp.

"I won't talk to anyone. Keep my husband out of thith."

A student nurse in surgical greens, who was a petite, pretty, Afro-American young woman, stood next to Zack in the crowded doorway. She had tight, kinky hair and wore white sneakers. "That lisp is due to her burns and multiple facial surgeries, Doctor," she explained to him.

"Getting close to Lani without her slashing her neck will be a challenge," Zack said to the student nurse.

As he wondered about his next step, Zack felt an elbow in his lower ribs. He turned to see the young student nurse looking up at him.

She whispered in his ear, "My patient is a famous model from the Islands. Her full name is Leilani Moana Kamehameha, but we just call her Lani, her model name. She's been in all the European magazines, like *Elle*, and others."

"Really? Impressive."

"She married our chief after she won Miss Hawaii three years ago."

Zack looked down at the petite student nurse, a third his size.

The resident surgeon tugged on his coat sleeve, "Dr. Sean O'Flanagan is out of surgery and is coming back. He's on his way. Maybe he can help."

Zack shook his head. "Keep him away. If they had a friggin' fight, as you said, then he'll only friggin' aggravate her," he said as he entered the room.

"Quite right, Doctor. It was a fire storm a few hours ago," said the petite nurse.

Zack stepped through the doorway. As he looked about the private room, he marveled at the plush amenities: luxurious furniture, designer wall hangings, and sculptured crown moldings.

He stepped onto Persian carpets which lay over thick, wall-to-wall Indian rugs. Zack recognized two prints of the old masters in ornately-gilded frames scattered on the floor. One was of Rembrandt.

Gold, brocade curtains covered expansive windows. The air was awash with scented flowers in crystal vases, sweet-smelling disinfectants, perfumed lotions and soaps wafting out of the private bathroom, and the whiff of an open, half-eaten box of chocolates. It was so unlike his psych ward that he smirked.

Sean O'Flanagan had only the best in this hospital for his wife. To dissuade her from the lawsuit, Zack surmised.

As he walked in, Lani pulled her bed cover up to her chin and partially hid her mutilated face. She wore fine, leather gloves, and she covered her head in a long, black Spanish scarf.

The diminutive nurse tugged at his sleeve, "Just tell her, Doctor. Tell her you're that famous psychiatrist, whom everyone read was the hero, written up in our papers after saving that young girl on the psych ward." She paused. "She'll listen to you. Tell her you're in charge here. Just tell her, Doctor. Go ahead."

At this point, the young nurse grasped the doctor's little finger and pulled him into the room. "This is Doctor…ah…ah…" She looked up to him quizzically and tried to read his name tag.

"Scarlatto."

She didn't wait for Zack to answer further, but instead continued, slowly but firmly, talking to Lani. "He's a psychiatrist, Lani; our new senior hospital specialist consultant, a highly-qualified psychiatrist. He's very smart, and very famous. He was in all the newspapers recently."

Zack, now in the room, was more surprised than Lani was with the introduction. The nurse clasped another two sweaty fingers with her small hand and pulled him toward the bed.

Zack, emboldened by the nurse's introduction, said, "Yes. That's right, Lani." He approached Lani's side. "My name is Dr. Scarlatto. I am a psychiatrist. Your doctor, Dr. Spinoza, asked me to see you."

"I heard about you thaving that girl from jumping off the roof, but shtay away, or I'll do it. Life is over for me," Lani lisped.

Zack held his ground. "The nurse and I will close the door, and everyone else will go away. She and I will just sit at the back of your room, far away from you, so please don't be scared," he said firmly, but with a warm smile.

Before Lani could respond, Zack told the nurse to close the door. She relished this novel authority, so different from scrubbing and handing sterile scalpels to surgeons in the OR. She dramatically pushed everyone out.

"Close that door; I don't want to be disturbed," Zack shouted with a determined voice, lending further authority to his presence.

At this point, he made his best move of the day. He looked at Lani, but raised his voice to the crowd behind him, "And that includes her husband, do you hear me?"

The young nurse nodded approvingly. The surgeon pushed others away. Lani jabbed at the air with her scissors. Others reluctantly stepped back. The door closed. All were disappointed to not be in on the theatrics.

Act three.

Zack looked about. There were two chairs in the room: one by the door, and the other by the bed. Zack took the chair by the door, moved it closer to Lani, and sat down.

He smiled at Lani. "I want your nurse to sit down, Lani; at the end of the bed. She's tired after working long hours through the night."

Lani, surprised by the turn of events, shouted meekly, "But no clother." She sounded exhausted. A dribble came out of the side of her mouth.

"Keep calm, Lani. Everything will be okay. But tell me now: what's going on here?"

The nurse was about to answer, but Zack put up his hand and hushed her. He had to divert Lani's attention from any dramatic attempts at suicide. "Why did you break that mirror, Lani? Very nice and pricey, it was. And it's bad luck, Miss." He pointed to the hand-held mirror shattered on the floor.

He sat back and crossed his legs in the brocade, Louis the 14th chair, pleased with his progress. He was in the room. The crowd was gone. Sean O'Flanagan was out. Lani accepted him. She was talking. The nurse sat close by. So far, so good, he thought. And Lani's in bed. Not on the ledge.

"I've had all the bad luck already. I'll never look in another mirror. Never," she wailed tearfully, hid her face, and blew her nose into a black, lace kerchief. The room reverberated with the rattle and snuffle of badly-blocked nasal passages after surgery.

Lani slowly looked at Zack and pulled her hair aside. She put the scissors on the bed and threw the glass shard on the carpet. She looked straight at Zack and slowly turned her face to the right, and then to the left.

Zack stifled a gasp, and forced himself to not react to the facial horror. He watched a Hawaiian woman who was in her late twenties slowly reveal her scarred face.

Zack's eyes followed the blue suture scars circling her nose, which was now partially flattened against her face. The rest of her face was contorted by the deep scarring of both cheeks.

Her upper lip was wide, pulled back from her teeth and grotesquely distorted. The poor woman couldn't close her mouth, since half her lip was stuck to one nostril. She had that golden, darker color of the Islands, but she had a pale skin graft sutured diagonally across her forehead. It was so light in color against her darker skin that it gave her a clownish effect.

"Lani, I'm so sorry to see you suffer like that. Tell me what happened," Zack asked sympathetically.

He stifled the nausea in his gut, partly from the sight of what was once a beautiful woman, and partly from the plastic surgery that was so blatantly botched.

"There was a fire in my van. On the highway to Thacramento." She paused. "My husband—that stho called famous, that stho called surgeon I'm divorcing!" She paused again. "He was following in his new sporth car." She paused. "Driving." She paused again. "Behind me."

She stopped, breathing rapidly, gasping for breath, wiping the dribble from her chin and trembling.

"You're having a panic attack. Probably post-traumatic stress, Lani," Zack said, wishing he had kept a lorazepam or two in his pocket just for her.

Lani took in a few deep breaths. "There was a thudden fire from the back." She paused. "In the van. It was the propane sthove we used camping. It tipped over and a spark thet it off."

She stopped, exhausted from talking. She snuffled.

"Go ahead, Lani," the nurse encouraged.

Lani continued, "I pulled over, and turned to put the fire out. The propane fire blew up." She paused. "Hit me." She paused. "In the face, neck, arm." She paused again. "I couldn't thee. The curtains caught fire. I wasth trapped, and couldn't get out."

She stopped and put her gloved hands to her face. Lani snuffled loudly through one nostril, cried, and dabbed at the nasal drippings with a tissue.

The young nurse's eyes teared up. She didn't hesitate for a second, and immediately moved to put her arm around Lani. The nurse soaked a small towel in water and gently wiped the tears from Lani's misshapen face.

The nurse took away the scissors and put them on the bedside table. Lani seemed relieved to be free of her weapon, and, in despair, threw her arms around the young girl.

Nurse and patient clung to each other as Zack remained silent.

He waited.

Lani breathed heavily, snuffled again and turned to Zack.

"He." She paused. "My husband." She paused again. "He only shtood on the thide of the highway. He did nothing to help me, nothing. Nothing. He was a coward—paralythed." She shouted and emphasized the word 'coward', again and again.

Zack, watching the tender scene of the nurse cradling her patient in her arms, moved to the edge of the bed.

"Lani, I'll talk to your physician and I'll help you," he said gently, as he took Lani's gloved right hand. He slowly peeled off the leather covering.

He was thinking fast of how he could use the situation to his advantage. Now he had Sean O'Flanagan's wife in his one hand, and perhaps Sean O'Flanagan's balls in his other, soon.

Maybe he would owe Zack a favor by getting rid of Forzani, if Zack could send her to his friend in London for a transplant. That would take the legal pressure off of Sean O'Flanagan, and get Lani out of his hair.

"I'm sorry this happened to you. It's a tragic loss. You've had many losses, Lani. Now that I'm here, I'm sure we can help you more."

"You're both tho kind to me. Yesh, many, many losses. Now I losht my husband; he hath another woman. That blonde bitch. I losht my face. I losht my career. I losht my youth," she wailed.

Zack looked at the slender, beautiful body outlined by the satin sheets. "You're suffering from a major depressive disorder and a post-traumatic stress disorder, Lani. I'll order an antidepressant and a tranquillizer for you. You'll feel better soon." He gently pulled her hand from under the sheets.

He turned her hand over and ran his fingers over the scars in her palms. The ring and little fingers were welded together by the intense heat, and her index finger and thumb were locked in a permanent spasm.

He gently held her hand while Lani rocked and wept in the nurse's arms. "This medication will also help the pain. There's good evidence that these newer anti-depressants also reduce chronic pain. You'll be more comfortable with the pills, Lani. Try to be optimistic and strong; like your famous grandmother, the Island queen from years ago. I read about her in James Michner's book, *Hawaii*; a very brave woman."

Zack moved closer and sat at the top of the bed, near her. He gently lifted her chin and looked into those frightened eyes, circled with dark shadows. Her right eyelid was pulled up and seared into the socket, chronically weeping, with a yellow puss still stuck to the lid.

Zack took her other hand. Lani recoiled at first, but she slowly exposed her right hand. He turned her hand over and saw the scarred flesh. The two middle fingers were now one; they were seared together by the flames.

"The other one ith better. I…" She paused. "I tried to put the flame…" She waited again. "Out with thish one."

Zack turned her hand over and he held her twisted fingers with both of his hands. He decided to take the chance.

"Lani, I have a good friend. He's in England and he's doing wonderful work with total facial transplants. It's a complete new face. I've seen his work in the medical journals, photos and all. I'll call him if you wish."

The nurse wiped Lani's nose and looked at the psychiatrist with a puzzled look. "Total facial transplants? You're not serious, Doctor?"

"For sure," Zack said to the nurse. Perhaps he had gone too far, he thought.

"A completely new face?" Lani asked.

"Total, and I mean total, facial transplants. He's so good that you can't even see the stitches. No scars, and the same beautiful skin color. I'll send you to his website."

He left out the part about the face being transplanted from a cadaver. Zack knew that his friend in England would have to wait for a Hispanic or some darker-skinned woman to die. Tragically, it would have to be a young woman somewhere in the British Isles.

"Oh, Dr. Sthcarlatto. That would be tho wonderful," Lani said, putting the box of tissues aside.

Zack was pleased to give her some hope; he saw her attempt a smile. He looked about. "Don't like that painting?" he asked pointing to a framed copy lying on the floor.

"I hate it."

Zack walked over and picked it up. "It's a self-portrait by the famous Dutch painter, Rembrandt."

"Too dark," she said. "It's so depressthing. My husband gave it to me."

"I agree, but I'm fond of the old Dutch painters."

"Well then, take it. It ish my gift to you," she lisped, pointing to the print with the gilded frame.

"Thank you. It looks just like my analyst, Abrahams, from my student days. I had to tolerate him for a whole year while he berated me for hour after hour," he said with a grimace.

Zack took the print and studied it closely. It was a painting of Rembrandt in his advanced years. It had the same piercing, beady eyes as his analyst, Dr. Abrahams.

"It's yours," she said again, dabbing at the weeping eye with a tissue.

"He even has the long, curly hair over his ears. The spitting image of Dr. Abrahams," he added with a laugh.

"Keep it. The eyes keep following me around the room. Too depressthing," Lani said, covering her face again.

Zack put the print under his arm. "I'll come and see you tomorrow. I'll leave an order for an anti-depressant, and I'll ask the psychologist on the ward to see you also. She's good at cognitive therapy, Lani."

Zack surveyed the opulent room once more, so different from his psych ward.

He winked at the nurse.

Zack walked out, tucked Mr. Rembrandt under his arm, and spied the chief down the hall, writing orders at a desk.

The snooping crowd of orderlies, nurses, and patients had dispersed. They were disappointed to not be able to witness some exciting melodrama, rather than the mundane, daily routine of a surgical ward. Nurses and doctors returned to their work—saving patients and lives who really needed their help.

End of Act three.

CHAPTER 18

The Really Big Deal

When Sean O'Flanagan looked up and saw Zack exiting his wife's room, he threw the pen and chart he had been holding down at the desk nurse, and nearly ran at Zack. "So what the fuck does she want? She's got me by the short hairs, Scarlatto." Sean O'Flanagan was nearly apoplectic.

Zack smiled and put the painting down, letting it rest against the sterile, white wall.

This was the first time Zack had met the chief of the hospital. He was a rugged-looking man in his late fifties, tall and well-built, with a mass of brown hair, small mustache, and dark, flashing eyes. He reminded Zack of the famous actor, the *Schindler's List* movie star, Liam Neeson. The chief, unlike Neeson, who wore a black, rumpled suit in the film, was still wearing his greens after coming out of surgery. He looked tired.

Zack decided to take a chance and be even more dramatic than Lani. He poured it on. Maybe this was what Seema suggested was needed: a weakness, an Achilles' heel that could be exploited. His wife.

"Well, sir. She's a real sick lady. Badly scarred, and she is one very angry puppy. Didn't say much to me. Wouldn't talk much at all. Wouldn't show me her burns or scars. Talked mainly, no, ranted and swore at me, and then at you, and she only wants to see her lawyer in her room," Zack replied.

"Lawyer? Shit man. No Goddamn lawyers. No lawyers, you hear. I won't let no fucking lawyers on my ward. She and they will suck me dry."

Zack loved this. "Yeah. I can understand that, sir. Hard to know what she said with that lisp. Something about a suit to wear? Sewed? Suet? Not sure, maybe something about your nice suit you must have bought. That's what she kept muttering over and over. What was she meaning, sir?"

It worked. Sean O'Flanagan bit his lip and Zack could see a bead of sweat running down his forehead.

Sean O'Flanagan cupped his hand and whispered into Zack's ear as a nurse walked by, "She's crazy. A fucking lawsuit, that's what she was saying. She wants to sue me for all I've worked so hard for. You got to certify her to the outlying mental hospital. Get her out of my hair, for Christ's sake."

Zack frowning, and appearing to be thinking hard, looked off into the distance and said, "Not very likely, sir. Not with a handy psych ward in your hospital, sir. Which, by the way, is filled with rats, silverfish, fleas, bedbugs, mice, and cockroaches. You wouldn't want your wife in there. Forzani is never there. He leaves it all up to me. But look, I've got a better idea."

Zack ushered Sean O'Flanagan by his arm to the end of the hallway and away from Lani's door.

"Yeah, yeah; well, it better be good. What've you got in mind? Send her back to Hawaii, for Christ's sake? Is that your idea? Bullshit, there's friggin' lawyers there, too."

Zack pushed his scheme. "Well, sir, she needs a proper facial transplant. I have a friend in London, England. He does them perfectly. I could get her there if you pay her expenses. I'll talk her out of the lawsuit against you for the van incident; your fault, she said, and the insurance adjuster apparently agreed, due to the faulty propane stove you bought, and you just stood there watching her burn. She said it over and over and over to the nurse as I left. I'll get her to just go for a proper, simple divorce, since she was ecstatic about the facial transplant idea."

"You can do that? I read about that plastic surgeon. Sam something-or-other. Do it," Sean O'Flanagan said, almost shouting now, almost jumping up and down from foot to foot, so relieved to get her out of town.

"Look, sir, I'll get her out of your hair, but I want Forzani out of my hair. He's old, failing, and behind the times. He'll be a legal liability for you soon with what he's doing, and not doing, on my psych ward. Like the lawsuit you had with his screw-up with Baker's uncle. Also, that very same Counselor Baker is now raising hell in the papers about the festering bunion of a building next to this palace of yours."

"I read about her shit in the papers. Going to cost a bundle, young man."

"Going to cost *you* a bundle with three lawsuits. First, your wife. Second, sure as hell if Forzani screws up, which he will, and now you've got Baker breathing down your neck."

O'Flanagan looked quizzically at Zack. "So, that's two. What's the third one?"

Here's the trump card, Zack thought. He laid it on the table. "Annie, a patient who was on the ward, is suicidal, hysteric, and has a wealthy stepfather. She left a diary describing Forzani forcing her to suck his dick in his office, underneath his desk. Doing the dirty on him under his desk while he sat there getting off. She made a recording of Forzani telling her how he wanted her to be his bitch and do what he said, to swallow his cum or else, shit like that. All on record, sir. Dates, time, and place verified."

"Sex? You mean sex? In my hospital? Holy fucking hell. Her

stepfather financially supports this place real good. I know him well. Play golf when he comes down here. I knew that fucker was kicked out of the Eastern hospitals for fucking around with young chicks. I gave him a chance here," Sean O'Flanagan said, breathless and seething again, hopping from one foot to the other again, more sweat pouring down his forehead.

"Yes, sir. Her stepfather has copies of that diary now. So does Baker. Annie's good friend and roommate, Kim, sent her diary to them. Kim was a witness, who is very reliable and credible. I'll send you a copy. What's your e-mail?" Zack offered, bringing out his cell.

Zack could see the wheels turning as Sean O'Flanagan mulled over the legal ramifications. "No, no, no copies. I don't want to look at that porn shit, or to listen to Baker again rant about her uncle's suicide. Look, I know that the Catholics with that nut case, Massimo, will help you fix up, or help you get a new ward. He's a loaded, off-the-wall psycho, and his priest, Roberts, has him sewed up. I think anything is possible."

They both just stood there, ignoring passing nurses who smiled at Zack and nodded to Sean O'Flanagan.

"I'll help you with Lani if you make it happen with Forzani. After all, you're the boss. I have my psychologist counseling your wife. I'll get my psych gal to tell her to forget about the lawsuits so that she is free of additional stress while undergoing the facial transplant. She'll enjoy living at the Ritz, in London. That will work, sir,"

Sean O'Flanagan looked at Zack, almost pleadingly again, and then he grabbed his hand and pumped it up and down. "Jesus Christ. You can do all that for me, young man?"

"Yes, sir. If Jesus Christ was here today, I could have made things different for him, too," Zack said with a grin.

Sean O'Flanagan squirmed, brushed the sweat from his forehead. He took the bait. "Get her out of my hair. But you keep her in London 'til this shit blows over. I'll get that pervert out of your hair and help you get what you want," he said.

A nurse came over and asked him to leave a prescription for one of his patients.

"Will do. She was screaming about taking you to the cleaners, sir. House, resort home at Manhattan Beach, your yacht, and your new Porsche."

"Jesus. She can have it all, but not my Porsche. Not my fucking Porsche, you hear?"

"Yes, sir. I hear. I'll do all that. Guaranteed. You have my word on this. But you move Forzani first. I don't want for you to have a sexual harassment suit on your hands also. Bad publicity for you and your hospital. Your friend, Annie's stepfather, will be out for blood."

"Yeah, yeah. Well, we'll watch Forzani take a slow bleed," Sean said with relief. He grasped Zack's right hand again and violently shook it up and down, and then walked away.

Zack grinned, wiped the sweat from his hand on his white coat after the chief's clammy grip, and looked at his watch to see what time it was in England.

CHAPTER 19

Alicia

Back on the psych ward that next morning, Zack asked the ward clerk where he could find Seema. "Her day off, Doctor. Our head nurse, Alicia, is back from holidays," the clerk replied, running off to organize the carpenters at the nurse's station, and to direct the movers handling the new beds.

He felt apprehension in his belly again, having to deal with a head nurse who may or may not be helpful to him. His neck muscles were still taut from the attack by Gomez, and he was still taking lorazepam almost daily in order to quell his anxiety. Plus, he also smoked the occasional joint.

He pushed those thoughts aside. He had one more ace up his sleeve to get rid of Forzani and that card, the black ace of spades, was called Baker. Once in his office, he turned on his laptop, and forwarded the photos he took of the ward to Councilor Baker at city hall.

Zack hesitated briefly, thinking of also including Annie's diary for Baker, but, after recalling Seema's advice, he decided to only show one card at a time. He signed off as Zack Scarlatto, MD, Psychiatrist. "That will impress the hell out of her, and get things moving around here," he said decisively.

He also decided to suck it up and try to look forward to meeting Alicia, the Chinese ward nurse in charge who was just back from Hong Kong. She was in the nurse's station telling the carpenter she wanted new, secured med cupboards with locks just as Zack approached.

She was sitting at the nurse's desk when Zack walked in, and he looked down at her shaved head. He almost burst out laughing at her strange appearance. He wondered what and who he would now have to be dealing with. She was a small, sinewy Oriental, wearing a short, skimpy skirt, a tight, V-neck cashmere sweater revealing an ample bosom, with crossed legs that were waxed and tanned. She had two black eyes.

"Alicia, what happened to you? Did some guy beat you up?" Zack asked trying to be sympathetic.

She looked up, smiling. "No, but I heard all about you from my staff. Welcome, and yes, you bet; by a surgeon. I had the slant taken out of my eyelids yesterday. What do you think?"

My, God, he thought. Another Jacinda with obsession about plastic surgery. "I think it must be blepharoplasty; that's what my friend Sam, a plastic surgeon, called it. He said that thousands of Asian women have it done in London where he practices."

"All I was getting at was that you white guys are a bunch of Rice Kings, all the fucking time," she said, throwing down her ballpoint pen after signing off on her report.

Zack smiled and thought: *Wow, she's my head nurse?* But he somehow liked this oddball. She was different, but maybe exciting.

"Really? Rice Kings?"

Alicia signed off her nurses notes on some other charts, got out of her chair, and filed the charts in a new cabinet that Zack had ordered for the office. "Oh, you don't know? They're all friggin' macho Caucasian men. They all want a nice, shy, unassertive, dependent, 'yes sir, roll me over and do it again' Chinese girl whom they can control. And screw.

And bully," she said with excitement in her voice now that she had clearly identified what she wasn't.

Zack put his hand on her shoulder. "Really? I'm sorry that was your experience."

"Yeah, well, they all think that all us Oriental girls aren't as assertive as the American chicks. They think we will just lie there and do their bidding for them: stay home, cook, screw, make babies, screw some more, and make more babies." Then she added for good measure, "I'm changing, man. For starters I got my eyes done. See."

Zack looked closely at Alicia. "Good for you Alicia. Don't take any abuse from anyone. Rice Kings? Really?"

She leaned over and touched Zack's hand and held it for a second, "Remember to come for dinner. This Friday. Let's say at seven. You bring the wine."

She took a piece of paper out of the desk and printed in large bold letters. She leaned into him. "Here's my address. It's suite number six, on the second floor. Red wine, white, blush, rosé, or bubbles: you decide. We'll talk about my ideas for our new ward."

"Our ward? Okay, I'll bring the merlot."

"And don't forget the rubbers, sport. I don't want another surgeon scraping out my uterus. He fucked it up the last time."

Zack frowned. He hated such personal confessions so early in a relationship that wasn't even there yet. It only meant she was too serious, and that it was far too early.

The tantalizing body lotion wafting up from Alicia, a delicate mixture of lemon, tangerine, and bitter orange, again reminded him of Maria's body. The aroma triggered his obsessive thoughts about her again, wondering where she was.

He carefully folded the paper and put it in his breast pocket. He knew that frantic sex with Alicia would help dispel those thoughts that still possessed him.

"I'll be there, Alicia. With at least a dozen rubbers, all of different colors."

CHAPTER 20

Alicia, Warts and All

It was a few days later when Zack took Alicia up on her invitation. He brought condoms, since he felt certain she must be promiscuous; she had been so loose with the invitation, and she had obviously had an abortion or two before, as she stated that her uterus had been scraped out.

When he arrived, Alicia threw her arms around him, gave him a slobbering-wet French kiss and pulled him inside, closing the door. She sat him down in the small living room, and put Zack's bottle of red wine in the kitchen, returning with an open, chilled bottle of prosecco.

He was aware that her tiny condo was all she could afford, located in the high-priced rental area in town. She plunked herself down next to him on her sofa.

She took a deep gulp from the bottle and set it down on the hardwood floor. Before Zack knew it, she was tumbling around on top of him, her skirt up to her belly button. She wasn't wearing panties underneath. She was a very agile young woman, not an ounce of fat on her, but still she had generous and voluptuous breasts, which pleased Zack.

Zack liked to take his time, and even get to know who he was having sex with. "Let's have a drink first, Alicia," Zack said, gently lifting her off him.

Alicia pouted, pulled down her skirt, but reluctantly agreed. As they sipped prosecco in paper cups, she lit up a rolled joint she had on the coffee table. They chatted briefly about her trip to China and the changes on the ward. The joint was a slow puff, passed back and forth.

Zack could see that she was in a hurry and horny. She was eager to please; she kept fondling Zack through his sport shirt and sending her nimble fingers down his pants. Then she quickly stripped his pants down, and, just as quickly, she doffed her own clothes, scattering them here and there on the floor.

After going down on him once, but holding back before he exploded, she pushed him along the sofa, and gently maneuvered his face down over her breasts, toward her crotch. Zack didn't mind giving a woman an orgasm with oral sex: cunnilingus. They all loved it, and were grateful to a man, or a woman, who had a good technique. Zack had a feeling she'd had both before.

Zack was sure that she had no idea that cunnilingus was once taboo, considered to be a perversion, and it was actually outlawed in England, throughout parts of Europe, and in many cultures.

The term came from the Latin *cunnus*, meaning vulva, which were the outer and inner lips of the female genitalia, and *lingua*, or tongue. It only became popular, and more acceptable, with the sexual revolution in the early sixties: articles in magazines like *Playboy* and *Hustler*, and Dr. Kinsey's discussions and exploration of sexual customs. Later, Masters and Johnson conducted more explicit research on sexual practices.

Prior to that, it was considered by most to be a perversion, and anyone who indulged in fellatio or cunnilingus was simply a pervert to be shunned. In fact, in some cultures and societies, including early England, it was illegal. One could be arrested, charged by the courts, and even hung by the neck, for indulging.

As Zack quietly agreed to help Alicia with sexual satisfaction, he was also quite fearful that there was the good possibility she had a sexually transmitted disease, more commonly called STDs.

She may have STDs without her even knowing about it, especially gonorrhea, since the gonococcus bacteria could sit in the female sexual and urinary system for years without demonstrating symptoms or problems, but still be contagious.

He thought of how he could develop gonorrhea, or even syphilis, or some other STD, if he went down on her. He could harbor it in his mouth, or elsewhere, if he has any other type of sex with her.

He wouldn't know for weeks after, until he has a discharge from his penis. Or worse still, she could harbor the spirochete bacteria that caused syphilis, which he hoped she didn't have. But could have. And any condoms that he used to block such bacteria during sexual intercourse could easily break if he entered her later that evening.

These thoughts, memories, and apprehensions followed Zack as he caressed Alicia's breasts, nibbled on her nipples, and continued to kiss her taut abdominal muscles. He continued his glide south as she opened her legs and spread them wide apart in hopeful anticipation of reaching the pinnacle of ecstasy once again.

As Zack continued, he noticed that her genitals were as bare as a newborn babe's, cleanly shaven. Her vulva, vagina, and rectal area was fully exposed for his pleasure, and for hers as well.

She waited.

He hesitated.

Zack gaped. His mouth was wide open, and then his tongue quickly receded back into his mouth. He stopped, clamped his lips tighter than a drum, reared back, and was unwilling to proceed. To his dismay and revulsion, he saw several small, dark, raised, wart-like eruptions. They were all imbedded into her skin around her vulva. And then there were several smaller warts that ringed her anus.

Alicia lifted her head from the pillow that she had been resting on. She peered down, and shouted, "Keep going. Keep going. Don't stop. I'm coming. What the hell are you stopping for?"

"What the hell is right, Alicia. Why the fuck didn't you tell me that you've got genital warts?" he asked in disgust as he began to get up.

Alicia partially sat up. She looked down toward her vagina, where she was hoping Zack would finish what he started. "Oh, shit, I know all about that. That's what my chiropractor friend told me. But he didn't mind going down on me."

"Well, fuck you. He can go down on you, but I sure as shit won't, because I *do* mind," he said as he got up and reached for his pants.

"Why?" was all she asked, disappointed, still breathing heavily, but hardly concerned about her warts, or what they meant to Zack.

By now Zack was furious as to how close he had come to being infected; if only he had kept his eyes shut, he could be infected, possibly for life, since such warts were very difficult to eradicate. "Alicia, as you know, being a nurse, those genital warts, commonly called condylomata acuminata, or venereal warts, are highly contagious."

Now it was Alicia who was mad. "They don't bother me, so why the fuck should they bother you? But they do itch, terribly sometimes," she added with some concern, disappointed that she wouldn't achieve the much-sought-after, pleasurable climax by Zack's tonguing. She didn't care about him, only herself and her immediate pleasure.

Zack felt her hostility but continued to dress. "Sorry, Alicia, but those warts are infectious, and are caused by the human papillovirus, or HPV. As a nurse, you know they are spread through direct skin-to-skin contact, and through saliva in the mouth. I'm outta here."

Alicia was more riled up than ever. "Fuck you, Doctor. I don't need to know that kind of shit from you, and I'm on the pill," she spewed out in anger. She got up, deflated, pulling on her skirt and reaching for the prosecco.

Zack shook his head in dismay. "You say you're on the pill, but that only prevents a pregnancy, not STDs. Gonorrhea is becoming very prevalent again, Alicia. And, worse still, it no longer responds to penicillin, or other antibiotics, like it used to. Because antibiotics are being used so frequently, including those hand washes and sterile wipes, bacteria are now becoming immune to antibiotics."

"There's other good shit for that stuff out there. My holistic medicine man told me. Herbs and stuff."

What Zack really feared even more, being somewhat of an obsessional-type himself, was General Paresis of the Insane.

"Sorry, Alicia. Being obsessional as I am, what really worries me is a severe, intense, paranoid psychotic state that happens with GPI, or General Paresis of the Insane. This means the person, usually a male, is irrationally suspicious, and, quite simply put, totally out of his mind: demented, psychotic, a goner, coo-coo, completely insane, due to syphilis infecting the fragile, delicate brain tissue," he said, watching her walk about in a rage.

"Never heard of that kind of shit happening, smarty pants."

Now that Zack opened the subject, he felt he should explain, "This insanity was due to the tiny spirochete, the little syphilitic bacteria, getting into the blood stream during intercourse and then invading the frontal, and other, lobes of the brain. It was called the spirochete due to its spiral, cork-screw appearance under a microscope. In those brief seconds I was down on you, I cringed as I imagined such a virulent bacteria slowly spiraling like a cork screw up my penis, into my pelvic blood stream. Pumped by my heart, it would go into and through the labyrinths of my cerebrum, the soft, jelly brain under the cranium, eating up all the nerves, dendrites, neurons, and blood vessels, just like the little wee maggots devouring the body after it is dead. But I would still be alive, and then gradually demented, my dear woman."

Alicia, still angry, but now somewhat subdued by this discourse, was listening intently. "So what then?"

"Well, over time, the spirochete turns the brain into a mushy, syrupy, bowl of jelly. A general paresis, or paralysis, of the whole body ensues, where facial muscles falter, vision goes dark, deafness prevails, hands shake uncontrollably, urine spills freely, feces erupts uncontrollably, anywhere and anytime, and then the loss of all reality. Utter and total insanity."

"I read in *Cosmopolitan* that the armies in Europe had that crap," she said, trying to be smart.

Zack went to her and patted her on the back. "Good for you that you're reading. It was quite common for most of Napoleon's troops to be thusly infected during their invasions of Europe. The whores always followed the armies seeking warmth, food, and money, and they were all infected with syphilis."

"Shit. Not worth the money."

"That's for sure; when those armies returned to their homes, they then infected their wives and girlfriends. The mental hospitals throughout Europe, but also some in America, were flooded with men and women suffering from General Paresis of the Insane. It was only after the Second World War that penicillin was prescribed freely. Doctors learned that one intramuscular shot cured all. But it was too late. Presently, that little spirochete, and the gonococcus bacteria, just stand up, dance about, and giggle at any attempt at a cure with penicillin. There is none. Not yet."

"Well, I ain't got that shit, and I ain't getting it," she shouted, stomping about the room again.

Zack, fearful of her wrath, but also concerned for her health, said, "Look, Alicia, I understand. I can see you're angry, but you could end up with cancer of the genital area, or, even worse, cancer of your throat after your chiropractor guy goes down on you and then French kisses you. That virus is passed around through oral sex, and any kind of oral kissing. Oral sex, anal, vaginal, or whatever, and it will also be in your mouth, and then you will be crushed with such disease and illness forever."

Now Alicia was really mad. She stomped her feet like a little child, naked but for her skirt, with her breasts flopping up and down. She clomped about, flailing her fists at Zack. Her ire raised her blood pressure; she turned red, visible even through her darker skin, and she began sweating from her vile temper. So much so that her fever and sweat caused her warts to itch.

Alicia began scratching at her vulva. "Damn you. See what you've done. Now I've got that itch again." She swore, pulling and scratching with her fingers at her vagina and on her outer vaginal lips, squatting on the floor in front of him.

"Sorry about your crotch, but you or your next lover could get oral throat cancer."

"No shit?" she said, calming down and pulling her sweater over her breasts. She knew the party was over.

Zack finished dressing. "Yeah, you probably read or saw that movie personality, that guy everyone knows, talk on TV, and in the rag papers about his throat cancer. He got it from oral sex."

"Yeah. I heard the girls talking and laughing about it."

Zack didn't like the fact that Alicia had shaved off all her pubic hair. In contrast, Maria was only partly-shaved, and he found that far more stimulating, more of a turn-on for him.

When he mentioned this to Alicia, she replied that the men she fucked on a regular basis liked a clean pussy.

"I get it, Alicia," he replied. "They find a hairless pubic area to be much more virginal, much more prepubescent, and much more alluring to them. It's like having sex with a very young girl-child for them. Some wouldn't go down on a woman if she wasn't shaved."

Alicia opened a drawer on the side table and pulled out a jar of antihistamine ointment. She squatted down on the carpet again and started spreading the salve all over her genital area. "Ah, that'll make it better." She sighed with relief.

"The custom started out with the porn magazines. The movies and the women's movement promoted it. Women felt more liberated without pubic hair. Pubic hair was confining, still suggesting male domination and dependency. Porn movie directors thought it would be more appealing, and certainly more revealing. There's nothing hidden, so to speak, but it was also more prepubescent: youthful, teenage, and virginal," he said as he got dressed to leave.

Alicia then grabbed a warm, soapy towel and wiped herself down thoroughly. She felt subdued by Zack's lecture, but also by his caring attitude. "I don't like it. It's itchy, scratchy afterwards, and I get small pustules when I shave myself," she said softly, muted, worried.

Zack just stood there watching as she spread her legs apart, kneeling down, washing and scrubbing her genital area again, and then spreading more ointment onto the warts.

"Yep, more shaved women end up with pubic infections because the hair follicles are now open to bacteria with the close shave. They have to keep shaving once they start; otherwise, the small hairs that grow back out are itchy. Pustules, boils, infections, and warts soon follow."

Alicia stopped scrubbing for a minute. "Maybe God had a purpose in putting hair down there. You could have been good at getting me to climax, Zack, if you would've carried on. You know women's anatomy, but you didn't go for my G-spot, like all those other men who try to find it with their fingers up my vagina, or by using my vibrator. That hurts. How come you don't do that?"

Zack watched her put other lotions all over her pubic area in order to calm the redness from the scrubbing effect. "That's a fallacy, Alicia. There is no G-spot, so to speak."

"The magazines and sex books don't agree with you, Doctor."

"Those who write that shit don't know that there are no pleasurable, spinal nerve endings in the upper surface of the vagina that can produce an orgasm for a woman."

"Really? I could never find it either if I tried to by myself, fingers or vibrator."

"That's right; the clitoris is the only place to be stimulated. Anatomically, it's the female answer to the penis. Gently caress that nub and away you go. Forget about the elusive G, for genital, spot."

Alicia nodded in agreement, and insisted on scrubbing down Zack's pelvic area, so he would be clean for her the next time. However, he had his pants on already, and it was getting late.

He was ready to leave, but Alicia kept holding on to Zack, clinging, not wanting him to leave. He reassured her that he would be back, but he kept that lie to himself.

Zack was worried about Alicia's clingy manner. She was too dependent, as far as he was concerned. She was good, yes, but still, not as good as Maria. As much as he tried to find another woman to take Maria's place, he couldn't find a replacement. Japanese, Chinese, Ghanaian, not even close. Damn! Where was that woman? Maybe it could be Seema and her little girl.

There was still some prosecco left in the bottle. Once Alicia was dressed, she took a sip and passed it on to Zack. He shook his head, wiped his mouth clean, and put the bottle down. Even that oral connection felt too risky.

Zack finished dressing and was about to leave her apartment when he told her to see a physician. "Get a blood check. Get some treatment for those warts. It will help that terrible itch."

Maybe she would. Probably not. As he walked out the door, he turned back as she called out to him. "Look, Doctor. Thanks. I can see that you really do care what happens to me."

"Yeah. Make sure you see a specialist. Maybe a gynecologist for a good check-up," he said, waving her a kiss good-bye.

"I better do that. This is the first time anybody really cared about me. Cared about me. Me. Everybody else just fucked me, warts and all, but you really seem to care."

Zack left, apprehensive now about his future relationship with Alicia, since she was still his head nurse. That was dumb, he concluded. He knew he should not have sex with a nut case who could easily accuse him of some kind of sexual abuse, or even lodge a sexual harassment complaint, since she was so angry at him. She could seek revenge and financial restitution.

Zack quickly drove to the nearest gas station, stopped, and scrubbed his hands thoroughly in the men's room. Next door was a pharmacy, where he bought two bottles of different types of antibacterial mouthwash. As he drove back to Jacinda's he took large swigs from each bottle, swirled the wash in his mouth, slowed down, and spat it out the window. He went through both bottles by the time he passed the gates into the gardens.

CHAPTER 21

Electro Convulsive Therapy

Zack was still fretting about his stupidity when he arrived at the psych ward early that next morning.

Seema saw him entering his office. He took off his sport's jacket and put on his white coat, and signed a requisition form on his desk to have the walls painted.

She almost ran down the hall to catch him. "Dr. Forzani asked me to tell you he wants you to give Massimo electro shock therapy this morning. He's gone haywire again. Manic," she said breathless.

"Forzani has me doing the dirty work for him."

"He's gone golfing for a few days. Said that O'Flanagan needed to see him urgently, so he left town."

Seema gave him a sly wink, and pulled him into his office, wanting to give him some further news. "I heard Baker called Forzani. Sparks went flying. Be careful with Forzani, big boy. You don't want to get into a pissing war with him," she warned.

Zack smiled, surprised that Seema, seemingly so culturally devout, would use those words.

"Where's Alicia?" he asked, not looking at Seema.

"Oh, she called and said she's going on an extended sick leave. Said she has an appointment with some specialist, a dermatologist, and won't be returning. She said I was in charge now."

Zack looked Seema in the eye, but didn't blink. Did she know about Alicia? If so, it certainly wasn't apparent on her face.

After a brief meeting to review what was going on in the ward, they both walked to the ECT room, where Massimo was having his shock treatments.

"What's the word on Annie? Anybody hear how she's doing?" he asked.

"She is still at the group home. Eating better. Some weight increase. She is still taken to Forzani in the evenings. She wants to go home to her stepfather's place."

"I hear her friend Kim is rooming with her. Annie's angel."

Seema reminded him that Massimo was waiting in the ECT room.

Massimo—Zack recalled O'Flanagan mentioning that name. He was loaded with money. And he was connected to some priest named Roberts.

"Massimo? Forzani ordered electroconvulsive therapy for him, but he's playing golf. Now he expects me to push the buttons on those electrodes," he said, hoping that O'Flanagan was going to keep his part of the bargain.

"Electrodes over the frontal lobes. Archaic stuff. Still in the Middle Ages," Seema said as they walked down the long corridor.

"I hear that Massimo is a businessman. Many business people now ask for this treatment, since they want to get back to work ASAP. Electroconvulsive therapy is now fast, safe, and reliable. It gets you back on your feet faster than the anti-depressants we use."

"True. Massimo runs an empire in auto parts, auto repairs, and sales. He also manufactures electric cars in my country and in China."

"He needs to be up and running as soon as possible. That's why he pays the big bucks for the ECT. I get *bupkis* for pushing the button."

"*Bupkis*? Something to eat, Zack?"

Zack laughed. "No, Yiddish. Means I get nothing at all."

"Still, it's medieval, this kind of therapy, but very common in my country."

Zack looked at his watch. He knew that the anesthetist wouldn't be in the ECT room for another twenty minutes. He stopped at the coffee machine he had installed in the common room on the ward.

A number of patients were sitting around, waiting to start the daily group therapy session with the ward psychologist, Emma, whom Zack had also hired.

Zack poured himself a coffee. Seema took a tea bag from her slacks pocket and put it into a steaming hot cup of water.

"It's not really medieval: it's from even before that, hundreds of years before. It was observed that people who were odd, strange, psychotic, or depressed got better if they fell, had a head injury, or had a fever from infections and then had a convulsion. With that seizure, that convulsion, they got better."

"You're kidding me. A knock on the noggin' got you better?"

"Yep. Those who had seizures due to infection, a fever high enough to cause a convulsion, were cured of their insanity. Epileptics were thought to never suffer from a mental disorder, since they had seizures and convulsions. Fevers due to infections, such as tuberculosis, pneumonia, or the Black Plague, were very common. It was a keen observation about that phenomenon by some so-called physicians and healers hundreds of years ago."

"But, Doctor, a jolt of electricity on the brain?"

Zack continued. "Egyptians used electric eels fished out of the Nile River and placed them on people to dispel them of the devil or evil spirits, as well as to cure them of nerve disorders in those days. Later, electric currents were applied to hands, feet, or buttocks in order to try and cure strange behaviors. Weird relatives who were out of their minds were brought to see those so-called physicians, who even used magnets on the body to try to find a cure."

"I never would have thought," she said, waiting for her tea bag to finish seeping.

"Years ago, we produced a convulsion using insulin coma. The insulin put the patient into a coma, then into a convulsion. Metrazol did the same. An intravenous injection caused the seizure. Many got better. Some died, unfortunately. We couldn't get them out of the coma, even by pouring sugared water down their gullets."

Seema sipped on her tea. "Yuck. That was an awful thing to do to people."

"Yeah, well prefrontal lobotomy was even more awful, Seema."

"I heard about that. Who started it?"

Zack sipped on his coffee. "Doctor Moniz, a Portuguese neurologist. In Lisbon, in 1935, he was interested in the brain, and he actually invented the procedure of cerebral angiography. That is putting a dye into the arteries leading to the brain, and then x-raying the brain in order to visualize the brain's vascular system."

"Today, we use this to test for tumors, aneurisms, strokes, and blot clots in the brain," Seema was proud to add.

Zack slowed his pace before arriving at the ECT room. "That's so. He then became interested in people who were very aggressive: belligerent murderers who were paranoid, insane schizophrenics. He first practiced on monkeys by cutting their frontal lobes of the brain, and he found that the monkeys were subdued: inactive, quiet, indifferent, passive, and no longer angry or hostile."

"Good that he monkeyed around with the apes first," she laughed.

Zack smiled, nodded. "You got that right, Seema."

Seema felt faint from the graphic description and stopped for a minute to catch her breath. "Did it work?" she asked, breathless.

"Sure did. They were cured, but they were devoid of all emotions, and were like zombies after that. But cured, so to speak. He received the Nobel Prize in Medicine in 1936 for his work."

"They are not done anymore, I hope, Doctor?"

"No, not any more. Over twenty-five thousand were done in America. The only guy who outlawed it was Stalin, in Russia. He said it was too brutal, too archaic."

Seema finished her tea. Outside the ECT room, Zack threw his coffee cup into the bin to be recycled. Seema pointed to the treatment room. "So, this ECT. Who got that going?"

Zack looked in the room through a window in the door. The anesthetist was preparing her needles: vials of intravenous injections. A nurse was reassuring Mr. Massimo, who was lying on the bed waiting for Zack. There was still a little time.

"A couple of Italians, Cerletti and Bini, fooled around with electricity and jabbed people who had uncontrollable muscle spasms with electric wires. By accident, they found they could produce a convulsion in dogs, pigs, and other animals by passing the current across their victim's frontal lobes. The manager of the local abattoir, located just outside of Milan, asked them to find a way to slaughter animals faster, less bloody, using an electric jolt."

Seema shook her head and asked, "Why at the abattoir, where they kill animals anyway? That's one reason why I don't eat meat. Yuck."

Zack chuckled. "Yes. The manager said it was too messy. Blood all over the place, he complained. He wanted the doctors to do it faster and more humanely. So they strapped down some pigs, and jolted their brains with the current. Unfortunately, all they found was that the animals just had convulsions. Didn't die.

"They then thought maybe, just maybe, they could cure mental ills with a convulsion. So they went to the local asylum outside Milan, and they tried it on a few chronic, insane schizophrenics, who stayed on the long-stay wards."

Seema was ready to open the door. "So? So what happened?"

"After three or four treatments, those severely ill men were cured. They insisted on going home. They did. After that, the next one was done in 1938, in Italy. No anesthetic, no muscle relaxants, no nurses, no oxygen mask to help the patient breathe."

"Just wires to the head bone?"

"No, they used an ice tong; you know: those tongs that pick up blocks of ice. The tong was then padded, oiled, and placed just over the temples. Then the doctors administered a jolt of one hundred and ten volts, for about two-tenths of a second. That's what we practice still, but we use an anesthetist to sedate the patient and watch his breathing and other vital signs. It's so much safer now."

"So, now it's your turn. Tell me all about Massimo, Seema," Zack asked before he opened the door to meet him.

"Yes, Doctor, good idea. Massimo was admitted into his private room again, early this morning. He is still hyper. Dr. Forzani said his manic-depressive illness is out of control, and he's now harassing homosexuals in the bars in town."

"Forzani? He's the one who's out of touch. It's called a bipolar illness now."

"You tell that to Forzani. Not me," she said, opening the door.

Zack held her back and closed the door. "Tell me about Massimo. What do we know about him?"

"Mid-fifties. Living with a young lady who is disabled and suffering from severe ulcerative colitis: Crohn's disease. He had her move in with him, but she adores him and takes care of him. He told me he's her purse and she's his nurse. Catholic. Some weight-challenged priest visits him, since he is a big donor to the church. Massimo is a big, big homophobe. Forzani sucks him dry."

"As in sexually?"

Seema laughed, embarrassed, whispered, "Monetarily, Doctor. Monetarily."

Zack found out Massimo had been the manager of the Hilton Hotels in addition to his automobile empire.

Zack was concerned about Massimo's failing memory. He thought it could be an early Alzheimer's. He learned his bipolar disorder always responded to a few electrical treatments.

Massimo had grandiose fantasies of being a famous movie star, alternating with his other conviction that he'd be the next pope. Zack heard he changed his identity every month, depending on what movie magazine he was reading.

When he'd arrived that morning, he was barefoot and convinced he was another movie mogul. He was wrapped in a Roman toga, just like the one Charlton Heston wore when he portrayed Moses in *The Ten Commandments*.

Zack opened the door to the ECT room, and they both walked into the small room where Dr. Olga Petrova, the anesthetist, was waiting.

"I heard the nurses in surgery talking about you. Our hero who saved Annie and then Sean O'Flanagan's wife. She was going to jump off the roof, was she?"

"You bet. Tenth floor, and hanging by her fingernails."

Zack didn't ask what she heard. Instead, he picked up the metal electrodes and cleaned off the head pieces with a cotton cloth. He apologized for keeping her waiting.

Massimo was standing near the bed and held his gown tightly behind his back. A nurse ensured the white cotton gown was wrapped securely around his body, so that his buttocks were not exposed.

Massimo was helped onto the bed by the nurse. He looked nervous, his lips tight and pale. His eyes darted about fearfully as one nurse gently pushed his head down on the pillow and covered his body with a sheet. Massimo crossed himself quickly, blurted something to Jesus, and then shut his eyes tight.

Massimo opened one eye and looked at Zack, who was holding the tongs that would discharge a jolt of current into his temples. "Another shot of Edison's medicine, doc?" he said fearfully.

Zack nodded to acknowledge that, yes, Edison discovered electricity, and now he was going to be able to use that discovery.

Olga replied. "Yep. Electro convulsive therapy will get you right again, sir. Just like last time."

Zack turned to the six young student nurses who were standing by. They were on his ward now, part of the teaching hospital. Zack made sure of that. "Hospitals get many private patients who voluntarily request this treatment," Zack said as he watched Seema talk soothingly to Massimo.

"Why, Doctor?" one nurse asked dutifully.

"The reason is that it is fast, efficient, and it has fewer memory-distorting side effects than it had in the past. It is much safer now that an anesthetist is present. Also, it is a unipolar current going across only one side of the brain, so there are fewer side effects. No major headaches or memory loss anymore. Patients who have to get back to work quickly prefer the procedure, as it produces a more rapid recovery than the slower acting anti-depressants."

She took out a pad and made notes.

"Time is money. I was told that by one financial director who insisted on the electro-convulsive therapy."

"Massimo donated a cool million to his local parish, Zack," Olga whispered in Zack's ear.

"That's a noble thing to do. One of his delusions, I guess."

"Nope. It was done. The priest blessed the check at mass, I heard."

"What did his young lady, his nurse, think of that?"

"It was her idea. She said you should get your hands on some of that money for your ward."

"Forzani keeps reminding me that it's his ward, not mine."

Olga lowered her voice. "He's a creep. Takes young women into his office late at night. Locks the door."

Zack looked at Olga. Could she be a credible witness to get rid of Forzani, if and when he needed her, in a legal battle? "What are you saying, Olga?"

Olga turned away. "Nothing. Just telling you. I tried his office once. Locked. Shouted back that he's doing psychotherapy."

Zack laughed. "You're kidding. He can't even spell the word. Strange. Late at night?"

Olga didn't answer. "Remember the priest and Massimo, young man. Lots of money there."

"Nice idea," he replied.

He and that priest will want something from me in return, Zack thought to himself. Seema came to his side.

As Olga prepared her anesthetic, Zack whispered to Seema, "Does the group home nurse still take Annie to see Forzani late at night?"

Seema nodded, sadly. "I checked the meds with the head nurse at that group home. He orders a sedative each night."

"What does Annie say about that?"

"Nothing. She's resistant, almost mute, and stoic. She says she wants her stepfather to take her home," Seema said. And then busied herself with calming Massimo.

Zack listened as Dr. Olga Petrova spoke reassuringly to Massimo: "The nurse will strap a small cuff on your finger to record your blood pressure and heart rate. The doctor will tape two small electrodes on your forehead, just above your eyes. This will record your electroencephalographic brain waves during the convulsion, informing him of the duration of the seizure, my dear man."

"Yeah, yeah. Yada, yada, yada; we heard it all before, Mrs. Nightingale."

Olga ignored his games. She stood at his side and tapped the vein in the crease of Massimo's left arm. He automatically tried to pull it away, but the nurse held on with a firm grip. Olga inserted a needle into his vein and slowly injected sodium pentothal, a sedative, in order to put Massimo to sleep.

Zack watched closely as the next needle, filled with succinylcholine chloride, a powerful muscle relaxant that prevented severe muscular contractions during the convulsion, was inserted. This drug relaxed patients so thoroughly that there were never any broken bones or dislocations, but it also quickly stopped all respiration. Massimo needed Olga to give him oxygen from a mask.

"Start counting down, Massimo," Dr. Petrova said as she injected the Pentothal.

"Ten, six, eight, one, seven, nine…" Olga put the oxygen mask over Massimo's face just as he stopped breathing, and she pumped in a few bagfuls of pure oxygen into his lungs. Seema inserted a rubber guard into his mouth in order to prevent injury to his teeth or tongue for when his body contracted with the seizure.

Zack moistened the electrodes with a jelly. He quickly wiped the patient's temples with alcohol in order to have his skin make a good connection with the jelly, and the electric impulse.

Olga nodded as she again checked Massimo's blood pressure and heart rate. Zack held the bilateral calipers to his forehead and pushed the button on the ECT machine. Eight hundred milliamps of electricity passed across both frontal brain hemispheres for two seconds.

Both physicians watched Massimo as he experienced a brief, but modified, grand mal seizure, which lasted twenty-five seconds.

Zack pulled the student nurses closer to the table. "You will see the only evidence of a convulsion are his toes going into a slight spasm, and in his eyelids briefly fluttering. Olga, and her injections, worked well to prevent a severe spasm of the muscles," he said as he put the calipers away.

The nurses made more notes.

Olga gave the patient another bag full of oxygen.

Massimo was turned onto his side by Seema in case he were to vomit, so that he wouldn't have to inhale the contents of his stomach. Not that he would vomit anyway, since he had not had anything to eat, and he had only a small drink of sodium citrate that morning in order to reduce the secretions in his mouth.

Massimo was breathing normally, and he looked like he was just in a deep sleep as a nurse wheeled him into a side room. Another nurse watched him slowly regain consciousness after a few minutes.

"Will he get better, Doctor?" the young nurse asked.

"Yes, for sure, Nurse. Massimo suffered a hypomanic episode. He was uncontrollably wild for three weeks before the police found him walking down the freeway. He told highway patrol that he was going to make a new movie in Hollywood."

"Wow, he had a long way to go."

"They are like that, and have no concept of reality. They buy cars, spend all their money, rack up debts, and change relationships like I change socks," Zack said.

"What does the ECT do?" she asked.

"Gets them better, that's for sure. We've known for a thousand years that mentally-disordered patients got better after they had a convulsion. Whether the seizure was precipitated by a fever, a blow to the head, or epilepsy, they all went into remission."

"So now we do it with this machine," the nurse said, pointing to the apparatus.

"You bet. You produce a convulsion when the blood sugar drops to zero. We used to do it with insulin. The British used to inject a drug called leptosol, which was effective, but risky.

"Glad it's him getting zapped, not me," she said with a shiver.

"Me too," Zack replied. He looked at Petrova. "From now on, we're going to do these treatments in the surgical out-patient day care clinic. I want a full team available, in case of some medical emergency after such treatments. Heart stoppage and so on."

"I agree, Doctor. I'll talk to my chief and the surgical resident about that. Good idea, young doctor."

As the room gradually emptied and the nurses went to take part in group therapy, Zack looked at his notes in his Blackberry. He had reviewed the charts of all of Forzani's patients. At first, he thought he'd mail the large number of shock treatments Forzani had prescribed to the hospital director. Zack had each patient's name and the extraordinary list of treatments each one received.

He brought up the American Psychiatric Association webpage. It had the standard policy for ECT quality assurance, as set down by the governing body for psychiatrists.

He put the package together for Sean O'Flanagan and was about to press the send button.

"Hell, they're golfing buddies. He might just delete the damn thing. I'll copy to Councilor Baker instead," he said to himself.

With that, Zack copied Forzani's e-mail from the elaborate web page and pasted it to an email intended for Baker. He also pasted his own document containing his concerns, and the APA's standard policy paper on ECT.

He added a short line: "Just a short note, for your attention. I have some concern about the excessive number of treatments prescribed for certain patients, and their questionable diagnoses."

This time he pushed the send button.

"Let's see what Baker does with that." He sighed and looked at his watch.

CHAPTER 22

The Bitch is Back

It was a few days after Massimo when Maria, the ever-scheming, eternally-seductive Maria, reentered Zack's life. Both he and Maria knew it was something he craved, needed, and ached for, but it was also something he dreaded. And that was because of Carlos.

Zack was lying on his bed in the late afternoon, wondering what the next best step would be to get rid of Forzani and take over the psych ward. Then he could tear it down, rebuild a new ward with Massimo's money, and become the director, and then professor, of psychiatry for the hospital.

The local radio station was playing *The Bitch is Back* by Elton John. Zack turned up the volume and listened.

It was a fever in Zack, waiting for Maria. Little did he know that she would be picking his brains, like the vultures on the beach in Acapulco, or that he would sell his soul to the devil just to have her.

He turned to see the Rembrandt painting, which was now hanging on his wall. The hot sun was flashing through his window, and Zack was focusing on the man in the painting who resembled his old analyst, Abrahams. Did he detect a sneer on that hideous face?

Duke sat up, growling. "Quiet, Duke, old buddy. I can't hear the words," Zack said, patting Duke lying next to him on the bed.

Zack didn't know how prophetic those lyrics would be. As Duke slobbered, drooled, and licked, cleaning his chops after wolfing down some leftover taco shells and bits of chicken, Zack sensed the different movements somewhere in the house.

Both dog and man could smell the odors filtering in from Jacinda's pots, cooking on the kitchen stove. The dog's nose twitched, confused by the other odors only a dog could be aware of. Duke was restless.

Zack sat back on his pillows and looked at the black lab, now nuzzled almost on top of his feet.

"Settle down, Duke. It will be dinnertime soon," Zack chided his pal. He got up and combed the lab's hair with a brush he found in the bathroom.

The dog leaned into the brush and perked up his ears, listening intently to a different noise somewhere else. He jumped down to the floor for a lap of water in the corner of the room, and he then went to the door and pawed at the frame.

Within two minutes, Zack called to his friend. "Settle down, sport. You know, sport, your mistress, Jacinda, may be suffering from a Munchausen's syndrome. She keeps getting plastic surgery to fix her face. She just finished getting a tummy tuck and an up-lift to one breast, after losing the other one to cancer."

Duke was curious, now standing on his tip-toes over the side of the bed, where his master returned for another stretch. He had never heard that strange name, Munchausen.

Zack patted Duke's head, and continued to talk to his friend and savior, "Baron von Munchausen, in the early eighteenth century, wandered about Europe, telling exaggerated lies about himself and complaining of bodily pains just to get surgical attention. He did that just to get love from people, old boy. He, too, had periodic surgeries on different parts of his body, and he received more attention for his apparent sorrow and pain. People still do that now. They go from one emergency room to another, in different hospitals, pretending to have some surgical ailment and asking for help."

Duke turned his head this way and that, trying to understand.

"Women, especially, get multiple plastic reconstructions all over their bodies for public attention, sport. They love the attention from surgeons and hospital staff. Tattoo artists make a fortune with black ink, adorning the bodies of those seeking adoration. People take selfies in order to admire themselves, just as the rich did hundreds of years ago, when mirrors came into fashion. Same thing now, fella."

The dog looked up, cocking his head. Suddenly, he gave a throaty growl, and Zack heard someone outside the door.

There was a soft rap on Zack's door. "Can't be Jacinda. We know her knocks. Could be dinner, but it's kind of early," he said to Duke. He got up and went to the door.

Duke heard Zack's loud gasp when he opened his bedroom door, and he was ready to spring to his rescue again in case of intruders.

Maria was there in all her glory and beauty, smiling as she seductively ran her tongue over her lips, nudging Zack aside. She made certain she brushed her breasts against his shoulder as she entered.

"Doctor Zack, I need you to examine my ribs. Please tell me if Maria needs her ribs taped after her fall," Maria asked coyly, looking him in the eye.

She closed the door behind her with her foot, and just stood there in all of her dark, ravishing splendor.

Zack stepped back, feigning displeasure, but inwardly pleased to see her.

She sensed his inner hostility and apprehension, "What do you think, *señor* doctor? Look at Maria. How she suffers," she said, pouting as Zack just stood there, mesmerized by her enticing charm, perfumed body, and intoxicating beauty.

Duke, at ease now that his master recognized the intruder, cautiously ambled back to his water dish and lay down, but he kept one eye open.

Maria has lost weight, which makes her appear even taller and slimmer in her high heels, Zack thought. He also thought she had never smelled so good. It was her body lotion, perfume, and after-bath spray that she always used that got Zack so excited. She stayed close to him. He began to feel his erection stirring in his groin.

After closing the door behind her, she stood in front of Zack and untied the string around her back of her sheer, light blue dress. His favorite color.

She momentarily cushioned the top of the dress with one hand, and then raised both arms above her head, dropping the dress to her waist. She proudly exposed herself from the waist up, recalling that this pose was one of his favorites.

"I pray that it is not broken. Just feel it here," she asked, gazing into his eyes. She placed his hand under her breast and gently moved it around.

Zack saw the familiar, finger-nail-sized tattoo of a small, black widow spider just above her left breast. It was the type of spider that voraciously ate its mates, and Zack feared she could do the same with him.

He knew she wanted something from him with her seductive, sexual manner. She wore a delicate, silver chain around her neck, with tiny silver bells that reached down to her taut, full breasts.

As Maria jiggled her breasts, the silver bells danced in unison. "These are pure silver, *señor* doctor. Each is from Taxco, our city of silver. My *tio*, my uncle Alfonzo, he bought them for me. You can feel them, here. I even have a small ring elsewhere. Maria, she will show it to you later," she said playfully, and, in a teasing manner, placed his hand over her other breast.

She again jiggled her breasts, allowing the bells to wiggle from side to side, from one nipple to the other. She enjoyed watching Zack's glowing face flush. He, again, sensed the growth swelling between his legs.

Zack desperately tried to control himself, but to no avail. All he could do was turn away. "We don't tape ribs anymore, Maria. You damn well know that."

She didn't flinch. She knew he would be angry with her. She was expecting that, but she had a plan. She knew him well, and she knew what to do. She gently pulled him to the chair next to his desk, and sat him down. She stood in front of him and dropped her dress. Then she slid off her panties. She kept her high heels on.

It was exactly what she used to do with him in Mexico City, in her small apartment. It was the high heels that excited him. She knew that.

Maria was a schemer. Zack also knew that. He would let her play her little game, but he would have the upper hand. Besides, sex with her would have a soothing effect on him.

He needed that.

Maria gently pushed Zack back onto the chair, straddled him, lifted his T-shirt up over his shoulders, and then deftly unzipped his pants. She dangled her breasts in his face and helped him enter her while she remained on top.

"Wait, Maria. I'm all sweaty. I'll have a quick shower," Zack said, giving her a slight push.

She pushed him back into the chair. "No. I like the smell of sweat on a man. It turns me on. Stay here."

Sex was slow and methodical, and she did all the work. She held his shoulders, but kept her gaze on his eyes, as she moved ever-so-slowly. She could feel the tension in his body gradually leave. She waited for him, so they would both come together.

Which they did. She could feel his muscles all over his whole body convulsing as he exploded inside her. He stopped breathing for what seemed an eternity. She waited. She remembered. When he finally inhaled, it was a deep, prolonged gasp for air. Satisfied, he just held onto her for the longest time.

After several minutes she stood up, feeling the moisture between her legs. She cleaned herself using the sheet from the bed next to her. She slowly slipped back into her dress as Zack pulled on his pants.

He looked aside to see the dog watching from the bed. *Was he grinning?* With his mouth open, panting, Duke rolled over, jumped up, and crawled under the bed.

Zack waited as he composed himself. He needed answers. It was easy for him to be gruff, trying to be dramatic and angry, and he tried to raise his voice at her. "Maria, you have to tell me what happened to you in Mexico City. Why didn't you meet me at the airport? It's been almost three months now since Acapulco."

She moved to Zack's bed and sat on the edge. She remained silent for the longest time. She said nothing as she pulled him to the bed and gently rolled onto him.

He waited as she held his body, one naked leg wrapped around him.

He put his hand under her chin and forced her head up close to his. He looked into her eyes. She finally answered. "I had to know what happened to Carlos. Some of his good friends in the Mexican mafia, *La Eme*, told me that Carlos had been killed," she whispered.

Zack brushed a genuine tear from her cheek, but, inwardly, he was glad that she was talking, explaining. "Carlos was your husband, then? Why the fuck didn't you tell me that before? That's who that fat Gomez and his one-eyed pirate were after?"

"*Si*, Zack. They cut up Carlos' face. They cut his face up, Zack. Salazar ordered it."

Zack pulled her dress aside, and, once again, felt her breasts, slowly massaging her still-erect nipples. "Salazar again. So that was why you were so interested in my friend, Sam, and facial transplants?" he asked.

As he continued to caress her breasts, she began to breathe heavily, but she allowed him to continue. She went on. "They told him they would cut off his *cajones* and force them down his throat, and then leave him to hang by his thumbs in the city square."

"Ouch. I know they don't fool around," he said, feeling the spasm in his neck muscles again.

"I'm sorry. When I learned he was still alive, I just had to wait and attempt to find him," she said, weeping softly into the pillow and taking his hands away.

"He's alive?" Zack asked, but waited patiently for her to continue. She was credible this time; her tears were genuine. He was certain of that, but he was also nervous about the mafia and those guys who could be after him.

Maria went on, and, this time, she told him the whole story. "My Carlos, he was with the Mexican mafia. Carlos was a drug runner, and made a lot of American money. Lots and lots of money."

Zack ever-so-slowly moved his hand down her belly, toward her pubic area. She still hadn't shaved, which turned on Zack, as it always did. He felt the small, silver piercing Maria had inserted near the top of her outer lips, just below her pubic bone. "Too bad you didn't get all that money, honey," he said sarcastically, fingering the ring.

Maria, uncertain at first, eventually, slowly, spread her legs further apart as his fingers gently searched. "He was very high up in the *La Eme* gang, with Salazar as leader. Later, Carlos turned on some of the *generalissimos*, the ringleaders, and moved money into his own account."

Zack slipped a finger into her, past the silver ring. "Not a good idea," he said as she gave a slight moan.

She allowed him to feel her outer lips as he slipped his finger in a bit deeper. "They found him, and cut up his face," she whimpered, and she became moist again.

"Yeah, yeah, so you said. So, what did he do with *La Eme*?"

"*La Eme* started as an organized mob in a prison in California. They were dealing with extortion and narcotics…ah, trafficking for sure. And murder of young girls, on both sides of the border."

Maria stopped, crossed herself, and said a silent prayer. She pulled his hand away, turned aside, and covered the bed sheets around her tense, sweaty body. She felt frightened of telling Zack too much, and then the expected rejection.

Duke, smelling the fear again and listening to Maria cry, crept out from under the bed, jumped up, and lay beside Maria. She held the dog's head close to her breast.

Zack lay there, not knowing what to believe, as her story continued to grow in greater detail. He pushed her away from him.

She rolled closer to Duke, and held him tenderly. Zack got up, walked about nervously, somewhat fearful of learning too much, but he went to her, and stood over the bed.

He was pointing a finger at her, glowering, with fire in his eyes. "Okay. So what are you after now? From me, what is it you want? I know your conniving ways, woman. Spit it out."

Maria tightened her grip on the dog as she felt Zack's impatience and growing hostility. She got up, only partly clothed in her dress, which had been torn open by Zack's groping.

She continued as she came to Zack, mascara running down her face. "Two very highly-prominent *politicos* in my country were arrested in Mexico, just before you left. I was worried for you. Those men knew I lay with you in the *Zona Rosa*."

"Pedro and Gomez: those two fucking pricks? They knew. They knew, bitch, and that's why they made a visit here, also. They almost killed Jacinda and me. It was your fucking stupidity that almost got me killed. It was Duke who saved us."

Duke, hearing his name, perked up his ears. Zack pushed her away, went to the bed, took a pillow, and threw it at her. He walked away, fuming.

Maria whimpered, covering her ears from the vitriol. "Wait, Zack. Please wait."

Zack held back. If he scared her too much, he would never get the full story. "Okay, okay. Calm down. Give it to me straight, but hurry up. So what happened back then, bitch?"

Maria took in a few deep breaths, settled down on the bed's edge, and carried on. "Don't call me that. Look, Zack, our famous President, Zedillo of Mexico, promised to fight the bad men and the drug trade. He wanted information, and he sent his men into the gangs."

Zack was walking about the room, Duke closely following behind, thinking it was a game. Both were not looking at Maria. "So I read in the papers."

"But poor Zedillo, for it was Zedillo's eldest son who was carjacked in full daylight. They tortured his son, and then left him for dead in the streets, near the opera house. Next, it was Zedillo's police chief. They gassed him in his sleep. He is brain dead forever."

"Sorry to hear that. They also cooked some mayor in your famous square in town. Could happen to me, and you, too, sweetheart. So how does Carlos fit into this, Maria?" Zack asked as he walked about the room, straightening the painting of Rembrandt that had gone akimbo when he threw the pillow. He could also think more clearly standing up and walking about.

Zack looked up at the painting of Rembrandt, but it was his analyst, Abrahams looking down, not the painter. His small, beady eyes watched him closely. *Was he mocking? Accusing me of being too sure of myself? Too aggressive?*

Maria's story brought him back to reality.

"Listen, my Carlos knew the drug lords. He was also giving information to the honest police. It was risky. The same assassins, those bad men who killed Cardinal Juan Jesus Ocampo and others at the famous Guadalajara airport, are now out to get Carlos."

Maria was nervous, jittery, walking about behind Zack, following him around the room. Duke jumped up, and, in turn, he followed Maria.

Zack stopped abruptly. He turned to face Maria. "Okay, okay, calm down and stop following me around," he shouted, opening a bottle and pouring her a shot of tequila.

Duke stopped, slinking away with the warning.

Maria composed herself as she sipped from the glass. She had to finish in order to persuade Zack to help her, to help Carlos. "They, the bad ones, tricked him at a meeting in Acapulco. There were many drug lords there. Some were happy with the new *politicos*, hoping the police would arrest some of them, so they would have more territory. The mafia killed twelve of their own, but very slowly, and only after three days."

Zack became gentler with her. "I read about it in your papers," he said calmly.

"This was a warning to the others. They were never found. Carlos, my husband, he watched as others were mutilated. Few just had their fingers cut off. Or their tongues pulled out. You see, Zack, Salazar wanted it to serve as an example to others."

Maria gagged at the vision she had just painted, and hid her face in her hands.

Zack, now impatient with her tears, berated her. "Enough sniveling. So, what happened to Carlos?" he yelled.

"My Carlos? They needed my Carlos. They knew he stole their money. But they needed him. They wanted to know what the *politicos* were doing next. They saved his life, but they cut his face from ear to ear."

"Wow. Slashed the poor bugger's face, did they?"

Maria only nodded, ignoring his ridicule, paused, and slowly continued after draining the glass. "My friend told me that Carlos was alive. And where he was. He was near to death."

She brushed her hair from her face. Tears ran down her cheeks. She was a drama queen. Zack knew that, but he also knew that those tears were real, sincere.

"So why the hell didn't you phone me," Zack shouted, opening the patio door to let in the cool, late afternoon breeze.

"I had to get a *medico* for Carlos. They had cut him badly. They put a terrible, blue tattoo right on his forehead while he was unconscious."

Maria went to the foot of the bed and opened her small purse. She took out two photos and placed them on the bed. "Here, see for yourself.

Look what they did to my poor Carlos," she said, pulling Zack back to the bed. She picked up the two photos and pushed them toward Zack.

Zack picked up the black and white snapshots. They were taken in a photo kiosk in a shopping mall, and were of poor quality.

"My God, woman. I've seen motor vehicle accidents and burn victims in my days in emergency, but not like this," he said with a low whistle. Duke perked up his ears to the sound.

One photograph was of a side profile of her husband. From the shoulders up, it was clear that Carlos was a big man, and at one time, perhaps, he was quite handsome. His face was cut from just above the eye, down his cheek, and right down to the center of his chin. The scar had tightened his face. He looked grotesque.

"Can you help Carlos? Detective Gennero wants him also, to help clean this country, your country, of Salazar and the bad men. I hate that pervert, Salazar," Maria begged, as she went to him, clasping his arm.

Zack brushed her aside rudely, and picked up the other photo.

The full frontal was even more hideous. Carlos had both sides of his face cut symmetrically. The sadistic slasher left an inch at the bottom of his chin. On his forehead they sculptured a large tattoo.

Maria came back to Zack, pointing at the photo. "*La Eme.*"

It was a large blue skull with bat wings sprouting out from its ears. Over the skull were the letters 'EME', and, under the skull, the larger black letters 'M—M'. Zack shuddered.

"Yes, Zack. *La Eme.*"

Zack pointed at the photo, "What the hell is that blue mark?"

Maria didn't look at the photo. "It is the famous emblem of the Mexican Mafia. *La Eme.* The M. That way, he couldn't leave or go anywhere. They knew he wouldn't go out in public. He couldn't tell the government, or Detective Gennero, anything. Anymore."

Zack threw the photos at her. Maria, startled, turned away, fearful he might strike her. Zack walked out to the patio. Duke followed.

Maria went to Zack. "Mr. Gennero said he would protect Carlos.

And me also."

"Gennero? Jacinda mentioned his name once. What the hell does he have to do with Carlos?"

She brightened up once Zack was calmer and he showed some interest.

"Mr. Gennero, a respected police man, talked to Carlos. That detective, he has been working on breaking up the Mexican mafia here, in your California. He said he would be certain to grant Carlos immunity. You know, if he becomes a state witness."

Zack shook his head. "Fat chance of that. He's a dead man."

Maria went back to Zack's bed, wiping her eyes on the pillow slip. "All my Carlos had to do for Gennero was one thing. To inform on all his known contacts. The police here want to clean up the drug trade. They needed help from Carlos, and Uncle Hector said he would help."

"What the fuck. Hector? Shit, this has nothing to do with me," Zack said, cursing for being involved again.

Maria had a card up her sleeve, and she threw her ace on the table.

"*Amigo*, Detective Gennero is worried. Another policeman is here from *México*. He is General Gomez, the bad man we met in our apartment. Gomez wants to kidnap Carlos and drag him back to *México*. General Gomez wants Carlos to give the government all the information on the mafia. He is a liar. He lies, and can't be trusted."

"Gomez? A general?"

"Yes, but that man, Gomez, he can't be trusted, and will give Carlos back to the mafia for *muchos* money," she said, her upper lip quivering.

"Gomez? Yeah, I remember that name. He's the guy with big friggin' braces holding up his huge friggin' pants, who was sporting a stiletto knife and held a baseball bat to my fucking neck."

"Please, just listen, Zack. The mafia would get to Carlos first and kill him. Then they'll kill me."

Zack swung around and pointed a finger at his own head, like he was using a pistol. "And then me, sweetheart. Me. You got me into this pile of horse shit."

"We will get out. Gennero will send us to the Canadian border."

"Well, good for you and Carlos in wanting to get out. Carlos is a dead man. With that tattoo and that face, he's a dead man. Even in a small town up north, he can't hide."

"Please don't say that," Maria begged. She wailed loudly and flung herself onto the bed.

A thump on Zack's door calmed the two combatants. "Maria? You okay? He hitting you? Maria? Sack? What happen?" Jacinda shouted from behind the door, still rapping loudly.

"No, it's okay, Jacinda. No fighting. Arguing only. Go back to the kitchen," Zack reassured her.

Maria, thankful for Jacinda's interruption, quieted and slowly arose from the bed.

"Sorry, Maria, but no plastic surgeon can fix his face. All his facial muscles are lacerated. His fifth cranial nerve, the facial nerve, was cut, and he has a bilateral facial paralysis."

Maria wasn't finished yet. Her eyes flashed as she stood up, and she showed her next card. "You could get your friend from London to come and see him."

"Aha." Zack laughed as the penny dropped. "And do what?"

"And do his *plastico* face work on my Carlos. We read in the papers what you might do with that model lady, Lani. The papers got a hold of the plastic facial story from the director of the hospital, and Gennero said he would help to protect Carlos. And you. And me."

"For Christ's sake, Maria. You've worked hard to set me up again. You suckered me into this in Mexico City."

Maria, sad and humiliated, slowly pulled on her tattered dress, ready to leave.

Zack, more dejected now than ever, walked about the room. Duke followed him again, but his tail was between his legs, sensing his master's despair.

Zack stabbed his finger at Maria. "I fell in love with you, Maria. You were good for me. I would have been good for you, too."

Maria recoiled from the hostility. She turned, deflated, thinking of leaving, defeated. She found one of her heels under the bed. "No one knew about Carlos. My brothers would have killed me if they knew I was secretly married to someone like Carlos," she almost whispered.

"Why Carlos?"

"He saved me, years ago, from Salazar."

Zack came to Maria and looked at her intently. "Did Salazar abuse you?"

"*Si*, as a young girl. Carlos took me away, and hid me from him," she replied, avoiding his eyes.

An old bottle of bourbon was in his closet. Zack went to the closet, sympathetic to her sad story of abuse, opened it, and took a deep gulp from the bottle.

CHAPTER 23

And Now the Hook, Line, and Sinker

Maria made her move. He was vulnerable, now that he was drinking. She wrapped her arms around his waist from behind, and she moved her soft hands over his chest, lifted his T-shirt, and pressed her breasts against his bare back.

"Zack, you're a doctor. Your newspapers wrote about you. You told Jacinda about your friend who can transplant a new face."

Zack broke the grip she had on him, and then he stormed off.

Maria brought out her trump card. She went to him. It was now or never. "Zack, I'll do anything for you. I'll stay with you. Forever. We can have sex every day, if you want. Any kind of sex you want. I'll meet you anywhere. I'll go away with you on weekends, and I won't say anything to Carlos."

Zack gave out a loud laugh. Duke, startled, thumped his tail and came to him. "That was a good line, and you have a sharp barb at the end of it in order to reel me in, Maria, but there's no big sail fish this time. You're not going to sucker me in, baby."

Zack bent down to calm his only real friend in the room, patting him and scratching behind his ears.

She had another hook. It was a good one. A good line and sinker. She threw it out.

"Zack, Carlos put a lot of money into a bank account in the Bahamas. It is pure and legitimate. *His* money. He earned it very cleanly. He will give you all of it. He'll transfer it all into your account."

Zack left her standing in the room, and he went out to the patio and watched the Japanese gardener trim the rose bushes in the distance. He started to enjoy the sadistic game. Now he was in charge, just like he was with Forzani, Sean O'Flanagan, Baker, and, soon, Massimo, and maybe even with that pedophilic priest who has access to all that money.

So, she knew about his account in the Bahamas.

He turned back and came into the room. "So…like how much, Maria?"

She thought for a second as she wiped the smudged mascara on her cheeks, still wet with salty tears. "He said he would give any man who was to help him the whole two hundred and fifty."

Zack frowned, deep in thought. He played for time, drawing the potentially deadly game out. He whistled softly. "A quarter of a million? Wow, Maria, is that in Mexican pesos, or American dollars? There's a big difference for me, you know."

"It's in American dollars, Zack. His good friend laundered it for him," she said with a wry smile, and then she grinned, indicating that she knew about Pedro and Zack's deals with him.

She watched him carefully. He licked his lips, and contemplated the next round in this possibly fatal game.

"Good friend? Hell, those kinds of friends and money are like oil and water." Zack glowered as Duke, now lying close by, listened intently to his friend, and followed him back into the room.

"Carlos is a man of his word. I'll transfer the money first, and then you can make the call to your friend to do the surgery."

"That damn Mexican cartel, and that whole fucking mafia, would come after me for that blood money. Carlos took it from them, sure as shit. They would squeeze the information out of him, Maria, and then out of me."

"I had my palm read, Zack. The old hag in the *zocolo*, the cathedral square, said you are my last hope."

He wrapped his hands around the bottle of bourbon and laughed. "Piss on your old hag, Maria. Look, the mafia would put Carlos' head in a metal vice. Then they would slowly squeeze his skull until his eyes popped out, and his brains oozed out his nostrils and ears," he growled, then popped the cork out and poured brown liquor on the carpet for effect.

Maria gagged again at the vision. Zack felt the power as the venom poured out: a rage-fueled rush of blood to his penis. His erection was huge and rock hard. He unzipped his fly, and put his hands on his crotch, pushing his pelvis toward her. "Then they'd catch me, and cut off my balls, and shove them down my throat. Like Salazar wanted to do to that gardener."

"No, no, don't, Zack," she pleaded.

He came right at her and forced her to look into his eyes. With the next fantasy that flashed before him, more of the venom surged out. "They would pick you up, Maria, and put you into a whore house at the Mexican border, fucking mills. You'd be screwed so often, in all three orifices, and for so long, that you wouldn't be able to piss, talk, shit, or walk," he yelled, forcing his erection between her legs.

Maria pushed him away, put her head in her hands, and she fell facedown on the bed.

Duke slinked away into the corner and covered his head with one paw.

"Money, money, money makes the world go round, honey. That's what it was all about. Like that tune from the musical, *Cabaret*, with Joel Grey and Liza Minnelli. I wouldn't take that money; I'd be a marked man, and my life wouldn't be worth shit."

Maria sobbed quietly into her folded arms. She pushed her hair back from her face, and made a final plea. It was her last and final trump card.

"Hector." She paused. "He said he would help Gennero. Hector and Gennero would be very grateful to you. And I know Hector would help you in your profession in this county, and on that psych ward. Gennero said he would get Carlos a hiding place in a small town, somewhere in the Cascade Mountains, somewhere up north. You wouldn't be involved."

"Really? Where the hell is that?"

"Outside some town. Seattle. Up north, somewhere."

As Zack paced the room, he took another mouthful of Jim Beam and pushed his erection back into his pants and zipped up his fly. Determined to savor and hold onto this moment of rage-fueled lust, Zack put the half-empty bottle on the night table. "I can't help you, Maria. Or Carlos."

He was exhausted by the hostility pent up inside him, but it felt good to get such sweet revenge.

Maria caved in and walked to the door, defeated. She took the only spiked heel she could find, looked up and begged, "Please, don't tell anybody about tonight. Please, I don't want Carlos to know I did this, ever. I did this for him, Zack, for him."

"Good for you, but not good for me, sweetheart."

"Carlos and Gennero will help me get Salazar someday," she vowed.

Now it was Zack's turn. He could feel the power surging throughout his body and into his groin again. "Okay, Maria. Okay. I'll tell you what I'll do for your Carlos."

Maria wiped tears away, stopped crying, listened intently, and felt somewhat hopeful by Zack's offer. "Yes, please, Zack. I'll do whatever you want. Tell me, please."

"Okay. I'll get Carlos to London to see my friend. That's a done deal. Guaranteed. You get that two hundred and fifty transferred into my account in the Bahamas. You divorce Carlos, just before I get him out of this country. I'll let you know when. You marry me immediately after, signing a prenuptial contract. You promise me three children, and to be faithful to me, or you leave, without two cents to your name.

"Lastly, you come to my bed anytime I call you," he said. His powerful erection throbbed again in his trousers. It was just waiting to be released after such an aggressive outpouring.

Maria hardly hesitated; she could see the massive bulge in his pants. "I promise on my mother's grave, Zack."

"That's worth shit to me. Do you agree?"

"I do, Zack. I'll do whatever you want and whenever you want it, but don't tell Carlos," Maria said, coming to Zack. She was just about to drop her dress again.

Zack stopped her. Instead, he almost tore the flimsy garb from her and threw her down on the floor, close to the bed. He pulled her up and forced the dress up to her chin. She was naked as he pushed her legs apart with his knees. With one hand, he guided himself into her, watching her reaction all the time. He was pleased to see she was not objecting or resisting, but was very accepting as she slowly moved her pelvis and tightened her groin muscles to make it better for him.

It didn't take long this time. It was a forced assault, and he relished in it. He pushed himself off her. She rolled over, pulled a sheet from the bed, and again cleaned herself from his sweat and semen between her legs. She got up, took her dress, and walked to the door.

"You can do me any time, Zack. Do you want this again? Shall we do it again, but, this time, on the bed, more slowly, like you used to like it? Slowly. But please, keep your promise," was all she said. She opened the door, hesitating, waiting for him.

"Not now. No more of that fucking. I'll call you when you transfer the money, honey. Now, fuck off," Zack said, walking away and taking another mouthful of bourbon.

She recoiled at his hostility. She had never seen him so verbally violent, and she had to leave him alone.

As he watched her leave and the door closed, Zack sat on his bed, alone once more, talking to a stray dog at his feet. He was very pleased with the deal he'd made.

He turned to his only friend. "It was that way in my late teens, while my senile mother wandered about, turning on and off the lights. My father never came home, and my sister ran into an early marriage in Jamaica, sport."

Duke rolled over. His ears were flattened against his head, fearful for his friend, feeling the anxiety.

"Maria's gone, and she took scar face with her, Duke, old chap. But we have a deal, and I know she'll honor our agreement."

He turned to Duke again. "Of all the Mexican relatives she has here, and of all the hotels and rooming houses in California, she had to come to Jacinda's shit hole."

Duke scratched at the covers on the bed and placed his head on his master's lap.

Zack patted Duke and scratched his ears again. He was pleased with the soon-to-be-his money, and now he would be able to have sex whenever he wanted, without looking for it elsewhere. Or having to pay for it.

"Sure, he could use a good cosmetic surgeon, like Sam, who will do the facial transplant. Sure, I will write a letter and say that a facial transplant would be essential. Sure, for Carlos' physical and mental health," he said to Duke, smiling as he walked to the patio, still carrying the bottle.

Zack looked back at the painting of Rembrandt hanging from the wall. He felt the old man's eyes following him as he walked back and forth. Just like Lani said he did with her.

The steely eyes squinted and turned red as the setting sun hit the fiendish-looking creature on canvas.

Zack pointed the empty bottle at the oil painting.

"I'd make a deal with you, or with the devil himself, and sell my soul, old man. All I have to do is get rid of Carlos, send him on the plane to

England. Then I will get my Maria to stay here with me; get Gennero to kill Gomez, Salazar, and one-eyed Pete, and finally send Forzani back to Italy—or to Hell—and then you can have my body and my soul," he swore as he finished the last drop in the bottle.

Duke cowered from the bitterness, uncertain where to go or where to hide. Zack walked back and forth again, and Duke followed. Zack was unsteady on his feet, and Duke slunk away with his tail between his legs.

The dog smelled Maria's shoe under the bed. He whined and began scratching the carpet.

"Damn, well I'll help that bitch after she screwed me in Mexico, but good. What Salazar did to her, she did to me. But, now, good-old Zack, the all mighty, the all-powerful, the all-seeing Zack, has Maria forever," Zack swore, slamming his fist against the wall.

His canine friend, resting on the floor and licking the wayward stiletto, looked up, and then crept under the bed.

"That's it, Duke, old boy. It's like Elton John's song, *The Bitch is Back*. Ever heard that one, Duke?"

He rocked back and forth on his bed, holding the empty bottle. Suddenly he had a wicked thought, as he sucked on the neck of the empty bottle, like a nipple on a breast.

"I could find Gomez easily enough. I'll make a deal, where he gets Carlos and I get Maria. It would be at the airport, just as Carlos leaves for England, and Gomez holds Maria back for my pleasure."

He sat up. His eyes suddenly focused again on the print of Abrahams'—or was it Rembrandt's?—mouth that was curled in a hideous sneer. Abraham? Rembrandt? Zack wasn't sure anymore, nor did he care. He was confused from the whiskey and anger that overwhelmed him. It was just as Zack spoke the horrid thought, that he felt the malice from that smirk on the wall.

He turned away, but felt the small, beady eyes burning into his back again. It was those eyes that suddenly overpowered him with remorse for what he did to Maria on the floor. "I hope I didn't hurt her," he said, looking at Abrahams.

He waited for an answer, some kind of a sign from the painting. The ghastly fantasy and his guilt were shattered by Jacinda calling out to him and banging on his door.

"Sack, it is my husband, Hector, emailed you a question. He left for 'Frisco City again," she shouted from the kitchen.

Zack went to his desk, threw the empty bottle into his basket, and turned on his laptop. The computer message light was blinking rapidly.

It was a brief, cryptic message from Hector. "*I have a friend, Georgette. She suffers severe nervousness and can't get out of the safe house. It is where street girls rest. I look after them. You are psychiatrist. See her for me. It's urgent. Massimo and I can help you with Forzani, and your good work at the hospital. Gracias.*"

"Piss off, man. I need a rest. I'm not seeing some hooker now," he swore. He went to his bed and fell asleep, exhausted and spent. It was Jacinda calling him after an hour for dinner.

CHAPTER 24

The End of Jacinda

Zack decided he would deal with Hector's whore some other time. He had more important things to do on the ward. He already knew about the safe houses throughout the city. Jacinda informed him they had been set up by Hector as places where prostitutes could rest, get cleaned up, have a medical check-up, add to the list of abusive johns on the bulletin board, and, hopefully, be rehabilitated by one of Hector's social workers. Maybe.

He was not ready to see some nervous hooker, or some vague psychotic complaint, just yet. Her 'nervousness', as Hector put it, could be pneumonia, gonorrhea, syphilis, a head injury from some brutal sex pervert, delirium tremens, addiction crisis, or a brain tumor. He wasn't going into a lion's den without help, and he might need some backup from a social worker or even a squad car.

Zack wasn't ready to confront Forzani yet, even though he was furious after Forzani discharged Annie. He was prepared to call Annie's stepfather again, or a nurse at Annie's group home, or even the police to report Forzani's abuse of a patient.

In addition, what made him even more furious was when Annie killed herself a few days later. Kim told him. She was beside herself as she told Zack that Annie had committed suicide while on leave for a day from the group home.

It was Forzani who signed her day pass, and Zack was ready for an all-out fight. He was remorseful for not taking action, knowing that Annie was vulnerable, and for not insisting she return to the ward. He was ready to use her suicide to get rid of Forzani.

He had already talked to Annie's stepfather about the tragedy, expressed his condolences, and sent him Annie's diaries, which Kim had secreted away.

Zack needed to talk this over with someone he could trust. That could only be his good friend, Sam, in London.

"Good to hear from you, buddy boy," Sam answered on his mobile, very pleased to hear from Zack; he vicariously enjoyed the drama Zack reported from time to time.

"Sorry to call you at the end of your day, Sam."

"Dinnertime here, bud. Out for a walk in Green Park. Clear the air after six hours of surgery. Good timing."

After a few more pleasantries and catch-up, Zack explained the situation with Forzani and Annie.

"Christ, man. You were the one to always get into some messy fuckin' situations. Even when we were in our internship together, I told you to stay away from the risky stuff, man. The lawyers do well suing guys like you."

Zack was ready to hang up. He didn't need this shit, or another Abrahams, berating him. "Yeah, yeah, Sam, but this is different. Listen, did you get that referral and medical letter on this guy, Carlos?" Zack asked, changing the subject.

"Got it. Just send him over. Good subject, from what I could see from the photos. Maybe his facial nerves are intact, and the contractures are just muscular."

Zack got back to his need for good advice. "What about Forzani, Sam? What would you do with this perv?"

"Listen, buddy. Play it safe. You've let her father, or whatever he is, and others know; so let them deal with that asshole. Just wait. You've done a lot. Wait, buddy. Take a deep breath and wait."

Zack listened and agreed, but he then talked more about Maria, and the deal he made with O'Flanagan. Sam was again amazed at Zack's energy in manipulating resources for his own upward mobility in medicine, and said so.

"Christ! You sound just like Abrahams, Sam. Remember him?" Zack swore, fed up with being chastised when he just needed some support and affirmation.

"Yeah, I remember him. But you go too far and too fast, Zack, and it's too risky for you to be so opportunistic in striving for that illusive brass ring. Take it easy, man; just stand back and let that boatload of Forzani shit hit the fan. You're too impatient. Bide your time, my friend: wait."

After hanging up, Zack felt better, and was actually even quite proud of Sam's analysis. *Just like that fucker, Abrahams*, he thought.

He decided to wait, as Sam suggested, and do no more. *Let the chips fall where they may,* he thought. He was sorry he told Sam about the deal to get Maria, and to send Carlos away. Sam thought that was too cruel and sadistic. Zack thought Sam was a wimp.

He finished his day at the psych ward, leaving orders with the group of nurses, some of whom he had just hired. He had arranged that day to have meetings with every nurse in order to talk about their role on his ward, and to deal with the trauma of Annie's suicide, since many knew her from her stay. It was a planning day, and he had scheduled an entire hour with each nurse, clerk, and orderly to learn from them how to drag the ward out of the Middle Ages and into the twenty-first century. It was a long day that ended with wine and a catered dinner for the staff that he, personally, paid for.

He made notes, dictated them, and sent a copy to Baker and Sean O'Flanagan. They would both be impressed.

By 7 PM, he was slowly maneuvering the sharp curves up the hill to Jacinda's home. He hoped Maria would be there, since it was one of those times she needed to come across, as she had promised. Sex with her would take all evening. Maybe throughout the night. He needed that.

It was then, just as he saw the rooftop of the mansion in the distance, when a black Hummer careened over the center line of the winding road, coming downhill. It came right at him, almost wiping him out. Zack swerved off the narrow road, braked hard, and swore at the idiot behind the blackened windows.

"Damn kids. Probably high on drugs in this posh neighborhood." He swore, giving them the finger out his window.

It was the passing glimpse of what looked like a dog's claw marks on the passenger's side that gave him a sickening feeling.

Zack pulled back onto the road, fearing the worst. He put his car in low gear and drove as fast as he could go up the steep incline.

As he pulled into the driveway, he leaped out of his car. Duke was always there to meet him. Not this time.

He whistled. "Hey, Duke! Where are you, fella?"

His friend always came bounding out of the kitchen patio doors to greet him. Panting, slobbering, wagging his tail, and jumping all over him.

However, there was no Duke as he approached the kitchen. He panicked when he smelled smoke when he was near the patio door.

"Jacinda, are you all right? Duke, come here, boy," he shouted as he opened the patio doors and ran into the kitchen.

He stopped at the stove, where a pot was bubbling over with chicken bits. Fat was spilling down the sides and sparking on the elements.

He turned the stove off. Then he heard an explosion in one of the back rooms.

The force rolled through the hallway and struck him in the chest, bowling him over against the kitchen table and spewing dishes against the wall.

As he picked himself up, he heard Duke whining. It was somewhere in the distance, in the back rooms.

Zack cleared his head as smoke rolled through the halls and into the kitchen, and then blew out the patio door. He got down on his hands and knees and crawled toward the bedroom. He found Duke, covered in grimy soot and struggling to get up on all fours in the hallway, just outside his bedroom door.

Duke's eyes were glazed over. His tongue was rolling out, and his legs gave out as he tried to stand. Duke was confused, but alive.

Zack grabbed him by the collar and dragged him out onto the patio deck through the kitchen. "Duke, you've got a large cut on your head, fella. Just lie still and the bleeding will stop. Where's Jacinda, boy? Jacinda?" he repeated, patting his friend down, expecting Duke to answer.

Duke crawled onto the cool grass, whimpering softly, but tried to wag his tail, happy to see his friend home again. Zack ran back into the kitchen and found a cloth, and then put it over Duke's head in order to stem the flow of blood.

Zack pulled out his cell and called 911. "House on fire. Lady inside. Call police and ambulance. Fire trucks," he yelled, giving his name and address.

He ran around to the back of the house, shouting for Jacinda.

Smoke and flames were spiraling out the windows of the back room. He stepped around broken glass.

It was then when Zack saw Jacinda, near the azalea bushes in the back garden behind the house. She must have crawled out, still wearing her housecoat after taking a shower with a plastic shower cap wrapped around her head.

She was facedown in the grass. The blood oozing out from her skull into the hyacinth beds told Zack that the worst had happened.

Duke was up on all fours by then, near Zack's side, as he kneeled beside Jacinda. "Is she alive, Duke? What happened here?"

Duke was whining softly, scratching at the ground near Jacinda's body.

Zack turned her over, still calling out her name and praying she would answer. As he did, he gagged at the sight. What he saw made him retch in horror and disgust.

Her forehead had been split open with a jagged rock lying at her side. Coagulated blood was heaped onto her chest.

On her forehead, an 'M' was crudely sliced into her skin with a sharp knife, just above her nose.

Zack kneeled down. Jacinda's eyes were staring at the darkening sky above. He turned away, cursing himself for not being there in time.

He reached down and drew her eyelids shut.

Zack looked at the wretched body now on its back. Jacinda's housecoat was open above her waist. She had had a breast reconstruction, and the plastic saline bag used in surgery had been brutally ripped open, leaving a gaping hole in her chest.

"Bastards tore her tits apart. That damn pervert, Pedro," Zack swore.

As he heard the wail of sirens slowly making their way up the hill, he looked down at poor Jacinda. Her belly was riddled with scars from liposuction and uplifts. Zack's eyes slowly moved down to her naked pelvis. Dark, red blood covered her heavy, muscular thighs.

"That bastard, Pedro, the breast groper also raped her before caving in her skull," Zack said as he covered the rest of her body with her housecoat.

He then carefully took Jacinda's right, clenched hand from under her housecoat and placed it over her chest. Jacinda's left hand was by her side, with fingernails loaded with skin scrapings from her attacker's chest or back. Her right hand had made a tight fist, gripping some piece of metal.

Zack opened her hand. In it was the gold cross of Saint Christopher.

"Salazar's cross! He was here with Pedro," Zack shouted.

Firemen were now all over the scene, pulling him from the degraded body. Zack took the cross away, and pocketed it before the firemen saw it.

Man and dog moved away as flames sparked and crackled, slowly receding and sputtering out as the firemen doused the back rooms with water hoses.

Tears misted over Zack's eyes as he left the body. "She must have been in the shower when those thieves came," he said to one fireman who was pulling a hose around to the back.

He left the body and walked to the side kitchen patio. Duke, still struggling to stay on all fours, weaved from side to side, dutifully following Zack.

Firemen were running through the house with hoses, flooding the back rooms, but the flames had died out by then.

Zack gently maneuvered Duke away from the chaos as three police cars raced over the grass and into the flowerbeds.

"You're lucky, Duke. They must have smacked you hard, but you'll be okay," Zack said, checking the cut on the dog's head.

Man and animal, both so close to Jacinda but for such a short period of time, stood aside and watched as an ambulance took Jacinda's body away.

The fire chief came over to Zack, patted Duke on the head, and told Zack that the house was saved with only the back room gutted. As the police questioned Zack, he feigned ignorance and said very little.

"Thieves, I guess. She must have struggled, poor woman. Duke here did his best," was all Zack said as he fingered the cross in his pocket.

He decided to keep the details of one-eyed Pedro and Salazar to himself, for now.

Zack walked back into the house once it was safe to do so. He needed to know what happened to Maria. He found her room empty and all her belongings gone.

Zack kicked at a broken rhododendron bush on the driveway, torn aside by the police cars. "We'll get revenge, fella. Don't you worry," he promised.

Duke gave a sorrowful yelp and brushed his head against Zack's pant leg. Zack, fearing for his own safety, packed his bags that were saved by the firemen—although soaking wet—and he decided to move into a dog-friendly, classy motel.

CHAPTER 25

Baker the Ball Breaker

Hector, Jacinda's son and daughter, Zack, and a few of their friends and neighbors attended the small memorial service in the local Catholic church down the hill.

Maria stayed away. "She's convinced she will be next," Hector said, comforting Zack with his arm around him.

"She's a nervous lady now, Hector," Zack agreed as he followed the family procession into the chapel.

"There will be a proper Catholic funeral in Mexico later," Hector added, eager to get away once again.

After the brief, but solemn, memorial service with Father Lopez presiding, the body was flown back to Mexico to be buried next to her parents and one sister in Guadalajara.

Before Hector left, he told Zack that Jacinda would have a family feast while her coffin was viewed by family and friends for several days before the burial in Mexico. Her favorite objects and mementos would be buried with her, he explained. He would see to it that *maize*, Mexican corn, would be placed in or near her mouth. Corn was highly-regarded by her culture. It represented rebirth and a new life.

Every year in October and early November, family and friends would, again, honor her and her family, during the Day of the Dead festival. It was a national holiday throughout Mexico with parades, festivities, and family gatherings, and with food and drink to remember those who had passed.

"You will have to come to our home then to again pay your respects to my wife," Hector said when he was about to leave, never to be seen by Zack again.

Zack had held Duke by the collar, sitting at the back of the chapel throughout the rushed service. There was no eulogy, no tribute to the poor woman. Only Duke's low, throaty growl, which added to Zack's sorrow.

The two children left that day. They were busy, they said. Zack could stay in the house while Hector made arrangements for repairs.

Zack shook his head at this kind offer. "*Gracias*, but no thanks, Hector. It's too risky living in the house anymore. Like your wife or Maria, I, and even Duke, here, may be next."

Hector only shrugged, as expected, and left saying he would have a security guard there day and night.

Zack checked into a local motel near the hospital that evening, and he took Duke everywhere with him after that.

He didn't tell anyone at the hospital about Jacinda. It was on the back pages of the newspapers, and no one connected him to the tragedy.

Work for Zack was difficult the next day. Rage and despair flooded over him as he tried to put the slaughter behind him with feverish work. His appetite was nil, and he didn't need to lose more weight. He forced himself to attend to his duties.

The nurse's station had privacy now that the carpenters had finished, and Seema, the new head nurse, even had her own office.

It was all thanks to Baker.

Zack sat in Seema's office reading a chart. The page blurred over in Zack's mind as he thought about Jacinda's murder and his own safety.

"You look sad and fidgety, Zack. You're depressed. Understandable," Seema said, kindly walking back with him into her office.

"Yes, and worried about Annie's suicide—and Forzani's next move."

Seema patted Zack on his shoulder and said, "Baker got Forzani to agree to all the changes on the psych ward. She thinks that O'Flanagan had something to do with it during their golf game."

"Great to hear, Seema." *O'Flanagan came through on his part of the deal*, Zack thought.

"Insisting that the hospital hire a registered psychologist was a good idea. Also, we could really use a social worker, extra-qualified nurses, and an occupational therapist."

Zack nodded and told her to hire all of them. Feeling grateful, he left the nurse's desk and returned to his office. He called his friend in London on the VOIP with his camera in place. He needed his friend again.

Sam came on. "She'll make history, Zack. Her husband sent Lani, first class, on United. She's in our hospital, and has a room at the Ritz on discharge," he said.

"When will you be working on her, Sam?"

"Quite soon. Had a major transplant three days ago. He has better control over his facial muscles already. Carl, my patient, loves his new self. I'll send you the photos."

"Motor vehicle accident on the M5?"

Sam made a face. "Nope. His face was torn off by a Rottweiler. Ugly, ugly mess."

"Ouch," Zack said.

They talked some more about Zack taking Sam's advice, and letting others deal with Forzani. He closed the laptop, knowing Sean O'Flanagan would be pleased to get Lani out of his hair. The psychologist who saw Lani several times before she left got Lani to reduce her stress load and to defer the lawsuit.

After hanging up, Zack left the office. He felt a tap on his shoulder as he closed his door.

"Got your e-mails, Dr. Scarlatto. I've been here while you were away from time to time. Absolute disgrace," the melodic voice sang behind him.

He turned and found himself facing a tall, dark woman in her early sixties. Baker was large for a Filipino woman, and was fairly attractive wearing a colorful, flowered dress. She had a long, thin face; dark, sparkling eyes; black shiny hair; and a bright smile. She was pointing to a man in the hallway snapping pictures.

Zack followed the dark, slender finger with nails painted a soft red. "That's Timberlake. I know him from his articles about this psych ward. He's your man, Ms. Baker?" he asked.

"Call me Marcia, Doctor," Marcia said with a lilt to her voice and a sly wink.

Zack was glad to have her onboard, and he warmed to the twinkle in her eyes immediately. Marcia smiled as she took him by the arm and sat him down in his office.

Marcia was intense. "I've already gotten shots of the entrance to this hell hole, and all the inside shit, before some of the restorations," Marcia said, showing him the photos on her Blackberry.

Zack watched as Timberlake kept sending her pictures as he snapped them.

"Nice to have the two of you here, Marcia. My God, the place looks worse in those color photos."

Marcia nodded. "We'll flush this shit hole down the toilet, and Forzani with it," she said with a vengeance.

"Great. Forzani, the boss, might not always be right, but he's still my boss, Marcia. He is very arrogant, prideful, and aggressive. You know the score. He believes in himself, and only himself. Could still be trouble for me."

"That prick had nothing but disdain for me after he refused

responsibility for my uncle's death."

"Prick or not, Marcia, he could still have my ass."

Marcia glowered. "I'll have his ass on a plate. I want revenge, and it will be sweet. He screwed up. My uncle was a sick puppy, and he should have treated him properly. You heard?"

"Yes, sorry. I heard," Zack said, regretting the sad story.

Marcia shook her head. "No need to be sorry. He was an alcoholic bastard. Abusive to me, my mother, and all the women he ever met. A fucking chauvinist pig that we had to live with after my father was killed in a road rage accident."

Zack sensed she wanted to talk about her father, but he held back at this time, and didn't encourage her to explain more. He had had enough grief for a while.

"A demolition would be nice," he said with a sweep of his hands, changing the subject from her father and uncle. No therapeutic stuff at this time.

"That's what we need, Zack. We need to tear this place down and build a new, four-story for you. I'll get O'Flanagan to appoint you the Head and Professor of Psychiatry here," Marcia said, turning off the photos.

Zack stood close, deeply breathing in the sweet scent of body lotion and perfumed hair. "You can do that? The city will do that? Kinda doubt it, Marcia. The State's broke."

"My Catholics, with all that Filipino money in this local cathedral, will donate, for Christ's sake, man. Our priest has Massimo San Marco in his hip pocket as a shoe-in major donor. All the priest has to do is tell our people to give more. Hector will help, and so will Sean O'Flanagan. Both are devout Catholics."

Marcia continued. "I heard what you did now that Sean's wife is out of his hair. He, Hector, and the priest own the university, and the university owes them a favor for all those millions of dollars, mister soon-to-be professor," she said not revealing any more as to what she knew about Lani.

Zack wasn't going to ask her what she heard. That was history. "Hector? You mean Hector Chapala?"

She nodded. "Yep. If you and I help Hector with the safe houses, my dear doctor, then he will help us to get rid of Forzani and build a nice, new psych ward for you. I heard he asked you to make a visit to one of those safe houses."

"Pleased to do so," he added, somewhat anxious and wondering if she also knew about Carlos and Maria via Hector. He was impressed that she knew so many details about all those people she referred to. Including Hector.

"Yeah, yeah. For the street girls. Then we can build it. Once we build it, they will come. You'll be in charge here and at all of those eight, safe havens for the street girls," she whispered, and promptly left to find Timberlake.

"Me in charge of the safe houses also, Marcia?" he asked, but Marcia was already gone, looking for Timberlake. There it was again: tit for tat. He had to do something to get something.

CHAPTER 26

The Safe House

Zack got a reminder again that next day from Hector, requesting him to see this nervous woman who was at one of the safe houses. Georgie was her name.

Duke looked up from his spot near the door at the motel when Zack got the call. Zack had given him an old blanket from his trunk, and Duke had made it into a nice, cozy bed for himself in the corner of the motel room; still close enough to the door, since he was always ready for a walk.

Duke's ears perked up when he saw Zack put on a leather jacket, and he jumped up, panting in expectation. He knew Zack was going for a drive when he reached for his car keys on the desk.

Zack gave him a hand signal to follow. The day was clear, and it would be a hot one again for late October. "Okay, sport. Come on. Let's go for a ride. I might need you to protect me," he said, laughing. And yet, he was somewhat edgy. He knew the safe house was in a very poor, neglected, seedy side of the city.

Zack opened the back door of his car, and Duke jumped in. He scratched at the blanket that Zack always had there for him, and maneuvered his big, black body into the warm space.

Zack turned the air conditioner on high and listened to the morning news. It was all about the fighting in Afghanistan, and the Taliban taking over parts of Iraq. It was the usual depressing news. He turned it off.

The drive took about thirty minutes. Zack recognized the sordid area in the old section of the city from driving through it, from time to time. He found the address easily, and maneuvered his car around the corner, close to the safe house, as Hector had described it.

He already knew something about the safe houses. They were for the street girls: a secure haven where some could move into low-cost housing, arranged by a social worker when it became available, through Hector.

This house, one of several owned and operated by Hector, was on the corner of a very busy street. The area was littered with stolen goods, and piled high with clothes in heaps: stolen bicycles, cell phones, radios, computers, and other tech stuff, all ready to sell to the locals and curious tourists.

Bearded, disheveled men, wasted from addictions, were scattered about, making trades or selling their wares as hookers—male, female, transsexuals and drug addicts—plied their trades. The alleyway behind the old, wooden, two-story structure was littered with garbage.

Zack slowly drove his car down the back alley, avoiding scattered tins, boxes, black plastic bags, and broken bottles. He pulled his car as close as possible near to the back of the house in the alley.

Other cars slowly made their way down the lane, some with women in them, and some stopping to make deals with men hunkered down in the shadows.

An ancient man, bald, with a scruffy white beard, shuffled out of a dark recess at the back of the house. He was wearing a black bandana around his forehead, dirty shorts that revealed infected, pussy ulcers on his legs, and grubby runners that didn't match. He was shirtless, revealing tattoos on his arms and a series of knife-wound scars on his chest from past battles he had lost. He looked like he was surviving, but barely.

He looked at Zack sitting in the car, and then at Duke in the back seat, who snarled at the sight of the unkempt stranger.

The man whistled between broken teeth as Zack rolled down his window part way. "It's okay, man. Hector, he says you was a' coming. Dunna know 'bout this dog, here, in you's car. Ladies gonna be scared of dis here darky animal. Maybe." He paused. "It's okay with me. I's gonna watch your hubcaps."

Zack opened his car door and walked out. He pulled out the leather leash from the floor of the car and clipped it on Duke's collar. He raised his hand in a partial salute to greet the old geezer. "It's okay, fella. He's with me. No fear of this here animal," Zack said reassuringly.

Duke accepted the leash readily, since he felt safe when tethered to his master. Duke followed, but he then had a sneezing fit from the man's stench as a slight breeze came through the alley, drowning the man and animal in disgusting odors.

The man flashed a stiletto knife as he kicked bottles and syringes away, clearing the way for Zack, but causing Duke to growl again.

Zack tightened the leash and kept Duke next to his body. In the dark shadows of the back lane, the man accepted the five dollars Zack gave him to watch his hubcaps.

Zack stepped over a broken syringe, several needles, and a half-filled condom as he peered down the alley. A woman came out of the back door of the house, followed by a man covered in a large, black jacket and a hoodie covering his face. That added to Zack's anxiety. He caught a glimpse of the man's face, which was badly scarred.

Zack reared back, pulling hard on Duke's leash. It was Carlos under the hoodie. He was sure of that, since the man looked both ways before entering a parked car in the alley. Zack recognized the scarred face from Maria's photos. The car sped away.

Zack and dog stood there for a time, with Zack wondering if he should go on. This he didn't like, and he was not prepared to learn that Carlos was being secreted in this safe house. He watched as the car turned the corner and was gone.

He thought of turning back, but decided to follow through with Hector's plea. After all, Marcia did tell Zack that Hector would be one of the Catholics to help, so he owed him.

Zack pulled Duke along, walked toward the corner of the block, and to the front of the house. Duke hesitated, but Zack gave him a strong tug. He slunk along, legs bent and body closer to the ground, but followed, hugging Zack's side.

Zack and Duke watched as men in the shadows of the street exchanged plastic packages with some of the women. Maybe some were women, maybe not. Someone climbed out of a large, steel, blue bin on the corner, carrying a plastic grocery bag while eating remnants of a hamburger.

Zack gingerly made his way to the front of the house, tugging at Duke to follow. It was an old house: a hundred years old, desperately pleading for a paint job, with a broken-down, white picket fence that was missing boards and was hardly protecting anything from the chaos of the street.

Zack nodded to a young, black woman walking by who was wearing a blonde wig, bright red lipstick, and who wore a blouse that hardly contained her massive breasts. She also wore red, very tight tights, which easily revealed her labia and even a glimpse of her asshole. She then propped herself up on her four-inch gold-spiked heels. She was unsteady, but she leaned against a mail post box for support.

Zack and dog stumbled over sheets of newspaper covering an old man huddled against the picket fence. He didn't stir. Zack thought of checking his pulse to see if he was alive, but Duke pulled him away.

Across from the busy corner, where man and dog hesitated awkwardly, there were many hookers wearing short, slit skirts and bikini bras, calling out to cars or pedestrians, looking for business and selling themselves to various bidders.

One of the girls saw Zack and started waving frantically. Her friend was leaning into a car window, talking to three men, totally preoccupied with making a few dollars, but taking a potentially-lethal risk, if she were to get into that car.

The first one who waved at Zack stepped off the curb, totally unconcerned about cars or bicyclists trying to avoid her, and putting her life at risk. She gave oncoming traffic the finger as drivers honked, trying to stop as she gingerly skipped across the street.

She quickened her stride when she spotted Duke, and yelled out to him, patting her emaciated legs in greeting and encouraging him, hoping, he would come to her.

Zack didn't wait for her. Instead, he opened the wooden gate to the house. He dodged a wire buggy, stolen from the local grocery market, full of clothes, bottles, tins, wood, and cardboard. It was pushed by a young, tattooed, shirtless man. He was only wearing a pair of ragged shorts and two different, odd-sized, dissimilarly-colored shoes. He was talking to an imaginary phantom.

Zack stopped at the gate to look back at a legless man. He was shouting at Duke to wait up for him, pushing his four-wheeled, wooden cart with his bandaged hands across the busy street.

The man maneuvered himself through the traffic, shouting obscenities as cars weaved about, trying to avoid him. He met the woman part way across the street, stopped and shouted, "Give you a ride if you straddle my cart, Imogene."

The woman snorted, not missing a beat as she crossed the road. "Fuck off, you legless prick. See me when you get your government check. Buy some of that Viagra shit, get a hard on, and then come find me," she spat, quickly sidestepping him as she made for the sidewalk.

The man, who had fought for his country and proudly wore a medal on his chest, gave her the finger as she ran at Zack, grasped his arm for support, and bent over to pat Duke on the head.

Zack slowed down while Imogene scratched the dog's ears. "Duke, you seem to be the most popular visitor in this place," Zack said as everyone waved, whistled or wanted to pat him.

A large, African-American community policeman was putting hand cuffs on a young man and pushing him into a marked police van. Zack was pleased to see the law close by, just in case.

The trio slowly made their way up the wooden steps. Duke recoiled as Imogene grasped his ears and roughly patted his neck again.

Zack looked at the woman squeezing his arm. *A pretty girl, perhaps, once upon a time, long ago, maybe when she was in her late teens, and she was probably of mixed racial origin*, he thought.

Imogene stood, dropped her hand on Zack's buttock, and squeezed. "Nice and firm, darling. Want to feel this one? What's his name, sweetie?" she asked, pointing at Duke.

"This here is my friend, Duke," Zack said. He gently nudged her aside and took the last step up to the door. He avoided a heavily blotched, dark stain that appeared to be blood. It was fused into the wooden planks of the landing. On the top landing was a large sign with a bare light bulb hanging over it.

He read, 'Parker House, a safe haven'.

Underneath was written in a black felt pen, 'In memory of Emily Parker'.

"Come, Imogene. I'll help you," Zack said as the girl struggled to maneuver the rickety stairs and landing, made of wooden planks, in her heels. Duke pulled on his leash, preoccupied with sniffing and smelling the blood-stained planks.

Imogene immediately began working on Zack. "Imogene, her usually only works nights, Doctor. Her needs money for today. Maybe two, maybe has three, children to support. Her husband, he murdered, he was in an overdose," she said of herself, hoping for a handout from Zack.

"Sorry to hear that, Imogene," Zack replied, giving her a five dollar bill and some loose change. He then opened the front door.

Imogene nodded, looked at the bill, and gave a sad smile at the small amount, revealing two upper broken teeth and one lower bicuspid that was missing.

She quickly composed herself, stuffed the money into her jean's pocket, stepped back, theatrically bowed before the doctor, and dramatically said, "Age before beauty."

Zack kept any comment about that to himself.

As the front door opened, she waved him into a large, dimly-lit room.

Zack heard the door slam behind him. Duke cowered. Zack coughed, sucking in the putrid air as his eyes watered from the smoke-filled room and plastered walls that reeked of nicotine.

As Zack peered in, he found a dozen women lying helter-skelter here and there. They were all dressed in flimsy, short skirts and tattered blouses or sweaters, with powdered legs that still revealed scars, open sores from infected injections, and blue varicose veins. Broken heels were scattered about the room.

Old, ragged sofas and broken-down chairs with stuffing coming out filled the room. Small, white, plastic tables were scattered about. The air stank of sweating bodies on display, all of different colors, sizes, ages, and shapes. Duke pulled back on the leash, uncertain of going further, snorting and coughing from the stink.

The women—perhaps they were girls; young and old, it was hard to tell—were all for sale. Cheap and cheaper, depending on the hour, the day, the time of the month or their government check, or, most importantly, the clientele.

Zack saw these kinds of people in the emergency wards when he was a resident working his last years in psychiatry. They came in psychotic, drug and alcohol addicted, suffering from liver failure, gonorrhea and other sex-related diseases, heart conditions, and brain injuries. They were treated for their acute, immediate disorders, kept overnight—at the most—and then they were discharged back to where they came from. Wherever that was, it was never good. And he always knew they would be back.

He also knew all these women in the room would be dead soon. Some would be murdered by sadistic, perverted men, who would then also steal the few paltry dollars they might have been lucky to amass that night. Or they would die of accidental overdose, using those paltry dollars to get impure, adulterated cocaine, fentanyl, heroin, or crystal meth from other sadistic, misogynistic men.

He looked at Imogene, who was now lying in the corner, twisted on the floor with legs wide open, talking to herself. She scratched open pustules on her emaciated thighs, and then licked the puss from her fingers. It was very unlikely he would ever see her again.

Zack saw a community worker, possibly a nurse, working on a small table in the corner, talking to a young street worker. He listened to the questions being asked about where the girl was living, what money she had, and what illnesses trouble her.

He saw a large sign posted on the wall nearby detailing the services available to the women. Hector's society provided dinner and breakfast, washrooms, clean clothing, nursing care, and, twice weekly, educational and work place resources.

He was impressed with the sign, which explained how the nightly mobile van service that carried both a nurse and a police woman drove about the neighborhood, stopping to ask street girls if they needed a coffee, police assistance, financial help, or a room for the night.

He had read that, last year, this very home provided over forty-five thousand meals, and over two thousand referrals to women needing emergency shelter. Forty women were referred to detox, and over six hundred individual women walked through the door that Zack and Duke had just come through, seeking warmth and shelter.

Zack stood there reading the bulletin board, listening to the nurse talk respectfully to the young woman. Suddenly, an older woman, black as coal and as large and as wide as she was tall, came out of the kitchen.

She was brandishing a huge butcher knife.

"Dere's no men 'lowed in here, you know that and with that dere dog dere. But maybe, oh, maybe, but I were expecting youse. A doctor, youse are? Hector says you is coming, man. Nice dog, dere," she said with a thick Caribbean accent, pointing her saber at Duke.

She was indeed a large woman, older beyond her years, in skintight jeans. A massive roll of belly fat hung over her rope belt.

Probably Jamaican, Zack thought as he noticed her thick lips, flat, wide nose, and poorly-streaked blonde hair. She was wearing large, gold, hoop earrings.

Zack nodded. He saw her forehead to be permanently wrinkled with heavy, deep, dark furrows. Zack thought he could lose a finger in one of them.

Zack smiled and offered his hand. "Yes, ma'am. Dr. Scarlatto," Zack replied, watching her wipe the sweat from her forehead. The atmosphere was stifling; there was no air in the room with all windows blacked out, barred and shut tight, as was the front door now, too.

The woman took Zack's hand and held onto it with a steel grip. "This is Holly, my name. I is the one in charge of Parker House, but Georgette, she the real boss. She da boss of all da houses for da real big honcho boss, mister Hector," she said to Zack.

Zack extricated his hand from the vice-like grip, rubbing it to get the circulation back into his fingers.

Holly stuck out her other plump hand, patted Duke, and said apologetically, "Glad you is here. Don' know what to do wit dat der child, Georgette. She has high anxiety, as her boss said to me," she said in her heavy accent with a worried look.

"Thanks, Holly. Where is Georgette?"

"In da back. Der is two rooms: her apartments, der. Go der and push the button. She's will let you in to her rooms. Take you big black horse wit you," Holly said, pointing to the back of the house with her blade.

Zack followed the point of the blade, past a number of girls preening themselves now that there was a man in the house.

He was cautious, uncertain what or who he would find. He walked into the back, pulling hard on Duke, who was even more hesitant in going further.

They came to a single, dark, tarnished door, with grease stains and paint bubbling off. Zack pushed the grubby, imbedded sticky button on the wall.

CHAPTER 27

Georgie Girl: or Was She?

Zack wiped the grimy oil from his finger after pushing the twisted button. He heard the hoarse voice of a heavy smoker shouting from somewhere behind the door. There was a small dog yapping in the background, and he thought he also heard a child's cry. Duke pulled on the leash at the sound of the yapper, pricking up his ears.

"Come in, detective."

Zack looked behind him to see who else she was talking to, when he heard a muffled ring from a buzzer. The door opened with a dull click.

As he walked in, he found the inner hallway bathed with stale smells of pizza, cigarette smoke, and yesterday's barbecued hamburger mixed in with Chinese.

Duke, now even more cautious than his master, slunk in tight to Zack and followed him closely as they both walked into the room.

A gorgeous redhead was standing near her mirror, admiring herself, but then waved frantically and shouted. "I thought it was detective

Gennero. You're not him, sweetie. Much more handsome though." She gushed as she ran to him, grabbed his arm and pulled him in.

As she moved past Zack, she hurriedly bolted the door. Her hand trembled as she slipped the heavy chain over the clasp, turned the key in the handle, and pushed another bolt across the jamb.

She leaned back and surveyed her guest and his dog.

"I'll give you the whole story. From start to finish, honey. How those bastards, those fucking cops, raped me. In the lock up. Sit down. Listen," she said, talking in short staccato sentences.

A slender wrist, greased in face cream, gripped Zack's arm. She pointed to a large, moth-eaten sofa, and she pushed Zack into it. She left him there as she moved to the corner by a badly-painted white end table with black legs, which was covered with make-up paraphernalia.

Reflected by a cracked, faded mirror, she began painting her toenails. Nail polish splashed all over her stubby toes as the fingers on her right hand twitched. She also tried to balance a glass in her other hand.

In the corner was a little girl playing by herself, but warily watching the intruders, man and beast.

The room was bathed in pink. Pink towels and pink, lacy curtains hung everywhere, while rose-colored mats and carpets, stained with cigarette holes, littered the floors. Vulgar paintings and photos of nude men, usually cavorting in a spa, or at the beach playing volleyball, covered the walls.

Zack unleashed Duke, who then left Zack's side and ambled over to the dark, little girl, who had a huge mop of black, curly hair on her head. She was playing with a soiled, black doll that only had one arm.

Zack smiled at the girl, who he decided was about four to six years old, and said hello. *Who was she, and whose was she? How did she get here, and from where?*

The little girl, dressed in a flowery, blue-and-white dress and sandals, had huge, wide eyes and a lovely, bright smile. She dropped her doll. She stood up, and followed Duke back to where Zack was dropped into the sofa.

"You my granddaddy?" the little girl asked, looking Zack in the eye.

"No, I'm not. You're a real cutie. What's your name?" Zack asked, not thinking of reminding her that their cultural color of skin was quite different, and, thus, no way could he be related as a grandfather.

It was Georgette who answered. "Katrina. Name Katrina."

Katrina came to Zack, spread his legs apart, pulled herself up, and sat on his right leg. "You my granddaddy?" she asked again.

"No. I'm not, sweetie but maybe I could be your uncle. How would that be, Katrina?"

Georgette came to Zack, patted Katrina lovingly, and whispered to Zack in his ear. "Got her from Haiti. After the earthquake. Momma, papa killed. Paid three big ones. From her auntie."

Katrina threw her arms around Zack and hugged him tight. "Uncle?"

"Sure thing," he answered, and held her warmly. She had beautiful, soft, dark brown skin, with twice as much curly black hair as little orphan Annie did in that movie.

Zack let the little girl just sit there, as he, too, sat back, nice and cuddly. He watched the strange scene unfold before his eyes. Duke sat quietly by his side, watching Georgette powder her legs. Her red, satin robe drooped down and hardly covered her small breasts, one somewhat larger than the other. As she crossed her legs, she revealed a highly-powdered limb that was badly shaved, but still quite muscular. There was a large penis hanging down, surrounded by two hairy testicles.

Zack pinched his nose at this half-woman, who was still a man, but small in stature; she was rather tiny, but was laden with overpowering odors. The heavy smell of nail polish, face powder, hair gels, perfumes, and thick cigarette smoke, coupled with the scent of a dirty, sweaty crotch, was overwhelming.

"I'm Dr. Scarlatto. A psychiatrist. Not a detective, Miss. Hector asked me to see you, Georgette," he said, using a tissue to wipe the grease off his arm where she pulled at him as Duke began sneezing spasmodically.

"Oh really? Lucky. Lucky for me. A psychiatrist? You say? I am Georgette. You big sweetie. You must psychoanalyze me. Shall I start? With my childhood? Or what those three pricks. What they did to me?"

"No. Start with this Gennero guy," Zack asked, recalling that Jacinda referred to him as some sort of savior. Jacinda never mentioned a transsexual; unless Georgette was the 'some whore' her husband was running around with, as Jacinda had complained once. Unlikely, as this person was neither female, nor any longer trying to be male, apart from what was between the legs.

Georgette was dressed in a colorful, candy-striped, short skirt beneath her red robe, which couldn't contain her outlandish breasts that were obviously laden with saline bags or silicone gel, but poorly done.

She ignored talk of Gennero. "A psychiatrist? Write a letter. Saying I'm perfectly sane, sweetie. I need a shrink. To do that."

Zack sat there quietly, somewhat intrigued. Duke settled down behind the sofa, now that both were talking with a little girl nearby. It was safe.

"Really? What for?"

"So I can have a surgeon. Work on me. Down here," she said, spreading her legs apart, pointing to the flaccid penis and balls Zack had observed a moment earlier.

"You really want to do all that painful surgery, Georgette? Just to become a woman?" he asked, clearing his throat of smoke wafting toward the trio.

She nodded enthusiastically. "I used to be George. Soon I'll be a sweet Georgette. Call me sweet Georgie. But listen up. You're a doctor. I get infections. It's my man. Paddy tells me. To see a surgeon. He complains; you know, that it smells," she said, almost in a whisper, somewhat embarrassed, as Katrina looked at her.

"Sweet Georgia Brown. Paddy? Which Paddy would that be?" Zack smiled, as he unconsciously hummed the tune, tiring of her inability to talk in whole sentences, but shocked by her paramour's name.

Katrina jumped down, and went to play with her doll with the amputated arm in the corner.

Zack looked at Georgie and asked her too many questions, all at once, something he never did as a psychiatrist. "A surgeon? Okay, to emasculate you? Who is Paddy, but tell me first: what smells?"

"No, no. I needed this dong. For Paddy. My boyfriend. You know. My partner and yours. He does well. Selling. So do you, sweetie. He used to dance in Vegas. Now stays here. Makes better money. With you. You know: pills. Off the ward. But look," she said, coming to Zack and turning away from Katrina. She lifted her penis for Zack to examine.

Zack reared back, surprised by the sudden graphic exposure. Composed, he looked at the swollen, infected member. "My God, Georgie. Your foreskin is infected. Medically it's called posthitis. You need antibiotics right away, and then you need to get circumcised, man. Er…I mean, lady. But, I thought you wanted to be a total female, to have the complete surgery? Removal of your genitals, and then a small vagina introduced. You already have the breasts."

"Shit, no. Well, yes. Paddy still needs it to suck on. I use it often into him. Some of my queer friends love it. The girls at the Pussy club play with it. But Paddy wants it off. It stinks. I need ten big ones, just for a meeting with the surgeon," she said, massaging her penis as it began to swell. Not embarrassed at all by its size and girth, she then pushed it gingerly back into her panties.

Georgie watched Zack intently to see if he was getting aroused by watching her play with her dick. Disappointed, she turned and stepped back.

Zack, aware of her attempted seduction, didn't respond or remark on her little show. He simply remarked, "Do you know why you weren't circumcised as a child? Look, Georgie, using it, or masturbating, is healthy. Men who use it, and do it often, find that it clears their prostate of potentially cancerous cells; they also don't have to get all dressed up, put on a tie and shave, before going out to find a woman and spend a lot of money on a dinner."

Georgie slapped her powdered thigh and gave out a squeal of laughter. "And for us ladies, Doctor? What about us ladies?"

"And by the way. Just for the record, it used to be called onanism. Onan, a man in the Bible, spilled his sperm on the ground lest he impregnate a woman. For you ladies? Well, women can do it by themselves, using their manicured fingers or a magic dildo, and no longer have to complain of a headache beforehand."

Georgie was intrigued, so Zack went on. "Masturbation for men and for women is healthy. Some say that it's a very pleasant hobby to have, and some dermatologists have said that masturbation, or other such sexual activity, is almost a guaranteed cure for teenage facial acne. For men, there's possibly a less chance of prostatic cancer, many urologists say. But listen, why weren't you circumcised as a young fellow?"

Georgie went back to preening herself in front of her mirror. She turned toward him, with her face cupped so the little girl couldn't hear, and whispered, "I guess mother said 'no'. Now, Paddy says yes. He wants a hole down here. After I get cut. You know: a vagina. Tired of ass-fucking me. Because I get a cheesy oil stink. Under the foreskin. Smells, he said."

Zack felt obligated to Hector, and as a physician, to assist this strange one in order to help her get healthy. He also needed more information on Paddy. How much did she know?

"Listen, Georgie. That accumulation is from the glands under the skin. Called smegma. Boys should be circumcised to stop such infections, and also to reduce the chance for other sexually transmitted diseases. In addition, some say they should get the human papillovirus vaccine. Surgery, and the vaccine, would help prevent throat cancers, which is getting more prevalent for those who have oral sex, males or females. Your Paddy is vulnerable to throat cancer. That vaccine would prevent cervical cancer in women after heterosexual sex, or after any sex of any kind."

Georgie looked in the large mirror at Zack, pointed her newly-painted finger at him, "Paddy took a medical course. Like his papa. At the hospital. At college. Very smart. He said if I get sized, I won't stink. But I need ten big ones. Paddy said you can pay me."

"Sized? You mean circumcised. Like hell I will. If Paddy is so smart, then get it from him. You're lucky to have him."

Georgie smiled broadly at Zack's confirmation about his business with her lover. "I have it. A referral to a surgeon. Help me with my nerves, too? Paddy will get pills for me."

"I'm sure he will. But I won't. No money from me, sweetheart."

Georgie got up, carrying another glass in her hand, pointing it at Zack and said, "Listen, Mister. You do. Or I write to Gennero that you're a pusher. Disbarred by the college, you will be. No fucking work. At that crazy place for you. Get it?" she shouted, spilling her glass all over the already-soiled carpet.

Zack looked around the meager room. He stifled a sneeze from the air, thick with a sweet body spray. "Okay, okay. No frigging letters. I guess I could do that, Georgette."

Zack was thinking fast. He would make up the difference by cutting Paddy's take.

Georgie blinked rapidly. Relieved, she winked at Zack. "Don't you think I look good, sweetie? Once I get the surgery, I'll be set. Write a book. Be on TV. Like those others who switched. But kept their dong for a while. I could tell everyone to get that papillo stuff. To stop all that infection stuff," she said, spreading her legs again and scratching her crotch.

"Listen, Georgie girl. Take my advice and join some of those LGBTQ groups that are now everywhere to help guys, er…sorry, I mean, gals, like yourself. They will give you lots of supportive group therapy, before and after the surgery."

"Yeah, sweetie, I know. Lesbian, gay, bisexual, transsexual. Yadda, yadda. What is? What's the 'Q' for, sweetie?"

"Q is for questioning. Still unsure, still questioning their sexual identity, Georgie. Unlike the lesbians and the gays—who we used to just call female or male homosexuals—that now have a strong identity, there are those who are still undecided as to what they are. Call themselves 'Q'."

Zack was happy to get her off her threatening stance. She could become aggressive. He was in her territory and vulnerable. "Okay. I still think you should get some help from the LGBTQ group here in the city. They are online, and they advertise in the local newspapers. They help out with meeting others, and organize events to go to movies, plays, artistic stuff together. Safer. Be careful, Georgie. Lots of perverts around, and they could get angry, and harm, or kill, you."

"Oh, sweetie. So kind. You are so kind. To Georgie," she said, running over and throwing her arms around Zack.

Zack let the hug stay briefly. "Listen, Georgie. Surgery is traumatic. You'll need female hormones all your life, and help to adjust. New identity, Georgie. Get some therapy."

Georgie sucked on another partly-finished cigarette and shrugged her big shoulders. She went back to her table and pointed with her toes at Zack, proud of her bright, blue toenails with silver sparkles scattered at the tips.

Duke sat up and scratched at Zack's leg in response to the yapping in the other room. Zack pointed to the back. "That dog that I hear barking. Yours?"

She cupped her hands and shouted, "Quiet, Fifi; be a good puppy now. Don't hurt the nice man. His dog—he will eat you for dinner."

"Hector said you might need help. For anxiety or depression?"

Georgette cupped her hands and whispered, "Hector told me. You, you would help Carlos, also. Georgette takes food. To Carlos. He is protected here. In our safe houses. No one knows. We move him from house to house. Moved him today. Elsewhere. In the state."

There it was again. Damn. Carlos. "Here in this safe house?" he asked nervously, not really wanting to know, but already saw him leave the house earlier.

She nodded. "Not here anymore, today. This is used only by street women. It's safe," she whispered, so Fifi wouldn't hear.

Zack said pointedly, "Listen, let's stick to just you, and only you, sweetheart."

"So sorry, Doctor. It is Hector. He hides Carlos, not me. Not your girl here, Doctor. I only look after him. Here, in this safe house that Hector set up. For the day at a time. He pays little Georgie. Then we move him elsewhere. He moves around. But it makes me so nervous."

"What's the problem with you now, Miss?" Zack asked, wanting to get out of this stink as soon as possible.

"I'm waiting for Hector. To arrange his flight. Carlos. Out of here: safely. So that Gennero won't find him. Or those Mexicans. Waiting is hard. Makes me frightened. You know. Nervous."

"I can see that you are anxious."

"Doctor, I can't stop shaking. It was after *mon amie*, my friend, Billie, was fucked in the ass, also. In the county jail. Can you imagine that? Almost murdered. She is a transsexual also, you see, and very…" She paused, looking for the right word. "How you say it? Vulnerable?" She smiled, and was now aware of Zack's own nervousness and vulnerability.

Zack was amazed she could puff at a cigarette, cough as she smoked, drink, and talk in spurts, all at the same time.

He scanned the photos hanging by thumbtacks on one wall. There were over twenty photos. They were all of a young, effeminate boy, starting from an early age. Some included his mother. In some the boy was dressed in tutus, performing at a ballet school. Others were from school plays where the boy was dressed as a girl. They gradually expanded to the present-day, older Georgie girl.

"You'll be better now. Don't be afraid. I'll write a prescription. Remember, the tough times don't last, but tough guys do. You were strong to get out of jail," Zack said as he pulled out a pad. He wrote out a prescription. He prescribed an anti-depressant that suppressed panic attacks at twenty milligrams, taken in the mornings. He added a sublingual tablet that disintegrates in the mouth and is fast acting, almost like a quick, intravenous injection.

Zack turned away from the photos. "Why were you in jail, Georgie?"

"That fucker. Asshole called Bob. He hit me, so I clobbered him. But good. Bastard called the police. It was at the club. Where I work."

"Look, Georgie girl, or Gorgeous, or whatever, it's a high-risk business. Hundreds of your type are murdered every year."

She turned away. "I know, but it's better for us girls, since we're talking about it these days. Hilary Swank got the Academy Award for playing the murdered Brandon Teena."

"She did? Who's he? She?"

"In the movie, *Boys Don't Cry*, from the early nineties. It was a good movie. I'm more careful. It's the fucking cops who screwed me. Not Bob."

"Bob could have killed you, Georgie. Trans people are murdered by perverts. Suicide is more prevalent. You'll have more of a problem getting proper health care from doctors. Proper schooling, and jobs," Zack explained.

Georgie was listening intently, but quickly countered, "We know, but it's getting better. Some of us started a helpline for trans people. We have a few counselors; we're on Facebook, online, apps. We need help. From doctors: your type."

Zack already had enough to do. "Sure, Georgie. Sure. Call me and we can set up something," he said, giving her his card and recalling the deal he made with Baker to help manage the safe houses.

"I need that big ten. Soon," she reminded Zack. She was intent.

That was enough for Zack. He was ready to leave.

However, suddenly, there was a violent kick at the back door, the entrance from the lane. Duke growled. Georgette was startled. She dropped her hairbrush and spilled her drink all over her cosmetic book. Katrina ran into Georgie's arms.

"It's the Mexicans. They're back," she screamed.

"I'll get it, Georgie, calm down," Zack said as he walked to the door. He ordered Duke to sit.

Georgie downed another hastily made Rob Roy and squealed, "It must be. It's him. Detective Gennero. It must be him. The detective."

CHAPTER 28

The One and Only, Detective Gennero

Hopefully it is Gennero, Zack prayed, *and not Carlos coming back.* Zack had to be careful. He didn't want Georgie talking to Gennero about his deals with Paddy.

He turned to Georgie. "No words to Gennero. I'll get you your money."

Georgie smiled, trying to remain calm as she walked back and forth. She nodded in compliance as she put on more makeup, and splashed lipstick on her previously-painted lips. Then she blew him a kiss.

Zack took the chain off the rear entrance, turned the key, and pulled back the bolt. He opened the door slowly. He kept his shoulder against it, just in case Carlos, or his handlers, wanted into the safe house.

Zack stepped back, surprised. Leaning against the doorframe was a short, scruffy man, with long, graying hair parted down the middle that cascaded down his back. He ground a cigarette into the concrete wall, and stuffed the butt into his jeans pocket.

He was short, stocky, but powerful, and, without difficulty, shouldered

Zack aside and walked in.

"Oh, it's him. It's the detective. Gennero," Georgette gushed, putting Katrina down, running at the man, and throwing her heavily-powdered arms around him. She pulled him in, held him in a strong grip, and danced him about the room.

"Detective, this is a real doctor. A specialist. He came to see me. He's going to fix me, too. He thinks. I'm a raging psychotic. He calls me…wait for it…Georgie girl," she said, proud of her astute diagnosis and new-found identity.

The detective pushed Georgie away at the end of the dance, brushed off the powder from his jacket, and looked Zack up and down. He spied the dog and whistled to Duke.

Duke didn't budge. He was settled behind the couch again. Katrina, instead, came to him.

Gennero patted Katrina on the head. "Go away and play, little girl."

She was miffed, but did as she was told.

Gennero scanned the room and turned to Zack again. "A real doctor? No shit."

Zack tried to hide a smile as he looked at this officially-bestowed, lawful protector of all citizens.

Gennero was in a black, woolen jacket with a yellow stripe rolling down each sleeve, and a ragged, coffee-stained T-shirt that was too large for him and hung underneath his jacket. He also wore tight jeans and white runners. As he talked, Zack noticed he was missing one lower bicuspid. He had to be close to sixty.

Gennero guffawed as he turned his attention to Georgette's self-professed analysis. "Psychotic? He's got that right. Psychotic, neurotic, hysteric, a mixed-up, fucking sexual screw-up. That's for sure, Georgie girl. I read your profile at the station." Gennero chortled, extending a strong hand to the doctor.

Zack took the nicotine-stained hand as Gennero pulled back and surveyed the real doctor.

"So! You're the one at Hector's house. Those fuckers! I'll get to Carlos first, and then that Salazar, and that Gomez, will be toast. I know what they did to Hector's missus, and to your nose," Gennero said, pointing to the small scar in Zack's nostril.

He swore at everyone and everything as he walked about the room, checking this and that and spewing a string of expletives.

"I hope so. Careful of your language, detective. Little girl here," Zack said. Zack was doubtful about Gennero getting Gomez, who was twice his size and had more armaments around his belt than half the city police force put together. His limos were also full of sawed-off shot guns and assault rifles. Gennero only had a small pistol at his side, with likely few bullets, at that.

Gennero turned abruptly. "So Hector told you where Carlos is hiding around these parts?"

It wasn't a question, but a statement. Zack blinked.

Gennero paused, waiting. Eventually he gave up, and turned to the wall that displayed the early photos of Georgie. He muttered something wicked under his breath, and snorted a few vile words at the nude hunks in the pictures playing volleyball.

"Not to me. Hector said nothing to me," Zack lied.

The detective pointed at Zack. "It's your duty to inform the police. That's me. You could be an accessory."

"Some big, black Mexicans are looking for him."

"Them and me. That motherfucker, Gomez, won't get him before I do," Gennero spat.

"Good luck," Zack offered, holding back another smile.

"Hector's a good man, a man of few words, but a good man. We can save Carlos from those mafia bastards."

Gennero slowly ambled around the room, picking up various trinkets, smelling a bottle of perfume, and looking down at Duke, who ignored him. He lifted the photos of men off the wall and placed them on the floor, back to front. "Little girl, here," he said.

He stopped in front of Georgie and put his hand on her shoulder, and then sidled up to Zack and pulled him back. "Georgie here was screwed up the ass when she was in jail. I believe her. Those bastards would fuck anybody or anything that crawls or bends over on two, or even four, legs."

Zack felt sorry for the half-man, half-woman who was listening to and taking such verbal abuse. Gennero looked at Zack and pointed at Georgie girl again. "Imagine putting your dick into a she male," he said holding his crotch. "It's not a he or a she, and she won't have a hole big enough to hold a small carrot after the surgeon gets a hold of her." He sneered.

Georgie girl simply knocked back another cheap gin, grabbed her crotch, forced her pelvis out toward Gennero, and gave him the finger.

Gennero blew Georgie a sarcastic kiss. He pulled out a tattered, black pad and searched for a pen. "You don't do double duty do you? Like one of those prictocologists, the asshole specialist? I saw one of you guys for my prostate last year. That bugger told me to bend over, and, before I knew it, he shoved his finger right up my ass. What a shitty job that would be."

"Good you had your prostate checked," Zack opined.

"Yeah, well I wasn't happy with this guy. I told him I wanted a second opinion."

"Really, detective? Did you get it?" Georgie asked, suddenly interested in someone else who had an object thrust into his anus.

"Yeah, yeah. The bugger put up two fingers and said to bend over again."

"Funny, funny," Georgie squealed. Katrina laughed in unison. Duke sat up at the loud guffaws. Zack just shook his head in dismay, having heard all those kind of prostate jokes before.

Gennero opened his dog eared pad, found a pencil in his jeans, and suddenly became very serious as he wrote down Zack's name.

Gennero kneeled down beside Duke, patting him gently. "Listen, doc, if you know where Carlos is, you better tell me. It's against the law to hide a fugitive in this state," he wheezed, patting Duke from head to tail with one hand. Duke licked the cigarette stains from Gennero's hand.

Zack shook his head. "I never met him; don't ever want to, and couldn't care less, Detective," Zack said.

Gennero seemed to accept that. He patted Georgie on the back and said he would look into her complaint about being raped in the jail house. He went to the back door, unlocked the bolts, and walked out into the alley.

Zack was glad to see the back of the famous detective. He went to Georgie girl, wished her well, and told her he was leaving after throwing the bolt in the back door again.

He whistled to Duke. "Come on, Duke. Let's go, boy. Good-bye, Katrina. Be safe," Zack said. He clipped the chain on Duke's collar.

"Bye, bye, Uncle," Katrina said sadly, waving her doll's only arm good-bye.

Both walked out into the main living room of the safe house. Both he and Duke were relieved to be leaving this surreal, unnerving, nightmare of a place.

CHAPTER 29

Gomez

Standing in the living room of the safe house, Zack hesitated for a minute. Holly espied him, and took him by the arm to the sofa, where a girl was lying unconscious. Someone in the kitchen was yelling to a woman that the soup was spilling over the pot, and to get the sandwiches ready.

It was then that the front door suddenly burst open. The noise made Zack rear up from checking the girl's pulse. Duke, in a frenzy, pulled on his leash and wanted to attack the gatecrashers.

The plywood front door exploded, splintering with a loud snap and disintegrating in a heap, almost on top of Holly, who ran to the front in order to confront the interlopers.

Zack tried to turn away as shards of cheap wood came flying, striking him in the legs. A sharp chip ricocheted off the floor and struck Duke in the underbelly. Breaking away from Zack's hold on the leash, he went howling toward the back of the room.

Holly screamed as two men burst in, stomping over the smashed door.

Zack, partly on his knees from Holly knocking him over, looked up. His gut went into spasm as he immediately recognized Gomez.

Holly, overweight but surprisingly agile, had recovered and quickly wheeled about and faced Gomez. She inhaled deeply, trying to puff herself up, standing on her tiptoes to confront Gomez. She reached out, punched Gomez in the chest, and tried to push him back out the open doorway.

Zack saw the large, black-handled Bowie knife at his side, almost a foot long in size.

As Duke started to bark at the mayhem, Zack grabbed him by the collar and desperately tried to restrain him. Holly had her hands on Gomez's massive chest and was pounding away. Gomez laughed, and with great force, punched Holly square in the face.

She staggered back with the blow; her nose was broken. He then moved forward, grabbed her by the head, and violently whipped her around.

Holly struggled, nose bleeding and swearing in Jamaican. But she was being strangled: Gomez had her neck in a tight grip from behind. She thrashed about in vain as he held her body with his left arm tight against his massive chest.

With one lethal swipe of his knife in his right hand, he skillfully slit her throat from one side of her neck to the other.

Her head wobbled momentarily, still held precariously upright by her cervical vertebrae and spinal cord. Her head then fell back against Gomez. She was almost totally decapitated. A flash of the French royalty passed through Zack's mind, as he recalled how the guillotine fell on their regal necks in the movies.

Georgie heard the clamor in the front. She came out from her room, with Katrina in tow, who was holding her dolly. Both saw the horrific sight of Holly with her throat cut, her two carotids still pulsating as they spurt, her body slowly sliding down Gomez's legs as they watched, transfixed with horror.

Georgie girl then vomited up her recent rum and coke and stale beer all over the floor, just missing Katrina, and then she ran at Zack for safety. She fell in a heap into Zack's arms, covering him in her vomitus. Katrina ran behind a sofa, and Georgie fainted in Zack's arms.

A hideous laugh erupted from Gomez as he reveled in Holly's bloody death scene and the chaos that he created. He bent down and wiped his knife clean on Holly's blouse, and, with another vicious kick, bowled her over.

Some of the girls scurried about, screaming and not knowing which way to go, and finally ran into the side kitchen. Others scrambled behind the sofas near to Katrina, trying to be as small as possible, toppling lamps and chairs onto the floor. The two women in the kitchen could be heard yelling, but they were nowhere to be seen.

Zack wiped Georgie's liquid lunch from his shirt and stepped back, knowing any attack, or even some attempted defense against Gomez and the large Bowie knife, would be futile.

Georgie was still out, either from too much rum and coke, or possibly from a massive coronary. He easily slid Georgie by one arm and one leg through her vomitus along the floor and away from Gomez, toward the safety of the wall.

This attempt for Georgie's safety freed Duke momentarily from Zack's hold on him. He snarled, baring his teeth at Gomez. His hair on the back of his neck stood on end. Duke remembered him from previous encounters.

Just then, Pedro rushed into the room. He scanned the chaos, wanting to get in on the action, hopping up and down from leg to leg, shouting and stuttering.

He brandished the large pistol that he was hoping would help find Carlos and take him prisoner once he uncovered him in this safe house. He pointed it at Duke. "Let me shoot that d-d-dog of a p-p-pig, Gomez. I want to t-t-test this fucker out," he stuttered, blinking, waving his huge pistol frantically. His other hand slapped his thigh rhythmically while he tried to take aim.

Gomez pushed him aside and barked out an order. "Later, asshole, later. You'll hit me instead. Check the rooms in the back. We came here for Carlos, not to shoot dogs or these other pigs," Gomez commanded.

Duke was ready to pounce at Gomez or Pedro, but Zack moved to grab him by the tail.

His hand, still slippery from Georgie's vomit, was unable to pull Duke back. He was too late. To his horror, he saw Duke charging at Pedro.

"Duke, no. Fella, come back," Zack shouted, and he ran to pull Duke away from Pedro.

The next motion was so fast that Zack only saw the huge blade flash again.

Pedro tried to protect himself as Duke jumped on him and scratched the patch off his eye.

Zack attempted to reach his friend and to pull him away when Gomez made one, fatal slash at Duke's exposed neck.

Zack was too late.

Duke, in his attack, slipped on Georgie's rum and coke and fell to one side, just as Gomez's blade struck Duke on the side of his head. Duke gave a throaty gurgle, slumped heavily into Zack's arms, and slipped onto the floor.

His dear friend rolled onto his side in a lifeless heap, unconscious from the blow to his head by the massive blade.

Duke's eyes, wide open at first, looked at Zack, but his pupils rolled up into their sockets and the lids slowly closed. He gave a shudder.

Zack called out, horrified when he saw Duke's head covered in blood.

"Duke…why did you do that? Duke!" he shouted in anger. He leaned down to hold his friend's head. Duke was unconscious, but alive.

Zack never finished his question.

A thick, hairy arm wrenched his neck back, and another hand pinned his arms behind his belt. Gomez held Zack in a vise grip; he loosened his stranglehold only long enough to let Zack take in a breath. He twisted Zack's arm into his back, took out his weapon, and held the blade, still dripping with blood, against Zack's neck.

Zack winced at the pain and looked sideways. The Mexican who used to wear a black eye patch was grinning at him.

"You'll end up next to your b-b-black b-b-b-b-bitch unless you tell us where th-th-th-th-that Mexican is hiding. We want C-C-C-Carlos," he stuttered, covering his disfigured eye, now free of the patch. He kicked at Duke's body.

Zack tried to turn his head as he felt the cold, crimson blade against his skin.

"Play it smart, Doctor. That Mexican whore from the beach in Acapulco probably offered you our money. We offer you something more. Your life," Gomez snarled. He pushed the point of the blade into Zack's neck.

Zack didn't struggle. He knew he could end up next to Duke or Holly, dead, and in some gravel pit in the hills.

Best to stay calm, he thought, as he pulled the hairy arm away from his neck. He thought quickly as he gulped for air.

"I don't give a rat's ass where she is or where her Carlos is. When I met Maria, I didn't know she was married to Carlos. That bitch lied to me. That's a fact."

Gomez snarled. "The fact, mister *medico*, is that Gennero knew where Carlos was hiding. We followed him here."

Zack tried to keep calm as his heart thumped against his breastbone. "I know that Gennero wants him, but I don't give a shit about Carlos, Maria, Gennero, you, or your money. You get him, and I get my Maria back; simple as that," he said, praying Gomez would swallow the line.

At this point, Georgie stirred and slowly crawled on her hands and knees through her puke and rum vomit behind a chair, near to Katrina's sofa. Pedro was determined as he kicked the chair away, pointing his pistol at her.

Georgie curled into a ball behind her over-turned, tattered chair, praying in gibberish to some unknown deity for safety. She put her hand up to deflect any bullets coming from Pedro.

"Leave the bitch, Pedro. You can have her later," Gomez shouted, as Pedro began groping Georgette's breasts.

Pedro swore at his victim after realizing her altered sexuality, and then he bashed her on the head with the butt of his pistol in revenge.

Pedro left her, and used a dirty kerchief to wipe the blood off his forehead where Duke had scratched him. He ran to the back, pushing two of the girls away who were cowering in the hallway.

Pedro ran back into the front room. "C-C-Carlos is gone. That f-f-fucker over there knows. Fuck all, G-G-Gomez," he said, pointing to Zack. "Let me shoot him in the head, and let's get out of here before some freaking c-c-cop comes," Pedro said, pointing at Zack with his pistol and kicking at Duke's body again.

With the kick from Pedro, Duke stirred and tried to get up on his front legs.

Zack looked up at Pedro. "Don't kick at the dog, Pedro. I'll get you for this one day," Zack threatened, despite the grip Gomez still had on him.

"Maybe you're right, and we should shoot him, Pedro, but I don't want a doctor's murder on my hands. We don't want that prick Gennero, and his police dicks, fucking things up for us. What we need is the motherfucker who took our money, and not the publicity of shooting a doctor. Don't do anything stupid, Stupid." Gomez sneered.

With that, Gomez lowered Zack's arm, pushing him down on his knees. In a quick motion, Gomez grabbed Zack's small finger on his right hand and bent it back.

"Cut off his fucking arm, Gomez; c-c-cut his arm," Pedro yelled, looking back while searching for his patch on all fours.

With one swoop of his knife, Gomez cut off Zack's little finger, just above the first knuckle.

Pedro was up. He chuckled at Zack, who was howling in pain, and he quickly picked up the bloody digit. He flicked it over a large cabinet, into the corner of the room where little Katrina was huddled.

The shorn-off pinky struck Katrina in the face as she looked up. Screaming and wiping some blood away, she leaped to her feet and ran for the open doorway, trying to flee.

Just as Katrina reached the door, the large, Afro-American policeman whom Zack saw earlier bounded up the wooden stairs with gun drawn and came through the open doorway. "What's going on here? I got a call from the neighbors," he shouted, stopping short of the body on the floor.

Pedro, excited by the police officer shouting and brandishing a pistol, immediately started firing without thinking first.

The first two shots felled the burly officer. He crumpled to the floor, almost on top of Holly's nearly headless body.

Katrina cried. She was confused, and pushed herself through the commotion, seeking safety in the open doorway.

Gomez tried to stop Pedro, shouting at him, but also feared being in the way of stray bullets, and stepped back.

Pedro wasn't finished yet, and kept firing at the officer, who was still struggling to get up. His hands were shaking, and he was now more confused and frightened by seeing a police officer, but Pedro kept brandishing his gun in all directions.

Zack, bleeding from his amputated finger, stepped forward and ran to Katrina to save her from possible death.

He was too late. Gomez pushed him aside, seeing that Pedro was out of control and devoid of all rational thought. Pedro let off another volley, and, this time, a bullet hit Katrina in the chest. Poor little soul, spared from the earthquake in Haiti, she fell in a heap over the now lifeless officer.

Zack had been flung against the wall by the strong arm of Gomez, and was helpless to save the little girl.

Georgie girl, still hiding behind the sofa in horror, shrieking at the top of her lungs, saw Pedro kill her adopted child and flung herself at

Pedro. He ducked aside, and simply bashed her on the head with the butt of his gun.

"G-G-G-Gomez, let's g-g-get the fuck outa here," Pedro shouted. He again aimed his pistol at the officer and pulled the trigger, but was out of bullets.

Gomez, not ready yet to do so, swore at Pedro for his stupidity, and he kicked Duke in the ribs again. "That's for grabbing my crotch at the house, bitch," he said to Duke, who was slowly still struggling to his feet. Pedro moved toward Gomez, ready to leave.

Zack, wrapping his bleeding finger in the tail of his shirt, faced Gomez. "You're in deep shit now Gomez; but I'll get better, and when I do, then I'll find you, and I'll kill you for what you did here: to Holly, to that little girl, and to my dog."

Gomez reared back in feigned terror, gave a throaty laugh, turned, and pushed Pedro toward the door. "That was just a sample, Doctor. The next time I'll gouge your eyes out, and cut off your ears and nose. You'll look just like that canary, Carlos," Gomez said, laughing as he bounded down the steps and into a waiting black Hummer, which quickly sped off.

Zack fell to his knees beside Duke, who was almost up on his feet, but he was still dazed. He used Holly's cell phone, which was near her body, and he called 911. He then gently covered the wound on his friend's head with a tattered kitchen cloth, which was also lying next to Holly's body.

Georgie pulled Katrina's body off of the officer, and then helped Zack to his feet. "We better get out of here, Doctor, before others come. You don't want to be here," she said, pulling a blanket off of a chair and covering Duke in it.

Georgie looked away from the nearly headless body on the floor, gripping Katrina tightly to her own body as Zack stepped around Holly's legs. He was still in a daze as Georgie pulled him along, helping him get Duke into her room and out the back door.

Once outside, Zack looked up and down the alley. It was already getting dark. The sun was setting, and a slight drizzle fell. He examined Duke's head, and only found a small wound that was sure to heal well.

Clouds had moved in, and the street scene was quiet. The pavement was slippery with the rain. The girls and their pimps had disappeared. The street quickly cleared as a lone police siren wailed, far down the street. He could see the lights flashing in the distance as he and Georgie pushed Duke into the back seat of his car. The man guarding his hub caps had disappeared.

"Georgie, wait here for the police to arrive. Tell them the story, and they will help you with Katrina's body. I'm sorry. Georgie. Sorry," Zack said. He had tears in his eyes as he touched the little body cradled in Georgie's arms.

"You go, Doctor. You were never here. You have work to do. Help us types. Help Hector with the safe houses," Georgie said. She was very composed again, in control, and thinking clearly.

With no sign of a black Hummer, Zack drove away, waving to Georgie. She didn't look back as she sat down on an old, wooden apple box in the alley. She was soaking wet, still holding her child and the one-armed, raggedy doll.

CHAPTER 30

<u>Baker and Sweet Revenge</u>

Zack, still feeling anxious and nauseous from the mayhem, wasn't sure where he was going as he drove cautiously, always watching to see if he was being followed. The image of Holly's head rolling about on her shoulders was vivid in his mind. However, his car knew the way; it continued up the hill. His steering wheel was slick from his sweaty palms.

Duke was uttering throaty noises, still pawing away at the blow to his head. He stretched out in the back seat. The drizzle of rain slowly coming through Zack's open window felt good, cooling Duke down.

Hector had texted Zack that he cleaned up his house and restored it back to how it was. Zack and dog were ready to move back in, with a twenty-four hour, well-armed guard on sight.

Zack pulled into the driveway, near the kitchen patio. A heap of burned lumber, windows, and doors still hadn't been cleared away after the fire. He swore at Hector for not getting that mess cleaned up yet. The heap stank as it smoldered in the rain, which was now pelting down.

Once the security man let him in, Zack helped Duke into his room, fed him, and filled his dish with fresh water. He then slapped a portion of antibiotics from a sample tube he kept stored in his bedside table drawer on to his severed digit, and he put a dab on Duke's head. He bandaged the stump. The wound was clean, and a flap of skin was ample enough to fold over the fractured bone. In retrospect, he was sorry he didn't retrieve the severed stump, as he was sure it could have been sutured back on.

The tape and bandage would hold it securely until he finished cleaning up Duke's head wound.

"I'll get that bastard for you, fella. I promise," he vowed as he kneeled beside Duke for a few minutes. He cleaned the small cut on the dog's forehead with alcohol, and then spread more antibiotic cream on it. The laceration would heal. There was no need to take him to the vet for stitches, he decided.

Zack took Duke outside for some fresh air. He walked around to the side of the house, and he felt safe enough with Hector's security man sitting on the patio, protected from the heavy shower, his pistol at his side. He waved at Zack, but didn't stir as he flipped through his copy of *Hustler* magazine and kept scrutinizing the grounds.

Zack went inside and changed into a clean shirt and trousers. He told Duke to stay indoors and just rest. He walked out and fired up his car, and then drove to the ER at another hospital. His finger was sutured by one of the surgical residents, who recognized him.

He lied as she taped his finger in gauze after the minor surgery. Zack forced a smile. "Really stupid of me, Carla. Cut it on a table saw. Bad carpentry."

Zack drove back, and was welcomed by Duke, who was getting back to his usual, frisky self. He sat at the kitchen table and drank the coffee he had picked up at the hospital cafeteria after his finger was cleaned up. He felt the buzz in his shirt pocket.

It was Baker.

No hellos or how are you. Just to the point.

"Too bad about Forzani; got beat up bad on the golf course. Must have been one of his crazy gamblers. He owed a lot of money to a lot of bad people," she said abruptly.

"Yeah, must have been," Zack said, disinterested, but glad to hear Forzani got his due.

"I'm meeting with the chief. Sean O'Flanagan has signed papers to oust Forzani at the end of next week. The hospital board has to approve his resignation, and your new position. Sean wants to see the architect's plans."

"Good for you. I'm grateful to your man for writing those articles about the psych ward."

"He's good."

"Damn good."

"We can have lunch at my place to talk more about the architect's plans. I need your input."

It was a command, not a request.

Zack agreed to lunch, but he also had an evening dinner date scheduled with Seema that night. He was looking forward to that. He could talk to her about the safe house, but without too much detail.

After a text message to Hector about Georgie and the attack on the safe house, without including any details about the shootings, Zack sent e-mails to the three social workers who were interested in helping with the safe house. They all agreed to establish a volunteer program in order to help Hector manage the other safe houses, but only if Zack agreed to be the consultant psychiatrist.

He agreed.

Zack's message light was on. It was from Hector again.

It was brief and cryptic. "*Heard from Georgie. Thanks for trying to help here. Sorry about Duke and Holly. Just like Jacinda. Good work with Baker and the new construction plans. The Catholics will help.*"

Zack didn't reply. There was no mention of the slaughtered police officer, or of Katrina. He propped Duke's photo on his desk.

His message light on his laptop was flickering again. He turned on his e-mail as he poured fresh water into the sink, and then buried his face in it.

There was spam about Epival, Viagra, Paxil and arthritic meds that he quickly deleted.

He reared back to see one was from Hector again. The rushed message was composed in lower-case letters and sent from a Blackberry.

"carlos is a good man. could help us clean up the mafia in my country, and here. you're a doctor—help him. mafia will kill him if they catch him. i read about you and facial transplants. general gomez works for the mexican government, but also for salazar. If he finds carlos, he'll take him back to mexico, but then the mafia will kill him before he testifies."

After a stiff shot of bourbon, he went to his computer and sent Hector a reply: *"Thanks for the info, Mr. Chapala; I'm sorry for Carlos and Maria. I'm not sure what I can do to help. Carlos needs a plastic surgeon in this country, not a psychiatrist. Maria needs therapy."*

He waited a few minutes, but didn't receive an immediate reply. He turned on both the radio and the TV to catch the local news.

The TV announcer detailed the deaths and the shootings at a safe house. Georgie was interviewed. She only said that her safe house was a haven in a dangerous part of the community, and such shootings were not unusual. She said that it must have been some addicts looking for drugs, and no one else was a witness, as all the girls had fled.

Georgie was seen crying huge crocodile tears: mascara was running down her cheeks as she focused her interview on the death of her daughter.

He would be glad to see Seema that night. She called and invited him for dinner and a birthday celebration for Aesha. "Spur of the moment," she said.

He needed that. He left his house to buy a nice gift for Aesha and flowers for Seema.

CHAPTER 31

Massimo

Late the next morning, Zack had to meet with Massimo, who was ill with a confirmed diagnosis of cancer in his lungs. He again listened to both the radio and the news on the TV.

The announcer said police had arrested two men, who were identified by a girl on the street. They were possibly involved with providing drugs to addicts in the area of the safe house. Zack sighed a breath of relief.

Back on his ward now, Zack discovered that Massimo had paid for the private room in the psych ward himself. He had made a good recovery after only one electro-convulsive treatment, but his prognosis, his medical future, was not favorable.

Zack asked Seema about Massimo. "That's right, doc. Money can do that," Seema said, who had been waiting for him near his office. Marcia was pacing up and down, still taking pictures.

"Thanks for the great dinner last night, Seema. Beautiful little girl, Aesha, and awesome curry. My favorite," he said, very gently touching

Seema's arm.

"She loved the small music box that played 'Happy Birthday'. She played it, over and over, until she fell asleep last night."

Marcia came over and gave Seema a hug, something Zack was able to do last night. "Too bad. We'll have to tear all this down after he dies," Zack replied, sweeping his hand over the ward.

Marcia laughed. "He's not going to."

Zack looked askance.

"Not going to die? Everybody does, Marcia."

"Yup. Not him. Not our man. You've read about cryogenics."

"You're kidding? Massimo?"

Marcia was in a hurry, as always, but explained, "Cryogenics. Life support technology, Zack, my man, and soon to be professor."

Zack whistled. "No kidding? It will keep him preserved on ice, until his cancer and bipolar can be cured in the future?"

"Not kidding. He's doing it. He has the bucks for that, but the bucks for the new ward will be up to his priest, doc," she said, nodding her head toward Massimo's room.

"The priest? How come? What's he got to do with the money, honey?"

"A lot, sweetheart. A lot. It's the Catholics that Massimo deals with. They are in his will and estate planning. Massimo and his so-called 'wife' will leave all future bequests and holdings in Father Robert's hands. It's the priest, man. He's in charge of the money. Honey."

Before Zack could say or ask any more questions, she was off, running to meet Timberlake, Councilor Baker's photographer, who was writing a story on Massimo, the Catholics, and the psych ward for the local papers.

Zack muttered to himself as Seema left with Marcia. He walked into Massimo's room, thinking about how he would deal with a priest now. A new wrinkle in his plans.

Massimo's private nurse looked up as Zack walked in. "I'm glad you came, Doctor. The surgeon was just here, and said our patient should be locked up in the mental hospital with the other crazies, and not in a general hospital, like this."

Zack frowned.

The nurse put her hand to her mouth. "Sorry. His words, Doctor. Not mine."

"He should know better. Not appropriate."

The nurse avoided the doctor's eyes. "Sorry, Doctor."

"It's okay, Maureen," Zack said, looking at her name tag and the small medallion on her uniform. It signified that she had graduated from a nursing school in Dublin.

Maureen was a likeable lady, attractive for her age, with flaming red head. She looked the spitting image of the starlet, Maureen O'Hara, in *The Quiet Man*, a film starring John Wayne from years ago.

She wore a light green, form-fitting surgical uniform that matched her olive green eyes. As she passed, Zack smelled fresh soap, "Irish Spring" body lotion, and the alluring scent of her still-slightly-wet hair.

Maureen pointed to the fat man sitting near Massimo's bed.

"Fortunately, his priest"—she hesitated—"he's with him always, now," she said with a strong Irish accent.

"Priest? He's not dying yet. I hope," Zack whispered, but now somewhat hopeful, since here was the priest Marcia had alluded to.

"Last night was just crazy, I can tell you." Maureen put her hand over her mouth again. "Oh, sorry about that word, Doctor."

"You're forgiven, again," Zack said, smiling. He thought about the fact that he loved Irish nurses, but he thought East Indian nurses were, to his taste, better cooks.

Maureen turned crimson, which hid the few freckles she had. "Thank you, Doctor."

"It's nice to see a green uniform on a nurse with red hair, green eyes, and that Irish lilt. Beautifully color coordinated," he added with a sincere smile, mimicking her Irish inflection.

Maureen's sudden blush, again, obliterated her delicate freckles and put a twinkle in her eyes. As she recovered, she coyly brushed her hair back and stood aside.

Sitting on a chair near Massimo's bed was a short, rotund middle-aged man. He was completely bald, with a very large head, an obese, flabby body, and pure, white, hairless skin.

Zack thought he looked like the fleshy, castrated eunuchs, like the ones who slaved in the Arab harems in the old Sinbad movies he had watched as a young boy, *Sinbad, the Sailor*.

This strange-looking man was dressed in a black, wrinkled suit jacket that was too small for him, or that he had outgrown from gluttony. It was one of the Seven Deadly Sins, and Zack was sure this man was guilty of other transgressions.

Stuck to his body with perspiration, he wore a soiled, creased, white shirt with a yellowed and dirty collar that was buttoned too tightly around his neck.

He held a small Bible, which rested on his crumpled, black trousers, and from which he was quietly praying.

As Zack approached the side of the bed, the man slowly pushed his corpulent body off of the chair with one hand. He clutched the aluminum rails of Massimo's bed with his other hand to steady himself.

As he looked up he said meekly, "Thank you for coming, Doctor."

"This is Father Esau Roberts," the nurse said, putting her hand gently on the fat man's shoulder.

Roberts nodded as he slowly sat down again in the chair.

"He's been here day and night, bless him," Maureen added, obviously an Irish Catholic as well.

Zack leaned on the rails, festooned with white and black rosary beads, and looked down at the priest.

"Dr. Scarlatto. Psychiatrist. Pleased to meet you, Father Roberts."

The fat priest set his Bible on the side table, pushed off from the rails, and stood again, looking around, uncertain where to go.

"Do you want me to leave, Doctor?" he asked, unable to move past

Zack in the small, tight space.

"No, it's okay. Stay if you wish," he answered, turning away from the sweaty body odor. He again recalled Baker and Alicia talking about the priest who was sucking Massimo dry, but controlled the money.

"Bless you, my son. Marcia told me about you."

Zack hated such blessings. He let it pass. "Marcia? Marcia Baker?"

The priest groveled. "Yes, my son. My parish has hired an architect, with Marcia's blessings. We have some tentative plans ready for you."

Zack, taken aback with such early information, asked quizzically, "You do? For the psych ward?"

"Yes, for your psychiatric ward, but thank you, Doctor, thank you. Bless you for letting me be with my parishioner. Thank you. I'll wait here as long as it takes, Doctor."

He was far too apologetic, oily, and groveling for Zack.

"Plans for a new building?" he asked again.

"I'll bring them to you, soon. Councilor Baker has a copy. To house a new psychiatric unit, my son. No one should be allowed to suffer like this in such a desolate, God-forsaken building," the priest said. He bowed slightly, and nodded toward Massimo, who was fast asleep and snoring softly.

Zack pushed it, needing to know what the priest knew. "The new psych ward?"

"With our benefactor, our angel, Massimo's, kindness. He mustn't suffer like this," he whispered.

The priest shuffled backward toward the door, wearing his heavy, black, Jesus sandals and dirty, white socks.

Zack recalled what Marcia had told him about Massimo, and his millions, everyone just waiting for his death, but he decided to hold that thought for later.

He turned his attention to his patient. Near Massimo's pillow lay a bejeweled Jesus who had been nailed to a small, wooden cross. Zack wasn't sure if it was Jesus or Massimo who shouldn't suffer like this, as the priest just pronounced.

The priest came back, neared Zack, and whispered in his ear, "The good Lord may take him soon, my son."

"Well, maybe. Maybe not, father" Zack said, "All in good time, priest. The Lord may have to wait a while. We'll see what the cancer specialists can do for him. In the meantime, he's responding to the medication for his delusional disorder."

The priest crossed himself. "God bless you, my son."

Zack wanted to tell the priest to stop calling him that. Such blessings only reminded him of Cuban priests in Miami. They all wanted to convert him to Catholicism soon after his mother died, wanting her pension money, which she didn't have much of.

The priest stopped, grateful to be included in the treatment process. "What will you do, Doctor? Give him something that will make him comfortable, please."

"Yes, we can do that," Zack said as he looked down at Massimo. He was snoring deeply, now that the sedatives had taken effect.

Zack was ready to walk back to the nurse's station when the priest clasped Zack by the arm. "Can I come and see you, in your office, soon? Do you have a card, Doctor? Please. I may need your help, my son."

It was the frightened look on the priest's face that made Zack relent. "I'm not your son, only a doctor. Here's my card," he said, deciding to be kind to the heavy man as he shuffled past.

Zack received yet another mumbled blessing from Roberts. In addition, Roberts also used his stubby fingers to give Zack the sign of the cross. Robert's fingers were pointed at Zack, still in midair, as Zack left the room.

CHAPTER 32

Sherman, the Contract Killer

It had only been a matter of days since Zack had seen the priest and Massimo. The weather had turned. Storm clouds had moved in. It was dismal and dark, with scattered rain and claps of thunder heard in the mountains.

Again, Zack checked the radio, the TV, the local and some national newspapers in order to see if there was more news about the safe house. There was none.

Zack couldn't put Annie's death behind him, yet, and he was still in physical pain from the amputated finger, which was also a further reminder of Katrina's death.

As to Annie, it was still a mystery. Why? She was near recovery, close to being discharged from the group home. Zack knew she had been suicidal. He secretly hoped Forzani would be blamed for her suicide, somehow.

It was quite late in the day, just as he was leaving the ward with

Seema—she had worked overtime, just to be with him—when he got the phone call.

It was Forzani's secretary. "Scarlatto? Come up here to Forzani's office. Annie's stepfather wants you here," she said anxiously, and then abruptly hung up.

"Why me?"

The phone was dead before he got an answer.

Zack dropped what he was doing, called Seema into his office, closed the door, gave her a kiss, and said he would see her for dinner soon. He made his way to Forzani's hideaway located in the glass wing.

As he walked into Forzani's waiting room, Josie was at her desk preening herself. Her hair was flaming red this time. She had a few more tattoos on her left shoulder, and her nails were so long he wondered how she could type. If she ever did.

Josie looked up from her copy of Oprah's *O's Summer Beauty Survival Handbook.*

When Josie saw Zack, she pushed Oprah aside. Almost immediately, she began spreading a perfumed hand lotion over her right hand.

"Oh, *ja,* is there absolutely anything else little Josie can do for the good doctor?" she asked in her Scandinavian drawl, keeping her mouth wide open and running her tongue over her ruby red lips slowly and enticingly.

"Very kind of you, Josie. No, thanks."

"*Ja,* vell, maybe next time. *Ja?*" she answered, somewhat disappointed. She waved Zack through to the inner office. She then promptly left, taking Oprah with her.

Zack knocked on Forzani's door, waited, heard guttural sounds, and walked in. He was anxious as to what and who he would find. Forzani must want to duke it out with him. But Annie's stepfather?

"Close the door, Scarlatto," Forzani ordered as he popped a pill and took a gulp from a bottle of water.

Forzani was sitting behind his opulent desk as Zack walked in. He was more ruddy, and heavier, than when Zack saw him last. He was sweating like a stuck pig, and he had a bruise on his forehead from a fight at the golf club.

Forzani was stuttering, slurring his words, 'aahing' and 'oohing' more than ever. "He's g-got a g-gun. Wants to…ah-a…shoot…um… me, Doctor."

Zack didn't correct him this time, thinking he must be paranoid, irrationally suspicious from all those pills he was gobbling down.

But then as he turned toward the windows, and he saw the other man in the room. He was a very tall, well-built man standing by the window.

The man looked at Zack, sizing him up and down. He was a large, muscular man, stoic, passive, sphinx-like. The big man turned and pushed a button on the wall. The whirring sound pulled the drapes together, cutting out any remaining light. He turned on the lights. It was near evening.

The man wore a shaggy beard, unruly mustache, and his long, scraggly hair fell down to his shoulders. He had a long face with deep, sunken cheeks, but his eyes pierced brightly out from under a massive, western Stetson hat.

Zack smiled and nodded. This couldn't be Annie's stepdad. He reminded Zack of Jeff Bridges in the movie *True Grit*.

The man tipped his Stetson to Zack in greeting. Zack looked down at the man's wingtip, snake-skin cowboy boots. *Nice boots. Expensive.*

Zack was amused. *Another doctor*, he guessed. *From Texas, but wearing an expensive black, double-breasted suit. With his pants tucked into his boots? Going to punch out Forzani? Sent by Annie's stepfather—or was this the stepfather? Couldn't be. It's a good idea to punch out Forzani,* Zack thought, but not if he was there as a potential witness.

Odd, he thought. He expected someone else, and something else, after he had talked to Annie's stepfather on the phone, soon after her suicide. The stepfather didn't have a deep Southern drawl. The man he spoke with on the phone several days ago was highly-educated, astute, and he was not from Texas.

The stepfather had been calm as they talked about Annie's suicide, and the details of her diary. He kept blaming Forzani for moving Annie off the psych ward. The stepfather ended by saying he was sending a message to Forzani. That was then.

Zack waited. Unsure what this was all about. The Texan said nothing. Obviously, he was very much in charge. Zack thought he must be the messenger.

Forzani started to fret. He was nervous, and started to say something. He looked at the door, made a move to get out from behind his protection, the large desk.

The man addressed Forzani. "Calm down, pard'ner. You're wound up tighter than a rattle snake," he said with a grin.

Forzani tried to calm down, but couldn't. "This here is…ah…you are a good friend of Annie's father, you said? A gun. You…ah, have, er, a gun," Forzani said, trying to make the introduction for Zack while trying to remain calm, sitting back down.

"That's so. Sherman," the man said with a deep Southern accent, walking to Zack and putting out his hand.

Zack shook the hand, wondering if that was his first or last name. "Oh, it's nice to meet you. I thought that Annie's stepfather was coming," he said, still bewildered by the meeting.

Sherman shrugged. "Couldn't make it. Sent me in his place, pard'ner. To take care of this pervert. Wanted me to cut off his balls. Take a load off. Have a seat, Doctor," he said.

It was an order; not a kindness, not a suggestion. A command. Sherman easily pushed over a large, leather chair with his boot. He pointed to it, and implied that Zack should sit.

"Castrate him? Hard to do. I can't be here, I'm afraid," Zack explained, thinking it was a bad joke. He was ready to leave.

Zack waited, and then Sherman pulled out an official document accepting Forzani's resignation. Dr. O'Flanagan had prepared it once his wife, Lani, was warm and cozy in London awaiting her facial transplant.

O'Flanagan got what Zack had promised him: Lani would be out of his thinning hair. Zack got what O'Flanagan had promised him: a resignation document that the big man brought with him. Forzani would be gone, once and for all.

Zack presumed that the Texan was there simply as a witness.

Zack got up and came over to Forzani's desk. "Thanks for the chair, Sherman, but let's get down to business. Dr. Forzani, I need for you to sign this paper, as prepared by Dr. Sean O'Flanagan. It's as good as a castration, but a lot less painful," Zack said, looking at Sherman and the resignation letter.

The man smiled. It was a pleasant smile, warm and confident.

"That's so, Mr. Forzani. You will be a 'mister' after you sign this note and retire; after the college suspends you for having sex with Annie. This gives Dr. Scarlatto, here, your title as chief of the psych ward," Sherman explained, patting the document now in front of Forzani.

Forzani was shaking uncontrollably, looking at the door, and, again, trying to stand up. He reached for another bottle of water on his desk.

"Sit," Sherman said emphatically.

Forzani sat down and opened a box of chocolates on his desk. Sherman moved to the door and locked it.

Zack turned to see Sherman take out a red bandana from his back pocket and wipe the door handle clean.

Zack said nothing.

"You have a lock on your door," Sherman said with a Texan drawl, looking at Forzani.

Forzani gave a meek smile, nodded, wiped his sweaty brow, and pulled a cherry-laden chocolate out of the box.

"For…ah…for security," Forzani answered, chewing on the chocolate for comfort. *Not a good idea for a diabetic,* Zack thought.

"You betcha…for security. While Annie was here? While you did 'therapy' with her?" Sherman asked, now standing between Zack and

Forzani's desk, handing Forzani a pen.

Sherman was in the way. Zack could only see part of Forzani.

Forzani shifted to the right and took a small bottle from a drawer.

Zack recognized it. Bronchial dilator. Asthma. Forzani shot a quick spray into his mouth, and ate another chocolate.

Forzani stuttered. "Well, yes. Therapists…they, they shouldn't be disturbed," he said, trying to be calm, but he was sweating like a stuck pig.

That didn't work. Certainly not for Sherman, nor for Zack.

Sherman turned to Zack. "This doctor is so crooked, if he swallowed a nail he'd shit out a corkscrew," he said, laughing at his own joke.

Zack didn't laugh. This was serious stuff. "That would be painful," was all he said.

Sherman's face was stern. He pierced his eyes in Zack's direction. "Do *you* do that, Doctor? You know, during therapy?"

Zack returned the look but blinked first. "No. Never do."

Sherman didn't blink. "Know anybody who does? Other therapists, maybe?"

"No. Not really."

Sherman turned back to Forzani. "I reckon Annie wrote that you always did. She wrote so. I reckon you did, just before the blow jobs or hand jobs," he said coolly.

Zack tightened. He looked to the locked door behind him, unsure of what was next.

"It's okay, Doctor. Please sit," Sherman said, turning and putting his hand on Zack's shoulder, gently maneuvering him back into the chair.

"What's going on, ah…Sherman, er, sorry, Mr. Sherman? Perhaps we should have, ah, you know…Josie here, as a witness…for legal reasons," Forzani meekly suggested. He took the pen and signed the document.

"No need. Video is recording."

Zack looked around. He couldn't see a recorder.

"Video?" Forzani squealed.

"Over there. On the table," Sherman pointed past Zack.

Zack looked around for a recording device. There was a large, pen-like piece that was blinking. It was scarcely visible amongst some books on the small desk.

Sherman gave a warm smile again and asked Zack, "Did you treat Annie?"

"No. I don't treat private patients. She was Dr. Forzani's, like a few others."

Sherman turned back to Forzani. "Did you have other patients here? With the door locked, Doctor?"

Forzani stood up again. "Now look here, Sherm-m-man," he stuttered, again opening his desk drawer, shuffling medicine bottles around with one hand, and holding his chest tightly with the other.

Before Zack knew it, Sherman was next to Forzani. He slammed the drawer shut, and pushed Forzani back down. It must have taken one second. No more than that for the agile Sherman.

Real fast for a large man with large, pointed boots, Zack thought.

"I said sit down, Doctor," Sherman commanded.

Sherman turned to Zack again. "Did you know about Annie's diary?"

Zack looked him in the eye and nodded. "A nurse and her roommate told me about it. She had it locked up. She kept the key around her neck."

"That's so. Her father read it, and passed it on to me. They all said you was a good, proper Doctor. Nurses said so. Annie wrote that, too."

"She did?" Zack asked. His throat was dry. He looked at the water bottle.

"Reckon she did. Her father said so. He also asked me to make a visit here. Didn't like what went on in this here shrink's office," he said sarcastically.

Zack didn't respond to the slur.

Sherman's next step was so quick that Zack almost missed it. He reached into his breast pocket, pulled out a pearl-handled revolver, and screwed a small pipe onto it.

A silencer. Zack paled. Forzani reached for more pills.

Sherman went to Forzani's desk, and, with his revolver, swept all of his medication onto the floor. Forzani's asthma bronchial dilators, coronary tablets, and other pills scattered all over the floor, mixing with the box of chocolates. Forzani tried to stand and to chase after the small bottles.

"My nitro. I need my nitro. My chest," Forzani gasped, now clutching his chest even tighter. He turned pale; as his eyes lost focus. Forzani, holding onto the desk, clenched. He was squeezing his chest hard. He gasped, sat down, and shouted for help. "My heart…it's my heart, exploding."

Frozen in his chair, Zack watched as Forzani's bladder emptied. Urine flowed down his pant leg, making a yellow stain on the carpet under his desk.

"He's having a coronary, man," Zack shouted and jumped up to help Forzani.

Sherman pushed Zack into his chair and reached Forzani first. He put the gun up to the man's head.

He was about to pull the trigger, but Forzani beat Sherman to it. While still clutching his chest, Forzani turned white, gasped, and slobbered. Spittle slithered down his chin. He keeled over onto his desk, face-first. Dead.

Zack jumped up from the deep leather chair he had been pushed into and ran to Forzani.

Zack didn't make it. Forzani was dead.

Sherman, surprised by the turn of events, comically blew apparent smoke away from the nozzle, just like John Wayne did in the old Western movies.

Not that there was any smoke from this gun, since it didn't fire, but Sherman was visibly dismayed that he didn't get to pull the trigger and shoot Forzani in time.

"Damn. The poor bugger died. How could he do that before I shot him? Fuck. But he signed the paper, just in time," Sherman said, walking about the room and eventually putting on his coat.

Zack checked Forzani's pulse. He was going to call for help. He was far too late, but still, he went to the phone on the desk.

Sherman again moved very swiftly. He took the phone from Zack and tore the cables from the wall socket. He looked Zack in the eye. "And don't use your cell, Doctor. Just don't do that. Yep. Dead as a doornail, I reckon. God fuckin' damn."

Zack then asked a rather naïve question. "Why did you want him dead?"

Sherman unscrewed the silencer and put the gun back into his breast suit pocket. "Why? Because society doesn't need guys like him. Besides, Annie's dead, and this is what I get the big bucks for. An eye for an eye, as they say."

"You got paid for this?" Zack asked stupidly again, knowing that he was a contract killer. Zack always liked to know why people did what they did, and just how much they made. That's why he asked the next question, "So, Sherman, just out of interest, can I ask how much you charge for something like this?"

Sherman smiled warmly and put his arm around Zack's shoulder. "I'll tell you the next time you need me."

Very dismayed he wasn't able to pull the trigger, he left Zack and walked about, fretting. "I better put a slug into him. Maybe I won't get those big bucks if I didn't kill him. Shit."

Sherman slowly ambled over to Forzani. He screwed the silencer back into his pistol, and was about to shoot Forzani in the head.

Zack moved quickly. "Don't do it, man. It's against the law to defile a dead body. He's dead. Done. *Finito. Kaput.* It's on your video. You'll be charged with the abuse of a dead body," Zack said stupidly to a killer as he ever-so-gently moved the gun away from Forzani's head.

Sherman, surprised by Zack moving his pistol away, pushed Zack away. "Fuck off, Doctor. I don't get paid if I don't kill him."

"I would think so, Sherman. Look, you can't kill a man again after he's dead. He's a goner." Zack was thinking fast and added, "Look, man, why not tell your people that you stuck your pistol in his mouth, and told him to suck on it. Get it?"

Sherman gave a weak smile, frowned, not sure where this was going. "Get what? Fuck, no."

"Well, you tell whoever pays you that you told him to suck on it, just like Annie sucked his dick. You were going to teach him a real good lesson. Save a bullet. No blood on the walls. Your people would love that scenario."

Sherman reared back and gave a loud laugh. "Aha! I like that. Christ, you're a fucking sadist, man."

Zack ignored that tribute. "Look, man. Tell your people that, just as you were going to pull the trigger, with the gun barrel in his mouth, the bugger died of fright. You simply scared the bejesus out of him. You killed him, man. Saved a bullet, and there isn't blood all over the place. Neat, tidy, easy-peasy: quick. It was your bright idea."

Sherman was almost ecstatic. "Well, what a smart motherfucker you are. I like that, man."

"That's the nicest compliment I ever had, Sherman."

"If there's any question about it, I'll just tell her father that you were the witness. I'll kill that video on his coronary and alter it. That will work, if we ever need it."

"Tell them you wanted Forzani's death to be symbolic; you know, prophetic kinda. You know, in honor of Annie. Oral sex. Fellatio with a loaded gun in his mouth. Her father will love it. You could ask for more."

"Fellatio? What is that shit? Sucking it off? No shit? I like that. Scared him to death? Yeah, I do like that," he said, taking the silencer off and putting the weapon into his coat.

"Well done, Sherman. Very decent."

"Yup. You won't see me again, sorry to say, fella, since I hear good things about you," Sherman said, as he took the signed document and gave it to Zack.

Sherman then moved between the video recording and Forzani, lifted his head, stuck the gun in Forzani's mouth, turned to have the video record the scene, and then let the head plop back onto the desk.

"The video shows he signed it willingly," he added, as he unlocked the door. He cleaned the handle again and sauntered out, cool as a cucumber.

Zack just sat there for a few minutes, warm and sweaty. There was nothing he could do. Forzani was dead, sure enough, and as dead as a doornail, as Sherman said.

Zack looked back to the small table that Forzani kept water bottles, next to his books.

Zack opened a bottle of water and emptied it. Forzani had a coronary. Simple as that.

"Thanks, Sherman. Damn. A contract killer from Texas," he said, gulping more water.

Zack walked out. It was the end of the day. Josie was long gone. He met a ward clerk at the elevator.

"Problem in Dr. Forzani's office, Miss. Check it out," Zack said.

There was a waste basket at the elevator. On top of the basket sat a large, white, Stetson. Zack picked it up. He smiled.

"They'll never find Sherman," he said to himself, as he fingered the Stetson, wondering if he should he keep it.

"Pardon, Doctor? Talking to me?" A nurse asked as she came out of the elevator.

"No. If that's even his name," he said to himself with a grin.

CHAPTER 33

Father Esau Roberts

I t was early the next morning when his phone rang in his office. Zack was still absorbing the tragic-comical scene from Forzani's office. He was wondering what happened to Sherman, and if he received more money from the stepfather for the way he killed Forzani.

Duke, snoring heavily, lying near his master's desk, awoke and snuffled rudely at being wakened. The ward aide was on the other end of the line. "A priest, a certain Father Roberts, is sitting outside of your office, Doctor."

Zack grimaced. He told the ward clerk to tell Roberts to wait. He had second thoughts about seeing the priest. He was in no mood to see the eunuch after dealing with Massimo, Sherman, and the sordid details of Forzani's cardiovascular demise. Now he had to deal with another fly in the ointment; someone who was probably a pedophilic priest who wanted something from him.

Just prior to the ward aide's call, Zack hung up after listening to

O'Flanagan's tirade on the phone.

"Fuck. Now I need to set up a hospital memorial ceremony in order to commemorate that prick Forzani's achievements here, after his fucking coronary. The hospital board voted on it this morning," O'Flanagan spat into the phone.

"I agree. A pain in the ass for you, sir, but a nice thing to do." Zack smirked.

He looked up at the painting of Rembrandt on the wall to the right of his desk. He had brought it to his office after the fire at Jacinda's.

"This will be another pain in the ass," he said, looking at Rembrandt, not quite aware of the significance of the remark, now that he would be meeting with a homosexual pedophile.

He was pleased to be the new director of the psych ward. Forzani's death had been ruled as a massive heart attack by the coroner.

Dr. O'Flanagan would pay homage and tribute to Forzani publicly, and then again privately at a large dinner in Forzani's honor. Graciously, the chief would bestow a small scholarship to a needy foreign medical student, as a tangible symbol in Forzani's name. Zack had made that recommendation.

"Nothing more was ever heard of Sherman, old man," he said, talking to the painting, walking about his office, again looking at Rembrandt. Zack was sure the old man had a critical snicker on his slim, pale lips, just staring down at him.

Zack pointed a hostile finger at the painting. "Fuck you, old man. I've got it all now. Three more issues that need to be taken care of, know-it-all. I need to get the hospital board to name me a professor at the university, as head of the psych ward; thus bestowing me a lifetime tenure with a fat salary, which O'Flanagan will agree to. Then, I won't need that second income and dealing with Paddy, who will remain silent once Georgie girl is cut. Third, I need to get that Frankenstein, Carlos, to London, and then I can have Maria all to myself."

His hostile mood was interrupted by the rap on his door.

"Okay, okay. He has to want something from me, but he, too, will have to give me something back," he muttered, as he reluctantly went to his door and opened it.

He thanked the ward clerk, who had been waiting and then rapped on his door again. He watched as Father Roberts rose from the chair outside his office and, with much effort, waddled in.

The priest was in the same dark, wrinkled jacket, which openly defied the struggling buttons. The off-color black trousers still needed pressing. His narrow belt, now a large, heavy rope, similar to what monks wore, couldn't contain the abdominal mass, which was desperately seeking liberty.

Zack closed the door. The priest stood in the middle of the small room. He remained silent. His fingers were locked in front of him, and his hands slowly rocked up and down, clutching a chain that held a large, silver cross.

"Nice rug," he said as he moved the small, Persian runner with his foot.

Did he know it was taken from Lani's opulent room the day she left for London? Zack had gone to see her to say good-bye.

"Thanks," was all Zack said.

Roberts looked at Zack's desk. "No photos on the desk, Doctor. You know, of family, or children? Your dog, here?"

"Family? No, don't have any here. Yes, my good friend, Duke."

"Nice. I like black Labs. Nice," he said, going to Duke and patting him on the head. He scratched his ears, and Duke gave a muffled growl. Roberts backed away.

"He won't bite."

Roberts looked around. "Just a picture of Rembrandt van Rijn? Nice."

Zack didn't respond. Instead, he motioned with his head to the chair, indicating the priest should sit. Zack moved behind his desk.

Duke got up, scratched his ear with his hind leg—ridding himself of the sweaty hand's perspiration—settled into the corner, and then peered at the strange-looking man.

Zack and dog watched the ample body fold itself into the seat. Roberts bent over and lifted his right leg across the other chunky one. A small, black, leather purse, so strangely tiny compared to the large body next to it, hung from Robert's shoulder.

He rested a Bible on his knee. He said nothing.

"What's this about?" Zack asked impatiently. He decided to be nice to the priest. After all, Baker told him that the Catholics would build the new psych wing, if they could swing the necessary funding from Massimo. That seemed to be the only fly in the still unresolved, sticky mess.

The priest was perspiring heavily as he shifted his body in the tight chair. Zack sat back and waited as Roberts used a large, red kerchief to mop his bald head. Roberts opened his Bible and ever-so-softly read a passage. He then kissed the gold cross that hung around his neck.

The priest uncorked his legs, stretched, and then walked over to one of the two windows in the room. He dabbed the beads of sweat at the back of his neck, and then tried to open one window. A hundred years of grime and dozens of coats of paint prevented him from opening the window.

He turned and looked at Zack. "The Catholic Church is threatening to expel me. They know that I was a pedophile. Some of the boys, now grown men, accused me, way back then. That now includes O'Flanagan's son. He used to be my altar boy."

Shit, Zack thought. *O'Flanagan's son is not a good mixture in my plans for a new wing. Another damn fly in the ointment, Paddy.* He got up and moved to the window. "Was once? Are you serious? Once a pedophile, always a pedophile. You know that," Zack said as he heaved open the other window with difficulty.

Sweaty body odor slowly cleared as a breeze blew in.

"Oh, God. I'm so glad you see it my way," the priest said with a faint smile.

Zack's eye twitched. He had been suckered in by the fat man, but

Zack was thinking rapidly, and he wanted to lead him on. Then he could spring his own trap. "See it your way?"

Roberts wheezed. Zack watched his belly jiggle as pulmonary bronchi gasped for oxygen, which was now flooding in from the open widow.

"You have to help me, Doctor. I read about you psychiatrists, and your work with long-term therapy, writing disability reports for men like me. Maybe there's some medicine, estrogens, prescribed by you, which could help suppress my libido. Not that there is much libido now, but the church would be impressed with the therapy. I could retire comfortably with a letter from you. Please. The church would think I'm trying to be therapeutically-compliant by taking meds," he pleaded, this time with his hands pressed in prayer.

Zack sat down.

"Sorry. Pedophiles can't be cured, especially homosexual pedophiles. They are born homosexual. They are immature characters who are attracted to young, immature males."

Finally, Roberts smiled. "Yes, yes, please go on."

Zack shook his head, and he pointed at Roberts with the pen on his desk. "Look, pedophiles aren't curable with hormone medication or psychotherapy, especially at your age. Maybe an endocrinologist, a hormone specialist, can help you."

"I read about your friend in the papers who does transplants. Could he give me two testicles from a young man? You know, to naturally provide hormones for me? I could change, Doctor. The Vatican would be impressed if I accepted surgery," he said, as his eyes misted over.

Zack softened. "Sorry. My friend doesn't do testicles."

Roberts looked up at Zack. "Well, can you please put that in writing: that I'm incurable with surgery, but hormones would help. I need something else from you. Please."

Here it comes. "Like what?" Zack stupidly asked.

The priest turned toward the window. He appeared solemn as he looked up at the bright, blue sky.

"I know that pedophilia is a classified mental disorder."

"So it is. You've been reading."

Roberts went on, slowly and methodically, as he pointed a thick, hairless finger, with bitten cuticles, at Zack.

"Since it is, and since you said what you did about pedophiles, I need a psychiatrist to write a letter saying I'm mentally ill, psychologically immature, or that I have a hormone deficiency, which is also a medical disability. Just state that: that I'm a pedophile, medically and mentally ill. And that I can't be cured but—yes. Yes, that's it. That you find I'm compliant with treatment, medication, and any other therapy you might prescribe."

"What good would a letter do?" he asked, finally understanding what the meeting was for.

Roberts smiled as he tightened the strands on the neatly-spun web. He clutched the Bible and the gold cross against his pendulous breasts, beneath the wrinkled jacket.

"Please listen. The church will give me a pension. If I'm mentally disabled then I'll get a disability pension. That's what the insurance contract the church has with me states. Let me get this right." He squinted and looked beyond the window at a robin, who had a worm dangling from its mouth while perched on the tree outside.

Zack knew what the priest needed. A report. A medical-legal letter. That letter from a psychiatrist would certify him disabled, and he could live well on a pension.

He waited. Duke shifted. Roberts sweated, and Rembrandt smiled, enjoying the circus unfolding before him.

The priest focused on Rembrandt, but he turned from the beady eyes, which stared back at him. He shuddered, but then the words came to him. "It said if the patient has a mental or physical disorder, then he's classified as disabled. I would get a disability pension, and I could live comfortably in the church hostel nearby until I die."

His eyes watered as he took out his cross again and kissed it.

Zack recalled Baker's and Hector's statements of the Catholics helping build a new ward. *A medical-legal letter in exchange for a new psych ward. That meant money. Lots and lots of money. That was easy,* Zack thought.

"I'll have to think about how to phrase it."

"Thank you, Doctor. Thank you. That disability, and Mr. Hector's financial gift to the parish to help hide a man out of the country, will see me through my old age," the priest said as he partially stood up and offered his hand.

Here was another unexpected zinger for Zack. Again it was about Carlos, and smuggling him from place to place, that made him uneasy. "Hector?" he asked, almost choking on his name. *Does anything get past this priest?*

"Yes, my son. I'll do it for him, and for this ward. Your ward. I heard about dear Dr. Forzani. All I need is a favor from you, and we can smuggle that man through the church, underground. We can hide him from parish to parish, as the Catholics did with the Italian Jews during the war. He'll be gone. His wife will be yours, my son," Roberts said in a hushed tone, with a sly grin on his thick lips.

Zack couldn't believe what he heard. *Who else knew about Maria?*

"I don't need that kind of info. Keep it to yourself, priest," Zack said angrily.

"I will. I will; sorry. I didn't mean . . ."

Zack cut him off abruptly. "Look, I'll give you a letter, and a referral to an endocrinologist to give you the prescriptions for estrogens, which hopefully will help quell your desires. Your parish head, whoever that is, and your church, will be impressed. I need something in return."

"Money? Yes, my son. I can pay you. Anything you want," the fat man smiled, having landed the fly in his web.

Zack appeared to be in thought, but he had it all planned out in his mind. "No. No money. Not your money. I want you to make a deal with Marcia Baker, and with Massimo's funds, to get Dr. Sean O'Flanagan to build me a new psych ward here."

The priest smiled. "Yes, my son, I will, I will. My diocese, with Mr. Hector and Marcia Baker's help, will build you a new wing. We must name it after Massimo, however. The San Marco wing, my son," the priest said quickly, as he pushed off the chair and stood, his head bobbing up and down in glee.

Zack nodded in agreement. "Okay, okay. Call it what you will, but stop calling me your son. It's a deal, but I want Baker to get it in writing—official like, from you."

The priest didn't show any emotion as he nodded. He came to Zack and offered his hand. Zack reluctantly embraced his sweaty palm and shook it. The priest bowed, and slowly backed out of the room, bowing again as he left. He smiled, and left the door ajar.

The priest turned to face Zack. "I have Mr. Massimo's check already. I am only the Lord's shepherd, Doctor. I tend to my flock, but we can help each other," he said, giving a low whistle to Duke.

"Sounds like it, Father Roberts."

"Oh, by the way, our Mr. Massimo will also need a letter from you. Just to say he is insane. For the judge. So we can care for him in the mental hospital, and not in a prison, since he made so many threats as a paranoid, and attacked a man at the bar."

Damn, Zack thought. *More medical reports, but for a new wing, it is a good deal.*

Zack decided to be nice. "Can do, Father," he said, emphasizing the paternal epithet.

The priest stopped at the open door. "You look sad. Did you lose someone, my son?" he asked, making a cross with his hand.

The priest must have known about Jacinda, or maybe Holly and Katrina, but Zack said nothing. The priest walked away.

Zack turned to look at the Rembrandt print on the wall. The old man was glaring down at him. He could feel the mean, ferocious look in his piercing, critical eyes. The thin, pursed lips turned into a scowl.

Zack pointed at the print. "What else could I do, man?" he asked, almost apologetically.

He waited, but there was no answer. Just the scowl.

"Fuck you. You know fucking well that they all want something from me. Maria and Carlos, Baker, Hector, Georgie, and now a friggin' priest connected to Massimo San Marco. I give all of them something, and I get a new wing. And now a prescription for estrogens for the priest from an endocrinologist, which he will get, and a set of testicles from a plastic surgeon, which he won't get."

Zack walked about the room. Duke was sitting up, nervous from the vile hostility. He got up and followed Zack from one end of the room to the other, close on his heels.

Zack and the dog stopped. He again turned to the painting. "I want something in return. I'll help Carlos and get him to Sam, after what that fucker, Gomez, did to Jacinda, and to Holly and the little girl," Zack shouted with a vengeance, as he again walked back and forth in his office.

Rembrandt's eyes followed him wherever he went. Duke cowered under the desk, fearful of the shouting. "Then I get Maria. The psych ward is mine. Forzani is toast. Baker and O'Flanagan are in my back pocket. Paddy will be happy with Georgie girl. Carlos will be out of my hair. Me and my Seema. And Aesha," he said softly, so only Rembrandt would hear the confession.

He peered at the print.

Was there a hint of a smile this time?

CHAPTER 34

The Last of Sam the Man

It was only a few short days later when Sam called Zack, breathless. "Hey, buddy. I read the latest Chicago Tribune sitting in Hyde Park this morning while having a coffee. What the hell?! Forzani's obit was in it; coronary, according to his stepdaughter's write up. No shit."

"No shit, for sure," Zack replied, but he was surprised that Sam had heard about it from in Europe. It was early morning—mid afternoon in London. He was also surprised that Selma, Forzani's stepdaughter, took the trouble to write up the obituary, after what Forzani did to her as a young girl.

Zack was glad to hear from Sam. "Yeah, Sam. Massive fucking coronary. Dead as a doornail, the surgical ward nurse said when she found him. He was sprawled over his desk that evening. 'Dead as a doornail,' she told everyone. She did."

"Fucker had it coming to him. Poor Selma. But she did well from the half-million he paid her for calling off the child sex abuse scandal back then. That would have put the nail in his coffin, if she would have signed that state attorney's document."

"Yeah. She called me and said she wanted to do that obit. It was in the local papers here, too. The obit was brief, but she said something about it gave her closure after her years of abuse and therapy."

Zack heard Sam take a gulp of his coffee. He then asked, "So you're in charge now? That was fortuitous. Coronary? Bullshit. Someone must have had something on him, and he beat the rap, did he?"

Zack wasn't going to tell his buddy the truth. He could never keep a secret, and he would have spilled the beans, no doubt. "Yep. No shit, Sam. Fortuitous, for sure. But listen up, man. This mafia type, Carlos, will be coming soon. You fix him up, man. Do your stuff on his face. Some local, wealthy bozo, who is a flipping do-gooder, will have a passport and first-class tickets for him to London."

Zack heard Sam opening the lid of a trash can and throwing his coffee cup into it. "I'll be glad to see him, and his gorgeous Maria, as you called her. Is she still the babe that she was? Good looker with nice tits?"

Zack was thinking fast. *Should he tell Sam everything? About the deal with Maria and Hector, the do-gooder?* "Well…uh, not quite…Well, yeah, she still has nice tits, but she's staying here, Sam."

Zack could hear the penny drop. "Aha, so you send Carlos, and she stays with you? You were always a fast one, Zack. Always a fast one. Thinking of yourself."

Zack scowled. *Should I tell him to fuck off?* "Well, shit, Sam. You'd do the same if you saw her, man," Zack said apologetically, and he attempted a slight chuckle.

"He would do better in recovery with his wife here, buddy. He'll need all the support he can get. Send her with him, man. Maybe, after that, you could have her," Sam said sternly.

Zack almost hung up, but he knew he still needed Sam to comply with the deal. If he didn't, all his well-laid plans would be scuttled. "Yeah. You're right, Sam. She'll follow him soon after. She told me she has to finalize the family estate, the will, and all that stuff. Sell their villa and city house, after her mother died. Then she'll be there once you've done your stuff. She'll be there, buddy, for his rehab. For sure, Sam. Okay?" Zack lied again.

"Okay, buddy. That's a deal. Deal?"

Zack hesitated. "Yeah, Sam. A deal. Right after the surgery. I'll send her. Got to go, Sam. The ward is calling me. Got to go."

"Listen, buddy: before you go. What's up with Georgie and her threats?"

"Yeah. That needs to be resolved. She wants ten grand for reconstruction. She'll give me the letter she wrote that could implicate me with that fucker, Paddy, who helped me sell the speed and Dexedrine, so I have to give her the cash, Sam."

"How you going to swing it?"

"At the airport. We know that Gennero will be there, and that's when she will threaten to give him the letter. I'll have the cash for her. Bitch."

"Yeah, you can say that again."

"Bitch."

Zack hung up. He knew Sam would keep his word. He was like that. Honest, reliable, straightforward, altruistic Sam.

CHAPTER 35

Salazar

Zack was unnerved for several days after that prickly call from Sam, feeling oddly exhausted. He was still angry at Sam for what he said about him. Bastard.

He didn't spend much time on the ward due to the chaos of demolition and rebuilding of the new wing. He had to discharge some of the healthier patients, and transfer others to a hospital on the outskirts of the city. It was tiring work. It was also risky and grueling dealing with complaining relatives, many whom were nervous about the move.

Zack was pleased to be honored at a ceremony hosted by the hospital board. It was attended by O'Flanagan, all the nursing staff, hospital, and university dignitaries. It was a celebration of the first stone, commemorating the new San Marcos wing.

Baker and her photographer snapped photos for the newspapers. Zack kept sending shots from his cell to Sam and a few other friends around the world. Everyone was proud when O'Flanagan unveiled the new plaque. Zack's name and new title were front and center:

Dr. Zacharias Scarlatto, M.D., Professor and Head

Of San Marcos Psychiatric Ward, San Diego

That will impress the hell out of Sam, he thought as he waited at Jacinda's home that afternoon for Georgie girl.

———

"Are you ready, sweetie?" Georgie shouted from the kitchen patio in a high-pitched voice. She was almost a soprano after all of the estrogen she had been consuming.

Zack was ready. He had packed a small bag, loaded with Duke's favorite biscuits and dry food. He had shut the place down and arranged for security to continue twenty-four seven. "I am, babe," he replied. They both gathered their things and went to the van.

Hector and Sam were the only other ones who knew he had already written an official medical report, outlining the psychological benefits of a facial transplant, for Carlos. Sam had already sent Zack a text message. He agreed to do the microsurgery on Carlos in England.

He, again, pushed to have Maria follow, soon after surgery, and he would let Zack know when that was. It might take a few weeks to find a good replacement for his patient after all the tests were finished on Carlos.

Hector was grateful for Zack's help in hiding Carlos and in helping to get him out of the country. He left two first-class tickets on United Airlines with Georgie. She was instructed to give the package to Zack, who would then give it to Carlos and Maria.

Georgie was excited to go to Vegas with Zack after the airport stop. She stepped out of the van and handed Zack the packet.

She had spent the day in the beauty parlor getting her tresses bleached, a manicure, and pedicure. She was wearing a flower-patterned blouse with a tight, layered, pink miniskirt. She'd had her legs waxed, and had slipped her feet into five-inch high heels. Her new, extended breast implants were accentuated by her height.

Zack smiled. She looked gorgeous as she announced, "I'm performing at the Silver Studs Club at the Silver Nugget, in Vegas, darling." Georgie cooed, twirling around on her heels, as she thrust her breasts toward him.

"Nice, Georgie, real nice," Zack said with a whistle. He walked back into the house, telling Georgie he forgot something in his room. He opened the packet once he was inside, and he looked at the tickets. He took Maria's ticket out of the packet, and put her ticket in his back pocket. She was going to stay with Zack, and he would be rid of Carlos, once and for all.

Zack locked the doors to the house, checked with the security staff, and walked back to the van. Just as he opened the car door to let Duke in, his cell phone rang. "Hope to hell it's not the hospital. I'm still off duty," he said. He closed the door, and then took the call outside, away from Georgie.

It was Maria. She was speaking in a muffled tone.

Zack told Georgie it was the hospital, and he instructed for her to wait a few minutes.

He moved away from the SUV and around to the side of the house, but away from the security guard, who was walking about, checking the doors and windows.

"I wanted to say good luck to you, Zack. I know I agreed to be with you, and I will. Carlos believes we have tickets, and we will go to Seattle, where he thinks he'll be safe. He will go alone, and I'll stay with you. Carlos is wearing a hat over his tattoo, and some of his beard has grown out. No one will recognize him at the airport."

The fear in her voice was palpable as she repeated, "No one will recognize him. Hector said we could meet at the airport to say good-bye to Carlos, Zack. Hector said you had some good news for us. What is it?"

He wasn't going to tell her over the phone that the ticket was for Carlos to fly to Heathrow, in London, and not to Seattle. "I'll be at the airport in an hour. The good news is that Carlos will have the medical certificate for Sam, and a first-class ticket for Seattle. Where will we meet?"

"Gennero, he said he'd meet us at the airport also. Just to make sure we got away safely on the plane to Seattle. His men will then meet Carlos and give him protection. The flight leaves at eight o'clock tonight. I'm so frightened, Zack."

"Wait for me. I'll meet you at the airport parking lot, outside near the departure hanger. Don't worry, I'll be there."

Zack said *adios* to the well-armed Mexican guard, and to his buddy patrolling the villa. He then jumped into the rear, pushing Duke aside to make room. Fifi was stretched out on the front seat, snoring softly after taking the tranquillizer tablet that both Georgie and Fifi were now addicted to.

"We have a brief diversion to Lindbergh Field, the airport just north of town. Have you recovered from that horrendous loss, Georgie?" Zack asked. Georgie only nodded, but said nothing about Katrina.

"Georgie has been on those little pills, for under the tongue. I gave some to little Fifi, too. Do you have the money for Georgie?" she asked, looking at Zack in the rear view mirror.

Zack nodded. "Yeah. In my case here. A money order made out to you, for ten grand, for your penile surgery and a new vagina. Drive quickly, Georgie, but carefully.

"Do you have the letter you said you would write, exposing Paddy and me to O'Flanagan and the university?" he asked.

"Yes, sweetie. In my bra. Next to my nice, new silicone tits. I got them with the first installment you gave me."

"That's the ten big ones, and no more after that, right, Georgie?"

"Right on, sweetie," Georgie replied, avoiding Zack's eyes in the rearview.

By the time they got to the departure hanger, the sun was a red, glowing ball in the sky amidst dark, threatening clouds. Zack easily spotted Maria and Carlos waiting beside an old van. It was in a deserted corner of the parking lot.

As airplanes lumbered by and then lifted off, Zack could feel the ground shake from the turbulence. Georgie slowed down. The lot was vacant. Zack looked around. No black Hummers. That was good.

"Get closer to those two over there," he said, pointing to Maria and Carlos. Georgie slowly maneuvered her car toward the two figures huddled in the mist.

Just as Zack stepped out of Hector's Mercedes SUV, another car pulled up.

"That's detective, Gennero," Georgie shouted. She was happy to see him again as he got out of his beat-up Chevy.

Another pale, young, and wiry man wearing a black leather jacket and blue jeans got out next to Gennero. The grungy detective slammed the door twice on the rusty old car. It had rolled a few times. The driver's front fender was missing, and the trunk was wired shut with bailing wire.

Zack held on to Duke and clipped the leash onto his collar once they were outside the SUV. Man and animal were hesitant as they approached Carlos and Maria in the rolling mist that was gathering about them.

The thunder of engines in the distance, and a sooty fog from the still-running motors, slowly covered the anxious group. Duke could sense the tension in the air. He slunk close to the ground, coughing from the thick exhaust fumes that surrounded him.

Zack motioned to Gennero to stay where he was.

Gennero gave a shaky salute.

"Let them have a minute, Billy. Settle down, fella. We have time, you know," Gennero yelled to his assistant, a young kid, as they both leaned on the Chevy, shining a flashlight at the small crowd. Billy the kid was jittery, bouncing about from foot to foot, sensing some action, and wanting to get in on it.

Zack looked at the worried pair. Maria wore a long, tan-colored raincoat, with a black scarf wound tightly around her head. She gripped her husband's hand, uncertain, as they both watched Gennero's movements.

Georgie stayed in her car with Fifi, who had stirred awake and started yapping. She was scratching at the windows, wanting to get out after she saw Duke.

Zack came closer. His knees were weak from tension. Duke wasn't so sure. He was straining on the leash, but followed slowly. Carlos had his arm around Maria, and he pulled her into his body. He had on a wide-brimmed, brown fedora, which was pulled over his face. He wore a heavy topcoat with its collars turned up.

The two were tightly-pressed against each other. The occasional passing cloud shed a few raindrops. A cold fog swirled about, circling Duke, sending a chill down Zack's neck, and forcing Maria into the arms of Carlos.

The beacon from Gennero's flashlight held Carlos in a rigid stance, but the frightened man kept blinking wildly in order to avoid the glare. The scars were still visible on both cheeks, and his face was distorted regardless of his miserable, scrawny beard; but the hat, and the developing darkness, hid the blue tattoos on his forehead. The fog gradually came and went, but the grotesque facial features were still visible to Zack.

Just as Zack approached Maria and Carlos, a black Lexus SUV suddenly appeared and skidded on the wet pavement. It came to a halt near the group.

Zack's neck muscles went into a spasm, recognizing Salazar's vehicle from the Acapulco meeting. Duke pulled Zack away, fearfully, as the SUV neared Maria and Carlos. Duke could smell danger.

A large and muscular man jumped out, slamming the door shut with a thud. Zack recognized the big Mexican immediately. It was Gomez. Duke tugged on his leash and gave a low, throaty growl. He was ready to have a go at Gomez once again.

Zack pulled up on the leash, "Steady, boy. Easy goes it."

Gomez shone a powerful beam at one, and then at another, in the group, using a heavy, two-foot-long flashlight, which could easily be used as a weapon, if need be.

Zack watched Gomez slowly approaching. He was wearing a tight-fitting, white T-shirt, bearing the logo of Zack's favorite hockey team. The Philadelphia Flyer's crest was partly covered by the blue denim overalls reaching up to his chest. An open army jacket covered his broad shoulders, and a black leather belt, encrusted with massive silver coins, circled his belly.

Zack, transfixed by the size of this gorilla, stepped back. He was uncertain of what to do, and looked about for an easy escape route. He recognized the massive blade dangling from Gomez's belt, the one that had felled Holly and his canine friend at the safe house. Zack was sure he had other armament dangling from that belt at his side.

No one moved, except for Gennero, who suddenly stepped forward. "Stay put, Billy. No funny stuff," he said to Billy the kid, who started to make a move toward the Mexican's SUV, opening his leather jacket, hoping to impress Gomez and show him that he too, had a weapon.

The big man turned and smiled broadly at Gennero, and then he sneered at the kid, waving him off like a pesky mosquito.

Gomez quickly found what he came for, and he fixed his light on Carlos. "Hold it right there, Carlos. You're coming with me, Mister. Your pretty wife can stay here, but I'm taking you back to Mexico City," he ordered gruffly.

Zack felt certain that there was someone else in the SUV; the back window slowly rolled down a few inches. Pedro? *Unlikely*, Zack thought. *Pedro would want to be in on any developing skirmish.*

Zack waited as Gennero came toward Gomez, and he slowly brought out the small, plastic bag from his back pocket. Zack recognized the rolling tobacco cigarette makings from his visit with Georgie.

Zack watched the man awkwardly fumble for a cigarette he'd already rolled.

The big brute ignored Gennero's actions, and pointed to the runway in the distance. "I've got a private plane waiting for us on the tarmac,

Carlos. Little man, you stay where you are," Gomez said, shining his light on Gennero, and then on Billy.

Gennero shrugged off the threat, and continued to mumble something under his breath about fucking Mexicans. He finally found the cigarette and stuck it in his mouth, again motioning to Billy to stop muttering out loud.

"Aha, Gomez. Welcome to America once more. Can I see your passport?" Gennero said with a sarcastic laugh.

Stupid to attempt humor and silly talk at a time like this, Zack thought.

Gomez disregarded Gennero's caustic welcome and pointed to Carlos, "Don't worry man; you'll be safe with me." He turned to his right and pulled back his jacket, showing off a leather gun holster that hung from the belt. Next to it hung a massive knife. A pair of handcuffs was also fastened to his belt.

Gennero took three steps toward Gomez. "How the fuck did you get through the border with that pistol, Gomez?" he asked with a pronounced wheeze.

Gomez gave out a sharp laugh and then dramatically bent back in fear. "You shoulda stuck to bringing in the crazies from those sleazy bars you drink at, Gennero. You're no fucking good here."

Gennero pointed to the SUV. "Where's that pussy pounder, that black, one-eyed, stuttering goon of yours, Gomez?" Gennero asked.

Gomez snickered. "Pedro? I put two slugs in his back in Tijuana. He was on top of my sister, that mother fucker."

"No shit. Well, at least the poor bugger died doing what he did best. Big loss to all the women in the Mexican hill towns, you know, Gomez," Gennero said with a grin.

Zack felt relief to hear about Pedro. He felt much safer now. He stepped back from Maria and Carlos, pulling Duke with him. He was convinced that Gennero was suicidal, and he was going to stay clear of any stray bullets.

"Yeah, I lost Pedro, but I've got Carlos," Gomez quipped with a toothy grin.

"Well, for fuck's sake, maybe you got me this time too, Gomez," Gennero said meekly.

"You're damn right I have," the big man sneered. "Now, you, and your Billy boy there, better just toss your guns down on the tarmac, and kick them away from you."

Gennero shrugged, but threw his gun down, and, after motioning to Billy to do the same, the kid reluctantly obeyed.

Gennero stood there, fumbling in his pockets for a match and sucking on a soggy cigarette as the clammy fog circled the group. He did as he was told, and kicked both pistols away in Zack's direction.

Gomez was still grinning as he looked down in disdain at the little detective who had finally found a match. Zack waited, helpless. He felt an eternity unfold before him as all the actors were standing still, frozen in this eerie scene. Everyone was waiting to see what Gennero was going to do, and if Billy was going to do something foolish.

Gennero slowly chewed on the old butt, and spat a few strands of tobacco at Gomez's feet.

The next brazen act was a sure way to get Gennero killed. He walked back, and stupidly struck the wooden match on the side of Gomez's SUV.

Zack winced, with heart pumping. *Dumb, stupid, stupid man. A reckless act if ever there was one.*

The heavy match, striking the silver truck, left a wide, sulfur mark on the hood, immediately setting off the high-pitched yowl of the car's alarm.

The set of high beams started blinking on and off. The alarm wailed, incessantly. Zack saw the back window close shut. The SUV rocked back and forth in unison to the wail of the shrieking alarm.

Gomez jumped back at the sound screaming in his ears and the flashing lights, which nearly blinded him. Gomez swore at Gennero as he tried to keep an eye on his quarry. He fumbled through his jacket pockets, searching for the remote.

Gennero was a dead man, Zack thought for certain.

Gomez wheeled back at the detective as he hung his right thumb over his belt buckle, near to his holster, and held his jacket back with his left hand.

"Too bad, Gennero. You lose. You had your chance. We had a man on Carlos all the time. I'm taking him back to Mexico with me."

Gennero said nothing. He slowly sucked on his cigarette and blew the smoke at Gomez. "You win, Gomez; I lose," Gennero said with a hangdog look.

Gomez grinned, and kicked one of the tires. He finally found the right button on his remote, and punched the button to shut the alarm off. The back window opened, slightly more this time.

Zack was thinking of slowly inching his way back to Georgie's car, pulling Duke. He was ready to take off, but he felt obligated to be near Maria, and do whatever he could for her. He sensed a gunfight developing, and he knew Gomez would be the winner, taking Carlos with him.

Gennero took a last, deep drag, coughed, and then flicked his cigarette on the pavement, right at Gomez's feet. It landed on his newly-shined black boots.

"Oh, sorry about that, my friend," he said sarcastically as he took five awkward steps forward. He stomped on the butt, at the same time kicking at Gomez's foot.

Gomez was thoroughly irritated by the kick, and the constant whine of the car alarm. He was angry with the scratch on his car, and irritated with Georgie's small dog, who was still yapping close by. Georgie, who was sobbing wildly, stood outside her vehicle and jumped up and down in fear. Billy the kid was making threatening noises again, puffing himself up. As if to have a run at Gomez.

Gomez shook his head and sneered, disregarded Gennero, and made his move toward Carlos. "I'm putting the cuffs on you, Carlos. It's just a precaution. Don't worry. You'll be safe. Your missus will go back with the detective, here."

Gomez reached around with his right hand to get his handcuffs for Carlos, and, at the same time, pulled out his huge pistol. Carlos looked into the distance as he considered running again, with or without Maria. He knew he'd be gunned down if he moved. Duke strained at the leash, wanting to jump at Gomez.

Gennero stood back, but it was Billy, the stupid kid, who bent down and pulled out a small, Double Tap derringer, a two-shot pistol, out from his sock. It was a tiny shooter, but he shouted and aimed it at Gomez.

Gomez was faster. He took aim and fired a round off at Billy. The bullet winged Billy in his left bicep, and went clean through the muscle. Billy, in pain, dropped his small gun, and wailed that he'd been shot.

Gomez took a few steps forward and kicked the gun away, letting Billy roll about on the tarmac, holding his left arm with his right hand. Then Gomez turned toward Carlos again.

Zack was frozen. He didn't know what to do. He suddenly felt Carlos nudge him in the ribs, and point at Billy's original gun, which was at his feet, kicked there by Gennero earlier. He mouthed something at Zack, "Shoo' the asstard." Zack looked down at the pistol just as Duke pulled himself away and jumped at Gomez.

Gomez, with his arm extended holding his pistol and still pointing it at Billy, whirled about as Duke jumped the Mexican and clamped his fangs on his right wrist.

The big man howled in pain and dropped his gun. It was then when Zack picked up Billy's gun off the tarmac.

Carlos' words propelled him into action, *"Shoot the bastard."* Zack fired at the open chest that was now facing him. Duke's jaw was still clamped on to Gomez's right wrist.

Gennero heard the loud pop. Duke still had his fangs on Gomez's wrist, and Gomez slumped down onto his knees, almost falling over onto Duke, who, only then, reluctantly let go.

Zack, still holding the pistol and aiming it at Gomez, lest he get up off his knees, was uncertain what to do now.

Maria pushed Carlos away, still fearing Gomez, uncertain if he was dead. Fifi was frantic, and Georgie sharply cried out and spun around, looking for her shoes, running behind her car, and hiding.

Zack, heart pounding and adrenalin rushing through his body at the courageous action, threw the gun down, and went to pull Duke away from the body that was slumped down on the tarmac.

Billy ran to Gennero's side, picking up his gun on the way.

Maria turned to Carlos, who mouthed something again in praise of Zack, and then he wrapped his arms around Maria and held her tightly.

The heavy fog whirled about the group as Zack peered through the rolling mist. He saw Gomez, wide-eyed, and incredulous on his knees, look down to see blood slowly saturating his hairy chest and oozing onto his white shirt.

His powerful body slumped to the ground and into a puddle of grease and oil. His white T-shirt had a red blotch right on the Philadelphia Flyers logo. It was neatly centered between his black suspenders.

Gennero quickly picked up his own revolver and pointed at Gomez, just in case he moved. He then told everyone to stand back. "Billy, you saw him go for his gun, didn't you? He was going to shoot me, you know, the bastard. Get the names of all the witnesses. I've been waiting to get this prick for years. He was out to get me, Billy."

"Yeah, he sure was, boss," Billy the kid said, having somewhat recovered from his arm wound. He walked over, and he kicked at the inert body. Billy was just happy to have something to do.

"Good shooting, boss. I never did like them there Flyers from Philly," Billy said, holding his wounded left shoulder with his right hand, and giving Gomez another sharp kick in the groin.

Gennero put his pistol back in the holster. He bent over Gomez and gave him a sharp slap in the face. Gomez didn't twitch.

Gennero took a kerchief from his back pocket. He then took Billy's gun, and wiped off Zack's prints from the hand grip. He then took the dead man's pistol and fired off a round into the air.

Gennero then jammed it back into Gomez's right hand, and made sure that those acts would be evidence enough that it was he, not Zack or Billy, who shot Gomez, since it was Gomez who was going to shoot Gennero.

Billy moved forward and looked down at the body. "Yeah, I sure did see him go for his gun, boss. That was a close one. He was going to shoot you all right…look at that, boss, he had it out, in his hand… shooting. He missed you. Bad shot. Bad shot. I'll write it all down. With names of the witnesses."

"Good man. Would have got me, Billy. Sure as hell, he would have."

"Sure as hell, boss," Billy said as he shoved his own small derringer back into his sock again.

Zack went to Gomez, freeing Duke from his leash now that it was safe to do so, and he put his hand on the dead man's neck. There was no evidence of a heartbeat.

"Serves you right, Gomez. This one is for you, Duke old pal," he said as he gave the head a little nudge with his elbow. Duke moved about, sniffing at Gomez here and there, making sure he was dead.

While Gennero was away for a few minutes, talking to Billy and telling him what to write in his notepad, Zack turned Gomez's hand over, and pulled out his huge pistol. He turned to Gennero and Billy, waving the shooter at both of them.

"Just stay back, both of you. Don't think I won't shoot, Gennero. I'll tell your men that Gomez got you and Billy. They'll believe me."

Gennero just stood there. Perplexed, worried. "Okay, okay. I'll just wait. I'll get Carlos when he goes up north. It will be easy to find him with that cut-up mug. Stand back, Billy," he said.

"Throw your guns on the tarmac again. Both of you, and hurry up," Zack ordered, nervous with a gun in his hand again. The pistol was shaking violently.

Both Gennero and Billy did as instructed. Zack kicked both revolvers away, toward Maria and Carlos. "And, you, Billy, toss that pea shooter over here, also," Zack added.

Billy said something under his breath, but he bent down, and brought out his derringer. He threw it at Zack's feet.

Zack tried to keep his gun aimed at Gennero and Billy, but it was difficult, as Zack was nervous holding such a pistol and also trying to think fast about Maria and Carlos.

He took Carlos by the arm and pulled him aside. "Look, we may not have much time. Here is a first-class ticket for you to London. It's leaving in a couple of hours. Be on it."

"Londah?" Carlos croaked, as his face went into a severe spasm.

Then Zack pulled the other airline ticket from his inside back pocket and handed it to Maria. Zack looked at Carlos. "I've got a medical-legal report saying you need a total facial transplant, for your psychological health. My friend in London, the plastic surgeon, said he'd meet you at Heathrow when you arrive."

Carlos took the packet with the ticket, and he made another attempt at a grisly smile. Zack pocketed the gun, not knowing what to do with it in case it went off.

Maria came to Zack, ready to stay with him, as she had promised. Zack pulled her aside and whispered, "I'm staying here with Gennero, Maria. To keep him occupied, while you get on that flight with Carlos."

"Me? Me to go with Carlos, Zack? I thought I was staying with you, as I had promised," she said, almost in tears, unsure of what she heard.

Zack took her hand. "You belong to Carlos. You always did. You always will, Maria."

"He knows I was with you that night in Mexico City, Zack."

Zack focused his eyes on Maria. "You told him about us?"

Maria pulled her scarf tightly around her head. "He knows I tried to convince you—with his money and with my body. I love him, and I'd do anything to help him."

"I know that now, Maria."

"I could have been with you, Zack. I really could have."

"You couldn't be with me, Maria. I see that now. I still have work to do here, and you can't be with me. It's always been you and Carlos."

"I did love you, Zack," she said and added calmly, "I'm carrying a child, but I was ready to be with you." She brushed away the tears that were streaming down her face.

Zack reared back. "Child. Pregnant? Can't be. Mine?"

"No. Carlos is the father. It's all right, Zack. It's his. It's all right," she whispered.

Zack nodded, and put his hand on Maria's shoulder. "Go to London. Have the baby. You'll be happy with Carlos; he's your husband. Wherever you decide to live, you belong together."

As she moved away slowly, crying still, Carlos gently took her arm. They started on their departure.

A shout from Gennero froze everyone again. They all turned to see the back door of the SUV open. And there he was. Salazar was in the back seat, trying to free a rifle from the gun rack.

Salazar pushed his obese body out of the car after freeing the automatic rifle. He plodded toward the small group, unsteady and limping from an arthritic knee. Zack was terrified and moved back. Suddenly, he saw Maria pick up Gennero's gun from where it had landed, close to her.

She took the pistol, walked several steps forward, and pointed it at Salazar. Salazar laughed as he forced his rotund body forward, raised his rifle at Maria, and kept coming at her.

Zack was sure Maria was dead. Her hand trembled so much that any shot was sure to miss.

He felt for the gun he took, but he had trouble getting the large pistol out of his tight, back pocket, where he had put it. He waited, and pulled Duke by the collar, closer to his body. Carlos backed away. Gennero and Billy just stood there. Then, they also retreated from the line of fire.

Salazar was close. He was surprised and rattled when he saw Georgie come out from behind her SUV, stumbling toward him wearing only one shoe, holding the other in her hand. She took a few steps forward, unsure which way to run.

Zack shouted at Salazar to not shoot, but that didn't matter to Salazar. He was only focused on his target. He raised his rifle and aimed it at Maria.

Maria held her ground. She fired at him as he closed in on her, but, with her unsteady hand, she missed his chest. Instead, the stray bullet hit Salazar in the left shoulder.

Salazar stumbled, stopped by the shot. He was partially winged, but equally stunned and surprised by Maria's bold act. He spun around, holding his shoulder, and dropped his rifle, swearing at Maria.

He turned back to face Maria, took a few steps, and tried to make a lunge at her. However, he had been turned sideways because of Georgie's frantic wails and arms flinging in confusion. Maria stood her ground. She took another shot. She missed his chest again, but the bullet hit Salazar in the throat, cutting his windpipe in half.

Gennero took a step toward Maria, but he saw her hand was shaking so violently that he hesitated, not knowing what she would do next.

Salazar staggered, gurgling blood filled his gullet and poured out his nose and his mouth. He bent over, picking up the rifle beside him. Maria stepped back, ready to shoot again.

Salazar croaked something that sounded like 'bitch'. Georgie, now frantic, was running about in circles. She was trying to push her ample breast back in place, which had flopped out, and she was squealing in a high-pitched voice. Salazar, confused by Georgie's sporadic moves, turned his rifle, and shot a volley at her.

Georgie screamed as the bullet from the powerful rifle hit her right hip, shattering her pelvis and lower limb. She shrieked in pain and fell over, grasping at her leg and writhing on the ground.

With Salazar preoccupied with Georgie, Maria fired again. Two more bullets hit Salazar, and, this time, they found their mark. Both bullets went through his newly-minted cross of Saint Christopher, which hung from his neck, centered on his chest.

Salazar stumbled and dropped to his knees, right at Maria's feet. The cross of Saint Christopher, Salazar's protective shield and good luck charm, had finally failed him.

Duke, who had been held by his neck by Zack, freed himself of the grip. He ran at Salazar, jumped on his back, and pushed him over. Maria calmly moved forward, took careful aim, and put another bullet into his neck.

"Fucking *cochino*. You pig. That was for my mother, and for what you did to me when I was a child," Maria sobbed.

Maria pitched the gun away. Carlos went to Maria, and he held her, wrapping his heavy coat around her as she wept, shaking uncontrollably.

Gennero finally made his move. He picked up his gun and wiped it clean of Maria's prints. He put the gun back in his holster, and walked back to find Billy.

"With Pedro, that's three down. Good shot, lady. I couldn't have done better myself," Gennero said.

Billy ran at the body. "Good shooting, boss. You got him real good, boss," Billy announced again, making notes in his little book.

Zack pushed Carlos and Maria away. "You better hurry, Maria. You'll miss that flight," Zack said, trying to regain his composure, but couldn't stop looking down at Maria's belly.

Maria followed his eyes, but only shook her head. "Too early, yet, Zack. Only three months," she said. She stepped back to join her husband, who was near the van.

She turned, looked at Zack, and waved. She walked away and didn't look back. Billy watched as she got in the car next to Carlos. They stopped briefly to look at Georgie, who was writhing on the ground, blood spurting from her leg.

"I'll help Georgie, Gennero. You call your police friends and get the ambulance," Zack shouted. He pulled the large pistol out of his back pocket and gave it to Gennero. He then ran to help Georgie.

He gasped as he looked down to see Georgie's right leg was blown to shreds by the blast. Zack bent over Georgie, and saw her leg was misshapen: at right angles compared to her body. She was screaming in pain. Blood spurted with each beat of her heart, soaking her pink skirt in bright, red blotches.

Georgie grasped Zack's shoulder as he kneeled down. She pleaded, "Help me, Zack. Help me. Call 911. Please!" she wailed.

"I will, Georgie; hang in there," he said. Zack put his hand on her hip, and he pressed hard, hoping to quell the artery from draining her dry. "I'll get a tourniquet. Take it easy. I'll stop the bleeding, but I need that letter, in case the ambulance takes you away, and they find the letter to Gennero."

"In my bra. Over my right titty. Tourniquet? Use your belt."

A large pool of blood had already formed around Georgie's pelvic area. Zack looked down at her right leg; her bone was protruding through the skin, where her thigh had been blown away. Blood was gushing like a geyser from the wound. He could see her heart was fading, as the spurts were slowly diminishing.

"Be strong, Georgie. I'll get it," he said, as he moved away from the blood. He reached into her blouse and found the letter and his money. He stuffed the bills in his shirt pocket, unfolded the note, just to be sure, read it using the van's head lights, and then folded it, and put it in his pocket.

Georgie stirred with his hand over her right breast. "The money. Put the money in my case. In the van…sweetie," she trailed off.

"Will do, Georgie. Ambulance coming. Couldn't find a tourniquet yet," he said, as she panted for breath, coughing.

She pulled him closer. "Put the check in my case in the van. Georgie will talk to Gennero, and your priest, if you cheat her," she said sternly.

"Will do, Georgie. Will do. Be brave," Zack said, patting her on the shoulder. He tried to twist her leg, ever-so-slightly, to quell the artery from spewing blood even more, but to no avail.

Georgie's breath grew shallow, and within moments, she stopped breathing. Zack felt for a pulse on her neck, but there was none. He walked away, shook his head, and put both thumbs down, indicating to Gennero that she was dead.

The ambulance would be too late.

Zack left the inert body and joined Gennero and Billy. "How's the queer one?" Gennero asked, nodding toward Georgie.

"Bled to death," Zack said, crumpling the note in his pocket into a tight, little ball.

"Pussy club will miss her, Doctor," Billy said with a hound dog look. "She was the best. Good legs," he added.

"She did her best, Billy," Zack agreed.

After a few minutes, the ambulance and two police cars pulled up to the scattered group. Lights were flashing, and sirens wailed. Duke was nervous with all the commotion.

Gennero hailed the paramedics and pointed to the three bodies, talking to the ambulance men, and joking with his police buddies. He waved to Carlos and Maria, as they began to drive away.

"Hey, take it easy, you two. I'll see you in Seattle, soon, you know," he yelled as the van sped away.

Gennero put his arm around Zack's shoulder as they left the scene. The paramedics shuffled the bodies onto stretchers as the police talked to Billy, who was in his glory, embellishing his role in the firefight. Gennero puffed on another Marlboro as they passed Georgie's crumpled body on a stretcher, and listened to Zack humming a tune.

It was *Unforgettable*, by Nat King and Natalie Cole. It had been Maria's favorite song to play when they made love together in Mexico City. It felt like another lifetime ago; a lifetime he no longer would inhabit.

The fog was as thick as pea soup, and there was a touch of misty rain coming down. Gennero put his arm around Zack's waist. "Ha. I'll have a stiff drink now. To celebrate popping that Gomez, and his boss,

Salazar. I've been waiting for those two motherfuckers. Things will be quiet around here now."

Both men laughed as they stomped on the oily puddles, as young boys are often wont to do.

"I was thinking of Maria, and what could have been. I'll miss her," Zack said, as he gently pulled Duke along toward Hector's van. He decided he would call Seema, and take her and Aesha to Vegas for a holiday, tomorrow.

He took Georgie's car keys just before her body was loaded into the ambulance.

Zack and Gennero waved back to Billy who shouted at them, "*Adios, Amigo. Hasta la vista*, my friend."

A 747 was coming in for a landing from the north, casting an eerie shadow on the group, and slicing a beam through the fog. Its powerful light struck the rear of Salazar's SUV. Zack absently glanced at the silver bumper sticker that prominently declared,

Give your life to Jesus. I did.

THE END

A BRIEF NOTE ON MR. VIDKUN QUISLING

Vidkun Quisling (1887-1945) was a military officer and politician in Norway before the Second World War. He became a close collaborator with Nazi Germany during the war. After Norway was invaded by Germany in 1940, he became the Prime Minister of the Norwegian government, but as a puppet of Hitler, known as "The Quisling Regime".

In 1945, after the war, Quisling was tried for embezzlement, the murder of many Jews, and high treason for collaboration with Germany. Found guilty, he was executed by firing squad in October, 1945. The word "quisling", often used by Churchill after the war, became synonymous with "collaborator," "traitor," and "rat fink" in many languages.

ABOUT THE AUTHOR

Dr. Lawrence E. Matrick received his M.D. degree in Medicine from the Manitoba Medical College. He subsequently worked at the Provincial Mental Hospital as a resident in psychiatry. He continued his studies in London, England and received his British degrees in Psychiatry. As a Fellow of the Canadian Royal College of Physicians and Assistant Professor in Psychiatry at the University of British Columbia, Dr. Matrick maintained a full-time private practice in Vancouver for almost 50 years. He also frequently served as a court appointed expert witness in British Columbia. A previously published nonfiction writer, he lives in West Vancouver. For more information visit his website, www.lawrencematrick.com. *The Quisling* is his first novel.